PRAISE FO
OF REN

What the Lady Wants

"*What the Lady Wants* has everything I love in a historical novel: impeccably researched details, a mix of real and imagined characters that are vividly and sensitively drawn, and a heroine who is true to her time yet feels utterly familiar. With *Dollface*, Renée Rosen crafted an unforgettable portrait of Prohibition-era Chicago; in *What the Lady Wants* she does the same for the city during its Gilded Age."

—Jennifer Robson, international and *USA Today* bestselling author of *Somewhere in France*

"Rosen skillfully charms, fascinates, frustrates, and moves her readers in this turn-of-the-century tale. Set on an epic historical stage, *What the Lady Wants* contains all of the hedonism, decadence, success, and tragedy of the great American novel."

—Erika Robuck, national bestselling author of *Fallen Beauty*

"*What the Lady Wants* is a story that opens with the Great Chicago Fire and keeps on smoldering to the end. Rosen's characters are finely drawn, and her love triangles are full of subtlety and sincerity. What the lady indeed wants may not be what you assume it to be!"

—Suzanne Rindell, author of *The Other Typist*

"Once again, Renée Rosen brings Chicago history alive in this fascinating story of Delia Spencer, trapped in a sexless marriage while desperately desired by a man she can't have—the arrogant, powerful department store mogul Marshall Field. A tale of tangled relationships and dubious morality, *What the Lady Wants* is captivating with a surprisingly contemporary twist."

—Stephanie Lehmann, author of *Astor Place Vintage*

"*What the Lady Wants* is as fun and addictive and Chicago-licious as a box of Marshall Field's Frango Mints. And, sadly, you'll finish it almost as fast. A delight."

—Rebecca Makkai, author of *The Hundred-Year House*

continued . . .

Dollface

"Rosen's Chicago gangsters are vividly rendered, and the gun molls stir up at least as much trouble as their infamous men."

—Sara Gruen, *New York Times* bestselling author of *Water for Elephants*

"Renée Rosen has combined her daring and vivid imagination with the rich history of Prohibition-era Chicago. *Dollface* is a lively, gutsy romp of a novel that will keep you turning pages."

—Karen Abbott, *New York Times* bestselling author of *Sin in the Second City*

"Pour yourself a glass of gin, turn up the jazz, and prepare to lose yourself in the unforgettable story of a quintessential flapper."

—Tasha Alexander, *New York Times* bestselling author of *Death in the Floating City*

"*Dollface* sheds a new light on Prohibition-era gangsters when we see them through the eyes of the women who kept their secrets and shared their beds. Rosen's Chicago is bursting with booze, glamour, sex, and power."

—Kelly O'Connor McNees, author of *In Need of a Good Wife*

PRAISE FOR THE OTHER WORKS OF RENÉE ROSEN

"Quirky and heartfelt." —*Chicago Tribune*

"Beautifully written, and with larger-than-life characters, this book will remain in readers' hearts for a long time to come."

—*School Library Journal*

"A heartfelt coming-of-age story, told with the perfect combination of humor and drama." —*Chicago Sun-Times*

"Absorbing. . . . As Rosen evokes her setting with a wealth of details . . . [readers] will empathize with the narrator's unique situation as a concentrated form of universal worries about finding acceptance, dealing with loss, and leaving home." —*Publishers Weekly*

ALSO BY RENÉE ROSEN

Dollface
Every Crooked Pot

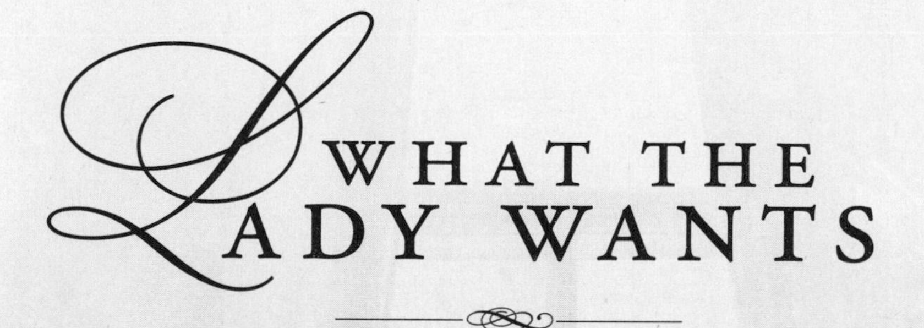

What the Lady Wants

A Novel of Marshall Field and the Gilded Age

RENÉE ROSEN

NEW AMERICAN LIBRARY

New American Library
Published by the Penguin Group
Penguin Group (USA) LLC, 375 Hudson Street,
New York, New York 10014

USA | Canada | UK | Ireland | Australia | New Zealand | India | South Africa | China
penguin.com
A Penguin Random House Company

First published by New American Library,
a division of Penguin Group (USA) LLC

First Printing, November 2014

LIBRARY OF CONGRESS CATALOGING-IN-PUBLICATION DATA:

Rosen, Renée
What the lady wants: a novel of Marshall Field and the Gilded Age/Renée Rosen.
p. cm.
ISBN 978-0-451-46671-6 (softcover)
1. Young women—Illinois—Chicago—Fiction. 2. Capitalists and financiers—Illinois—Chicago—Fiction. 3. Great Fire, Chicago, Ill., 1871—Fiction. 4. Chicago (Ill.)—History—19th century—Fiction. I. Title.
PS3618.O83156W47 2014
813'.6—dc23 2014017729

Printed in the United States of America
10 9 8 7 6 5 4 3 2 1

Set in Bell MT
Designed by Spring Hoteling

PUBLISHER'S NOTE
This is a work of fiction. Names, characters, places, and incidents either are the product of the author's imagination or are used fictitiously, and any resemblance to actual persons, living or dead, business establishments, events, or locales is entirely coincidental.

To Debbie Rosen, my mother, my best friend
and the first person to take me to Marshall Field's.

ACKNOWLEDGMENTS

I would like to thank the following people for their expertise and assistance with the writing of this book: Craig Alton, John Hancock, Sally Sexton Kalmbach and the research staff at the Chicago History Museum and the Newberry Library.

For their ongoing support and friendship, I wish to thank the following people: Karen Abbott, Tasha Alexander, Jill Bernstein, Katherine Eley, Lisa Fine, Andrew Grant, Nick Hawkins, Rick Kogan, Lisa Kotin, Chris Lee, Julia Liebilch, Marianne Nee, Kelly O'Connor McNees, Amy Sue Nathan, Charles Osgood, Javier Ramirez, Dennis Rosenthal, Beth Treleven, Hollis Turner and the whole Sushi Lunch bunch.

To the hardest-working agent in the business, Kevan Lyon—thank you for your patience, guidance and ongoing support. I couldn't ask to be in better hands.

To my editor, Claire Zion. You've been a wonderful collaborator and have made me a better writer. Thank you for always asking the right questions and pushing me (ever so gently) to the next level. It's been a joy to work with you!

To the rest of my team at Penguin, especially Jennifer Fisher,

Jessica Butler, everyone in marketing and sales and, of course, the extraordinary Brian Wilson, who always goes above and beyond for his authors and his booksellers.

A special thank you to the following: Joe Esselin, my first reader, my mentor and friend. Mindy Mailman for being who she is—which is just amazing. Brenda Klem, who no matter how near or far is always there for me. Sara Gruen, who held my little paw on this journey from the very beginning, and John Dul, the man with impeccable timing.

I couldn't follow my dream without the love and support of my wonderful family—Debbie Rosen, Pam Jaffe, Jerry Rosen, Andy Jaffe, Andrea Rosen, Joey Perilman and Devon Rosen.

“Give the lady what she wants.”

—Marshall Field

WHAT THE
LADY WANTS

BOOK ONE

1871–1886

CHAPTER ONE

1871

She supposed she fell in love with him at the same time the rest of Chicago did. The Great Fire had raged on for two days, and the flames didn't discriminate: they devoured businesses and residences, mansions and shanties alike. In the end, miles of streets and buildings were ravaged. But from this smoldering ash, a handful of men came forward to rebuild the city. Marshall Field was one of them.

The day before the fire started, seventeen-year-old Delia Spencer was walking down State Street in search of hair combs needed to complete an outfit for a party the following evening. She was strolling along when her heel got caught in a loose plank on the wooden sidewalk. Oblivious to the throng of horse-drawn cars, wagons and coaches rumbling by, she worked to free her boot. It was only the train whistle, from several blocks over, that seized her attention. She could feel the ground juddering as the locomotive barreled through town, coughing clouds of black, oily smoke. The soot remained after the train passed, clinging to the facades of the restaurants, tearooms and dime museums. Even the Nicholson paved roads were covered in a thin coating of locomotive residue.

She was moving again, and in the time it took her to walk less than a city block, half a dozen peddlers selling everything from chicken feet to slabs of lard tallow soap approached her. She crossed the street to get away from them, lifting her hem and watching her step to avoid the road apples left behind by the horses.

The whirl of chaos surrounding her reminded Delia of the time her relatives from Boston had come to visit, telling their friends and neighbors that they were going to a trading post out west. They'd been appalled by the fetid smells of the Chicago River and said that the city was a noisy, vile, dangerous place. But Delia argued that no other city could boast a three-tiered fountain like the one in Courthouse Square or the marble and limestone buildings along State Street that stood four and five stories high. She couldn't imagine a more vibrant place to call home. The city was barely thirty years old and it was changing all the time, maturing, ripening with each new day. Her father was fond of saying that Chicago was coming into its own in 1871.

"The clover is upon us now," he'd said to her just days before the fire as Delia had stood with him on their velvet green lawn that their gardener faithfully watered each day to combat the months of drought. "Yes, indeed," her father had said again, "we're in the clover now."

Mr. Spencer was a proud Chicagoan and one of the men who'd built up the city in the very beginning, long before the boom began.

"When we moved here back in '54, we were pioneers," he'd told her. "You weren't even a year old. There was a cholera outbreak that year and everyone—including your mother—thought I'd lost my mind, moving my family to this desolate place. They said Chicago was uninhabitable. And they weren't entirely wrong," he'd chuckled. "The roads were nothing but dirt and mud. Thickets of weeds were everywhere. The city was full of nothing but cottages and shacks. There were miles of marshland all around, and if people think it smells bad now, they should have been here back then. Hard as you tried, you couldn't get away from the stench of sewer water."

Standing next to him on their lawn, she'd followed the line of her father's gaze toward the downtown horizon. "Didn't you tell me once that you found fish in your drinking water?"

He'd smiled, giving her a nod. "You'd fill up your basin and there'd be fish this big"—he held his fingers an inch apart—"flipping and flopping right before your eyes."

Delia had laughed. "Why did you want us to live here back then?"

"Because I saw promise in Chicago. I knew this swampland in the middle of the country was going to be the key to prosperity. This city has waterways and railroads, and we're smack in the center of everything. I knew if anything worthwhile was going to happen in this country, it was going to have to go through Chicago."

Her father had been right. Delia found it hard to believe that just twenty years before the Spencers arrived, Chicago had been a fur trading post, home to the Indians and just four thousand brave pioneers. Since then the Potawatomi had been replaced by more than ninety thousand intruders, come to seek their fortunes.

When Delia arrived at Lake Street and Wabash Avenue, a horse-drawn streetcar let dozens of riders off in front of a group of dry goods stores—one of which belonged to Delia's father.

Hibbard, Spencer & Company stood three stories proud, dwarfing the blacksmith, the umbrella repair shop, the cordage shop and the other merchants surrounding it.

Delia went inside and wandered up and down the aisles, letting her fingertips graze the different bolts of brocades, chambrays and gossamers piled one on top of the other. She lost herself among the white and yellow beeswax candles and spiced soaps when her father called to her.

"What a surprise. What are you looking for, Dell?" He removed his spectacles and gave them a polish on the bottom of his waistcoat.

"Hair combs."

"Well," he said with a laugh, "you won't find them in this aisle."

"I know, I know. I can't help it, I got distracted."

As a young girl, before her mother taught her to know a woman's place, Delia had spent many an afternoon down at Hibbard, Spencer, hoisted up on the counter, watching her father ring up all the sales. Oh, how she loved the sound of the till each time the cash drawer sprang open. She had wanted to become a merchant like her father. She wasn't afraid of hard work, or put off by the responsibility. She wanted the satisfaction of making her own way and had even thought of taking over her father's business someday. But she was a girl and a Spencer girl at that. She grew up on the exclusive Terrace Row, in a rusticated stone block home with a majestic mansard roof and dozens of servants. She'd studied piano and dance and had attended the city's finest finishing school. Her mother wouldn't even allow her to take painting classes at the Academy of Design, let alone work in a dry goods store. No, her only job was to find a suitable husband and raise his children.

• • •

The night the fire started, on October 8, 1871, Delia was getting ready for Bertha and Potter Palmers' party in celebration of the opening of their new hotel, the Palmer House. Sitting at her vanity, she gazed into the looking glass while her maid pinned her long brown hair and fastened it with the sterling hair comb she'd purchased the day before. This was the first party Delia would attend after having been formally introduced to society in September, and she wanted to make a good impression. She chose an emerald gown with forest green velvet ruches and beading along the bodice. It had been designed for her by Emile Pingat on her last trip to Paris the summer before.

"Quit your dillydallying," Abby said, standing in the doorway. "Don't you worry, Augustus will still be at the party when you get there."

Delia saw her sister's cheeks flush at the mention of her beau. "It's not Augustus I'm worried about. It's Mother."

"Oh, she must be seething down there," Delia said as the maid gathered her long train and fastened it to the hook at her waistline.

"You know how she is about being prompt." Abby stepped closer to the looking glass and adjusted the bow atop her curls, which their maid had styled for her before reporting to Delia's room.

Abby was four years older than Delia. Her piercing blue eyes and light blond hair came from her mother, whereas Delia's dark coloring belonged to the Spencer side of the family. After studying themselves in the cheval mirror one last time, the girls went downstairs to join their mother at the foot of the staircase. Her mother's hand was gripping the banister and Delia just knew her fingertips must have long since turned white inside her gloves.

Mrs. Spencer raised her hand and summoned her girls to her side. "Come now. Your father has the coach waiting out front."

It was half past eight on a Sunday evening. There was a chill in the air accompanied by fierce winds that whipped around their carriage. Delia noticed that even the gaslights, protected by glass domes, flickered from the wind's force.

They were nearing State and Jackson when they first heard the alarm bells sounding from the courthouse tower. Delia peered out the carriage window but saw nothing.

"Not again," her mother said as she adjusted her hat. It was the fourth time that week that the fire alarms had sounded.

"It's to be expected," said her father. "After all, we haven't seen a drop of rain since July."

"Look," said Abby, pointing toward the west.

Delia turned and saw a sweep of red and yellow on the horizon, rolling in like waves on the lakefront. It seemed ominous to her, but her father didn't appear concerned, so she pushed her misgivings aside and shifted her thoughts to the coming party.

Bertha had been telling Delia and her sister about the hotel's grand opening celebration for weeks. Bertha and Abby were both twenty-one and had been friends for years. Being younger, Delia had always tagged along, the unwelcome shadow. But this past year the awkwardness of their age difference seemed to have vanished. In fact, many now mistook Delia for the older sister, and in recent months, she'd become closer to Bertha, even closer to her than was Abby.

Age obviously didn't matter to Bertha, who had married a man twenty-three years her senior. And what would the richest man in Chicago give his young bride as a wedding present? If you were Potter, you'd give her a hotel with your name on it. It seemed like an odd choice to Delia, but the Palmer House was spectacular. Even the smallest guest rooms started at three dollars a night.

The Palmer House had opened its doors less than two weeks

earlier and everyone had been looking forward to the grand opening party. As the Spencers made their way around the corner, Delia saw the finest carriages in the city lined up out front.

A uniformed doorman, imposing as a statue, greeted them, while another uniformed man inside helped the women off with their manteaus. Entering the lobby, Delia paused in the rotunda, eyeing the oversize chandeliers. The stenciled ceiling was breathtaking and the plush royal blue Axminster carpeting seemed to swallow her footsteps whole. At last she got to see the Carrara marble that Bertha had been talking about and wherever she turned she saw gold—gold trim on the portrait frames, along the wainscoting, the moldings, the winding staircase banister and the glowing wall sconces.

The ballroom on the second floor was even more elegant with high-buffed marble floors that reflected every image from above. Delia guessed there must have been close to two hundred people in the ballroom and yet Augustus Eddy had no difficulty finding Abby and sweeping her onto the dance floor.

Augustus had been courting Abby for the past three months, which pleased Delia's parents. He was a good prospect for her sister. At just twenty-four Augustus was the youngest director the Rock Island Railroad had ever had. He was also the youngest man Delia had ever known to wear a monocle. She thought perhaps he did this to offset his boyish face, round and seemingly full of innocence.

Delia remained with her parents, though she lagged a bit behind, testing her independence and very much aware of the newspapermen eyeing her and jotting down notes on their tablets. Abby had been mentioned countless times in the papers over the past several years and now it was Delia who was about to capture the reporters' attention. For as far back as she could remember, her mother had stressed the importance of fashion. The

Spencer girls, as they were known, made annual fall visits to Europe for their wardrobe consultations and fittings. For years Delia and her sister had been known for their sense of style.

With a cool eye, she observed the women who no doubt were still wearing last year's pannier crinolines beneath their bejeweled bustled gowns. They were each an elegant statement, but a statement of the past. They had unwittingly passed the fashion baton to the younger generation of women such as herself, and Delia wondered if they were even aware of this as they sipped champagne and sherry. She drifted on, passing before a group of men drinking brandies and talking business. All around her handsome couples glided about the dance floor to the music of a twenty-piece orchestra. Delia watched her sister and Augustus waltz, twirling and spinning, wondering when her turn would come.

While the orchestra played on, Delia smiled, thinking that this was the world she'd been groomed for and at last she was old enough to embrace it. She loved everything about the party—the music, the glowing candles on the tables, the scent of fresh flowers in the air, even the Negro servers balancing sterling silver trays of hors d'oeuvres upon their white-gloved palms.

In the center of it all, Potter and Bertha mingled with their guests. Potter, in a white jacket and tie, paled alongside Bertha in her satin ruby-colored ball gown adorned with silk floss and metallic lace. The diamonds in her tiara sparkled each time she moved. Delia would have guessed she was wearing ten pounds of jewelry that night.

"Come," Bertha said, as she looped her arm through Delia's, whisking her along. "Let me introduce you around."

Delia met so many people she could scarcely keep the names and faces straight—except for one.

"Mr. Marshall Field," Bertha said with a sweep of her hand, "may I present Miss Delia Spencer."

"Charmed." The elegantly dressed dry goods merchant leaned forward and kissed her hand. "You wouldn't by chance be related to the Spencer of Hibbard & Spencer, would you?"

"I would indeed," she said. "Franklin Spencer is my father. And please don't tell him this, but I'm a great fan of Field, Leiter & Company."

He laughed. "Obviously you're a young lady with impeccable taste."

She smiled, feeling very grown-up and glamorous. Being a Spencer, Delia had met plenty of important figures, but something about Mr. Field intrigued her, though she couldn't say why. He stood bandy-legged with his right hand parked in his jacket pocket like he was posing for a portrait. And he was impossibly too old for her. Judging by the hint of gray at his temples, she guessed he was nearly twice her age. Delia preferred fair-haired men and Mr. Field had dark brown hair and an even darker mustache, bushy and in need of a trim. But he did have captivating blue gray eyes. That he did. Bertha excused herself to tend to her other guests, and while Delia continued talking with Mr. Field, she noticed that he wasn't wearing a wedding band.

"Shall we see what all the commotion is about?" He motioned toward the crowd that had assembled near the windows, stepping aside so that she could precede him.

Delia looked for her parents and Abby as more people squeezed in to look out the windows, watching what was growing into a raging fire in the southwest. Delia heard the alarm bells ring again as the partygoers *ooh*ed and *aah*ed over the flaring flames in the distance. It was as if they were watching a fireworks display.

"I've never understood the morbid fascination with other people's misfortune," said Mr. Field.

Delia glanced around, looking again for her family, and when she couldn't find them she followed Mr. Field off to the side. The orange glow from outside bathed the wall of windows near them. But Mr. Field wasn't watching the fire. Instead, he turned and gave her an appraising look.

"I know it's impolite to ask a lady her age, but exactly how *young* are you?"

"Seventeen. I'll be eighteen next month."

He closed his eyes and patted a hand over his heart. "My oh my, but you are an enchanting creature, Miss Spencer."

She smiled timidly, uncertain of what to say or do next. No man had ever spoken to her like that, had ever looked at her like that before, either. She stared at his hand covering his heart and noticed his crooked index finger. The joint just above his knuckle was hyperextended. Delia chanced another bashful smile just as a white-hot blaze cannonballed across the horizon. Even from where they stood they both saw it and rushed back toward the windows.

Seconds later there was a loud explosion that shook the building with such a force that the chandeliers clanked and a server dropped his tray. Delia shrieked and grabbed hold of Mr. Field's lapel as couples cleared the dance floor and the musicians put down their instruments. Delia saw a glimpse of Abby's blond curls before she lost her again in the crowd. Everyone squeezed in around the windows, watching the night sky, alive and wild with streaks of red, blue and orange.

Delia released her hold on Mr. Field's lapel and clutched her chest. "I'm sorry. That frightened me so."

He didn't say anything. His eyes were trained on the inferno. The winds had picked up, howling against the windows, feeding the flames. The fire was gaining on the city. There were more explosions and rumblings heard from miles away.

"Must have been the turpentine plants or else kerosene tanks," said one of the guests.

"Don't forget there's half a dozen lumberyards over there, too," said another man with a full goatee that hung from his chin like a whitewash brush.

The next explosion happened closer by and Delia watched in horror as a fireball appeared just blocks to the west and consumed an entire building as if it were made of paper. The room filled with screaming and shrieking. This was not like the fires of the summer. Delia was paralyzed with fear.

Before the flames got any closer, Mr. Field grabbed hold of her hand. "Come with me," he said. "We have to get out of here."

Everyone at the party had the same idea, as they all quickly rushed for the doorways. Delia thought she spotted her father, but then he disappeared in the chaos. She saw Potter Palmer climb onto the stage where the orchestra had been. Cupping his hands about his mouth, he shouted above the panic and commotion. "Everybody—it's time to evacuate. Please, everyone leave the hotel now!"

The room exploded into even more mayhem as people shoved one another out of the way and rushed the doors. Hats and evening bags flew as people tripped over their own feet, trying to escape. Delia's gown rustled as she raced down the staircase, holding tightly to Mr. Field's hand until someone pushed her from behind and she was separated from him.

"Mr. Field? Mr. Field—wait!"

She was caught in a blur of people shoving past her, rushing toward the exit. Delia thought about her manteau, but there was no time to get it. Frantically she searched for her parents and Abby, but all she saw was the chaotic barrage of strangers. By the time she made it outside, the street had turned to pandemonium as people fought to flee the buildings and restaurants nearby. There was no sign of Mr. Field anywhere. No trace of her family, either. She was all alone, surrounded by confusion. All she knew for certain was that the fire was growing closer and that she had to find a way to escape it.

CHAPTER TWO

Delia soon found herself among a mass of people heading north. She'd lost track of time as alarm bells continued to sound and fire shot out of the windows and doorways she passed by. The flames rose from the ground up, reaching far above the rooftops and leaping over entire buildings.

People were hauling drays and carts filled with clothes and blankets, dishes and a jumble of other personal belongings. It seemed as if they had grabbed whatever they could find to fit inside their carts as they'd fled their homes. Even small children lugged suitcases at their sides, banging into their knees and shins as they ran. Spooked horses galloped madly, careening through the streets, dragging carriages behind them as their passengers desperately held on to the side rails.

Even as Delia steadily moved north, she could feel the heat rolling in from behind as the flames drew closer to her. The air was hot and thick with smoke. Tiny orange cinders alive with fire swam before her eyes, floating about like dust motes. The strong winds blew burning planks of wood across half a city block, setting off new fires wherever they touched down.

The heat soon became unbearable. Delia stepped onto a tarred walkway, her shoes sticking to the blistering, bubbling surface. Something stung her arms and legs and she noticed the sleeves and bottom of her dress were smoldering. She screamed, frantically swatting at the live embers that landed on her. She'd never been so frightened in all her life as she slapped out the cinders with her gloved hands.

She trembled even after she'd extinguished the embers, but did her best to keep moving. The roads were becoming congested, crowded with carriages at a standstill while pedestrians like Delia squeezed their way around the clogged streets and walkways. All the while, she tried not to think about what might have happened to her family. She had to keep a watch on her emotions for fear that if she eased up, the panic would swallow her whole.

She lost all sense of where she was until she passed the post office engulfed in flames. Just beyond that, she saw a wooden swing bridge ignite and disappear within seconds, slipping beneath the water of the Chicago River. At last she recognized Courthouse Square. People stood in the fountain, trying to escape the suffocating heat. The alarm bells from the cupola continued to sound even as twelve-foot flames licked the sides of the building. Delia watched the guards marching prisoners from the courthouse jail out onto the street. Red-hot embers landed on one of the inmates, and before her eyes, she saw his uniform burst into flames. Terrified, she turned away and moved on, passing a series of saloons that had been broken into, their windows shattered by men helping themselves to every bottle they could get their hands on.

Though Delia was surrounded by people, could feel their

steaming flesh pressing up against her own skin, she felt utterly alone. Another wave of tears rose up on her, but she pushed them back down as a blast of wind caught her from behind and carried off her hat. She watched it rolling down the sidewalk like a tumbleweed, gone forever. Her feet were blistered, her legs throbbed and she wasn't sure how much farther she could go. She was hungry and tired. The noise was deafening: people crying, hooves pounding the pavement, explosions going off and buildings collapsing. She couldn't comprehend the suffering she was witnessing: grown men sobbing, people and animals set aflame, women rushing back inside burning homes for their children. Delia didn't want to see any more. She wanted to go home. More panic rose up inside her and she feared she'd never see her parents or Abby again. She was fighting back another round of tears when a familiar voice called her name.

"Delia, Delia—" her father shouted from inside the family carriage as their driver pulled back on the reins and brought the coach to a stop. The horse's coat was shiny with sweat and foam oozed from its mouth. Part of its mane looked singed and she saw the blood seeping from a gash on its hind leg.

"For goodness' sake, child, get in." He opened the door and grabbed her around the waist, hoisting her up.

Delia couldn't speak. Her family finding her in the midst of the chaos was a miracle. As soon as she felt her father's arms around her, she released her tears, letting the fright she'd been trying to suppress come to the surface in full, gulping sobs.

Her mother plucked a handkerchief from her satchel and dabbed Delia's eyes while at the same time scolding her. "Why did you wander off alone? We were looking everywhere for you," she said. "You scared us half to death."

"Shssh, she's all right. That's all that matters," said her father.

Abby scooted closer to Delia and reached for her hand. Her sister had torn her glove that evening and the seam along her index finger had opened. Even in the dark, Delia could see that Abby had bitten that exposed nail down to the quick.

The carriages were still backed up and it took an eternity just to round the corner. Once they'd made it around the bend, though, they picked up speed and traffic started moving again. Yet, everywhere Delia looked, there were more wagons, drays, even stray horses heading north. She realized they were just one in an endless caravan that night, trying to stay ahead of the fire.

When they reached the southern tip of Lincoln Park all the coaches came to a stop. Some of the horses, like their own, were injured and overheated from the flames, frothing at the mouth. Looking out the window, Delia saw hundreds of people sitting on the ground with horse blankets wrapped about their shoulders. Others used their suitcases as stools, their elbows propped on their knees. They were in the midst of a refugee camp that had sprung up out of nowhere. She was struck by all the different people—the Irish, the Germans, the rich, the poor—all united in their need to escape the fire. A man in a Prince Albert coat with a velvet collar streaked black from smoke stood next to a man in a fraying nightshirt and a tattered cap. It was the same with the women, some in ball gowns and hats and others draped in work dresses with babushkas covering their heads.

Delia joined her father when he stepped out of the carriage to stretch his legs. Everywhere she turned, she saw mothers sobbing because they couldn't find their children, while their husbands stood by helpless to console them. Her father said he was going to speak with some of the other men and Delia watched him walking away, his broad shoulders sifting through the crowd until she lost sight of him. That was when a kernel of panic formed in her gut. She realized that she'd been expecting her father to fix this—this impossible catastrophe—just as he'd fixed her skate, or the roof on her dollhouse, or splinted her dog's hind leg after he was hit by a wagon. He'd always fixed every other problem in her life, but this was bigger than him, bigger than anything they'd ever seen. That terrified her but it also marked a change in her. She knew she couldn't afford to crumble and something deep inside her solidified. It was as if she could feel her inner core expanding with a force she didn't know she had. Looking back, she would remember this as the moment she found her strength and came to understand the meaning of self-reliance.

When her father returned to the carriage he told them that everyone had decided to wait it out. "We're far enough north now. The fire will never come all the way up here. We'll stay here tonight and in the morning, once they've put this beast out, we'll be able to go back home."

Home! It was the first time anyone had mentioned *home* and the very word brought to mind the question that had haunted Delia through the whole ordeal. It was Abby who finally asked, "What if our house is burned down? What will we do? Where will we go?"

"Now you listen to me," Mr. Spencer snapped. "The fire's spreading north and all those buildings that burned were nothing but balloon structures. They were made of wood frames. Our house is stone and we live far enough south. Our house will be fine, you hear me?"

"Now not another word about houses burning down," their mother said, giving both Delia and Abby a warning glance.

Delia tried to take comfort in her father's words, picturing their home among the other limestone mansions that lined Terrace Row. She listened to her mother and sister talk about needing a hot bath, wanting a cup of calming tea, wondering if McVicker's would be open for that Friday's matinee show. Delia wanted to join in, but she couldn't take her eyes off the flames still breathing in the distance. It didn't seem possible that anything could stop the inferno.

When dawn broke Monday morning, the sky was still dark with thick black smoke. The only light Delia could see came from the flames, still shooting a hundred feet into the air. The fire looked to be about a mile away and that was too close. The carriages started moving again as the fire pushed their caravan farther and farther.

An hour or so later they stopped in a stretch of prairie land, surrounded by shanties and cottages. Delia was hungry and tired. Time seemed to hang in the air, just as thick and unmoving as the smoke. There was nothing to do but wait. A man who had salvaged his accordion began playing oompah music while other men passed around lager and whiskey that she assumed they'd taken from the looted saloons back in town. People were eating raw corn that they'd found growing in the nearby field, juice from the kernels dribbling down their chins. Her father commented that it was the first time he'd ever seen the Germans and the Irish tolerate one another's company. They had no choice.

As the day stretched on, Delia moved from the carriage to the field, where the blanched-out grass rose up past her knees, just waiting to feed the fire. But still, it felt good to walk around after being cooped up for so long. Their coachman was tending to their horse, inspecting the gashes on its leg, shaking his head as he muttered something to her father. Delia distanced herself from them, thinking how she couldn't bear another night inside that coach. She had barely closed her eyes the night before. The winds had howled so, beating against the sides of the carriage, rocking them to and fro. She'd been freezing one minute, sweating the next. The sounds of the fire had terrorized her during the night, but now, in the daylight, she had become accustomed to the booming roars off in the distance. She thought only vaguely about it, just another lumberyard igniting or perhaps more buildings collapsing.

At dusk she had no choice but to retreat to the carriage again with the rest of her family. They all slept fitfully. It was almost midnight according to her father's pocket watch when they heard a steady *tap, tap, tap* on the roof. At first Delia feared it was cinders showering down on them, but then she heard the yelping and clapping. She looked out the window. *Rain!* It was raining. She held out her hand and let the droplets pelt her open palm. A gift from the heavens! The harder it rained, the more it lifted people's spirits. She watched them, young and old, standing with their heads thrown back, letting the rain wash over them. She could almost hear the hiss of the fire losing ground as giddy relief spread throughout her body.

By Tuesday morning, the fire was out and the black smoke had given way to a gray smoldering haze. Tears sprang to Delia's eyes. They had survived. They were going to be all right. These were the only thoughts circling her mind as their carriage slowly began making its way back through the city and toward their home.

"Everything's so quiet now," said Abby, who had worried the open seam of her glove so that now two additional fingers were exposed along with their nibbled nails. When she started in on a fresh fingernail, her mother swatted her hand away from her mouth.

All was calm now but Delia found the stillness haunting. As they made their way back through Lincoln Park, she could see that the city had been broken to its core. The wooden sidewalks were gone. The trees were gone. So were all the houses and buildings. The rain continued to fall, turning the streets, already filled with heaps of debris, into gray sludge. Without any landmarks to guide them, even Delia's father had difficulty knowing where they were. Through his clenched jaw he called out to the driver, trying to decide which paths to take. Despite the coachman's prodding whip, their horse was barely inching along. Block after block of buildings that had stood four and five stories high days before had now been reduced to piles of charred wood. Delia's mother kept her hand clamped over her mouth, her eyes blinking back tears.

At last, up ahead in the distance, Delia spotted the turrets of the Chicago Avenue Pumping Station on Michigan Boulevard. Two days earlier, they'd simply blended into the background, but now they were everything, an anchor for her hopes. The pumping station was still standing. All was not lost! Hope rose up inside her.

"Look," she shouted, her pulse jumping with enthusiasm. "It's going to be okay!"

But as soon as those words left her mouth their carriage came to a halt. The driver cracked his whip over the horse's hide, but it refused to move. Delia's father got out and climbed up onto the box. Again and again the driver whipped the animal until its legs buckled and it collapsed.

Delia and Abby cried out and their mother covered her eyes as the carriage violently jolted forward. Mr. Spencer and the driver jumped down off the box to check on the horse. Delia watched through the window. The horse was dead, its eyes bulging open, its mouth covered in froth, its coat slick from sweat and rain. Delia turned away, thinking she might be sick despite having nothing in her stomach.

Now they had no choice but to go the rest of the way on foot. The mud and ash covered Delia's bottines as they walked, coming across odds and ends lying in the carnage. Delia saw a rag doll in the muck, her button eyes looking up to the sky, and a ceramic bowl or perhaps a vase, melted into a twisted shape. A pocketknife had survived along with a man's shoe, its tongue hanging out thirsty and covered in soot.

The downtown streets and walkways had become impassable and unrecognizable. Any minute now Delia expected to see McVicker's Theatre or Colonel Wood's Museum. She was desperate to see the opera house or the Green Room, even the State Savings Institute, anything that looked familiar. But other than an occasional wall or storefront left standing, the city had been incinerated. The fire had been so hot that even the limestone had decomposed into heaps of sand and grit. Even the metal and steel cores of the buildings that everyone believed were fireproof had melted into globs still glowing red from their centers. If those had melted in the inferno, what could possibly be left of their home? Delia swallowed hard and pressed her hands to her throbbing temples.

Her father looked at her, as if he knew what she was thinking. He had two days' worth of whiskers covering his face, dark circles looming beneath his eyes. "We're going to be fine," he insisted as they forged ahead. "The entire city can't be in ruins."

Delia prayed he was right, for if not, she feared they would never survive. There would be no clean water, no food, let alone anything else.

The rain stopped as they continued to slog through the ash. A man in the middle of the rubble held a coveted copy of the *Chicago Tribune* and called out the headlines: "Tens of thousands homeless. More than three hundred dead. Medill declares, 'Chicago shall rise again!'"

Delia walked alongside her father as they came across heaps of dead cinders, soaked from the rain but still hissing and sending plumes of steam rising ten and twenty feet high. One lone pole remained standing with a cardboard sign nailed to it. When Delia saw what it said her stomach lurched.

CASHBOYS & WORK GIRLS
WILL BE PAID WHAT IS DUE THEM.

MONDAY 9AM OCT. 16 AT
60 CALUMET AVENUE.

FIELD, LEITER & CO.

"Oh, it can't be," Delia said to her father. She thought of Mr. Field as she bent down and picked up a handful of damp ash, collecting it in her hand like a snowball. "This can't be all that's left of Field, Leiter & Company." She was choking back tears because she knew then that her father's store, just a few blocks over, must be gone as well. "This can't be all that's left of State Street!"

Each step after that was harder to take, their spirits sinking in the mud along with their shoes. Delia and her family continued walking south, heading deeper into the heart of the destruction. As they approached Terrace Row, Delia's heart dropped down in her chest and she felt as though she couldn't breathe. All they found was a charred wall, not more than six feet tall, looking as though it was a single wind gust away from tumbling over. Smoke rose from the piles of debris like campfires on the prairie. She felt hysteria mounting inside her. Where were all the trees? The gardens? The mansions? There was no neighborhood left. Their home was gone. Everything was gone. She promised herself she wouldn't cry. She had to be strong for her father, who held her sobbing sister, and for her mother, who had already dropped to her knees, landing in a heap of ash as she wept into her hands.

Delia had to distance herself from her broken family. Their

tears and sobs echoed through her body, draining what little courage she had left. As she walked among the ruins, she wondered, *Could this rubble possibly be where the parlor stood? Is this what's left of the music room? Where was my bedroom?*

Then she found a gooseneck copper teakettle lying on its side. It must have been in the kitchen, or maybe it had belonged to a neighbor. She'd never seen it before and yet it was the only thing they had left. She picked it up and cradled it in her arms as a single tear leaked from her eye.

CHAPTER THREE

Five days later, Delia and Abby lay on their sides facing each other, crowded into the same bed. Not that Abby didn't have her own bed just a few feet away, but she'd had a nightmare and come running to Delia.

Delia covered Abby's shoulders with the blanket and propped herself up against the walnut headboard. She could smell her sister's breath, sour like yeast. As she turned up the lamp on the nightstand, a warm glow filled the room, bringing objects into view: the intricate wood carvings around the mirror of the bedroom hutch in the corner, the Persian rug, the blue velvet draperies on the bay windows. It was a fine house, but it wasn't home.

Delia and her family had taken refuge at a relative's house down on Eighteenth and Michigan, on the fringe of where the fire stopped. Her aunt and uncle had welcomed them without question. It had been less than a week since the fire, but Delia felt as if the first seventeen years of her life had all but faded away like fragments of a dream she couldn't fully recall.

"Do you think Augustus is okay?" Abby whispered to Delia.

"You'll hear from him soon." She'd been telling Abby that every night since the fire.

"But how will he know where to find me?"

Delia didn't have an answer. She didn't know where to begin to look for friends. Her father told her that several families had already left the city, heading for Philadelphia or New York. But he wanted to stay in Chicago and rebuild his home and his business. Thankfully he had insured everything, so Delia knew that the physical could be rebuilt—but what about everything else? She thought about her father, the strongest, proudest man she knew, and how this fire had taken something vital out of him, like the marrow from his bones. His confidence, that part of him that always knew what to do next, seemed to have been buried in the rubble.

Her mother was even worse. She'd stayed in bed for two days, refusing to get up, unable to eat. "I can't face it all," she'd cried into her fists. "I tell you, I can't face it."

Delia, like her parents and everyone else, walked around in a stupor for days, trying to grasp what had happened. She couldn't comprehend that the city was gone. The tasks ahead were overwhelming. The cleanup seemed insurmountable, the repairs and rebuilding too daunting. At times she had to stop and sit, catch her breath, for fear that she might faint.

"Try and get some sleep," Delia said to Abby, reaching over to turn down the gaslight. "Don't you worry, it's going to be all right," she said, stroking Abby's hair. "Somehow everything's going to be all right."

As Delia's eyes adjusted to the darkness, she heard Abby's breathing deepen. She had fallen back asleep, but Delia remained awake. She rolled onto her back, thinking about how in another few hours she'd have to get up and face another day. It had been less than a week and already she was exhausted. It wasn't physical fatigue she suffered from, for nothing visibly demanding had been put upon her. It was emotional, a steady draining from her mind, her heart. She was worn down from the inside out and no amount of sleep could revive her. How was she going to find the energy to keep going? God, how she just wanted everything to go back to the way it was before the fire.

Delia remained despondent for days. She spent her time in her aunt's front parlor, sketching the scenes she'd witnessed the night of the fire: two men laying wet carpets on a rooftop hoping to spare it from the blaze lapping at the house next door, people running into Lake Michigan, rats and other rodents coming out from underground, seeking escape from the heat. Though she knew better than to think of herself as a real artist, she had a modest talent. Despite her mother seeing no point in Delia studying art, drawing and painting had always helped her make sense of the world around her. That was how she connected all the fragments she experienced, giving it order in her mind. She turned to drawing now, but even after she'd done a pile of sketches, the fire's devastation was beyond her.

Putting her sketch pad aside, she reached for the newspaper and came across an advertisement on the front page of the *Chicago Tribune* that surprised her:

FIELD, LEITER & COMPANY
REOPENING
ON THE CORNER OF TWENTIETH AND STATE STREET

She recalled the sign outside the rubble where the old Field & Leiter store had stood at State and Washington and realized that Mr. Field must have started looking for a new location the moment the fire was out. Even Delia's father—considered one of Chicago's most astute businessmen—was still months away from being able to reopen Hibbard, Spencer & Company. How could it be that in less than two weeks, and in the midst of such suffering and chaos, Mr. Field had been able to get a new dry goods store up and running? Though she wished her father's store had been the first to reopen, she couldn't help but feel a surge of admiration and gratitude for Mr. Field. He was bringing life back to the city.

Delia grabbed the newspaper and ran into the drawing room. "Look," she called to her sister as she waved the *Tribune*. "Let's go! Please, say you'll come with me."

Abby didn't need much convincing. She was heartened by the news as well. They needed to replace *everything* and Abby especially loathed having to wear her aunt's and cousin's hand-me-downs.

So that afternoon Delia and Abby headed on foot from Eighteenth and Michigan over to Twentieth and State. It was a cold fall day, gray and overcast. The air still carried a stale smoky smell. As they walked they didn't see a single hack or omnibus go by, but they did hear the trains, which had been spared from the fire. Their whistles blasting in the distance were a welcome sound.

Many of the streets were impassable, so they had to take the long way around, walking east toward the lakefront. With collars turned up and hands stuffed inside their coat pockets, Delia and Abby passed city workers clearing pathways, shoveling heaps of rubble toward the water, dumping it all into Lake Michigan. They saw planks of wood, half of a piano, a parlor chair and other debris floating along the choppy surface.

As they headed on, they noticed a carriage or two passing by and when they turned south onto State Street there were more carriages and phaetons rumbling past them. Half a dozen more.

When they arrived at their destination, Delia stopped and checked the address.

"This can't be right," she said. "It's nothing but an old barn."

"And in the middle of nowhere."

Delia observed the horse barn, which sat on a barren stretch of overgrown grass. The ground was dried out with more cracks running through it than a broken eggshell.

"They must have made a mistake in the newspaper," said Abby.

A group of women trudged past them, trampling through the rough terrain with their dresses hiked up to their ankles. They were elegantly clothed, one in an inverness cape, another wearing a bonnet with a lace-embroidered brim and the third with a jacket with a pannier that cascaded past her bustle.

"Excuse me," said Delia, "but we're looking for the new Field, Leiter & Company."

"This is it," said the woman with the bonnet.

"Here?" Delia pointed at the horse barn.

"Well," said the woman with the cape, "the line starts around the corner, but yes, this is it."

The line? Delia and Abby peered around the side of the barn and there were women—a hundred or more—lined up, chatting among themselves and eagerly anticipating their turn to step inside. Delia and Abby took their places at the end of the line and within minutes another dozen or so women had joined the wait behind them.

Delia caught a glimpse of Mr. Field standing in the doorway. With his white gloves and plug hat, he looked as proud as if he were standing before a castle.

"Plenty of merchandise inside, ladies," he called out. "New shawls and silks just arrived this morning from New York and Paris."

She watched him greet his customers as they crossed the threshold, and when their turn came, he looked at Delia and took her hand in his. "Miss Spencer," he said. "What a lovely surprise. Welcome to Field, Leiter & Company. And who is this you have with you?" he asked.

After Delia introduced Mr. Field to her sister, he welcomed them both inside. "Please," he said, "come have a look around. Stay as long as you like."

When she and Abby entered the makeshift store, Delia was amazed by what she saw. It may have been a horse barn on the outside, but inside, it was a genuine dry goods store. Not as grand as the one that had burned down, but a real store nonetheless. Mirrors had been mounted on the whitewashed walls, and the floors were wide planks but sanded, so that the surface was smooth and even. The salesclerks stood eager and erect, the men in black suits, the women in dark dresses. The horse stalls had been converted into display counters, filled with bolts of fabric—brocades and tweeds, satins and merino. There were beautiful silk mantillas and velveteen bonnets, and next to that, rich lisle threads for embroidery, an assortment of cattle bone, jade and pearl buttons and other notions. There was a counter just for toilet waters, one for handkerchiefs and lace, another for hosiery and bloomers.

The sisters paused before a handsome display of inkwells, fountain pens and desk blotters. Then they moved on to another fabric stall. Delia felt the need to touch each item, run her fingertips over the different textures, the taffetas, velvets and satins. It was crowded inside with women entering through the doorway more quickly than others left out the exit. With the exception of the trains, this was the first sign of normal life she'd seen since the fire. It was uplifting and invigorating to be surrounded by people ready to get on with their lives.

Delia had been admiring an ivory-handled parasol when she looked back at Mr. Field still standing in the doorway greeting more arrivals. After nearly two weeks of despair and devastation—when even her own father admitted feeling broken and beaten up—this man was the one person she'd seen radiate hope and confidence. While everyone else doubted the city's resilience, he was forging ahead. She found his optimism contagious. Apparently, so did the hundreds of other women who had gathered at the store. It was as if he was restoring their spirits, giving them a reason and a way to carry on.

Though she recalled that the night they met, Bertha said he was thirty-seven—twenty years her senior—Delia Spencer recognized that there was something rare, something extraordinary about Marshall Field.

CHAPTER FOUR

Delia welcomed the sound of hammers pounding, of saws slicing back and forth, their blades chewing through marble and granite. She took comfort in the workmen shouting from stepladders and rooftops as she made her way down Michigan Boulevard with Abby and her mother. It was December and the ground was a solid mass of frozen ash, covered in snow. And yet, over the past two months, even as winter set in, Delia watched with wonder as the city started to come back.

"Oh look," her mother said now, pointing to the construction on a snowy lot, the site of their future home. "They've started on the chimneys."

The three of them paused to look at the progress the builders had made. Stacks of masonry blocks and brick were scattered about, as the city had outlawed wooden construction right after the fire. The Spencers were rebuilding at Michigan and Sixteenth, near where they were staying with their relatives. It was to be a twelve-thousand-square-foot Romanesque-style home designed by an up-and-coming architect, Henry Hobson Richardson.

"I can't wait until we're back in a home of our own," said Abby.

"And just think, now you'll live even closer to Augustus," said Delia.

As it turned out, Augustus's family home on Wabash and Twenty-second Street had been spared in the fire. It had taken him about ten days but eventually he had located Abby. Delia could tell that the temporary separation and fear of losing each other had only intensified their budding love.

"Come along, girls," said Mrs. Spencer. "We mustn't be late."

In an effort to return to some semblance of normalcy, Delia's mother had been taking her daughters to the dressmaker for weekly consultations so that the Spencer girls could replace their lost wardrobes. The dressmaker, like so many other small businesses, had set up shop in a makeshift shack. When they arrived, she hustled Delia behind a flimsy drape that served as a changing room.

"Of course this is just temporary," the dressmaker apologized for the umpteenth time while pinning the flouncing to Delia's dress.

Delia looked in the mirror and frowned. "I'd prefer the trim a little higher on the hip," she said.

Delia always involved herself in the dressmaking process. Weeks ago she had presented the seamstress with sketches illustrating how she wanted her evening, afternoon and even walking dresses to look. She'd even given her a design for a new skating outfit. As much as she had carefully chosen her designs and as talented as the dressmaker was, Delia knew that none of these new dresses would compare with the work of the Paris designers. But the Spencer girls' annual autumn trip to Europe had been postponed because of the fire. Mrs. Spencer did not want to leave her husband, who had started running Hibbard & Spencer from William Hibbard's home.

"And remember," said Delia, "use the silver floss embroidery, not gold." She caught herself in the mirror and felt a stab of regret. She didn't like what she saw and it wasn't the dress that she was unhappy with. It was her own image. How could she be concerned about things like embroidery and flounce when so many others had nothing at all?

Immediately after their visit to the dressmaker, Delia went to the First Presbyterian Church and signed up to help distribute warm clothing and food to those who had been left homeless.

"Are you certain you're up to this?" asked the petite woman in the vestibule, folding blankets, rising on tiptoes, straining to reach the top. "You're one of the Spencer girls, aren't you?"

"But I want to help. I'll do anything." Delia stepped in, took the blanket from her and placed it on the pile.

The woman looked at her and smiled. "Very well, then," she said with a nod. "You can fold those over there," she said, pointing to a heap of dull, rough blankets the color of olives. "And when you're done, we just got a new donation of shoes. They need to be sorted and arranged according to size."

After that, Delia reported to the church seven days a week to help the fire victims. And oh, the things she saw! Children without warm clothing, the soles of their blistered feet bleeding and peeking out of their torn, tattered shoes. Men and women so beaten down and frail, their eyes seemed sunken in their sockets. Delia would stay at the church as long as she could, reading one last story to a child or rubbing an old woman's tired shoulders with liniment.

Despite her efforts, Delia still felt guilty when she returned to her relatives' home, knowing her aunt's cook prepared their supper, the footman chopped wood for the fireplaces, and the maids made sure they had warm beds. How could Delia enjoy these comforts? Instead she lay awake at night, unable to escape the forlorn faces that haunted her memory come sunset.

After volunteering for two weeks straight, Delia took a day off and accompanied Abby and Augustus to the Palmers' country home in Hyde Park. It was a lovely estate on a large plot of land with a fine stable and sprawling gardens out back. Inside, the house was beautifully decorated with a Mathieu Criaerd commode and several gilded wood fauteuils, which Delia recognized as the work of Jean-Jacques Pothier. Delia's eye for design wasn't limited to just fashion. No, she was equally interested in home furnishings. From the time she was a young girl, she had pored over her father's back issues of *Godey's Magazine and Lady's Book* and devoured every issue of *Harper's*, studying up on the latest designers.

That Sunday afternoon in December, Bertha hosted a small gathering that included her neighbor Paxton Lowry and his friend Arthur Caton.

"Well, if it isn't the Spencer girls," said Arthur as soon as Delia and Abby entered the drawing room.

They had both known Arthur since childhood, but this was the first time Delia had seen him in years. He came from an extremely wealthy family; his father was one of the most powerful judges in Chicago. Like his father, Arthur had gone to law school out east and he had recently been admitted to the bar. He had moved back to Chicago just three days before the fire.

Paxton explained all this before saying, "Arthur comes back to Chicago and the whole town falls apart."

Delia and the others watched Paxton in silence as he moved to the bar. No one could think of anything to say in response.

"Oh, come now," he said, plucking a bottle by its neck, letting it swing like a pendulum. "It was a joke."

"Not a very funny one," said Bertha.

"Forgive me." Paxton hung his head in mock shame.

Delia found Paxton to be an unusually pretty man with long lashes, smooth, almost whiskerless skin and a tender smile. She watched as he refilled Potter's glass and then Arthur's. Augustus adjusted his monocle and waved his hand, saying he'd had enough. Delia and Abby were drinking tea along with Bertha.

While the men talked about the vigorous rebuilding of the city, Bertha and Abby summoned Delia into the hallway. "Well, what do you think of Arthur?" Bertha asked.

Delia peered back into the drawing room. Arthur was sitting casually in a cane-backed chair with his long legs stretched out before him, crossed at the ankles. He was very stylish with sandy blond hair combed back off his forehead and rugged-looking muttonchops.

"I don't remember him being so handsome," Delia admitted.

"And don't forget, he is a Caton, after all." Abby said this as if no further explanation was needed. Of the two girls, Delia knew her sister was the one more concerned with appearances.

As they started back toward the drawing room, the butler appeared in the hallway announcing the arrival of Mr. and Mrs. Marshall Field.

Mr. and Mrs.? Delia turned abruptly. She felt an unexpected burst of disappointment, as if an unspoken promise had been broken. She'd had no idea he was married. Even after all she'd read about him in the newspapers, she'd never seen even a single mention of his wife.

Mr. Field smiled generously when he saw her. "And so we meet again, Miss Spencer."

"Very nice to see you, Mr. Field."

"Please, call me Marshall. Or better yet, Marsh."

"But only if you'll call me Delia. Or better yet, Dell."

They laughed in agreement. She couldn't help but notice how easy and comfortable she felt talking to him. It was that way every time she saw him, like they were old friends rather than recent acquaintances.

Delia felt his wife's eyes on her even before Bertha introduced them.

"This is Marshall's wife, Nannie. She's from Kentucky," said Bertha. "Like my people."

Nannie patted her hair in place as she said hello, her voice carrying a hint of Kentucky drawl. "Well, isn't it nice to meet you."

Delia found that she was every bit as intrigued by Nannie as she was with Marshall. Or maybe it was because she'd been so intrigued with Marshall that she took an interest in Nannie. She couldn't help it. Delia was fascinated by the woman who had captured Marshall Field's heart. She noticed every detail from Nannie's brown hair, fastened in a Gordian knot, to her slender figure and the Japanese silk day dress with gathered flounces. She was very stylish, befitting the wife of the city's most successful merchant. She was older, closer to Marshall's age, probably twenty-seven or twenty-eight. Whereas Marshall moved about with ease, shaking hands with the men, Nannie held back. She appeared self-conscious one minute and then, as if to overcompensate for her insecurity, she would make bold gestures. She would interrupt conversations with non sequiturs or suddenly sit down at the piano to play a song that she clearly hadn't mastered. Delia suspected that Nannie was who she was by virtue of marrying Marshall Field. It appeared that she'd been thrust into a world she'd hadn't been groomed for.

"Nannie's starting a new club for women," said Bertha.

"Yes, you must come join us," said Nannie. "We're going to be discussing books and plays, and the opera. We're going to recapture the culture that was lost in the fire. We've already received a shipment of books from England for the city's library."

"But we don't have a city library," said Delia.

"Well, we certainly have the start of one now," said Nannie with a cunning smile.

The more they talked, the more Delia liked her. Nannie, for all her quirks, had spirit. She realized that must be what had attracted Marshall Field to her; she seemed to be a woman whose energy could match his.

Delia sipped tea from Bertha's delicate jeweled cups while Potter told everybody of his plans for the new Palmer House Hotel.

"Construction is already well under way," he said. "And this time, by golly, that hotel will be fireproof."

"I no longer believe there is such a thing as a fireproof building," said Augustus.

"Mark my words," said Potter. "The Palmer House will be one hundred percent fireproof. In fact, I challenge any man who thinks he can set fire to one of my new guest rooms."

"Let's not encourage the guests to set fire to the rooms, dear," said Bertha.

"You just better hope Mrs. O'Leary doesn't check in," said Nannie with a cackle.

"Oh, that poor woman," said Abby. "Did you see the horrible things they wrote about her in the newspapers?"

"Poor woman?" Marshall sat up straighter. "Her cow nearly destroyed the entire city."

"They don't know for certain that her cow started it," said Delia.

"If Marshall said her cow started it," said Nannie, "then the cow started it. He's never wrong. About anything." She smiled, but Delia noticed that Marshall did not.

"Oh please," said Arthur. "Is anyone besides me tired of talking about this fire? What on earth did we talk about before the fire? Can anyone remember?"

As the day wore on, the ladies exchanged their teacups for glasses of sherry and Delia found that while Marshall and Augustus were engrossed in conversation with Potter, Arthur and Paxton were quite attentive to her. Arthur was explaining that he'd just sold his telegraph company to an outfit called Western Union.

"It all sounds very exciting," said Delia.

"Actually it's rather boring," said Arthur. "A lot of paper signing and handshaking."

"Will you stay on with this Western Company?"

"Western Union," Paxton corrected her.

"Western Union, then." She smiled at Paxton and turned back to Arthur. "Will you be tending to their legal matters now as well?"

"Hopefully not. Really, Delia," Arthur added with an inebriated grin, "I only did it for the money. I never have to work another day in my life because, you see, now I'm very rich."

"You've always been very rich," Paxton pointed out.

"Well, then, now I'm very, *very* rich." Arthur looked at Delia and raised his glass.

Arthur and Paxton were laughing, but Delia felt a bit dismissed, as if he thought she wasn't intelligent enough to follow the workings of a business deal when truly she wanted to hear more about it. That was the sort of thing she found interesting, but she wouldn't ask again. She wouldn't beg to be taken seriously.

Before the afternoon was over, Arthur had asked if he might call on Delia. She hesitated, still miffed over the way he'd disregarded her interest in his business affairs earlier. Yet she couldn't ignore the fluttering in her body each time she looked at him. He was a very handsome man and he was certainly charming and educated.

"Oh please," Paxton said finally. "Say yes or he'll only keep asking."

"Well, in that case," said Delia, "I'd be delighted."

CHAPTER FIVE

1876

Delia Spencer married Arthur Caton five years later. Arthur had courted her for nearly four of those five years before proposing. Delia hadn't hesitated to say yes. No one made her laugh like Arthur and no one tried harder to make her happy. Whether they were sailing or horseback riding with Paxton or picnicking with Abby and Augustus, Arthur made her feel like the luckiest girl alive. He had become her favorite person to do *anything* with—it didn't matter what as long as they were together. She couldn't imagine finding a better man to spend her life with, to raise a family with and fulfill her role as a wife and mother.

Delia knew her wedding was the most anticipated social event of the season. And while Abby's wedding to Augustus Eddy two years earlier had certainly been elaborate, it paled in comparison with Delia and Arthur's.

When Delia arrived at the First Presbyterian Church, the paved sidewalks were lined with newspapermen and onlookers hoping for a glimpse of the fashionable bride. She wore a tulle and white satin gown by Worth and velvet ball slippers with jeweled embroidery. Her white Marseilles kid gloves were embellished with jewels as well. The press would later write that "she sparkled," which pleased Delia and many others. She knew that her wedding was as much for the city as it was for her. Even before the fire, people in the East had looked down on Chicago as a filthy, backward prairie town; and the fire hadn't made the situation any better. The people who lived in Chicago longed to be seen as residents of a refined and sophisticated city, and because of her position in society, Delia knew she had the ability to help enhance their reputation. And she did it with grace and pride.

Following the ceremony, the new Mr. and Mrs. Caton boarded Arthur's elegant coach drawn by four black stallions and made their way through streets packed with cheering, waving admirers. Delia had never been happier. Her handsome, wealthy groom was every girl's envy. He was taking her to Europe for their honeymoon and the two were eager to start a family right away. Everything seemed perfect.

Their reception was held at the Spencers' home on Sixteenth and Michigan, a house filled with multiple archways and elaborate stonework. Delia and Arthur took their places in the receiving line along with the other Spencers and the Catons. Delia knew her father-in-law had prominence with local politicians and she realized that by virtue of this marriage, her own social status had been raised, but it was overwhelming. She had already greeted Congressman Wentworth and a group of city officials and was relieved when she saw Bertha and Potter making their way through the line. At last people she knew.

While she was chatting with Bertha, Delia's new mother-in-law appeared at her side.

"Delia, darling," she said in a discreet whisper, "you can talk with Bertha later. General Sheridan and his wife are waiting."

Delia felt her shoulders tense up the way they always did whenever Mrs. Caton spoke to her. "Of course, Mrs. Caton. I was just—"

"Delia—" Mrs. Caton raised her voice along with an eyebrow. "The Sheridans. Please."

From the very beginning Delia had tried to ingratiate herself to Arthur's mother, but her efforts had proved fruitless. She remembered the first time Arthur introduced the two of them. Mrs. Caton had asked so many questions that day Delia would have thought she was the judge in the family: *How many languages do you speak? What is your favorite opera? Your favorite play?* With each answer, Mrs. Caton pursed her lips and nodded. But as soon as Delia and Arthur became engaged, the competition began. Delia quickly realized that Mrs. John D. Caton was the most important woman in her son's life and she planned to remain so. If Delia suggested a show, Mrs. Caton was quick to say that it had received unfavorable reviews and would make another recommendation. Everything from Delia's tastes in music and restaurants to the charitable organizations she supported was challenged.

It was while Delia was speaking with General Sheridan and his wife that she looked up and saw Marshall and Nannie Field working their way through the receiving line. She found she couldn't concentrate on General Sheridan's words because she was so eager to receive the Fields. She noticed that Nannie looked a bit disheveled, as if the wind had gotten hold of her. She wore a peach basque with a matching scarf that wasn't draped quite right and her squared train looked as if it had been stepped upon. And yet, Delia was grateful to see her, as she was ever so fond of Nannie. After all, it was because of Nannie that Delia had become a member of the Fortnightly Club and the Chicago Women's Club, two very prestigious organizations that hosted some of the city's most impressive social events. Already that year they'd invited Henry James to a speaking engagement that had people lined up out the door and around the block. Mark Twain had also drawn an equally large crowd.

When the Fields finally reached her, Nannie kissed her cheek and whispered, "We wish you well, my dear." She then moved on to Arthur while Marshall approached Delia.

"Best wishes with your marriage," said Marshall. "Arthur is certainly a lucky man."

Delia could think of nothing to say in response because she was so distracted by how distinguished Marshall looked. His once dark hair and mustache had turned snow-white. It seemed to have happened almost overnight. She remembered Nannie telling her about it and saying that he looked like an old man now. Delia couldn't have disagreed more.

"Again," he said, kissing the back of Delia's hand, "best wishes to you." His eyes locked on to hers and for a moment everything around her ceased to exist; the music, the guests, the fanfare, all blurred into a soft focus. As soon as she caught herself, heat began filling her cheeks and she forced herself to turn to the next person in line.

As the party got under way, Delia and her new husband danced to Handel's "Largo" and the "Danube" waltz. It already felt different to dance as man and wife. It was as if a lifetime of hopes and dreams were embracing her.

"Look at Paxton over there, will you?" Arthur whispered in her ear. "He seems positively bored."

Delia glanced over Arthur's shoulder and saw Paxton waltzing with the girl he was currently courting, Muriel Brownville.

She was talking, her mouth moving as quickly as her feet. Paxton wasn't even looking at her.

"She won't last another week," said Arthur.

"That poor girl. She's obviously very fond of him."

"Aren't they all?"

"I'm afraid Paxton's running out of young girls' hearts to break," said Delia.

"What a pity," said Arthur with a roll of his eyes as he whisked Delia across the room, to where Paxton and Muriel were waltzing. As the two couples danced side by side, Arthur and Paxton carried on, the two of them talking about an upcoming polo match.

At the end of that dance, Delia shared an incredibly awkward waltz with her new father-in-law. Judge Caton was an older, but crankier, version of his son, muttonchops and all. But he wasn't half the dancer.

"We're pleased that he's finally settled down," said the judge as he clumsily swept her along the dance floor. "It certainly took him long enough to get around to it, didn't it?"

"I assure you he was well worth the wait. I'm a lucky girl."

The judge paused for a moment in the middle of their waltz and looked at her. "Ah, yes, spoken as a new bride," he said with a jeering laugh. "We'll see what you have to say a year from now."

Delia was grateful when the dance ended and she could retreat to the safety of Bertha and Abby. As the hour grew later, the crowd in her parents' ballroom thinned out. Delia was able to watch from across the room as Arthur, Paxton and some of the other remaining young men raised their glasses in toast after toast. Muriel Brownville was sitting by herself at one of the round tables, waiting on Paxton, her chin cradled in the heel of her hand.

When it was time to say their good-byes, the new couple

headed to the Palmer House, where they would spend their wedding night. Delia felt nervous but excited. Abby had prepared her, explaining things that her mother never would have addressed. Delia wondered if she would be as lucky as her friend Annie Swift, who had become pregnant on her wedding night.

The bridal suite was adorned with tufted chairs, a settee and a marble-topped commode with gold escutcheons. Enormous vases of roses and calla lilies were placed about the room and on either side of the canopy bed. Her maid, Therese, helped Delia prepare for her husband, then retired to her own staff room down the hall. Delia waited nervously for her husband, standing in the bedroom wearing her nightgown and a matching wrapper made of satin with a lace jabot.

"There you are," said Arthur when he entered from the other dressing room. He struggled his way out of his bathrobe and dropped it over the back of a chair. "And here we are."

Delia's heart was pounding as he crossed the room toward her. The smell of whiskey reached her before he did. Her mind raced as he led her over to the bed and ran his fingers through her hair. Arthur had been reserved when it came to displays of affection and passion, but she knew he was merely being chivalrous and respectful. Now they were man and wife and there was nothing that couldn't be expressed, couldn't be shared or shown. This one night would crown their marriage, seal their love and complete them as a couple.

She was expecting something tender, something slow and filled with emotion. According to Abby, the marriage act was so beautiful it could move her to tears. But instead she found Arthur's gestures clumsy, his kisses hurried and sloppy with whiskey. She longed to feel his skin on hers, but he kept his union suit on the whole time. His body was crushing her as he fumbled with his buttons and hastily hiked up her satin gown. He struggled to find his way to her beneath the bedsheets. Delia didn't know whether she should have helped. And then she felt him. Suspended above her, he rested the weight of his hips against her and pressed his legs into hers as the tip of him pushed against her most private opening. All at once, he forced his way inside her, and she felt a sharp tearing sensation. From what Abby had told her, she knew that meant her husband had taken her virginity, as he should. But Abby had not mentioned that the pain would continue, would grow even more intense as his body moved inside of hers. She stared at the bedpost shaking back and forth, back and forth as he pushed his way into her again and again. She might as well have been an ewer, for not once did he look at her, speak to her, kiss her. She gritted her teeth to keep from telling him to stop. She was his wife now and she wanted children. This was her duty. So she stayed silent until he finally stopped, suddenly stilling over top of her.

Arthur sighed.

She didn't move, wondering whether that was it.

He sighed again, deeper this time. "I knew I shouldn't have had that last brandy with Paxton." He rolled off her and pulled her head onto his chest.

Delia paused, wondering what to say, how to respond. She certainly didn't feel the elation her sister had promised. Instead she felt strangely lonely. Confused and left cold.

Before long, she heard Arthur begin to snore.

CHAPTER SIX

Delia and Arthur honeymooned in Europe for six months. They visited Paris and London, Italy and Spain. He took her to Germany and Switzerland, too. The judge had arranged for them to dine with princes and dukes, duchesses and earls. Delia had the time of her life, attending elaborate parties and balls, drinking and laughing into the early hours of the morning. She felt as if she had waltzed her way across the continent.

It was the second week of their honeymoon, after their evening with the infante of Spain, that Arthur returned to Delia's bed. Hurried and intrusive, it was no better for her than their wedding night. Apparently Arthur felt the same, for he did not visit their marriage bed again the entire time they were abroad. Honestly, if it weren't for wanting children, she would have been content to forgo the act altogether. Yet she loved Arthur so completely and adored their time together.

Once they returned to Chicago, Delia and Arthur moved into

a twenty-two-thousand-square-foot mansion at 1910 Calumet Avenue designed by the architects Burnham and Root. It was a grand home with a terra-cotta brick exterior and striped awnings along all the top-story windows. They had three master bedrooms, seven guest rooms, thirteen fireplaces and eleven servants, who had their own quarters off the kitchen.

Their house was just a few doors down the street from where the judge and Mrs. Caton lived. Arthur's middle sister, Laura, and her husband lived next door to the judge, and the mansion directly across the street belonged to the eldest daughter, Matilda, and her husband, completing what they affectionately referred to as "the Caton Colony." Delia had wanted to live elsewhere, away from the Colony, but at the judge's insistence, the newlyweds moved to the Calumet Avenue address.

She didn't like being under her mother-in-law's eye, but nonetheless she threw herself into making her new house one of the city's most elegant homes. She spent her first three months outfitting each room in the highest fashion. Her dining room table seated twenty and was designed especially for her by Charles Coolidge. The Herter Brothers did all her millwork and cabinets. The luster tile treatment in the drawing room was created by De Morgan and the wallpaper throughout the main floor was William Morris. She was eagerly awaiting the arrival of two settees, her sideboard, an armoire and several other pieces from Georges Jacob and Charles Cressant of France. Once everything was in place she could begin entertaining. Although the truth of it was that she and Arthur had enough social engagements on their calendar to carry them through the next two years. Just that evening, in fact, Delia and Arthur were attending a celebration at the Field mansion in honor of Marshall's forty-second birthday.

The Fields lived just one block over on Prairie Avenue, directly behind Delia and Arthur. Delia could look out her windows and see their mansion. Their backyards faced each other and were separated only by their coach houses, the stables and a narrow alleyway. Perhaps it was due to their close proximity, but since they'd been home from their honeymoon, Delia and Arthur had become especially friendly with the Fields.

Her maid, Therese, was helping Delia dress for the party in a *grenat* satin gown trimmed in velvet. Delia stood still, arms held out to her sides, while Therese fastened the fifteen buttons on the kid gloves that stopped above her elbows.

Arthur appeared in the doorway of her dressing room in a white silk waistcoat and a red cravat. "My, aren't we going to be the most natty couple there tonight." He caught a glimpse of himself in the cheval mirror and smiled approvingly.

"Would you expect anything less?" She smiled, too, and stood behind him in the mirror, smoothing her hands over the slope of his shoulders.

On the night of Marshall Field's birthday, August 18, 1876, Delia strolled around the corner arm in arm with her husband. While Calumet Avenue was home to the Caton Colony, one block east, Prairie Avenue was home to the rest of Chicago's elite. They had already gone past the Second Empire–style mansion belonging to Philip Armour, the meatpacking tycoon, and were coming up alongside George Pullman's stone-carved house with its glassed-in court and ornate terraces. George was best known for his invention of the Pullman luxury sleeper train cars and was a firm believer in the importance of opulence. A few doors down was the home of Levi Leiter, Marshall's business partner and part owner of Field, Leiter & Company. Everywhere Delia looked she saw houses with glorious terraces and Athenian marble facings, covered carriageways and decorative stonework. And while Delia's home was certainly on a par with the houses that lined the neighboring streets, Prairie Avenue had its own cachet and had earned the sobriquet "Millionaires' Row."

Soon they arrived at 1905 South Prairie Avenue. The Field mansion was a simple but massive redbrick home, flanked by two giant elms. Delia saw the white sheer curtains billowing in the windows as the silhouettes of partygoers moved about inside. There was only one carriage out front and she recognized it as the white brougham belonging to Bertha and Potter Palmer. The Palmers lived over on Michigan Boulevard. Apparently they, along with Abby and Augustus, who were still living with Delia's parents, were the only guests that evening from outside the immediate neighborhood.

"So sorry we're late," said Delia, clasping Nannie's hands while kissing her on both cheeks.

"No apologies needed," Nannie replied, going from Delia to Arthur. "The birthday boy isn't even home yet. He's working late as usual. Go on inside," she said. "Enjoy yourselves."

"Well, there you are," said Abby as soon as Delia entered the main room. It was a small, intimate gathering, just a handful of couples: George and Harriet Pullman, Philip and Malvina Armour, and Levi and Mary Leiter along with a few others.

Bertha was dressed in the height of style, a yellow silk gown stitched with golden embroidery and a delicately draped overskirt. She wore her dark hair in a high knot that supported her signature diamond tiara. Her many bracelets clinked as softly as wind chimes each time she moved.

As usual, Bertha held court surrounded by the other ladies at the party. But Delia noticed that Nannie appeared more interested in straightening a portrait on the wall than she was in what Bertha had to say. Though they were friends, Delia always sensed that Nannie felt threatened by Bertha and it was easy to understand why. After all, at twenty-six, Bertha was six years younger than Nannie. Bertha was beautiful and bubbly and everyone adored her. Mrs. Potter Palmer was always the first name on everyone's guest list and Delia suspected Nannie felt that as Mrs. Marshall Field, that was an honor she deserved.

Bertha was talking about Charles Frederick Worth, her favorite fashion designer. Delia's and Abby's, too.

"I'm going back to Paris next month to see him for my spring wardrobe," Bertha said.

"The man is a true artist. A genius," said Delia.

"I can't wait to see his latest collection," Abby added.

"Oh, when it comes to fashion, you Spencer girls have such an incriminating eye," said Mary Leiter.

Delia was certain she'd meant to say *discriminating* eye. She had only recently gotten to know Mary, but she'd already noticed the woman had a baffling habit of confusing her words.

Mary followed up her gaffe by saying, "You all have such a sense of style. The rest of us can't keep up."

"That's the whole idea," Delia teased.

They were having a good laugh over that when Delia noticed eight-year-old Marshall Junior standing in the corner, his eyes wide, watching all the glittering guests. He was a sweet young boy, exceedingly polite, always thanking Delia for the lollipop or chocolate she produced from her pocket whenever she saw him in the neighborhood with his governess. When he noticed Delia looking at him, he scampered out into the hallway and perched himself on the bottom step of the staircase, his nightshirt pulled down over his knees and skimming the tops of his slippers.

Delia went over and crouched down beside him. "Hello, Junior. How are you tonight?"

"I'm fine, Mrs. Caton." He offered his hand and gave hers a firm shake.

"Where's your sister?"

"Oh, she's already in bed. She's just a baby."

Delia laughed. Ethel was three years old. "Shouldn't you be in bed, too?"

"Please don't tell Mother I'm down here. I'll get a whipping if she sees me."

"I won't say a word as long as you go back up to bed right now."

With that, Junior sprang to his feet and Delia watched him scurry up the stairs. Just as she stood and turned around, Marshall came through the front door.

"And there he is," said Delia. "The guest of honor. Let me be the first to wish you a happy birthday."

"Oh please." He winced mockingly, handing his plug hat to the butler. "I've been doing my level best to forget what today is."

"Not much chance of that happening here tonight," she said.

He removed his gloves, handing them to his butler as well. "I suppose everyone's arrived already, then?"

"Afraid so."

Marshall leaned toward Delia and whispered, "My wife's going to have my hide for being late, you know." He offered a smile just as Nannie came around the corner.

"Well, look who decided to grace us with his company." Nannie folded her arms across her chest. "Maybe you'd like to greet your guests. They've been waiting over an hour for you." She gestured with her chin toward the grand hall.

"Hello, dear." He leaned in to kiss her cheek, but Nannie pulled back and turned her face away.

"Well, then," he said, unfazed by Nannie's snub, "if you'll both excuse me."

It wasn't until Marshall left her side that Delia realized she was flushed and stirred to her core. It seemed like the mere sight of him always did that to her. She reentered the party, watching as everyone rallied around Marshall. In his quiet, unassuming way, he made a statement wherever he went. Even if it hadn't been his birthday, he would have been the center of attention. He just had one of those magnetic personalities.

The party continued and Delia tried to keep an eye on Arthur, who always seemed to have a fresh drink in his hand. Of course, their life had seemed like one long party, so drinking wasn't unusual, but lately Arthur didn't just keep up with the crowd; he often seemed ahead of it. Depending on the circumstances, he could be either the source of great amusement or the cause of embarrassment. Just the week before, during a party at the home of the meatpacking giant Gustavus Swift, Arthur, after a few too many whiskeys, had taken command of a loud and boisterous game of charades. Delia found herself apologizing to their hostess, Annie Swift, and she and Arthur had a terrible argument about it when they got home. The next morning he didn't remember a thing. Delia glanced over at him now. He sat in the corner talking with Potter, Augustus and Marshall, and he seemed perfectly fine as far as she could tell. But she still worried.

She went back to chatting with Harriet Pullman, George's wife. "Has the rest of your furniture arrived yet from France?" she asked.

"I'm still waiting on a few pieces," said Delia, finally taking her eyes off Arthur.

"Well, I simply can't wait to see what you've done. I'm certain your home is going to be spectacular." She smiled warmly, her full round cheeks shining like small, polished globes. From the neck up you'd think she was a heavyset woman, but in fact, Harriet was quite slim.

"We'll be entertaining soon enough, but I'll have you over beforehand for tea and a private viewing."

"Oh, that would be marvelous." Her cheeks rose even higher on her face.

"Did I hear something about a private viewing?" Sybil Perkins interrupted, her fingertips fluttering as she pressed her palms together.

Delia gazed at her as if she didn't understand, hoping to dodge the question. Sybil was the neighborhood busybody. She reminded Delia of a little birdlike creature with her pointy nose and chin, her arms always flapping about excitedly, her hands gesticulating energetically each time she spoke.

"Delia here has agreed to give me an advanced showing of her home."

"Marvelous," said Sybil. "I'd love to join you."

"But of course," said Harriet before Delia could think of a reasonable objection. It was to be expected. Why Harriet and the others tolerated Sybil's nosiness was a mystery to Delia.

"I'm available Thursday afternoon. Or next Tuesday as long as it's before three o'clock . . ." Sybil was saying.

Delia glanced over to check on Arthur and noticed Marshall looking her way. It was just a passing glance, but it grabbed hold of her for a moment. She couldn't look away from him even though she knew she should.

"Well?" Sybil was waiting.

"What? I'm sorry. What?" She hadn't heard a word Sybil said. "You'll have to excuse me now, Sybil. I just remembered there's something I need to tell Arthur."

Delia had been desperate to get away from the woman. When she reached Arthur's side, she noticed the waiters serving hors d'oeuvres and whispered, "Don't you think you should eat something?"

Arthur didn't seem to hear what she said. He turned to Delia and smiled. "I was just talking with Marshall about a polo match in New York City." She noticed his eyes were unfocused, as if he were speaking to the air. "Fascinating. I find him just fascinating. Don't you? Really fascinating."

"Yes, yes, he is fascinating," Delia agreed, reaching for Arthur's empty glass, grateful that he didn't resist. When a tray of petite cheese soufflés and quail eggs nestled in puff pastry passed by, Delia insisted that he have some.

She stayed close to Arthur after that, until dinner was called. Her seat at the table was stationed in between Lionel Perkins and Philip Armour. From across the table, she watched as the footman refilled Arthur's wineglass. The dinner was a five-course extravaganza, and thankfully, by the time it was over, Arthur had sobered up.

For dessert, the footmen rolled out a grand cake standing four tiers high and lavishly decorated. Nannie led everyone in a round of "For He's a Jolly Good Fellow" while Marshall shook his hands, trying to wave off the attention. For someone who was such a showman in his place of business, Delia found him to be quiet and introverted in social situations. It was an interesting contradiction and it intrigued her.

Nannie stood at her husband's side with her fingertips on his shoulder. Her pose struck Delia as oddly possessive. After they sang, she said, "Happy birthday, dear. I can only hope that someone gives you a timepiece for a present so you won't be late next time we have company."

Marshall smiled graciously, his hands raised in surrender as everyone laughed politely. But Delia saw something pass between Nannie and Marsh and realized it hadn't been a good-natured gibe.

"Well now," said Bertha, "let's hear from the birthday boy."

"Speech, speech," said Potter, raising his champagne glass by its stem. "Come on, Marsh, let's hear it."

But Marshall waved his hands in protest.

"Oh, please." Bertha clapped her hands, setting her bracelets clanking. "Speech! Speech!"

"Go on, dear," said Nannie. "Your guests are waiting for you. Again."

Marshall shifted in his chair, stalling.

It was Delia who finally raised her glass and said, "On behalf of Mr. Field I would like to announce that all imported fabrics will be on sale tomorrow."

The room erupted in laughter and Marshall covered his heart with his hand and bowed toward Delia in appreciation. An unexpected glow welled up inside her as she basked in his praise.

"Well done," said Potter.

"Your wife has quite a wit," George Pullman said to Arthur.

"That she does." Arthur reached for Delia's hand. "Indeed she does."

Mary Leiter turned to her husband, utterly confused and a bit miffed about it. "You didn't tell me there was a sale on fabrics tomorrow."

Everyone looked at Mary Leiter and burst out laughing again.

CHAPTER SEVEN

After they'd finished dinner, the men retreated to the library for their brandies and cigars, while the women retired to the parlor. Nannie had furnished the room extravagantly, in the style of Louis XVI. A gold birdcage stood in the corner, home to her two gray, yellow-faced cockatiels with matching orange blush spots near their eyes. Delia, who'd always been afraid of birds, sat as far away from them as possible in a black and gold chair with fluted legs and a pair of golden sphinxes for arms. She found it as unattractive as it was uncomfortable.

While sipping her sherry, Mary Leiter announced that her daughter was starting piano lessons. "She practices her scales morning, noon and night," she laughed lightly. "I tell you, her piano playing is going to be the vein of my existence."

No one bothered to correct her. They were all accustomed to Mary Leiter twisting up her words, coming out with a string of nonsensical statements that everyone politely ignored. After all, like Nannie, Mary was a simple woman whose husband had come into a great deal of money after establishing Field & Leiter. While the men seemed to have transitioned gracefully into their positions of power, their wives appeared to be struggling with their own elevated status. Especially Mary, who found herself ill equipped to mix with high society. She wore couture by designers whose names she could not pronounce and sat through operas without grasping a single word. But she was kind, so everyone overlooked her naïveté and malapropisms.

Harriet Pullman continued the conversation, talking above the squawking of the birds, about her twin boys and then her two older daughters. Bertha chimed in about her sons and Sybil Perkins spoke at length about her daughters. After Nannie told stories about Ethel and Junior she asked Abby about Spencer.

"I can hardly believe he's almost three years old," said Abby.

Delia folded her arms and pressed her ankles and knees tightly together. It was painfully obvious that she was the only one in the room with nothing to contribute to a conversation about children.

Harriet turned to her. "You know, dear, you're really still a newlywed. I'm sure that a year from now, you'll be raising a family, too."

"Oh, of course she will," insisted Abby while the cockatiels batted their wings.

"We do hope to start a family soon," Delia said as she leaned her shoulder blades against the chair. She and Arthur had been married eight months and so far nothing. Arthur was the only Caton son, and the judge and Mrs. Caton were eager for an heir to carry on the family name. Delia's own mother had mentioned countless times that she wanted more grandchildren. But no one wanted Delia to have a child more than Delia. If only Arthur would come to the marriage bed more often, she knew they would stand a better chance of becoming pregnant. Not a month had passed that she hadn't cried at the first sign of her own blood.

While the women carried on, Delia excused herself and slipped out of the parlor. She was light-headed and rested her forehead against the wainscoting in the hallway, drawing deep breaths. Maybe something she'd eaten hadn't agreed with her or maybe she was just overwhelmed by the talk of children. With each new breath she felt the stabbing jab of her corset digging into her rib cage.

While standing there she overheard the men down the hall in the library. It sounded like they were having some sort of a gentlemanly disagreement, with Levi Leiter and Marshall at its center. Though Levi and Marshall were successful business partners, Delia had heard that the two rarely saw eye to eye on most matters. Apparently that night was no exception. What surprised her, though, was that they were willing to debate their business disputes openly in front of their friends.

"This is where you and I differ," she heard Levi saying. "Wholesale is more lucrative and yet, you insist on focusing on retail. Retail is nothing but a bunch of women with too much time on their hands."

"Time. And money," she heard Potter remind him.

"Especially when it comes to our wives," George Pullman added with a laugh.

Marshall spoke over the others. "That's precisely why I want to continue importing merchandise from Europe. I've always said, 'Give the lady what she wants.' "

"And I'm sick of hearing it. That's nonsense," said Levi. "Women aren't all that particular. They'll purchase whatever we offer them."

The conversation drifted on, but Delia lost track of it as another wave of vertigo came on. She flattened her hands against the wall and studied the swirling grains in the wainscoting, trying not to faint. She felt like she'd been there for hours when she heard a voice calling from behind.

"Are you unwell?"

Delia turned with a start and there was Marshall.

"My goodness, you're white as a sheet," he said, placing his hand on the small of her back and steering her into the library. "Get me a glass of water," he called to his footman.

Arthur rushed to her side. "Dell, what's wrong?"

"Nothing, nothing," she said. "I'm just a little light-headed is all. I'll be fine."

The men turned and stared at her, unaccustomed to having a lady in their company while enjoying their cigars and after-dinner drinks. Levi Leiter and George Pullman nearly dropped their glasses and Potter just about choked on his brandy. Augustus adjusted his monocle, while Lionel Perkins flicked his cigar and missed the ashtray by an inch.

"Please, gentlemen," she said, breathing in their smoke. "Forgive me for intruding. I'll just be a moment."

Arthur helped her over to the settee. "Just rest here until it passes, Dell."

She took the glass of water from the servant. It felt ridiculously heavy in her hand. After a few sips she felt better, and the light-headedness subsided, but still she couldn't bring herself to return to the parlor. She couldn't bear listening to the other women going on about their children. And besides, what the men were saying intrigued her, so she stayed in the library, feigning illness. Before long, the men turned away from her and resumed their conversation.

". . . You give these female customers far too much credit," Levi insisted. "Most of them wouldn't know a piece of Pekin wool from a bolt of tweed."

Delia couldn't help but laugh.

"Excuse me?" Levi gave her a sharp look.

"Oh, surely you don't believe that, Mr. Leiter." No sooner had the words left her mouth than she regretted saying them.

Arthur reached for her hand and gave her a warning squeeze. "You'll have to forgive Delia," he said with a chuckle. "I'm afraid my wife gets a bit passionate when it comes to ladies' fashions." He laughed again.

"No. No," said Marshall, leaning forward. "I'd very much like to hear what she has to say. Delia," he said, addressing her directly, "you certainly represent the modern woman. And, Levi, I'm sorry, but the modern woman is precisely our customer. Please"—he gestured to her—"go on."

"Well . . ." Delia cleared her throat and began. "For one thing, I believe that fashion is essential to a lady. Particularly a lady of means. It's an expression, a form of art if it's done properly. Mr. Leiter, I think you'd be surprised by how astute most women are when it comes to fashion."

"That is precisely my point," said Marshall.

Delia eased back in her seat and smiled.

Levi drew hard on his cigar. He was a big barrel-chested man with a reddish beard and dark hair combed straight down onto his wide forehead. When he spoke, he always sounded as if he had a head cold. "I tell you," he said to Marshall, "you're wasting your time and our money by catering to these women." He gazed over at Delia, hands raised in apology. "No offense."

"Oh, none taken." She smiled. "But I do think Marshall here raises an interesting point."

"Is that so?"

"Well, let's face it," she said, "for any woman of means, the dry goods store is our gathering place. If we're not attending luncheons or women's meetings, we're at the dry goods stores.

We go in the morning and we're there until we either need to powder our noses or we're about to drop from hunger."

The men laughed.

"I'm quite serious. Where else are we women going to go? Of course we can visit a tearoom or attend our meetings at one another's houses, but we're not allowed in your clubs and we can't very well congregate in saloons, now, can we? More to the point, we don't have a place of business to go to. Keeping up with the latest fashions, and making sure you men live in the finest homes—those are the very things that have become our jobs. And we tend to our business at the dry goods stores."

"Exactly," said Marshall. "Levi, are you hearing what this young lady is saying?"

Delia smiled, practically beaming. She'd never felt so validated. She was filled with a sense of acceptance and pride. She had a mind to fire up a cigar right along with them.

Still, Levi wouldn't let the subject go, so the discussion escalated with both men nearly shouting. Levi started pounding his fist against the arm of his chair and he went red in the face as a vein in the center of his forehead stood out, pulsing. "Marshall Field, you are no businessman." Levi slapped his glass down on the table.

The conversation continued and after finishing their cigars, they decided to rejoin the women in the parlor. When Delia walked in with the men, the wives rose from their chairs. Abby and Bertha stayed back while the others stood side by side with their arms crossed over their chests, forming a wall of disapproval. The cockatiels were flapping their wings like mad, chattering away in the corner.

"There you are," Nannie said to Delia in a cool even tone. "We were wondering where you'd wandered off to."

"I'm afraid I was a bit light-headed. The men brought me some water and I waited with them in the library until it passed."

"Thank goodness you're feeling better," said Nannie. Her lips were curved upward in a forced smile.

When the women and men began chatting again, Bertha pulled Delia aside and lowered her voice. "As your friend, I'm telling you to watch your step. It's no secret that the Fields are unhappy, and you don't want to cross Nannie."

Delia glanced at her hostess and then back at Bertha. "What are you talking about?"

"After you left the parlor, some of the women were saying that you were coming across as being awfully *familiar* with Marshall."

"That's ridiculous—"

"I'm telling you as your friend," said Bertha. "You don't want to cross Nannie."

Later that night after Delia undressed and dismissed Therese for the evening, she ran her fingers over the tender indents along her rib cage and waist caused by the boning of her corset. Her unpinned hair hung down in glossy brown ringlets caressing the bare skin at the center of her back.

She eased into her wrapper and went to the door, pressing her ear up close, listening, hoping to hear the sound of Arthur's footsteps making their way down the hall. All was quiet. She thought about going to his room, but it was never good when she did the approaching. She knew it had to be his idea.

She went to her dressing table and brushed out her hair. As she worked through a snarl, she tried to remember the last time she and Arthur had had relations. It had been at least a month and she was at a loss as to why. She couldn't force her husband to try more often. Perhaps this was normal for a man and wife. Maybe the problem was her and she should have been able to conceive with the least amount of effort. But still she so desperately wanted a child, especially after listening to the women talking about their children that night.

She set down her paddle brush and went over to the windows. Looking out across the backyard, she could see the lamps still on inside the Field mansion. Bertha's warning came back to her as she gripped onto the velvet drapery and wondered if maybe she *had* been too familiar with Marshall. She admitted she was fond of him and yes, they did seem to share many of the same interests. Oh, but it was absurd. After all, he was married to her friend and far too old for her. Besides, she was a married woman herself.

She drew the drapes closed and turned down the lamp on her side table, watching the pink globe darken as the wick went dead.

CHAPTER EIGHT

"What brings you down here?" her father asked, as Delia followed him about the floor of Hibbard, Spencer & Company. The store had been rebuilt at Wabash and Lake, at the same location as before the fire.

"Can't a girl visit her father at work?" she said as they moved up and down the narrow aisles. Delia could stand in the center and touch both sides with her fingertips. They were in the sporting section, going from a heap of lawn tennis rackets to a pile of fishing poles and tackle boxes, to the mountain of golf clubs and croquet sets.

"You know I welcome your visits anytime." Mr. Spencer picked up a baseball. "Look out, Dell—" He tossed the ball. "Here it comes."

Delia caught it in one gloved hand. "You really should have had a son," she said with a laugh, throwing it back.

"Nonsense, I'm counting on you for another grandson. And

besides, you're still the best shortstop there is." He smiled and set the ball down.

Delia changed the subject and got to the point of her visit. "You'll never guess where we were last night," she said, hoping to sound casual.

"And where was that?"

"I attended a birthday party for Marshall Field."

"Oh, no! Fraternizing with the competition again. There's been quite a bit of that lately, hasn't there been?" He shook his head in mock disapproval.

"After all, we are neighbors. And Arthur and I are awfully fond of Marshall. And Nannie, too. What do you make of him? Of Marshall?"

"Marshall and I have known each other for years. You know that. I see him all the time at the Chicago Club—he sits at the Millionaires' Table with Cyrus McCormick and Potter and the rest of them. I join them there occasionally, when I have the time."

"Yes, but what's your impression of him?"

Her father paused and thought for a moment. "Decent enough fellow. A few of my clerks used to work for him, though they didn't much care for his style of management. He's got a reputation for being overly demanding. Tough to work for. *Persnickety* is the word I've heard associated with him. And cheap—at least when it comes to salaries."

"Oh . . ." Delia felt a wave of disappointment. *Persnickety* and *cheap*. Not flattering words at all.

"But then again," her father said, "I suppose that's what makes him so darn successful. When it comes to business, he's brilliant. That's why they call him the Merchant Prince." He paused to straighten his cuff. "Why the sudden interest in Marshall Field?"

"Oh, no reason," she said, waving his question away with a

sweep of her hand. "As I said, we were socializing with him last night. Arthur is simply mad for Marshall, that's all."

A few days later Nannie invited Delia to tea. She arrived wearing a purple silk Madame Gabrielle dress with two gathered flounces and a rolling collar trimmed in velvet. But Nannie greeted her in a simple skirt with a *tablier* hanging down the front. At first Delia thought she had arrived too early, but it became apparent that Nannie had no intention of changing. Delia ended up feeling terribly overdressed and awkward.

Still, Nannie had a lovely table for two set near the window in the parlor. The cockatiels were perched in their golden cage, squawking and flapping their wings in a fury as Delia passed in front of them.

The weather had called for rain according to the newspapers, but so far it was a crisp day, not a cloud in the sky. The sunlight coming through the window shades landed directly in Delia's line of vision. She could see the bands of sunlight running across her arms and hands and no doubt across her face.

"Excuse me," Delia said, squinting to block the sunlight, "but would it be possible to adjust the shades?"

"Oh, of course, of course," said Nannie, toying with her earrings and then her brooch.

Delia waited patiently, but Nannie never called for her butler and made no attempt to adjust the shades herself. Instead, Nannie went on talking. "You and Arthur are such a fun couple," she said. "Everyone always says you're the life of the party."

"Well, Arthur's the instigator, you know."

"That's not what I've heard. Weren't you the one who started everyone playing charades at the Swifts' dinner party?"

Delia cringed inwardly, remembering that night when Arthur had behaved so badly. She was surprised that Nannie had mentioned this and told herself that she was just making conversation. Still, Delia tried to deflect the insinuation. "Who doesn't love charades?" Delia forced a smile as she gazed at the bands of sunlight slicing across her arms. A trickle of sweat rolled down her back. She was terribly distracted by the heat and the cockatiels, who were now squawking again, beating their wings madly.

"I've always been very fond of Arthur," said Nannie. "Still, I'm sure you must find it lonely in that big house. No children. Just the two of you."

"I manage to keep busy," said Delia, as she lifted her teacup, telling herself it was an innocent observation, and that Nannie intended no malice by the comment.

"You know," said Nannie, drumming her fingers along the tabletop, "Marshall is quite taken with you."

"Oh?" Delia nearly spilled her tea.

"He adores Arthur as well," she said. "But there's something about you he finds particularly fascinating. He's always admired high-spirited, vibrant women. His mother was like that. That's why he and Bertha get along so well."

The light coming through the window went from blindingly bright to suddenly dark and ominous.

"Well, it looks as though it might rain after all, doesn't it?" said Delia, desperate to change the subject. The birds began acting up again and Delia shuddered.

"I gather you don't care for birds," Nannie said, noticing Delia's reaction.

"They're very pretty," she said. "But actually, I'm terrified of birds. Someone threw a dead bird in my lap when I was a child and I've been frightened of them ever since."

"Well, then, there's only one way to get you over your fear." Nannie got up and went over to the cage, causing the birds to extend their wings and let out a string of more shrill calls.

"Really, I'm fine," said Delia, watching in horror as Nannie laughed and threw open the cage, letting the birds loose.

They came flapping out into the room, soaring and swerving in opposite directions. Delia's heart raced as she ducked each time one of them flew overhead.

"There's nothing to be afraid of." Nannie held out her hand and waited until one of the birds landed on her, its talons gripping onto her flesh. "Here now," she said, walking toward Delia with the bird. "See how sweet he is?" She lowered her hand, letting the bird hop onto Delia's shoulder.

Delia let out a gasp and froze. She could hardly breathe. The bird's claws dug into her shoulder while the other bird perched on the base of the chandelier, eyeing her with a menacing gaze. Delia was too terrified to move.

"Oh, relax," said Nannie with a laugh. "That way he won't bite." She smiled at Delia, clearly enjoying this.

"Please." Delia begged with her eyes. "Please get him off."

"Oh, all right." Nannie reached over for the cockatiel and with a gentle toss sent the bird soaring into the air. She went back around and sat down while the birds flew about the room. "Did I mention that I'm taking the children to Europe for the winter?"

"Oh?" Delia couldn't take her eyes off the birds, which were now perched along the windowsill, dangerously close to her.

"The Christmas season is so taxing on Marshall," said Nannie. "He's down at the store from morning till night. If it were up to him, he'd just as soon sleep there. So I'm going to take the children and have a real holiday by ourselves."

"What a shame that you can't all be together." Delia flinched as the birds took off again, circling the chandelier.

"Junior's used to it. Ethel's too young to know the difference." Nannie paused, closed her eyes and began massaging her temples with her thumb and middle finger.

"Are you unwell?" Delia asked.

"Just this headache. I've had it for two days now. I was feverish all day yesterday and now I have a migraine. I can't seem to get rid of it."

"Perhaps I should leave and let you lie down."

"Would you mind, dear?"

Delia was only too happy to get away from the birds. There was a crack of lightning followed by the roar of thunder as Nannie rose from her chair and drifted out of the room without so much as a good-bye.

Delia raced out of the room, closing the doors behind her while the butler fetched her shawl. As he led her down the hallway, the front door opened and in walked Marshall, shaking the rain from his top hat and umbrella.

"It's pouring like the devil out there," he said to his butler before looking up and noticing her. "Why, Delia"—his eyes grew wide—"what a wonderful surprise."

She couldn't conceal her smile. It was ridiculous that she should be so happy to see him. Just one glimpse and she'd forgotten about the birds. "I was having tea with Nannie," she said. "She wasn't feeling well and went to lie down. I was just leaving."

Another crack of lightning lit up the foyer, followed a beat later by the thunder.

"Oh dear," she said, "I was sure the weather report was wrong. I didn't even bring my parasol."

"Don't you worry," he said, opening his umbrella. "I'll walk you home."

"Didn't anyone ever tell you it's bad luck to open an umbrella indoors?"

"Pfft." He held the umbrella over her head as droplets of rainwater ran off the edges and onto the floor. "I don't believe in silly superstitions. Don't tell me you do."

"Guilty, I'm afraid. No shoes on the counter, no walking beneath ladders—I've always been that way."

He smiled as if he found it refreshing, or perhaps just immature and foolish. She couldn't tell.

He looked out the window. "It seems to be letting up. Shall we make a run for it?"

"You don't need to walk me home. Really. It's just rain. I won't melt."

"Nonsense. I insist." He stepped out onto the porch and waited for her to join him beneath the umbrella.

Halfway around the block the rain started up again. They were walking side by side, shoulder to shoulder. She could feel the heat coming off his body, could smell the scent of his shaving soap along with the damp leaves and soaked grass. Maybe it was because of what Nannie had said to her—the sheer power of suggestion—but Delia felt as though she and Marshall were engaged in some illicit act. The rain was pelting the umbrella just as intensely as Delia's heart was beating. Neither one of them spoke; she found herself at a loss for words.

Marshall let the umbrella veer too far to the left, sending a trickle of rain down Delia's side. She reached up to center the umbrella and as her gloved fingers brushed against his hand, an unexpected jolt surged through her. They stopped walking for a moment, turned and looked into each other's eyes. Delia swallowed hard. Her fingers were still touching his. A crack of lightning lit up the sky and before the thunder struck, they'd started walking again. Faster this time.

When they reached her home, they stood beneath the front awning, looking at each other while rain trickled down the gabled rooftop.

"Thank you for walking me home," she managed to say.

"My great pleasure."

He was so close she could breathe him in, feeling her chest swell. His brilliant blue gray eyes never left hers. Something inside her, at her very center, responded to him against her will. His eyes dropped to her mouth and as he studied her lips she felt herself drifting closer and closer to him, as if pulled by an invisible string. Just when she was sure he was going to kiss her, the front door opened.

"Why, Marshall." Arthur smiled and reached out his hand. "Good of you to see Dell home. I was getting worried and thought I might go fetch her myself. Come in, come in. Dry off and have a brandy with me."

Marshall tried to beg off, but Arthur insisted. "You can't deny me the chance to beat you again at a game of chess, can you?"

While Marshall and Arthur went into the library to play chess, Delia slipped away and went up to her bedroom. She was flushed as she stood before her vanity, refusing to look herself in the eye. Nannie was her friend. Arthur was her husband. She pressed one hand to her damp forehead and the other to her heart, thinking, *What just happened out there?* She wasn't sure if she was frightened or excited, but she knew something had just started and that nothing would ever be the same.

CHAPTER NINE

"No, no! Stop it!" Delia screeched as Arthur clamped his hand over her mouth. She squirmed in every direction, trying to get away.

"Ssshh. You want the servants to hear you?"

Her sides were aching from laughing so hard.

He reached across the bed and tickled her again.

"No! Stop it!" Delia squealed, pulling away from him.

"Okay, all right." He held up his hands in surrender. "Truce."

The tears were oozing from her eyes as she giggled and rolled on top of him, their legs entangled. She sighed and smiled at him, letting down her guard just as Arthur reached up and tickled her ribs.

Delia shrieked and laughed again. "I beg of you, stop. Stop!"

"Okay. All right. I promise—no more."

She watched him guardedly, and once she was certain that he meant it this time, she drew a deep breath and dropped her head to his shoulder. Her nightdress was hiked up to her waist, her hips were pressed hard into his and she felt the heat building inside her.

He'd come to her room earlier that night and climbed into her bed. After turning down the lamp, he pulled the bed linens up over their bodies and reached for her. She always felt the initial sting of him entering her, but then her body would relax and make room for him. But just as she'd begun to relish the feel of him, the sense of fullness and completion, he was done. Usually, as soon as he finished, he'd put on his robe and be halfway down the hall before she'd even sat up. But that night he stayed in her bed afterward. They talked, they laughed, he found her ticklish spots—under her arm, the side of her ribs, the arch of her foot. Now that they were quieting down, she found herself wanting him again. Lifting her head, she looked into his brown eyes, leaned in and kissed him.

He returned the kiss, and her excitement spiked immediately. She was panting, her core filling with expectation when he reached up and cupped her face in his hands.

"It's getting late, my pet." He scooted out from under her, peeled back the covers and sat up on the side of the bed.

"You don't have to go yet," she said, rising to her knees, pressing herself against him with her arms wrapped about him from behind. "You could sleep in here tonight."

"And keep you up with my snoring?" He undid her hands, stood up and reached for his robe hanging off the bedpost. "Get some sleep, Dell. It's late." He turned back and kissed her on the lips. Then he left.

Afterward, Delia lay in bed staring at the ceiling. She placed her hands on her belly, wondering if maybe this was the night she would conceive. Her body was still longing for Arthur as she let her hand drift down the slope of her stomach to the top of her coarse dark hairs. That night she let her fingers explore the parts of her that Arthur had never searched out.

Delia woke early the next morning. And like all mornings after, she placed her hand on her stomach feeling for a difference, some indication. Her skin was warm, warmer than usual, and though she knew it was foolish, she told herself that it was a sign.

It wasn't quite seven o'clock when she eased out from under the covers and rang for Therese to help her dress before she headed downstairs. From the dining room she could tell the kitchen maid was hard at work. The room filled with the aroma of coffee brewing and the scent of pastries with cinnamon and sweet cocoa baking in the oven. The *Chicago Tribune* and the *Chicago Daily News* were folded neatly in front of Arthur's place setting. Williams, their butler, must have just pressed them, because she could feel the heat still on the pages when she reached for the *Tribune.*

She skimmed through the columns, reading about Rutherford B. Hayes's quest for the presidential nomination, a labor union rally and a man in Grand Rapids named Bissell who'd invented something called a carpet sweeper. Delia, who'd never beaten a rug in her life, couldn't imagine such a thing ever catching on. She turned the page and saw a large advertisement for Field, Leiter & Company.

Delia hadn't been down to Field, Leiter & Company in nearly two weeks, not since the day Marshall walked her home in the rain. Harriet Pullman and Annie Swift had invited her to join them that afternoon for shopping and Delia was debating whether to go. She was beginning to think that avoiding Marshall and his store was in and of itself an admission of guilt. After all, she hadn't done anything wrong. She'd probably only imagined that he'd wanted to kiss her that day in the rain. For the umpteenth time she reminded herself that he was a married man. They were neighbors. They were friends. Just friends.

It was all so ridiculous. Delia made up her mind that she would indeed meet the others at Field, Leiter & Company that day. She would purchase the last of the decorating touches for her home so that she would be set to entertain in time for the winter season.

The footman brought out a plate of hot tarts served on Delia's Spode breakfast dishes. She liberally spread the sweet cream butter over the top of the steaming pastries and let the delicate layers melt in her mouth. The coffee was good and strong. While she continued reading the newspaper, Delia absentmindedly nibbled at the tarts until the plate was empty.

By the time she'd finished her coffee, it was going on nine o'clock and Arthur was still in bed and showing no signs of stirring. She took a fresh cup of coffee and went into the library to see if she needed anything at the store to finish the room.

It was a handsome room with an antique Robert Adam mahogany hutch in the corner and a wall of shelving devoted to Arthur's law books, their uniform gold-embossed lettering running down the spines. A spectacular tiger skin was splayed out in the center of the floor as a rug, its head and tail still attached. Arthur had shot the tiger while on safari with Paxton in Africa before they were married. At first the rug had frightened her. The eyes were so intense, the teeth so sharp and menacing, she'd nearly expected the beast to leap up from the floor. But over time she'd grown to admire its sheer ferocity. In fact, she liked it so much that she'd agreed to the bear rug that now lay in her parlor as well as the buffalo head mounted over the mantel in the drawing room.

Delia was making a mental note to pick up some lace doilies

for the sideboard when Arthur appeared in the doorway, still in his bathrobe and slippers, his heels riding over the back edges.

"Good morning, my pet." He came over and kissed her forehead. "You're up early."

"Or perhaps *you're* getting up *late*?" She raised her cup as if making a toast.

"Well"—he lowered his voice—"someone kept me awake very late last night."

She laughed, thinking of how much she'd enjoyed having him in her bed. "What are you going to do today?" she asked.

"I thought I'd go riding with Paxton."

Arthur was an accomplished equestrian, having learned to ride almost as soon as he was able to walk. He kept a stable behind the house on Calumet for his six geldings and four mares. Downstate in Ottawa, he had a horse-breeding farm with two stallions and twenty mares that produced fifteen to twenty foals a year. The horse farm was adjacent to the Caton family's country estate, a Queen Anne–style mansion that was unquestionably the focal point of the countryside. Its many chimneys could be seen from every direction.

"Or on second thought," said Arthur, "maybe I'll go to the Chicago Club instead. Pick up a hand of cards and visit with the fellows down there."

The Chicago Club was exclusive: men only, and only very wealthy men at that. Marshall belonged there, as did Potter, Cyrus McCormick, George Pullman and even her father. Delia didn't say a word, but she desperately wanted to point out that he'd been to the club nearly every day that week. Instead he could have gone through the household expenses and seen to it that the servants were paid on time that week rather than having them come to her with their hands out. Arthur could have met with Augustus, who had been asking for legal advice on a business matter. He could have been doing much more than spending his days drinking and playing cards at the Chicago Club.

Sometimes she wished he'd go back to work at the law firm, but she knew he never would. Between his windfall from Western Union coupled with his trust fund, Arthur Caton didn't have to work. He didn't want to work, either. And this bothered Delia. She was accustomed to men like her father who worked twelve- and fourteen-hour days and not just for the money. Hardly. Her father was wealthy enough to have retired when he was young. But he loved his work, and as far as she was concerned, hard work was what made a man a man. After all, Marshall Field didn't need to work, either.

Delia stopped herself. It wasn't fair to compare Arthur with men like her father and Marshall. Arthur had grown up in a family of privilege, whereas her father and Marshall had started with nothing. They had no choice but to work and work hard unless they wanted to starve in the streets. It was a way of life for them.

She remembered the stories her father told her about arriving in Chicago with just fifteen dollars in his pocket. And then there was Potter, who had opened his first Chicago business with a small loan he'd obtained from his father. Nannie had told Delia about Marshall growing up as a poor farm boy in Massachusetts and coming to town to make a name for himself. Delia found it all so inspiring. To think that these men had achieved so much, and out of nothing but their own determination to succeed. What she wouldn't give for the opportunities that men had, and yet her own husband wasn't even interested in trying to achieve something of his own. It bewildered her.

"Well," she said, "I for one have a very busy day ahead of me. I'm heading down to State Street for a bit of shopping and then I'm meeting your mother here later to walk her through the house."

“Just as well then that I disappear for the day, isn’t it?” He chuckled.

Delia patted the cushion next to her on the davenport. “Come. Sit next to me.”

After he sat down she rested her head on his shoulder and said, “I think last night may have been the night.”

His eyes opened wide. “Can you tell so soon?”

“Oh, I know I’m being silly, but I’m just so hopeful.” She looped her arm through his and repeated, “I’m just so very, very hopeful.”

CHAPTER TEN

Later that afternoon, Arthur and his coachman drove Delia downtown in his four-horse tallyho, which drew attention from nearly everyone they passed. Arthur was known about town for his four black stallions and black carriage with gold trim. He loved to ride up on the box with his coachman just so he could see all the admirers.

After being let off at Washington and State, Delia had to wait several minutes for a break in the trail of omnibuses, wagons and hacks barreling past before she could cross the street. And even then, she had to rush before the next cavalcade raced through. The fall winds blew in from the west, whirling a pile of dead leaves in a circle above the sidewalk. Chisels and hammers pounded all around her as more buildings—theaters and restaurants and shops—went up. Delia joined the wash of pedestrians weaving in and out of the jammed crosswalks. Pushcarts lined both sides of the street, tended by men in soft caps waving to her and the other passersby, peddling their wares, everything from caramels and sweetmeats to cabbages and tomatoes.

The city's resilience struck Delia each time she visited State Street. It had been five years since the Great Fire and in that time the heart of Chicago had been rebuilt, and then some. All the buildings that Delia remembered being charred to the ground had been resurrected, and in grander style than ever before.

As promised, Potter had rebuilt the Palmer House to even greater splendor. With silver dollars tiled into the floor, marble soap dishes and fresh-cut flowers in the guest rooms, Potter Palmer had created the most luxurious hotel in the country.

Field, Leiter & Company was back stronger than ever, too. Having left the horse barn on Twentieth, they'd moved to the Singer Sewing Company Building at their old Washington and State Street location.

Delia stepped inside, leaving the chill behind her. It was a large building with two elevators and a wide staircase that led to the upper four floors. All was very sleek and elegant inside with long maple display counters that ran the length of the main floor. There was a flurry of activity as clerks feather dusted their merchandise while cashboys made their rounds to the counters, picking up bills and dropping off change. The customers were mostly women, all of them elegantly dressed. They wore fashionable riding habits, street suits with formfitting bodices, stylish hats with clusters of plumes sprouting out the tops.

Delia spotted Annie Swift's white blond ringlets. She stood with Harriet Pullman and Sybil Perkins before a satchel display. Delia was disappointed to see Sybil there, but with no women's meetings scheduled that day, where else would Sybil be on a free afternoon other than at Field, Leiter & Company?

As Delia greeted the women, she admired the needlepointed evening bags from Vienna and beaded faille styles from France.

Annie was commenting on a velvet swag design from Italy when they all heard someone shouting, "Out! Out! Get out of my store!" Delia turned and saw Levi Leiter flailing his arms at a bewildered man. "I don't care how much money you have," Levi was saying. "Put those sleeve garters down this instant." The women watched as Levi chased the man out of the front door.

It wasn't the first time he'd done something like that. Levi was known for chastising customers he didn't like, so Delia and the others simply pushed onward through the store as if the outburst had never happened. They stopped at a counter of tonics and salves, including magnolia balms and remedies that promised to remove warts and unsightly blemishes, while others guaranteed to restore men's hair or make a woman's wrinkles vanish. Delia breathed in the scent of lilac, rose and lily toilet waters wafting from a nearby display.

While the others stood around discussing an upcoming charity ball, Delia drifted down the center aisle, pausing over a display of delicate lace handkerchiefs from France. At the next counter, she picked up a bar of tonquin musk soap and inhaled deeply, relishing the subtle spicy fragrance. As she set the soap down, another display captured her attention, an array of beautiful silk shawls with crystal beading.

She was running her hands along the fine fabric when a deep voice from behind said, "I don't think orange is your color."

Delia turned and nearly dropped the shawl. "Marshall!" She felt an unexpected rush course through her body. "Aren't you supposed to talk women *into* buying things?"

"I'll never lie to a lady." He smiled with an open hand splayed over his heart. The other hand with his crooked finger was stationed in his pocket, almost as if he was hiding it. "Now this blue right here," he said, reaching for a moiré shawl. "This is a much better choice for you. They call it verdigris. It brings out the color of your eyes."

"My eyes are brown," she said with a laugh.

"Then would you believe that the color complements your fair complexion?"

"Now that, Mr. Field, I will accept." She laughed again.

"Do you have a moment? There's some items that I'd like to get your opinion on."

This time it was Delia who placed an open hand over her heart. "You, the Merchant Prince, are seeking *my* opinion?"

"Mrs. Caton, with all due respect, when it comes to ladies' fashions, there is no one whose opinion I value more."

Delia took in his compliment, feeling it spread throughout her chest and limbs, making her cheeks flush. "Well, in that case, Mr. Field, I'm all yours."

She was laughing when she glanced over and noticed Harriet, Annie and Sybil watching her. Sybil gave her a long, puzzled look that made Delia uncomfortable, as if she'd been caught doing something wrong. Harriet turned away and soon after, Annie did the same. Delia knew she should rejoin them, but Marshall wanted to show her some things, and besides, he'd said that he needed her opinion. That was too great a request to turn away from.

He guided her with his hand behind the small of her back, walking her down the aisle. Stopping before a millinery display, he rotated one of the hats. "Remember," he said to the shopgirl, "feathers and enhancements face out."

The young clerk apologized, looking as though she'd committed a grave mistake. Marshall moved on with Delia at his side. She couldn't help but notice the way the salesclerks stood at attention when he passed by, nearly holding their breath. Delia remembered her father calling him "persnickety" and "tough to work for."

Marshall walked her into the back storage room where wooden crates, just off the freighters and trains, were stacked floor to ceiling, stenciled with thick black lettering on the sides: PARIS, MADRID, VENICE. Half a dozen men checked inventory lists as they unpacked the items.

Grabbing a long flat rod, Marshall began prying open a wooden crate. She observed the way his thick hands wedged the lid open. Sensing that he was a perfectionist, she imagined that one crooked finger must have seemed like an immense flaw to him, which probably explained why he kept it in his pocket whenever possible.

As he opened the first crate, Delia's pulse took off. She was getting a private preview of the latest styles. There were sable-trimmed cloaks imported from Spain, Persian paisley shawls with fringe, satin underskirts and silk hosiery from Italy. Delia was fascinated. Of everything he showed her, there was only one item—a Dolly Varden bonnet—that didn't impress her.

"I think the lace *and* the crystals are too much," she said.

"Hmmm." He held the bonnet, tilting it to the side. "I was wondering that myself. I asked a couple of the shopgirls for their opinions, but none of them gave me a straight answer. They were just waiting to see what I thought. Why can't more women just speak their minds?"

"Is that really what you want women to do?"

"As long as they agree with me." He laughed and called over to his office boy. "Send the Dolly Vardens back."

Delia stood back in amazement. She'd never felt so important. This was a man who was respected by all for his tastes and here he had followed her advice. She realized she'd never really been taken seriously—listened to—and by a man she respected to this extent. A burst of confidence awakened inside her. She held her shoulders back, standing proud. It was as if Marshall had shone a light on her, allowing her to see her true self.

Marshall turned again to the boy. "And use Burlington & Quincy this time. They're less expensive than Chicago & North Western."

"Yes, sir." His office boy jumped to attention and began at once to seal up the crate.

"You're very frugal," commented Delia.

Marshall looked at her, amused. "And is that a *bad* thing?"

"Not at all. I'm just making an observation." She noticed his office boy trying to suppress a smile as she spoke.

"I'm frugal whenever it makes sense to be frugal. That doesn't mean I won't spend like the devil when something strikes me."

They went on talking and looking at merchandise. Delia traced her fingers along the different silks and lace as she asked about Nannie and the children.

"They're in Europe."

"Already? I thought they weren't leaving until the holidays."

"So did I, but apparently Nannie changed her mind. They just left yesterday, in fact."

"What a shame."

"It's better for her. She suffers from migraines, upper respiratory infections and just about any other ailment you can think of."

"Isn't there anything that can help her?"

"I've already taken her to half a dozen doctors. They haven't got any answers other than to give her laudanum. She claims the air in Europe is better for her condition. So off she goes." Marshall looked at her and his smile vanished.

She couldn't read the expression on his face and assumed he was brokenhearted over Nannie's chronic illnesses. She found his loyalty to his ailing wife just one more of his admirable traits.

Realizing she'd been staring at him, she nervously dusted off her hands. "I'm sorry," she said. "It's getting late. I need to be heading home now." It was going on three o'clock and no doubt her mother-in-law would be waiting for her.

"It gets lonely in that big house with just the servants," he said. "Perhaps you and Arthur would care to join me for dinner sometime?"

"That would be lovely." She was still dusting off her hands as she looked at him. "I know Arthur would enjoy that very much."

He gave her a penetrating look with those blue gray eyes, and she felt that same pull toward him that she'd felt that day on her porch in the rain. She backed away from him. She had to.

On her way home Delia tried to conjure up excuses for keeping her mother-in-law waiting. *She'd run into the girls from the Fortnightly Club . . . She'd been tied up in traffic . . . She'd been too busy shopping . . .* In truth, she had been so swept up with Marshall that she'd forgotten to even look for the items she'd gone there to purchase.

Though she knew she'd catch her mother-in-law's wrath for being late, Delia had no regrets. Marshall made her feel valued and useful. He took her opinions seriously and this feeling of being respected by a man like Marshall Field was worth any reprimand awaiting her.

For the first time since she'd met Mrs. John D. Caton, she didn't care what her mother-in-law thought of her. Delia realized it didn't matter how she decorated her house, which social engagements she attended or committees she chaired, because as long as she didn't produce an heir, and preferably a son, Delia knew there was no pleasing Arthur's mother. And yet even if she did bring a male heir to their family, Delia supposed she'd be regarded only as the custodian.

When she arrived home, her mother-in-law wasn't waiting for her.

"You've been spared," said Arthur. "Mother isn't coming today."

"Oh." Delia walked into the library and set her satchel down on the chair in the corner. "I'm sorry to hear that." She actually was a bit disappointed that she wouldn't be able to test her new-found indifference on her mother-in-law.

"I sent her home." His voice was flat. He was sitting on the sofa, his shirtsleeves rolled up and his hair in a rumpled mess. She saw the opened bottle of bourbon in front of him on the table.

"You're drunk? Already?"

"Possibly. And please don't start scolding me again about my drinking. I've had one hell of a day."

She inched closer to his side. "What's the matter? What's wrong?" She reached for his forehead, feeling for fever as he pulled away from her.

He looked miserable as he refilled his glass.

She paused for a moment, listening to the ice crackling, breaking down as the bourbon hit it. "Please, tell me what's wrong?"

"It's Paxton," he said, taking a long sip. "He's decided to move back to New York. Apparently he's got some girl there."

"Oh." Delia nearly laughed. "You know how fickle Paxton is. He'll be back."

"You don't understand." Arthur set down his glass hard. "He's my best friend and he's leaving."

"You still have me. Aren't I your best friend?" She smiled, but Arthur just gave her a long, blank stare that she couldn't decipher. She felt the sting of rejection as he drained his glass, got up and walked out of the room.

CHAPTER ELEVEN

Candlelight glinted off the blue topaz diamond on Delia's finger as well as the crystal goblets and sterling silverware. She was dining at the elegant Kinsley's on Washington between State and Dearborn. Arthur was on her left and Marsh—as they'd taken to calling him—sat to her right. Their waiter had just opened their third bottle of wine.

In the past few weeks Delia, Arthur and Marsh had spent a good deal of time together. Delia adored Marsh and told herself it was perfectly fine as long as Arthur was with them. Besides, it was Arthur who sought out Marsh's company even more than she did, especially now that Paxton had moved back to New York.

It was at Arthur's insistence that Marsh join them for a play the week before, followed by a visit to Wallach's down on LaSalle and Erie for hot toddies. The previous Sunday, Marsh had come over to the Catons', and he and Arthur played chess while Delia curled up on the settee with her sketch pad. At first she'd drawn the two of them, deep in concentration, hovering over their respective sides of the chessboard. But then it was Marsh that she sketched, focusing on his classic features, his straight nose and narrow chin, the strong line of his jaw, the intensity of his eyes, the fullness of his mustache. With the tip of her finger, she blended the harsh charcoaled edge of his mouth, blurring the line between fact and fantasy as she caressed his lips and wondered what it would be like to kiss him. Catching herself in this reverie, she set her pencil down and tore up the sketch.

After that, she'd sheepishly excused herself and went into her room, feigning sleep until she'd heard Marsh leave. Later that night, she was so racked by guilt she hardly slept at all. All she could think was that her thoughts had betrayed Arthur and Nannie, too.

In the morning, though, her guilt dissipated. By noon she forgave herself, taking comfort in the fact that she hadn't actually done anything wrong. She hadn't done anything at all; she had just been fantasizing. She was still reminding herself of this the night at Kinsley's.

"So I've been thinking about this horse-breeding business of yours," Marsh said to Arthur.

"Actually, it's not a business. Really just a hobby," said Arthur, as he refilled everyone's wineglass.

"But why not expand your operations? Make something of it," said Marsh.

"Why would I do that? I don't need the money."

"It's not about the money. You do it because you can. It's about making your mark. Leaving something behind that your children and grandchildren will carry on. That's why we get up every morning and do what we do. We're the backbone of this country. Just think about all the people you could put to work."

Arthur looked at him, confused, but Delia knew exactly what Marsh was saying and it made her blood pulse a bit faster.

"Think about it for a minute," said Marsh. "Whether it's a city horse or a country horse, even a trotting horse, those animals keep a lot of people employed. You have harness makers, carriage makers, blacksmiths, stable hands, coachmen."

"And don't forget there's uniforms for the coachmen, their driving gloves and such," said Delia.

"Exactly," Marsh agreed, thumping the table. "Expand your operations and you'll join the ranks of the men who helped build this city and this country."

Delia marveled at how Marsh's mind worked. He was a visionary and it was his brilliant ideas that separated him from other merchants, from other men. She only hoped that Arthur was taking it all in.

"You certainly have the land to expand," Delia said to Arthur.

"I've never thought about turning it into a *business*," said Arthur. The word came out as if coated in something bitter. He lifted his wineglass and shrugged. "I just like breeding horses."

"I think it could be a wonderful opportunity," said Delia, reaching for Arthur's hand, squeezing it tightly.

When they got home that night, Arthur poured himself a brandy and followed Delia upstairs to her bedroom. "It's certainly an interesting prospect," he admitted. "But I wouldn't know where to begin."

"Why not ask Marsh?" Delia was already in bed, hugging her arms about her knees. "I'm certain he would be willing to advise you."

"He's really quite remarkable," said Arthur, reaching for his brandy. "The more time we spend with him, the more I realize that." He took a sip and continued. "Maybe with his help I could make a go of this. And then what would my father say?"

"You'll show him." Delia laughed. There's nothing she would have liked better. Judge Caton was a demanding man and severely critical of his son, calling him lazy and spoiled, neither of which Delia could deny. But she believed in Arthur. All he needed was some encouragement, some guidance, and Marsh was the perfect person to do just that.

Arthur set his glass down and lay beside Delia on her bed. "I think I could learn a great deal from Marsh. Certainly more from him than I ever learned from my father."

"I was just thinking that very thing." Delia scooted closer to Arthur and rested her head on his shoulder. "There's a chill in here," she said. "Why don't you get under the covers."

"Marsh is very wise. Don't you get that impression?" He stretched out his legs, crossing them at the ankles. "You know, the more time we spend with him, the more I like him. He's really quite remarkable," he said again.

She smiled, realizing that Arthur was repeating himself, which was what he did whenever he drank too much. But just the same she was thrilled that Arthur saw what she saw in Marshall Field. The fact that Arthur admired him as much as she did made her feel less guilty about her attraction to him. It was as if this lure toward Marsh was something that she and Arthur shared together. In their own ways, she realized they were both falling a little bit in love with him.

Arthur reached for his glass and balanced it on his chest. "I think I'll make some notes and see if I can discuss them with Marsh."

"That's a wonderful idea."

Arthur nodded and set his empty brandy glass on the night table and sat up.

"Where are you going?" Delia felt a jolt, a tug at her heart.

"To write down my notes."

"Now?"

"Marsh has me inspired. I don't want to lose any of these ideas."

Delia pulled the covers up over her shoulders and slouched back down. She could hardly protest. She was pleased that Arthur was finally motivated to do something. When he kissed her on the forehead, she willed herself not to wrap her arms around his neck and pull him back into her bed. She turned and looked at the indentation his head had left on the pillow.

Delia sat in the library, studying her social calendar and watching the snow fall. It was early December and icicles hung down from the mullions along the window frames. Several weeks had passed since Marsh suggested Arthur start his horse-breeding business. As far as she knew, Arthur hadn't done a thing about it. He wouldn't even show her his ideas when she asked, making her think that he'd never bothered to write them down in the first place.

Delia glanced again at her calendar. She had a full schedule. There was a Fortnightly Club meeting and Frances Glessner, a leading socialite, had invited her over for a reading group she was starting. A lover of books, Delia was especially looking forward to that gathering. She was also having tea with Bertha one day and lunch with Annie Swift the next. There was a charity ball that weekend, along with a hospital dedication ceremony Sunday afternoon. Because the judge had donated fifteen thousand dollars to the project, the whole family was required to attend. Just thinking about it and all her other social obligations left her exhausted. She closed her calendar and rubbed her temples. As she stood up from her desk, a dull ache spread across her lower back. Her head throbbed and her stomach knotted up with the first sign of her monthly cramps.

She called to Therese for a hot water bottle. She didn't need to bother checking the date or counting the days. She already knew that another month had come and gone. Once more she had failed to conceive. Delia went upstairs, stepped out of her dress and loosened her corset. She no longer cried at the sign of her monthlies. She was used to it and had come to expect the disappointment.

In just her chemise and drawers she stood near her bedroom windows looking out across the way at the Field mansion. It was daylight, so the lamps weren't on yet, but she could see people milling about inside, probably the servants. Delia felt the knot in her stomach tighten as she pulled the drapes shut.

She went over to the bed and rolled onto her side, curling her body around the warmth of the hot water bottle. If she wasn't meant to have children, then why was she here? What purpose did God have for her?

Oh, if only she and Arthur could have children—even one child—all this nonsense with Marsh, this infatuation with him would go away.

She dozed off and when she got up she found Arthur hovering in the doorway.

"I just got back from lunching with Marsh. Therese said you weren't feeling well. I came up to check on you." He went over and sat next to her on the side of the bed, his hand gently rubbing circles along her back. "What's wrong? Is it your head? Do you feel feverish? Tell me what it is, my pet."

With her back toward him, she said, "Another month. I've failed you, again."

He leaned over and wrapped his arms around her. "You haven't failed me, Dell."

She rolled onto her back and reached up to stroke his face. "I was thinking maybe we need to try harder. Try more often," she said. It was a subject she rarely broached, but she was desperate. It had been nearly three weeks since he'd touched her.

"Who's to say? Some things can't be forced."

"But I do think we need to make more of an effort."

"Relax," he said with a soft smile. "You need to relax and it will happen." He unlaced his shoes and slipped them off before he stretched out on the bed beside her. "There, there." He yawned as he placed her head on his shoulder.

It took all her will to lie there and let him hold her. Delia needed him to say he'd try harder, too. How was she ever to become pregnant if they didn't try more often? She watched the shadows growing longer on the wall as they lay there in silence.

After a while, Arthur yawned and said, "I do have something that I think will lift your spirits."

"Oh?" She glanced up at him, thinking he was finally doing something about the horse farm.

"I was thinking it might be nice to build a solarium out back. I spoke with Marsh about it and he's recommended an excellent architect. Solon Beman—he's the one who did Pullman's conservatory." Arthur yawned again. "I have a meeting set with him and I think we can break ground on it this summer."

"Won't you be busy with the horse farm business all summer?" She waited, and when he didn't answer, she gazed up at him. His eyes were closed, his breathing deep. It was three in the afternoon and he had fallen asleep.

CHAPTER TWELVE

It was the height of the holiday season, and since Nannie was still in France with the children, Delia and Arthur continued to extend invitations for Marsh to join them for dinners or accompany them to special events and parties. As a result the three of them became a fixture on the Chicago social scene that season. They were out together three, sometimes four nights a week.

One Saturday afternoon, Arthur had even convinced Marsh to take a day off and go skating with them. The three of them ventured to the lagoon in Lincoln Park. It wasn't quite round, shaped more like an egg that just hit the skillet. Blade marks of previous skaters gone by were etched into its frozen surface. Bare trees peppered the land that separated it from Lake Michigan. Delia cleared a space on one of the snow-covered benches and sat to tighten her skates while she watched Arthur and Marsh whirling around. They swerved this way and that, in between the other skaters. A rosy pinkness filled Marsh's cheeks as the wind blew his white hair back off his forehead. He was naturally athletic, as was Arthur, and the two of them glided effortlessly until Arthur's front skate caught the back of Marsh's blade and they both went tumbling down.

They were still laughing when Delia skated across the ice, reaching them in the center of the lagoon. As she tried to help them up, she lost her balance and went down, too. The three of them had their arms and legs entangled, laughing. Delia looked over and saw Arthur rest his head on Marsh's shoulder, his body shaking as he fought to compose himself.

After that, they skated three in a row with Delia in the middle, her arms looped through both of theirs. She felt like the luckiest girl, surrounded by two of the finest gentlemen she'd ever known. It seemed to her that there, on that ice, in that one moment, the three of them had achieved a perfect balance—each of them leaning on one another, each of them advancing.

But the spell was to be broken the following night. It was a blustery cold evening and the three of them attended Annie and Gustavus Swift's annual winter pageant at the Edgewater Club. Actually, Delia and Arthur had gone together and Marsh met them there later when he was done at the store. When Marsh arrived Delia was talking to Nathaniel Fairbank, an industrialist best known for his Gold Dust Washing Powder and Fairy Soap. As soon as she noticed Marsh standing in the entranceway, she broke away from her conversation with Mr. Fairbank. *Marsh is here! Now the party can begin.*

As he made his way over to her, Delia offered him a playful smile. "Don't you look handsome tonight, Mr. Field."

"And you, my dear neighbor, look ravishing as ever."

Delia wore a burgundy silk taffeta gown she'd had made just the week before. She set her hands on her hips, posing as if modeling for him. Marsh laughed, giving her a devilish grin. Delia was still smiling as she glanced over and saw that some women from the Fortnightly Club were watching her. She dropped her hands to her sides and felt her shoulders sink forward. *What was she thinking? How could she have been so indiscreet?* She immediately reined herself in, excused herself and went to her husband's side.

"Is Marsh here yet?" Arthur asked, taking a sip from his drink.

"I'm not sure. I haven't seen him." As the lie left her lips it bewildered her. There'd been no reason to deny having seen Marsh. It was as if she'd just handed herself something tangible to feel guilty about.

As the party progressed, she was constantly aware of Marsh's whereabouts. In the foyer, in the ballroom, everywhere she turned, he was there. When their eyes met, her body flooded with a sensation she couldn't quite name. It was all-consuming, thrilling and unnerving.

When it was time for dancing, the guests moved into the ballroom and the orchestra played while couples joined in. Gowns twirled this way and that as partygoers looked on, sipping champagne, enjoying the merriment.

When Delia asked Arthur to dance, he said, "In a minute, my pet. Just give me a minute here." He'd been chatting with Lionel Perkins and Cyrus McCormick. "Or better yet," he suggested, "go ask Marsh. He'll dance with you."

The orchestra had just started the cotillion and Delia went over to Marsh. "Arthur's engrossed in conversation. He sent me over to ask if you'll be my partner?"

Though her invitation had been perfectly proper, she was surprised when he said yes. They took to the floor with three other couples: Bertha and Potter Palmer, Harriet and George Pullman and Malvina and Philip Armour.

The music swelled around them and they all joined hands as

their circle moved through the steps. There was a rigadoon followed by a sideways glide to the right and then a glide back to the left before their hands moved toward the center to form a star. Delia felt a spark each time her fingertips touched Marsh's, and each time their eyes met, the other couples ceased to exist. She was terrified but elated. It was this clash of emotions that only Marsh roused in her. She didn't know what to do or where to go with these feelings. He overwhelmed her so. After they'd turned to the right and then to the left, the four women stepped toward the center and then glided back toward their partners before the men did the same.

Delia was so lost in the dance that at first she hadn't noticed Arthur standing at the edge of the dance floor with a wounded expression on his face. She watched his eyes move from her to Marsh and back to her. With just a glance she knew that he was sulking. She could tell by the way he made his eyes go sad and full of self-pity. It was the look he mustered whenever he wanted something that he couldn't come right out and ask for, leaving it up to Delia, or whomever he directed the pout at, to figure out what was bothering him.

As soon as the dance was over, Delia excused herself and left Marsh's side to rejoin Arthur. "Oh, there you are, darling," she said, reaching for his hand. "Come," she purred. "Come dance with me."

Apparently, her attention was enough to restore his good mood. He let her lead him onto the dance floor. Delia danced with a flourish, accenting her every move with a sway of her hip, a tilt of her head, a graceful wave of her arm. Halfway through the dance she acknowledged an ugly truth to herself: even though Delia had changed partners, she was still dancing with—or rather for—Marsh. His eyes never drifted from her performance—

and that was exactly what it was: a performance. As soon as she realized what she'd been doing, she shifted her focus and went back to dancing solely with and for her husband.

The dancing went on until the party thinned out and the orchestra played its final number. Delia and Arthur laughed as he kept twirling her even after the music had stopped. As they stepped off the dance floor, Delia fanned herself with her hand, trying to catch her breath while Arthur dabbed his forehead with his handkerchief.

She excused herself, and as she was walking into the lavatory, she overheard a cluster of women talking. She didn't pay attention to them until she heard her name.

". . . and Delia calls herself a friend. Poor Nannie . . ."

Delia knew that voice. Sybil Perkins. She froze in place and leaned against the wall for balance.

". . . Oh, and the way they carry on. Levi says it's just a pigment of my imagination, but I know better." That comment was clearly the unmistakable mangling of Mary Leiter.

"She calls him *Marsh* now and he calls her *Dell*," added Sybil. "And did you see them dancing earlier tonight? Shameful."

Delia drew in a deep breath. *How dare they talk about me like that! I haven't done anything wrong.* She deliberately took a step forward and then another until the women saw her reflection in the vanity mirror. Eyes flashed wide, mouths gaped open and Mary Leiter stopped speaking midsentence. They were embarrassed and Delia was satisfied that she'd made her point; she was aware of them gossiping about her and they knew it. Before they could say or do anything to minimize their guilt, Delia turned sharply on her heels and left the powder room.

When she stepped back into the ballroom she felt certain that everyone was watching her, judging her. It was as if she were becoming larger, more obvious, more central to the room. She wanted to go home. But Marsh, who usually turned in early, was instead suggesting to Arthur that they get a nightcap.

"What do you say, Dell?" asked Arthur.

"I'm sorry, what?" She was lost in her own thoughts, distracted by all the eyes on her.

"We're going to get a nightcap across town," said Marsh.

"Shall we?" Arthur held out his arm to her.

Anything to get her out of that room. She accepted her husband's arm and walked past a group of women watching as the three of them left the party.

Soon they'd arrived at the Sherman House lounge. It was a large, cavernous room, dark with a giant fireplace that crackled and sparked, casting the room in a warm glow. After she'd had a glass of brandy, Delia put the gossips out of her mind. She felt happy again, even giddy. She was sitting with Marsh on the settee, while Arthur took the armchair across from them. Delia and Marsh were doubled over, chuckling, recalling how George Pullman had told his wife while they were dancing not to complain about being dizzy because "waltzing was the way of the whirl."

"Oh, it was just too funny," said Delia as she dabbed her eyes with the backs of her hands. "Especially coming from George."

"I've never heard him even attempt a joke." Marsh pulled a handkerchief from his breast pocket, for his own eyes were tearing. His shoulders were shaking as he continued to laugh.

Delia glanced over at Arthur, who sat expressionless, watching them. She composed herself enough to say, "I'm sorry, darling. I guess you had to be there."

"I guess so." Arthur wrinkled his brow and skirted a finger about the inside of his shirt collar as if he felt constricted by it.

Delia tilted her head, trying to catch his eye, but Arthur seemed more interested in his brandy. She saw on his face that same look she had seen earlier while she was dancing with Marsh. He was feeling left out and she attempted to pull him back into the conversation.

"Arthur," she said with too much enthusiasm, "don't you think this was by far the best winter pageant the Swifts have ever thrown?"

Arthur rolled his eyes and signaled to their waiter for another drink.

By the time Delia and Arthur returned home that evening, Arthur had snapped out of his sour mood and was happy again. He was drunk as usual and Delia was even tipsy herself. They waved to Williams, their butler, indicating that the servants were not needed that night.

The two of them laughed and danced their way up the staircase. Arthur twirled her round and round until she collapsed onto her bed, woozy from their twirling. Pushing herself up from her elbows, she sat until the room stopped spinning and then made her way over to her vanity. Arthur sat on the side of the bed, working his way out of his necktie while Delia unclasped her earrings and tossed them on her vanity like a pair of dice.

"Marsh does like his late-night brandies, doesn't he?"

"As if you don't," said Delia playfully, shooting him a glance through the threefold mirror.

"It's good to see him relax, have a little fun. Next to my father, I've never seen a man who works as much as ole Marsh. Frankly, I don't think it's healthy."

"Oh, I don't know," said Delia, unpinning the braids from the crown of her head. "I think hard work is good for a man. Makes them useful and productive. A little hard work wouldn't hurt you at—" Delia did a quarter turn on her vanity stool, letting the air escape from her mouth before she clamped her lips shut. Arthur looked deflated and she instantly scolded herself, blaming the slip on her last brandy.

"If this is about the horse farm, I'll have you—"

"It's not about the horse farm."

"I've been waiting to see how long it would take you to bring that up."

It had been nearly two months and Arthur had yet to follow through on any of the plans Marsh had worked out with him. Each time she asked about the farm, Arthur had responded with a million excuses, and if pressed, he turned it into an argument. She should have known he'd never do anything with it. He was lazy. She hated to admit it, but it was the truth.

Arthur turned away and tugged on his waistcoat. "I suppose I could work myself into an early grave, but personally I'd rather enjoy my good fortune. If that's a crime, then I suppose I'm guilty as charged."

"I'm not accusing you of anything. You know I think you'd make a brilliant horse breeder. And a brilliant lawyer, too."

"I *am* a horse breeder *and* a lawyer in case you forgot. Practicing law bores me to tears. Is that what you want for me? Being chained to a desk and pushing papers about all day long? You sound like my father."

She got up from her vanity and went to his side. "I only want you to be happy."

"Then quit comparing me to Marsh." Arthur got up and went down the hall to his bedroom, slamming the door behind him.

Delia stayed in her room, refusing to run after him. She had to admit that he was right, she did want him to be more like Marsh. She couldn't help it. Nor could she help her attraction to Marsh. But at least she had no intention of doing anything about it. Didn't that count for something? And didn't it matter that she was sick inside over it? That she felt like a despicable friend to

Nannie and an even worse wife to Arthur? She had no right to complain about her agony, but surely Arthur knew she hadn't chosen to feel this way about Marsh.

About an hour later, Arthur knocked on her door. "May I come in? I couldn't sleep."

She scooted over in bed, making room for him next to her. They lay side by side, wide awake, neither one speaking.

Finally Delia slipped her arm across the bed and stroked Arthur's cheek. "I'm sorry," she said.

He murmured and put his arm around her, pulling her head onto his chest, "You're infatuated with him, aren't you?"

She could hear his heart beating against her ear. "I don't want to be."

"But you are."

She went silent.

"People were talking about you and Marsh tonight. They were watching you."

"But you were the one who told me to dance with him—"

"Don't insult me. This isn't about the dance, Dell. It isn't about what people say, either. Dammit. Don't you see? It used to be the three of us, but lately it just seems more like it's all about you and Marsh. I saw the way he looked at you while you were dancing. And then again later, when we went for a nightcap. I might as well not have even been there. He adores you and I'm just in the way. I'm on the outside looking in. I feel like I'm losing you. And him. I'm losing you both to each other."

"You're never going to lose me." She breathed in deeply, taking in a mixture of his sweat, the brandy and that familiar scent that was uniquely his. "I don't want you to feel left out. Neither does Marsh."

"So you've discussed this with him?" Arthur slapped the side of the mattress.

"No. Never." She leaned up on one elbow. "I'd never do something like that to you. I'm just saying that I can tell how much your friendship means to Marsh. He'd never want you to feel excluded."

He didn't answer. She slouched back down onto his chest and fiddled with a button on his nightshirt.

"It's hard with three," she said. "Someone always feels left out. It's unavoidable. Don't you think I feel like the outsider whenever you and Marsh are so engrossed in one of your chess games? Neither one of you even notices when I leave the room. Or what about the times when you and Marsh go to the Chicago Club? I can't step foot in there and you both know it."

"He's my friend, Dell. He's my friend and he wants you. Even when he's with me, you're the one he wants. I can tell."

She sat up abruptly and looked at him, a splinter to her heart. She was just then realizing that this was more about his losing Marsh than her.

"And you want him, too," he said. "I can tell—just admit it."

Delia squeezed her eyes shut. There was that trace of jealousy, of possessiveness; the words she needed to hear. She clung to them, relieved. "You need to know that I'm fighting this, Arthur. I'm fighting it with everything I have."

CHAPTER THIRTEEN

1877

Delia stood on the top deck of the *Baltic* with Arthur, Marsh and Nannie. A steady breeze moved clouds across the sky as a February chill swept over their shoulders. The trip had been Marsh's idea. He had business to tend to overseas, and even though Nannie had recently returned from London with the children, he had persuaded her to leave the children in the care of their governess and arranged for the four of them to make a vacation of it in France.

Originally Bertha and Potter, along with Robert Todd Lincoln and his wife, Mary, were going to join them. But at the last minute, Potter had business in New York and the Lincolns were called away to Springfield for a family matter dealing with his mother, the wife of the late president. Delia expected the trip to be canceled, but Marsh insisted they still go. And so, Nannie, Marsh, Delia and Arthur and their servants had traveled by train to New York before boarding the *Baltic* bound for Cherbourg.

Delia held on to the railing, waving to the crowd below, as the giant steam engine let out a roar followed by the fierce rumblings from below. Its force broke through the thin sheet of ice and churned the water like champagne bubbles. The gun of departure sounded as the cheers grew louder, the good-bye waves grew longer and more strident. They were on their way.

Delia was certain that this trip was exactly what she and Arthur needed. Arthur needed to know that he wasn't being left out, and Delia needed to get away from Chicago and give the gossip about her and Marsh a chance to die down. She hoped that traveling *with* Nannie would help in that regard.

As the steamer picked up speed, Delia looked out toward the stern. The winds shifted sharply and they all moved to the opposite side of the ship to avoid the steady plume of thick black smoke blowing from the engines.

Marsh, for all his frugality in business, was true to his word: he knew how to spend "like the devil" when he wanted to. He had reserved their own stateroom on board the White Star line with plush green velvet seats that had brass nailhead trim. Above the cherrywood wainscoting was a series of large paintings housed in enormous gilt frames. There were two stewards at their beck and call. They dined on roast beef and lobster, served on Royal Worcester china with Duhme sterling silver, and drank fine wine and champagne from Richards & Hartley crystal goblets. They joked the first night, saying that the *Baltic* was like the Palmer House on water.

The first night at sea Nannie dominated the conversation with stories about her recent stay in Europe. She spoke ad nauseam about her London friends whom no one had met and about the various dinner parties and balls she'd been invited to.

Delia caught Marsh's eye, just shy of a roll. No one spoke of it directly, but Delia knew that Arthur and Marsh realized, too, that things were different now with Nannie back. She wasn't part of them. She was out of step, oblivious to the rhythms of their friendship. Clearly she sensed something was amiss and was desperately trying to ingratiate herself with their circle. But despite the polite attention Delia extended to her, Nannie's efforts were falling flat. After exhausting the topic of her travels Nannie launched into an awkward string of tales about her early courtship with Marsh.

"Do you know that he chased after a moving train and jumped on board at the last minute just to propose to me?"

"Now, Nannie." Marsh tried to stop her. "Let's not—"

"Oh, but it's true. He did that. He thought he'd never see me again if he didn't. Can you imagine Marshall here making such a gallant effort?"

Marsh's cheeks went from pink to red.

He looked at Delia but she turned away. Picturing young Marsh in love tied a knot in the pit of her stomach. She hated being jealous of Nannie. She had no right to that emotion. It was ludicrous and yet she couldn't help herself. She reminded herself that he was Nannie's husband, not hers, but still the jealousy persisted. She tried to tell herself that Nannie wasn't happy in her marriage anyway, but there was no way to justify her desire for Marsh.

Trying to quash her guilt, Delia began overcompensating, laughing too hard at Nannie's jokes, listening too intently and agreeing too emphatically with everything she said. It was absurd to think those gestures could make up for the fact that she was falling in love with the woman's husband.

After the eight-day crossing they docked in Cherbourg. One long train ride later they arrived in Paris. As she stepped off the platform, she drew a deep breath and was instantly reminded of how old Europe was. The air smelled of centuries gone past. It was late morning and the cobbled streets were damp from a light snowfall the night before. At the far end of the Champs-Élysées Delia saw women holding wicker baskets and men with fancy walking sticks going about their business. Delia had been to Paris several times but never before in the wintertime. She was taken with how quiet and quaint it seemed, how charming it was this time of year. Not to mention how very different it was from Chicago. The pacing was different, more languid, less chaotic. The lack of noise and bustle was calming, and yet somehow the city was invigorating. She breathed in deeply again, appreciating the air free of soot and dust.

The Hôtel Le Meurice, where they were staying, was magnificent with a granite entablature and sculpted stone detailing. They had a floor of suites to themselves and in addition to their personal maids and valets the two couples had a staff of eight hotel servants to tend to their every need. Delia's four steamer trunks had set sail days before they did and were already waiting for Therese to unpack when they arrived.

Tired from travel, they had dinner their first night at the hotel. Not that doing so meant they were deprived. They feasted on Caviar Russe, Potage Tortue Claire, Turbot à la Hollandaise and Salade Lapérouse. During dinner they discussed their plans for their trip. Marsh had suggested the Cathedral of Our Lady of Chartres, or the Palace of Fontainebleau, perhaps the Notre-Dame Church in Melun. "Or we could visit the stained-glass windows at the Saint-Aspais Church and stay over—"

"Oh, for God's sake, Marshall," said Nannie. "I'm exhausted just thinking about all that. Can't you just once—just for once in your life, relax! Just *relax*, dammit."

"Nannie, please," he said in a low voice, "you're embarrassing yourself."

"I am not! Am I embarrassing myself?" She looked to Delia

and Arthur for agreement but turned away again before either could think of how to respond. "See, they don't think I'm embarrassing myself."

"All right, then you're embarrassing *me*."

"Oh," said Nannie with a taunting laugh, "the great Merchant Prince has spoken. Well, too bad. Too damn bad. You're always going, going, going."

"I think you've made your point," said Marsh.

"That's all you ever do"—Nannie whipped her head from side to side—"is go, go—"

"Nannie, dammit, that's enough!" Marsh thumped his fist to the table, making the wineglasses jump.

The table went quiet. Nannie drew a deep breath while Delia held hers. Were the Fields done arguing or was there more to come? Delia didn't know what to expect, but for the first time she realized that Marsh and Nannie didn't actually like each other.

Later that night, Arthur followed Delia back to her suite.

"I think it's all the laudanum she takes for her migraines," said Delia. "Poor Marsh. I don't know how he puts up with her when she's like this. Did you hear the way she talks to him? And if she speaks to him like that in public, can you imagine what happens when they're alone? He must be miserable with her."

Delia had been brushing her hair when she stopped midstroke, realizing in shame that she'd been taking pleasure in discussing Nannie's troubled marriage. She set the brush down and looked at herself in the mirror. What was she doing? Nannie was her friend. *My God, what is happening to me?*

Delia got up and went to Arthur's side, looping her arms around his waist as if that would return her to her senses and stop the bad thoughts from poisoning her mind. "I love you," she said. "I really do love you."

He had been silent until now. "I love you, too. You are my treasure."

She kissed him, wanting him to pull her closer and remind her of where she belonged.

Arthur ran his hands over her back in a slow easy circle. When she went to kiss him again, he brought her hands to his lips and said, "I think I'd best turn in. Don't forget we have a full day tomorrow."

She stood at the doorway long after he'd left her hotel room. She looked down at her open hands, wondering what she had to hold on to. How many more times could she be turned away, how many more times could she reach out for Arthur and get nothing in return?

Yes, she yearned for a child, but she also wanted to feel like a woman. She needed him to want her. But suddenly she saw it so clearly. Just as she had realized Nannie and Marsh disliked each other, she understood that while her husband might love her, he did not desire her.

And she needed to be desired. That much she knew. And she also knew the man that wanted her was Marsh and she couldn't deny that she ached for him, too.

CHAPTER FOURTEEN

The next morning the four of them had breakfast at Café de la Paix. The moment she stepped inside, Delia took in the lovely frescoes that played along the walls, the plush interior of greens and burgundy and the heavenly scents of buttered pastries and rich, strong coffee.

Everyone was pleasant, acting as if nothing had happened the night before—especially Nannie, who was cheerful and full of energy, despite complaining that she'd been running a fever before bed. It wasn't until she excused herself and went to the lavatory that Marsh leaned across the table and apologized for her behavior.

"I'm sorry if she made you uncomfortable last night."

Arthur placed his hand over Marsh's. "This is us, remember? You don't have to apologize for a thing."

"Of course not," said Delia, still looking at Arthur's hand resting over top of Marsh's. "There's no need to apologize to us."

"Well, now," said Nannie in a cheerful voice when she returned to the table, "we're so close to the Opéra Garnier. Should that be our first stop?"

When they were done with breakfast the four of them went to the Salle des Capucines, which had been completed the year before, specifically to establish a home for the Opéra. They could see the cupola from the café. A golden figurine topped the dome, a crowned goddess with servants at her feet.

Inside the opera house Delia stood before the grand staircase, absorbing the breathtaking opulence surrounding her. Her eyes traveled from the frieze along the ceiling to the gold and red marble archways and columns that led to the balconies. Statues of Gluck, Lully, Handel and Rameau looked on from their golden pedestals. When they entered the hall, Marsh planted his hands on his hips and stared up at the bronze-and-crystal chandelier flickering from above.

"Come, take a look," said Marsh, ushering them all into the center of the room.

"It's magnificent," said Delia.

"Isn't it, though." Marsh leaned in over Delia's shoulder, pointing out the detail work of the bronze. But she couldn't focus with him standing so close to her like that. Her head filled with the intoxicating scent of his shaving soap. She felt his chest press against her back as his breath brushed over her neck, filling her body with a rush of heat. Reluctantly she stepped away from him and went to Arthur's side, slipping her arm through his.

Delia still felt flushed from the feel of Marsh an hour later when they left the Opéra and hired a carriage to take them to the Sacré-Coeur Basilica. Once they arrived, they strolled around the interior of the church.

"Oh, isn't it stunning," Delia said as she nuzzled up to Arthur's shoulder.

"We didn't see this on our last visit," he explained to Marsh and Nannie. "It truly is amazing."

"Oh please." Nannie looked all around and threw up her hands. "It's a church. We have plenty of them back home."

The rest of the day, Delia found herself walking with Marsh on her left and Arthur on her right. Nannie seemed to always be lagging behind, complaining that it was too cold, or her feet hurt, she was hungry, or tired. It seemed that nothing could please her.

The second week of their trip, Arthur accompanied Marsh by train to Milan for business. Delia had wanted to go along, eager to see the textiles Marsh was purchasing, but out of duty she remained in Paris with Nannie, who suffered from another migraine.

After saying good-bye to the men, Delia went to Nannie's suite and gently rapped on the door. Nannie's maid, Sheila, showed her inside. She was a young girl, no more than seventeen or eighteen. She was quite pale with red hair and a spray of freckles across her nose. As Delia stepped into the light she noticed the girl had a bruise on her cheek, a palette of purples, yellows and reds.

"My goodness, Sheila, what happened?"

"Nothing, ma'am." She covered her cheek with her palm and shook her head, her eyes pleading for silence. "Nothing happened. My clumsiness is all."

"Delia?" She heard Nannie calling for her. "Dell, is that you?"

Delia peered around the corner into the sitting room.

"There you are," said Nannie with a flick of her wrist. "Come here."

Delia went over and perched on the chair opposite Nannie, who was lounging on the settee with her legs up, crossed at the ankles. "I received a letter today from Sybil. She had quite a bit to say."

Delia was taken aback by Nannie's tone but tried to keep the mood light. "Doesn't she always have a lot to say?"

"Oh, this time she was especially informative."

"Anything I should know about?" Delia asked warily.

"I haven't decided yet," said Nannie.

"That's very mysterious."

Nannie propped a cocarette between her teeth. "Would you care to join me in a smoke?"

"Thank you, no." Bertha had told Delia that the cocarettes were laced with cocaine. She knew a number of women enjoyed them in private, but they held no appeal for Delia.

Sheila stepped in and produced a light for Nannie, who lit her cigarette and inhaled deeply, releasing a stream of smoke through her nose and mouth. Nannie drew another puff, and when Sheila stepped forward, holding an ashtray, Nannie flicked her ash and then shooed the maid away with a wave of her hand. "Never around when you need her and then you can't get rid of her when you don't."

Delia offered Nannie's maid a thin smile.

After Nannie finished her smoke, she suggested they visit the antiquity shops nearby.

"Are you certain that you feel up to that? With your migraines and all . . ."

Nannie was already on her feet, motioning for Sheila to fetch her coat and muff.

With Therese and Sheila accompanying them, Delia and Nannie went about their shopping. For someone who claimed to be suffering from a migraine, Nannie managed to weave in and out of stores with great ease, barking instructions to her maid while snapping her fingers. "Pack this. Ship that. Put this back."

Sheila trailed behind, her arms loaded down with parcels. Yet in the midst of this whirlwind of shopping, Nannie turned to Delia and said, "She's absolutely useless. Can't do anything right. I'm going to fire her as soon as we get back to the States."

Delia didn't say a word, but she thought about the bruise on Sheila's cheek. She wouldn't have been surprised to learn that Nannie had something to do with it.

The rest of the week passed more quietly, and four days later Arthur and Marsh returned from their trip to Milan. That night the four of them dined at the elegant Tour d'Argent. It was one of Delia's favorite restaurants. With a corner table by the windows overlooking the scenes of Paris, and tapered candles all about, Arthur and Marsh talked about their visit to Milan.

"The Madonna statue is something to see . . . And the architecture in general . . ."

Delia noticed that Nannie turned her back to Marsh ever so slightly each time he spoke. Right in the middle of Marsh telling them about their visit to Piazza della Scala, Nannie excused herself from the table to powder her nose. Marsh continued on with his story.

The following afternoon they all bid Paris good-bye and started their journey back to the States. Everyone seemed in a good humor until their last night on the ship.

The four of them were dining in the Fields' stateroom when Nannie took hold of the conversation. Without warning she turned to Delia and said, "Sybil Perkins wrote to me again. I received her letter just before we left Paris."

Delia couldn't imagine why Nannie was bringing up Sybil's letter, but she saw that it upset Marsh. He frowned and turned a stern eye to Nannie. "Not now," he said.

Nannie ignored him. "She told me you spent a great deal of

time with my husband while I was away in Europe with the children."

"Oh, Nannie." Marsh shook his head. "This is ridiculous. You promised."

Delia felt cornered, her face and neck growing hot. She set her glass down, careful not to spill her wine. Her hands trembled. Nannie had obviously been stewing over this for days.

While she took a moment to gather her thoughts, Arthur spoke up. "Both Delia and I saw a great deal of Marsh while you were away. It seemed like the neighborly thing to do, seeing as he was all alone during the holidays." Arthur gave Delia a conspiratorial nod and she had never been so grateful to him in all her life.

"I apologize for my wife's outburst," Marsh said.

But Nannie pushed on, her Southern accent suddenly more exaggerated. "I did hear that you and Marshall were dancing at the Swifts' holiday pageant."

"Indeed they were," said Arthur. "In fact, I suggested that Marsh stand in for me. It was completely innocent."

Delia looked at Arthur, who was holding her hand. She realized that he was defending his friendship with Marsh as much as he was defending her honor. Now that Paxton was gone, Marsh had become Arthur's closest friend and confidant. Arthur needed to see himself as a vital cog in their tidy little circle and Nannie had just given him the opportunity to be indispensable, especially to Marsh. The whole thing put a lump in Delia's throat.

"Oh, come now, Arthur," said Nannie. "Don't you see it? Don't you see how they look at each other?"

Marsh plucked the napkin from his lap and threw it onto the table. "That's it," he said, reaching for her arm. "I'm taking you to your room."

"I'm not ready to go back," Nannie protested.

"Oh, yes you are. I'm not going to subject our friends to any more of your rude behavior." He yanked her out of her chair and escorted her by the wrist through the stateroom.

As Delia watched them leave, Arthur turned to her and said, "And you worry that *I* drink too much." He poured himself another glass of wine, filling it nearly to the rim.

After dinner they went into the lounge on deck and found Marsh sitting by himself on a settee in the corner.

"I'm terribly sorry about tonight," he said, dragging a hand over his face and letting it drop to his lap. "Nannie can be very hurtful. Very cruel."

Arthur slouched down in his chair and ordered a drink despite the warning look Delia had given him. "I hope she'll be feeling better tomorrow when we arrive in New York."

Marsh pressed his lips into a thin smile. "That's awfully polite of you to put it that way—especially after her little performance tonight. I used to think it was the laudanum. But there's something about Nannie. Something that can be so hateful, so spiteful."

"Is there nothing you can do for her?" asked Delia, perched on the arm of Arthur's chair.

"Nothing but take away the laudanum those damn doctors keep feeding her. And even then, what good would it do? She's a hypochondriac, you know. Always imagining she's plagued by fever, certain that she's dying."

Arthur patted Marsh on the back and said, "No need to worry, old man. Not with us." He leaned back in his chair and took a sip of his drink. "Not with us," he repeated, his words slurring together.

While Marsh and Delia made small talk about their expected

arrival in New York the next day, Arthur let his eyes close, his glass tilting in his hand. Delia retrieved it from his lax grip before it spilled, and set it on the table. Within a matter of minutes Arthur passed out and Delia fetched his valet to take him to his room before someone saw him like that.

Afterward Delia walked back over to Marsh. "Now it's my turn to apologize for my spouse's behavior."

"No apologies needed." He checked his timepiece. "It's still early," he said. "There's no reason why the two of us can't have a nightcap, is there?" He looked at her and patted the seat cushion next to him.

The corners of his eyes crinkled up as he studied her face. A smile came upon his lips and then hers. Something unspoken yet understood was happening between them. It made Delia nervous and apparently it affected Marsh the same way, for he cleared his throat and looked away at something over her shoulder.

"So," he said, turning his eyes back toward hers. "Shall we stay and have a drink, then?"

Delia joined him on the settee and ordered a glass of sherry.

"Poor Arthur is going to have an awful hangover tomorrow, isn't he?" said Marsh.

She shook her head and tossed her hands in the air. "He drinks too much. He just never knows when to stop and I can't make him stop. God knows I've tried."

"So much for the four of us getting away together. Seems we brought our troubles with us. We would have been better off leaving Nannie and Arthur back in Chicago."

She turned to him, surprised by his candor.

He gave his wine a swirl. "Sometimes I think Nannie and I were doomed from the very start. Did you know her sister died on our wedding day?"

"Oh, my goodness—how awful. No, I didn't know."

"We were supposed to be married in June of '62—you were just a child then."

Delia smiled. Until he'd said that, she'd forgotten the difference in their ages, but she was in fact twenty-three and Marsh forty-three. By the time she was born, he'd already been through school, had arrived in Chicago and was working as a top salesman at one of the city's biggest dry goods stores. Marsh had practically lived a whole life before Delia could even walk.

"So there we were in the parlor about to take our vows and there was a terrible explosion. Shook the whole house. One of the kerosene lamps blew and Jennie's hair caught fire. She died later that day."

"That's horrible. I had no idea."

"Nannie was inconsolable. Jennie was her best friend. She was even going to move to Chicago with us. Months later, when we did finally get married, Nannie still couldn't get past her grief and I didn't know what to do for her. So I made a lot of money and bought her one big house after another. Nannie's all about appearances, you know. Has to have the right address, the right clothes, the right circle of friends. She doesn't mind spending my money. She just resents my working in order to make it. If Jennie hadn't died, we might have had a chance. But after that, I didn't know how to make her happy. I still don't. I've tried everything I can think of." He thought for a minute and stroked his mustache. "She certainly knows how to make a man feel like a failure."

Delia saw the pain in his eyes. She realized then how sad he was, how his marriage both disappointed and frustrated him. She got the sense that there was nothing he could do to change Nannie's feelings, or lack thereof.

"She dutifully gave me two children," he said. "I wanted more. She didn't."

Delia pressed her hand to her heart. "I can't imagine not

wanting children. That's all I've ever wanted and I can't have them. Arthur doesn't seem to want to try." She was surprised that she'd blurted out something so personal, so intimate. But then again, she trusted him and felt as though he understood her, already knowing such things without her having to say a word.

"I'm afraid that Arthur, like Nannie, has his own demons," said Marsh. "We're married to two very complicated people, aren't we? I don't know about you, but for me it's a very lonely existence."

"I love Arthur, but at times I think we would have been better off as friends, rather than husband and wife."

"At least you have a friendship. I'm afraid Nannie doesn't like me very much. She certainly doesn't love me—if in fact she ever did."

Despite having witnessed the animosity firsthand, she still found it hard to believe that Nannie didn't love this extraordinary man. Didn't everyone want him? Didn't they all see what she saw in him?

Marsh shook his head. "She tolerates me—*if* I'm lucky. But she's still the mother of my children and for that, I have no choice but to forgive her a million sins."

He looked at her and they both went silent. She wanted to tell him that she respected his loyalty to Nannie, but the words wouldn't come. He was stirring her with his eyes, and if she didn't know it was wrong, it would have been so easy to fall into his arms. He must have known what she was thinking because he cleared his throat, which she noticed he did when he was nervous and at a loss for words.

The tension was unmistakable. Delia studied her hands, paying attention to the bump beneath her glove. Her wedding ring. She glanced at Marsh, watching him drum his fingers along his thigh. Thankfully the steward came by and broke the silence.

After their drinks arrived, Marsh turned to Delia and clinked his glass to hers. "I hope Arthur knows what a lucky man he is."

Delia swallowed hard and went quiet, unable to think of anything to say. She could feel herself slipping, about to lose control. They couldn't keep coming back to this point. This dangerous place where one wrong move could destroy everything that they'd vowed to honor and keep sacred.

"I should probably turn in for the night," she said.

"Don't go." His voice was hushed, the fine features of his face partly eclipsed by a shadow.

"I really should." Though she didn't want to leave him—God, no—she forced herself to get up, walk away and not look back.

As she turned the corner, she knew she couldn't bear the solitude of her room, and despite the cold night air, she went out on the deck. Gripping onto the railing she looked out at the inky sea, the cloudless night sky. A cool sweat broke out along the back of her neck. She felt as though she'd just traveled some perilous passage. She heard footsteps approaching from behind and cursed her heart for rejoicing when she turned and saw Marsh.

"Isn't it ironic?" he said, coming up behind her. "They're talking about us back home. Can you imagine what they'd say if they saw us now, in the wee hours of the morning, up on this deck?"

"We haven't done a thing wrong," she said, only half believing it. But as she looked into his eyes, she'd never felt more alive.

"Of course not, but we might as well have, seeing as they've already accused and tried us." He looked at her and smiled.

She met his gaze, and felt a connection to him that was palpable. Without warning he reached for her waist and drew her closer to him. Less than an inch separated his body from hers and it nearly took her breath away. "Yes"—she raised her fingertips, unable to resist the urge to touch his cheek—"and tomorrow we go back to face our jury."

"To hell with them."

She shook her head and eased out of his embrace.

"Delia, wait—"

But instead she turned and walked away. She walked away even though she'd never known she could want anything so badly.

CHAPTER FIFTEEN

The day after they arrived back in Chicago, Delia went to a Fortnightly Club meeting at Sybil Perkins's home down on Prairie Avenue. When she arrived, she heard the chattering of twenty-some women as she left her coat with the butler in the foyer. Yet when she entered the parlor, the room turned very still, and deathly quiet. Heads turned and all eyes were upon her. She realized with a start that they had been talking about her. All of them.

"Oh, Delia," said Sybil, rising from her chair, fluttering her arms about. "We were just wondering about your trip to Paris. How was everything?"

"It was fine," Delia managed to say. Her throat felt dry. She took a seat in the back of the room with her sister, Abby, on one side, Bertha on the other. Abby squeezed her hand, and slowly the focus left her as the other women began making proper conversation.

"I told them it's not true," Abby whispered when no one was paying attention to them.

"What's not true?" Delia whispered back.

"You and Marsh carrying on while you were in Paris," said Bertha.

Delia closed her eyes and shook her head. She wasn't wrong about the jury waiting for them back home. *But I haven't done anything wrong.*

"They're just jealous," Bertha added.

Flanked by her sister and Bertha, Delia suffered through the long meeting. She was hot and restless and willed herself to stay seated and as inconspicuous as possible, not wanting to give the others anything else to find fault with. But all the while, she felt herself crumbling in anger and humiliation. She couldn't wait to escape.

After the three of them left the meeting, Delia gave in to her anger. "Who are they to sit back and judge me?"

"They're frightened," said Bertha as her driver helped her into her white carriage.

"Of what?" But Delia knew exactly what they were afraid of. They assumed she was having an affair with Nannie's husband, and if Marsh could stray, so could their husbands. And then what? If they lost their husbands, they'd lose their livelihoods, their social status, their everything.

It was after that meeting that Delia decided it would be best if she stopped socializing with Marsh. Though the thought pained her and she would miss him—God, how she'd miss the sound of his laugh, the way his eyes crinkled up when he smiled at her, the way she felt just being in his presence—she knew it was best for everyone if she let Arthur continue the friendship without her.

"Aren't you going to join us?" Arthur asked Delia as he took his hat from Williams, the butler.

"Not tonight," said Delia. She was staring at the porcelain figures in her curio cabinet, her slippered feet resting atop a needlepoint footstool. "You go on without me," she said. "And do send my regrets to Marsh."

"You're sure I can't convince you to change your mind?"

"Go. You'll miss the opening curtain. Go on. Enjoy." She forced a smile, still looking at the figurines.

The three of them had planned to see a play that night. Nannie was in Kentucky with the children, but Delia couldn't allow herself to be seen out in public with Marsh—even if her husband was with them. It would only fuel the scandal. After Arthur left to meet Marsh, Delia reached into her curio cabinet for one of her Bloor Derby figurines of a young woman sitting on a bench alone, sipping tea. She seemed so lonely. Delia felt a kinship to that woman cast in porcelain, breakable yet unable to break free.

She remained in the drawing room, paging through a book but not retaining a word of what she'd read. All she could think about were those women, her so-called friends, gossiping about her, spreading lies. She'd done nothing wrong. Was it wrong to think about another's husband? A friend's husband? Of course it was, but the more she tried to suppress her feelings, the stronger they grew. Still she had resisted. And it hadn't been easy when her own husband didn't desire her. When she knew that Nannie was horrid to Marsh, that she didn't love him. *Still, she had resisted.* Wasn't there something to be said for that?

She was about to turn in for the night when she heard Arthur and Marsh coming through the front door. She wanted to run and see Marsh, but instead she stood very still in a shadow of the stairwell, hiding like a child. Arthur had his arm slung over Marsh's shoulder, his overcoat was buttoned wrong and his hair was tousled. Even before she heard him speak, Delia knew he was drunk.

"Is Mrs. Caton still up?" Marsh called to Williams.

Delia receded a step deeper into the shadows, away from the railing.

Williams took Arthur's hat and tried to help him off with his coat, but Arthur shooed him away, keeping his arm clasped about Marsh's shoulder. "Oh, we did have fun tonight, didn't we?" said Arthur. "Wasn't it fun? Thank you for going with me." Delia watched as Arthur brought his other arm around Marsh's shoulder, embracing him as he said repeatedly, "Thank you for going with me. Did I thank you for tonight?"

"Several times in the carriage." Marsh laughed and gave Arthur's shoulder a pat.

"Oh, Marsh," Arthur sighed. "We did have fun tonight, didn't we?" He pressed his forehead to Marsh's and closed his eyes.

Delia was about to turn away when she saw Arthur run his fingers across the nape of Marsh's neck, caressing his snow-white hair—just as she'd longed to do. She moved closer to the railing, disbelieving what she was seeing. She could barely breathe. She broke out into a cold sweat as she ran her clammy palms down the front of her wrapper. There was something so intimate in the gesture, something so offensive to her. Perhaps she had suspected it before, but she had never allowed herself to admit it.

Marsh reached behind him and removed Arthur's hands while stepping out of his embrace. "You've had too much to drink, my friend. Williams—," he called for the butler. "Please help Mr. Caton to his room."

Delia slipped away and raced into her bedroom, swallowing back tears as she leaned against the door. She still couldn't believe what she'd seen. She wanted to deny it, but the truth had just stared her in the face. Her marriage was a farce. She thought back to their wedding night and to all the nights Arthur had shared her bed. He'd made her a beggar. A groveler. A fool. All that time she'd been wanting him and he'd been wanting something—someone—else. What was she to do now? How was she ever supposed to have his child when clearly he didn't want her? The rejection pierced her heart. She felt betrayed, used. Wasted on a man who could never love her the way she wanted and needed to be loved.

And to think she'd felt guilty about her feelings for Marsh when all the while, Arthur had been pursuing him himself. She thought about how Arthur would pout when he felt Marsh was ignoring him, or favoring Delia over him. And now she realized it had nothing to do with jealousy over her. It was *all* about Marsh! Everything made sense now and it sickened her and broke her heart.

She cried all through the night as she lay awake, contemplating a future that looked nothing but bleak to her now. She hoped for answers to come along with the daylight creeping in from the parting of her drapes, but only despair remained. All she could think was that she no longer had a husband. She'd never had a husband. Not in the true sense of the word. And what was she to do now? The obvious answer would be to leave him. But the courts would never grant her a divorce without her exposing him, and that she couldn't do. Even if she could have been so heartless as to shame him, what would she do if she left him? Where would she go? Was she supposed to buy a home for herself? She'd never heard of a woman owning property. She wouldn't know where to begin. And even more than that, Delia couldn't imagine her life without Arthur. He was her best friend.

It was then that something else took hold of her. A new layer unfolded. She stepped out of the cloak of the rejected wife, and thought about Arthur, her friend. Her best friend. How could she not feel sorry for him? It was all so complicated. It was obvious to Delia, but she wondered if Arthur understood his attraction to

Marsh. Each time Arthur turned to Marsh for advice, sought out his approval, craved his attention, she knew he was gaining the very things he'd never gotten from the judge. And when the two sat down at the chessboard, or played cards at the Chicago Club, he found the friend he'd lost in Paxton. Delia had always understood that, but now—now she realized there was something else he was seeking, something more—something she couldn't comprehend. And she had to wonder if Arthur even understood it himself.

She rolled over in bed and thought about what Arthur would remember in the morning. Would he remember that he'd been rejected—just as he'd rejected her? Would he recall that he'd made a fool out of himself? She clutched the spare pillow to her side, letting its feathers fill the hollow in her body as she realized that she was more saddened than angry. It was just such a sorry situation. For both of them. For all three of them.

CHAPTER SIXTEEN

There was only one person Delia could talk to about Arthur, so the next day she went to see Marsh at Field, Leiter & Company.

When she arrived at State and Washington, the chaos of the city swept her up. A string of bustling carriages and wagons jammed the intersections, while the peddlers crowded the sidewalks and shoppers wove in and out of stores.

Upstairs in the executive offices she found Marsh standing behind his desk, staring out the window, his palm pressed against the glass, his fingertips tapping the pane. He must have seen her reflection in the glass because even before he turned around and saw her face, he asked her what was wrong.

She dropped into the wooden chair opposite his desk and took a moment to muster her courage, find her words. His desk was neat and polished, not even a smudge visible on the mahogany surface. Pencils stood erect in a cup at the edge of the blotter, next to a crystal inkwell. The day's mail had been opened and filed.

"Dell," he broke into her thoughts. "What is it? What's wrong?"

"It's Arthur." She fidgeted with the buttons on her gloves. "I'm worried about him."

"How so?"

"It's just that he doesn't seem quite right when it comes to . . ." She struggled for the words. She'd never spoken of this aloud before to anyone.

Marsh came around to her side of the desk. "What is it? Is he ill?"

She studied her hands, her fingers intertwined.

"Dell, tell me, please."

She lifted her head and stared into his eyes, letting the words tumble out. "He's in love with you, Marsh."

He drew a deep breath and looked away. "Dammit." Taking the seat opposite her, he leaned forward, resting his elbows on his knees, rubbing his face with his hands. "I'm sorry, Dell. I've sensed it for some time. Dammit." He sighed again and shook his head. "Arthur wants something from our friendship that simply can't be."

Delia sat up straighter, feeling the tension across her shoulder blades. The room spun around her. She couldn't think of anything to say.

"You must know that I'd never do anything to hurt him," said Marsh. "I'm very fond of Arthur, but . . ." His voice trailed off for a moment and then he began again. "He loves you, Dell. Of that I'm certain. But Arthur is longing for something—something you can't give him. Something I can't give him, either." Marsh leaned over and took her hand.

She told herself to pull away, but the warmth of his touch seemed so right. The feel of her hand in his was the very thing she needed, especially after her long night. She'd been sick to her stomach, crying so hard that she had to turn her pillow dry side up. As he ran his thumb over the back of her hand, she felt her eyes watering up. "Marsh . . ." She couldn't finish her thought.

"We've always known where this was heading, haven't we?" He reached over with his free hand and tilted her chin, making her look into his eyes. He sighed from deep within his chest. "I'd never want to hurt Arthur, you know that. But I can't deny how I feel about you. Perhaps I'm just an old fool. But I'm an old fool who's fallen in love with you."

"Marsh, no."

"Meet me tomorrow."

"I can't." Her hand was still in his. "Nannie—"

"Nannie doesn't love me."

"But she's my friend."

"Is she really? Trust me, you don't need a friend like Nannie. Please, Delia. Nannie's in Kentucky with the children. Come meet me tomorrow. I can get a room at the Sherman House. Please."

"I can't." Freeing her hand from his, she stood up and walked to the door. She paused in the doorway, her hand resting on its frame, unable to pull herself any farther from him.

"If you change your mind, I'll be there. Waiting."

She shook her head and left his office, rushing out of the store and onto the street. It was just as loud and raucous as ever, with carriages, omnibuses and people scurrying about, but she paid it no mind. It was just background noise as she replayed her conversation with Marsh over and over again in her head.

She was already at State and Jackson when she stopped and leaned up against a building, catching her breath. For the first time, she asked herself, *Why?* Why couldn't she meet Marsh? A chilling wind swept across the street and with it came a sense that something very deep inside her could change, had changed. For underneath all the hurt and disappointment, the frustration and anger, was a new understanding. A calm, clear understanding. Her husband was incapable of fully loving her. Nannie was not a friend. The other women in town had already condemned her. There was no defending her reputation. No one would believe she hadn't done anything wrong. So why? Why—when every cell in her body wanted him—why couldn't she go meet Marsh?

The next morning, after a restless night's sleep, Delia mustered her courage and had her driver drop her at the corner of Clark and Randolph. The temperature was dropping and it had started to snow. Slush seeped through her soles, but she was too preoccupied to notice.

She had a million scripts running through her head as she entered the hotel, shaking snow off her coat and hat. She rehearsed lines inside her head as she stepped off the elevator and knocked on the penthouse suite door. There was no answer at first and Delia began to fret, thinking that Marsh changed his mind. She was about to turn away when the door swung open and there he was standing on the threshold freshly shaven, a towel slung over his shoulder and his shirtsleeves rolled up. His mouth dropped open as he reached up and pulled the towel from his shoulder, letting it fall to the floor. He looked stunned, as if he hadn't expected her to show.

Despite how much she'd prepared for this, now that she was face-to-face with him she couldn't think of a thing to say.

He walked her into the suite and locked the door behind him. Her mind was racing and she felt flushed. *What was she doing there? It wasn't too late to turn around and leave.* She stared into the roaring fireplace as the flames lapped the crackling logs.

She kept telling herself she'd made a mistake, she had to

leave. And she still hadn't spoken a word. Neither had he. Instead he reached for her cheek, stroking her skin with the back of his hand. She was trembling. She'd been denying what she'd wanted for so long and now here he was, right in front of her. She stood on the brink, just a step away from the fall that she'd never be able to rise back up from. She was about to become guilty of everything she'd been accused of. Marsh's face was just inches away from hers. The ache inside her opened wide. She'd never been so vulnerable and she didn't care.

"Oh, Marsh," she said finally, "what are we doing?"

And without a word he leaned in and kissed her ever so gently. She'd never been kissed like that before. It filled her whole body, warming her and warming her spirit. As he wrapped his arms around her, she knew that they could never take this moment back. And she knew she'd never want to. His kiss told her everything she needed to know. There was no doubt that he desired her as much as she did him.

They were still kissing as he unfastened her dress and she fumbled with the buttons on his waistcoat. She felt only pleasure as he slid the fabric down past her shoulders, her breasts heaving toward him from her corset. He unlaced her with such a seductive touch, as if he were unwrapping a present. She didn't remember how they had moved into the bedroom, but there they were, working their way through the last traces of their clothing.

When she saw his body in the flickering glow of the bedroom fireplace, the desire that welled up inside her seemed insatiable. At forty-three he was still firm, lean yet muscular, and now he was offering all of himself to her. She was overwhelmed when she felt his skin touching hers, knowing that nothing was between them, separating them any longer. He explored her, slowly, lovingly, even caressing and then kissing a scar along her thigh that Arthur never knew was there. She'd never been touched so gently, so lovingly before and yet, for all his tenderness, she was aware of his power, his intensity. It was immeasurable. That same raw energy and strength that he'd put into building the city and his business, he now poured into her. She felt it in his kisses, in his embrace, in the way he never let his eyes leave hers. She could barely breathe. There was no more holding back. Her body responded in ways it never had before, opening itself up to him, moving with him, lost in this moment they were sharing. She'd never known such pleasure. Her whole being ignited and nothing had ever felt so right. She belonged with this man. The ripples of satisfaction coursing through her body overrode whatever guilt, whatever misgivings, she may have had. This was right. This was where she belonged, and when she shattered in his arms, it was a complete surrender. She had given herself over to him wholly.

Afterward as he kissed her softly on the lips, he confessed, "When Bertha first introduced you to me, I was mesmerized and nervous as a schoolboy. I knew I was in trouble the moment I set eyes on you."

"I knew right away, too. I didn't want to admit it to myself, but I knew it, too."

She lay on the bed and felt the details of the hotel room coming back to her consciousness. Suddenly she was aware of the coffered ceiling, the wainscot armchair in the corner, the secretary and note cards resting on top along with the inkwell. It all began floating into her line of vision.

So accustomed to Arthur, who always raced back into his bathrobe, she was pleasantly surprised when Marsh circled her in his arms and held her close, kissing the sweat that had formed along her shoulder blades and across the nape of her neck. He held her like that for the next hour and they talked, telling each other things they might not have shared, had they never shared their bodies.

Marsh told her about growing up in the Berkshires. "There

were eight of us children, living in a two-story farmhouse. My father sent us to school in the winter and out to work the farm the rest of the year."

"Is that how you broke your finger? Working on the farm?"

He held out his right hand and studied his crooked finger. "That's another story, for another day." A sadness filled his eyes as he wrapped his arms around her middle.

"Well," she said, hoping to restore the close mood they had been enjoying, "I can't picture you as a farm boy."

"Apparently neither could I. When I was sixteen I got a job at a dry goods store. Five years later, I came to Chicago, determined to become a merchant. Nobody thought I could do it because I was so shy and quiet. They started calling me 'Silent Marsh,'" he chuckled. "My mother was the only one who believed I could make a go of it."

"Smart woman," she murmured.

"Yes, she was. I should have listened to her when she told me not to marry Nannie. She told me I'd never be happy with her. Actually, she came this close to telling me Nannie would make me miserable."

Delia's mood began to sink at the mention of his wife. How could she ever face Nannie again after this?

He sighed and nuzzled his cheek close to hers. "My mother would have liked you, though," he said, kissing her neck, making her forget about Nannie again.

"You think so?"

She could feel him nodding. She ran her hands over his forearms and smiled, content to stay there like that with him forever. And then, just like that, he released his embrace and sat up, stretching his arms overhead. Delia reached for a blanket heaped at the foot of the bed. The fire had died down and she was suddenly aware of the chill in the room.

"And now what?" she said, pulling the blanket onto her shoulders. "Where do we go from here?"

"You mean in terms of Arthur and Nannie?"

She nodded.

"We tell them."

Delia closed her eyes. Even though he had betrayed her in his own way, she dreaded what this would do to Arthur. "I don't want to hurt him."

"I don't want to hurt Arthur, either. Or Nannie. But we have to tell them," he said. "I won't cheapen this by sneaking around and I won't lie about you. We need to tell them."

Delia nodded. She knew he was right, but then what? "Do you think Nannie will grant you a divorce? I know Arthur never would. We both know there's a reason why he married me in the first place."

"I don't expect Arthur to divorce you, but my marriage is over," he said. "It has been for years. I'm tired of pretending. I just want out. I'll go back to being a bachelor. I practically am one now as it is. I just can't stay married to Nannie anymore. I'm telling her as soon as she gets back from Kentucky."

CHAPTER SEVENTEEN

The next day, Delia went into Arthur's room and sat on the bed that she'd never been invited into.

"We need to talk." She reached for his hand. "Please, come sit with me. It's important."

"Are you unwell? What's wrong?"

She bit down on her lip, hard enough to make it hurt, as if she wanted to punish herself for what she was about to say.

He studied her face while deep lines sank into his brow. "What's this all about?"

"It's about us." She sighed. "I know you love me. And I love you, Arthur. But I can't go on pretending that everything is fine between us."

"Is this about the horse farm?"

"No." She could have laughed had the worry in his voice not been so heart wrenching.

"Is it about having a baby?"

"Oh, Arthur, let's not kid ourselves. How can we have a baby when you don't want to try?"

"That's not so. I do."

"When? Once a month? Once every six weeks? And it's always me begging you. And when you do want to, you're too drunk." She reached over and stroked his hair. "Oh, Arthur, you try—I know you try—but I don't want a husband who has to try. I want a man who wants me."

"But I do want you."

"Not enough. You don't want me enough. You don't want me in the right way. And I'm sorry, but Marsh does. He does want me."

He pulled away from her. The color drained from his face.

"I'm sorry but I can't pretend anymore. I'm in love with him." Hearing the words aloud for the first time both thrilled and terrified her. "I didn't mean for it to happen, but it has and I can't help the way I feel."

"He's my friend. He's taking you away from me and you're taking him away from me, too." Arthur stood up and went to the other side of the room and dropped into a chair.

She went and knelt by his side. "No one's taking anyone away from you. I love you, Arthur, but what we have here in this marriage—this just isn't enough for me." She rested her cheek on his knee. "I never meant to hurt you. Marsh and I . . ." She couldn't finish her thought because he had started to cry.

His shoulders shuddered and he hung his head, fisting up his hands. "You can't leave me." He looked up as the tears streaked down his cheeks. "You can't disgrace me like this. I can't have a divorce in my family. My parents will disown me. My father is a judge. He'd never understand."

She swallowed past the lump in her throat, unable to speak.

"Do as you please with Marsh," he said. "I'll look the other way. I'll do whatever you ask, but please don't divorce me. Don't shame me like that. All I ask is that you let me have my dignity. Please, Dell, I beg of you—don't leave me."

"Oh, Arthur, I'm not going to leave you. I don't *want* to leave you. But I can't lie to you, either. I can't sneak around behind your back."

"What are people going to say? You'll ruin yourself in this town, you realize that, don't you? Your reputation will be destroyed. Along with mine." He shook his head. "My God, you're going to make me a laughingstock."

"No, you won't be. I promise. I won't lie to you or Nannie, but no one else needs to know. I'll be discreet, you know I will. This is our business. I'll keep your secret and you'll keep mine."

The next morning Arthur walked into the dining room with a packed valise in his hand. He set his bag down next to the sideboard and sat beside her at the table. "I'm going down to Ottawa for a few days."

Delia nearly missed the saucer when she put her coffee cup down. "Are you sure?"

He nodded. "I just need to be alone right now." He stroked her face with a tenderness that she now understood to be a gesture of kindness and friendship, nothing more.

She wrapped a shawl over her shoulders and walked him outside where his coach was waiting. Both of them had tears in their eyes as they embraced.

"It's cold out here," he said, running his fingers over the fringe on her shawl. "You shouldn't be outside without a coat."

"Don't stay away too long," she said, gripping onto him.

"Take care of Marsh while I'm gone." There wasn't a trace of resentment in his voice.

She stood on the walkway, waving long after his four-in-hand turned the corner. Seeing him ride off like that left her feeling lost, ungrounded. All she wanted then was to run to Marsh, the only place where she belonged now. Knowing that Nannie was still in Kentucky, Delia clutched her shawl about her shoulders and hurried off for the Field mansion.

Marsh was in the sitting room with a stack of Sunday morning newspapers piled on the table next to his wingback chair. As soon as the butler brought her in, he stood and waited for his butler to disappear. When they were alone he embraced her, filling Delia with a clash of relief, remorse and guilt.

"I told him," she said, clinging to Marsh, speaking into his shoulder.

"How did he take it?"

She felt his hand pressed against the back of her hair. Delia shook her head. "I don't envy you having to tell Nannie."

Marsh didn't say anything. He released her from his embrace and backed away, refusing to look at her and instead gazed at a shelf of books.

Her blood quickened. "Marsh?"

He ran his finger along the ledge as if inspecting for dust.

"What's wrong? What's the matter?"

"I can't tell her yet."

"What?" Delia's stomach roiled.

"I received a cable this morning from Nannie's cousins in Kentucky. She's unwell. It appears as though she's had some sort of a nervous breakdown. They're worried for the children. I'm leaving on the six o'clock train tonight to get her. There's a sanitarium in Rochester—"

"A sanitarium?"

"I've decided to take her there for a while. Her cousin is bringing the children back here in a few days."

Delia was speechless. She heard Nannie's cockatiels sqawking in the parlor next door.

"I knew she was headed for trouble," he said. "The woman's been a wreck ever since Paris. Every time I turn around she's taking more laudanum."

Delia dropped her eyes to the floor. "Oh, Marsh . . ." She looked up, tangled in a million emotions. Their plan had just taken a detour and then another concern struck her. Delia pressed her fingertips to her mouth. "We did this to her, didn't we?" She said this as if thinking aloud. "We've destroyed Arthur and now Nannie. We're bad people. Something bad is going to happen to us."

"Don't talk like that. We've fallen in love. That's not a crime."

"Yes it is. It is when you're married to other people. Maybe we should stop this. Stop it right now."

He reached for her wrists. "Don't. You've told Arthur. You've done the right thing, and as soon as Nannie is well, I'll tell her."

"But she was fine until Paris."

"She was never fine. Don't take that on." Marsh went and stood over by the windows and rubbed his eyes. "Nannie has been unwell for a very long time. Who knows what set her off this time. They tell me this sanitarium is the best place for her. I need to take her away from Chicago. Let the gossips here assume she's back in France vacationing. The fewer people who know the truth, the better."

Delia thought she detected a slight mist collecting in his eyes and she didn't know whether to be touched or jealous. She'd never before seen Marsh show any genuine feelings or tenderness toward Nannie.

"I have to figure out what I'm going to do with the children once they get back to Chicago," he said. "Their governess will take care of them while I'm in Rochester with Nannie, but I don't like the idea of leaving them at a time like this. I don't know what they've seen, what they've heard. I don't even know what they've been told about their mother."

"I'll look in on them," she said. "I'll check in on them every day if you want. Arthur will, too, when he gets back in town."

He pressed his lips together, his mustache covering his mouth completely. "Thank you for that."

"Of course." She stroked his face with the tips of her fingers, letting them slide down his jaw and land in her lap. "Of course."

Delia stayed with him, the two sitting quietly side by side, their fingers laced together, her head on his shoulder. It was not romantic. It was real. She knew she had just complicated her life exponentially and yet she felt it was right to be with him. She belonged with this man and had never felt closer to anyone, not even her sister. She and Marsh were lovers now. They were connected, sharing everything, both good and bad. She wanted him to know that his problems were now hers. They didn't speak then. They didn't have to. He knew what she was thinking. Certain things were understood.

Several hours later, knowing she couldn't see him off at the station, she said good-bye to Marsh at his house. He gave her a quick kiss rather than a long, passionate one intended to sustain them during their separation, and this, too, she understood. It was easier for him to leave her that way.

As he left for the depot, she went around the corner, back to Calumet Avenue. When she walked back into the house, she was acutely aware of being alone. All that warmth and belonging that Marsh had cocooned around her was gone. Now she was exposed to the raw consequences of her actions. She felt Arthur's absence as never before. The kitchen maid fixed her a cup of tea and Williams brought it into the drawing room, where Delia sat before the fireplace. She saw faces in the flames, like drama masks flickering, both laughing and crying. It was exactly how she felt. So happy to have Marsh, so guilt-ridden by what it took to have him. She couldn't stop thinking about Arthur. And Nannie. And those children. How many lives were they disrupting and what right did they have to do so? She knew Marsh thought her superstitions were silly, but she worried that there would be retribution. There had to be. Without Marsh there to quell her fears, she was certain that they'd just invited trouble into their lives.

One week later Arthur returned from Ottawa, acting perfectly normal, as he would after a return from any trip. He handed off his valise to Williams, kissed Delia's cheek and asked how she'd been. Before she had a chance to answer, he was already pouring himself a drink.

"How are you?" she asked, following him to the bar.

"Better," he said, taking a long pull. "Much better now. Just needed to sort through some things in my mind."

"I understand."

He smiled sadly. "Oh but you couldn't possibly, my pet."

"I'm sorry. You're right. I don't understand."

He set his glass down and reached for her, hugging her fiercely. Her cheek was pressed against his shoulder. He held her with such strength it was bewildering. How could it be that he didn't want her the way a man was supposed to want a woman?

"I know it isn't natural," he said as if reading her mind. "I don't understand it myself. I don't know what comes over me. I only hope that you don't find me too revolting."

"Oh, Arthur, I could never . . ." She held on to him tighter.

"You need to know that I don't want to stand in the way of your happiness," he said, kissing the crown of her head. "You'll let Marsh know that, won't you?"

She nodded, unable to speak as she clutched onto him.

Later that same evening at the judge's house, Delia took her rightful place next to her husband at the dining room table along with the entire Caton Colony. Her mother-in-law's tastes were quite different from her own. Everything, from the sack chandelier to the marble-topped buffet, was done in the Second Empire style.

Delia was never at ease in their home, but on this visit, she was especially tense. After an icy cold greeting from the judge and Mrs. Caton, Arthur's sisters, Laura and Matilda, barely said hello. It was as if they'd heard the gossip about Marsh and had already condemned her.

The judge sat at the head of the table. The dining room filled with the smells of roasted garlic, sautéed onions and a host of other rich flavors. As the footman began serving, Mrs. Caton turned to Arthur. "And how did you find everything down at Ottawa?"

"Never better, Mother."

His voice was too bright, too forced. Delia felt a stab of guilt. She couldn't bring herself to look at Arthur. She sank down in her chair, wanting to hide.

Then the judge turned to Arthur. "What did you make on the stallion you sold to that fellow in Highland Park?"

Arthur dabbed his mouth with his napkin and smiled proudly. "Two thousand. Cash."

"What was your asking price?"

Arthur's smile receded as he smoothed his napkin across his lap. "Twenty-five hundred."

"I figured as much." The judge shook his head. "You never did understand the art of negotiation, did you? If you'd asked three, you would have gotten twenty-five and if you'd asked four, you would have gotten three. Everything I've taught you has gone in one ear and out the other. You practically gave that horse away. Just gave it away."

All eyes were on Arthur. His cheeks were growing red and Delia saw the pinpricks of perspiration forming along his forehead. She wanted to protect him, the way a mother protects her child.

"Bad enough you don't work," said the judge. "And now you're giving your damn horses away."

Delia couldn't take any more. "Please," she said. "Please let Arthur be."

Everyone at the table gasped and turned to her. Mrs. Caton froze with her hand splayed over her chest, her mouth hanging open. Arthur's sisters and their husbands stared at Delia. No one ever spoke to the judge like that.

"I beg your pardon." The judge cocked his head and squinted as if he hadn't heard right.

"I'm sorry," Delia said, instantly recoiling. "Forgive me."

The judge turned to Arthur. "So you let your wife fight your battles for you, is that it?"

Delia waited for a moment, hoping Arthur would speak up, defend himself, but he just sat with his eyes aimed at his plate. Delia glanced around the table and saw that everyone was avoiding one another, all their expressions set in stone.

The judge's eyes narrowed in indignation. "Well, is that the case?"

Arthur hesitated and then mumbled, "No, sir. That is not the case."

Delia reached under the table and took Arthur's hand in hers. His palm was damp and clammy. She wanted to scream, wanted to tell them all that Arthur was perfectly capable of fighting his own battles, but she knew that would only make it worse for him. She'd unintentionally put him in a position where he was torn between her and his father. Instead of helping him, she'd made things infinitely worse. Her heart was breaking for him beneath the weight of her own guilt.

CHAPTER EIGHTEEN

Marsh was still away. It had been almost three weeks. He was splitting his time between staying in Rochester with Nannie and tending to business in New York.

As she had promised, Delia had been looking in on the children several times a week. She introduced Junior to her nephew, Spencer, and despite his being almost six years younger than Junior, the two took an instant liking to each other, playing checkers and making drawings together. They were competitive, but good-natured about it, especially Junior, who recognized that his years of seniority came with the price of responsibility.

One Saturday Delia brought Junior and Ethel to her house only to find they were fascinated by how different her home was from their own. Junior especially loved the tiger and bearskin rugs. He lay down on the floor in the parlor, face-to-face with the bearskin, making growling sounds. Ethel was captivated by the globe that spun round and around on the brass stand in the library. But those amusements were short-lived and soon Delia was at a loss as to what to do with them. Ethel and Junior were sitting with their elbows on their knees, their chins resting on their knuckles, eyes looking heavy and glum, when Arthur wandered into the parlor. He turned to the children and then at Delia, who gave him a helpless shrug.

"Who's up for a horseback ride?" Arthur asked, bringing his palms together in a vigorous rub.

The children lifted their chins. "Me! Me! Can we? Please?" asked Ethel, already rising to her feet.

When they went back to the stable, the spring sun beat down on them, and the air smelled of manure and hay. Delia swatted at the horseflies swarming all around as she went in to see the horses. She'd brought carrots from the kitchen and reached in her pocket, holding a carrot out for one of the geldings, loving the velvety-soft feel of his muzzle against her palm. She patted his neck and pressed her nose in close to fill her lungs with his heady scent.

"Okay," said Arthur, walking a gorgeous Arabian named Tia up to the mounting block. "Who wants to go first?"

Ethel was already jumping forward, hand raised. "Me, me! Let me."

Junior didn't challenge her. Instead he sat on a bale of hay while Arthur hoisted little Ethel up on the mare and walked her around the arena, warning her to hold on tight. Her pretty little face burst with laughter as she squealed in delight. Junior sat with hands planted back on his knees, chin on his knuckles, watching his little sister. Arthur never let go of the reins and after a few times around the arena it was Junior's turn.

"Now, don't let her know you're scared," said Arthur, as he helped the boy into the saddle.

"I'm not scared," Junior insisted. But when Tia whinnied and stomped her foot, Junior let out a cry, making his little sister laugh.

"Be quiet, you," Junior said, as Ethel covered her mouth and continued to giggle.

"It's okay," Arthur assured him as he led Junior out of the stable and into the arena. "Hold on now. Here we go."

"He's a baby," said Ethel.

"Shhh." Delia pressed her index finger to her lips.

Delia watched Arthur with these children and her heart ached. He would make such a wonderful father. She felt a tenderness toward him then that she didn't know what to do with. She loved Marsh with all her heart, but in the moment she questioned if she'd given up on Arthur too soon. She thought she had moved beyond all that and shook her head as if to ward off the thought, cast it from her mind. She recalled all their failed attempts at childbearing and reminded herself that she could never be fully loved by him. How ironic, Arthur bred horses, as many as twenty a year. But together they couldn't produce a single child.

Two weeks later, on a Saturday afternoon, Delia went to the Field mansion to pick up Spencer, who had been playing all morning with Junior. When the Fields' butler showed her into the drawing room, she was taken aback. A rush of emotions raced through her body. Spencer and Junior were tumbling about on the floor. With Marsh. She wasn't sure what surprised her more, the fact that he was home or that he was wrestling with the boys. Marsh preferred more dignified activities: chess, reading, visiting museums and the theater. His white hair whipped around and his blue gray eyes grew wide the instant he saw her standing there.

"Delia!" He pushed himself up off the floor, dusted off his knees and straightened his necktie.

"You're home." She was thrilled to see him, but the children kept her reaction in check. Instead of running to him she concentrated on removing her gloves, one finger at a time, as if it were a monumental task.

"Just this morning. Didn't you get my telegram?"

She shook her head, peeling off the second glove. The boys were rambunctious, jumping around, hoping to lure Marsh back for more wrestling.

He smoothed down the front of his waistcoat. "You boys carry on without me," he said. "I need to have a word with Spencer's aunt."

He led her into the music room and closed the double doors behind him. Sheet music on the stands rustled as a breeze blew in through the windows. It wasn't until Marsh put his arms around her and drew her close that she believed he was really there, right before her.

She could scarcely breathe as she whispered into his ear. "I've missed you."

"I don't like being away from you. I'm no good without you. I need you, Dell."

She would never tire of hearing him call her name. The sound of it made her go weak. She melted into his words and his touch, letting the spicy smell of his shaving soap envelop her. It was one of life's most perfect moments. She closed her eyes and breathed in deeply. God, how she loved this man.

He broke away first. He always did. It was just his way. The sheet music fluttered again in the breeze.

She reached up and stroked his face. "Tell me how you've been. Tell me everything."

He sighed and looked toward the ceiling as he ran his hands up and down her arms, leaving behind a trail of goose bumps.

"That bad, was it?" she asked.

"Nah, I'm fine."

"And what about Nannie? Dare I ask how she is?"

He sighed again, deeper this time. "You see the beast in someone's eyes when that poison is leaving their body. I never knew just how dark her soul was until I saw her like that." He shook his head. "Watching her go through that was excruciating, but at least it's out of her system now. They say she needs rest and I'm of no use to her where that's concerned. All I seem to do is agitate her. So I went to New York, took care of some business, and now I'm back."

"I wish I'd known you were coming home. I was worried when I hadn't heard from you."

"I wired you last week. I don't know what could have happened to the cable."

When Delia returned home later that afternoon with Spencer, she asked Williams if any telegrams had arrived for her.

"Just the one," said Williams, helping her with her satchel and parasol.

"Which one?"

"It arrived last week. Mr. Caton said he would deliver it to you."

Delia stormed into the library, where she found Arthur stretched out on the divan with the newspaper in one hand, a drink in the other. His left foot was on the ground, skimming the edge of the tiger rug.

"Sorry, it must have skipped my mind," he said after she'd confronted him. She could hear it in his voice. He was drunk. He got up and teetered his way to his desk and retrieved the telegram. "It's right here." He handed it to her.

She noticed that it had been opened. "You read it?" she asked, surprised that he would have done such a thing.

"I couldn't help myself," he said with a mea culpa hand placed over his chest.

Delia quickly skimmed the telegram:

> LEAVING NEW YORK FRIDAY NIGHT STOP
> WILL BE HOME BY SUNDAY STOP I MISS YOU
> DELL . . .

"It arrived about a week ago," Arthur volunteered.

"You held on to this for a whole week? You kept this from me?"

He looked away. "I couldn't bring myself to give it to you after I'd opened it."

"Why would you have opened a telegram addressed to me in the first place?"

"Because"—his cheeks reddened—"I assumed that it was meant for both of us." He paused and rattled the ice in his glass. "He didn't even mention me."

She felt his embarrassment and in an instant her anger had been replaced with guilt.

Arthur went over to the bar and fixed himself another drink. He shrugged. "You see, I had to open it. I was so excited to hear from him, I couldn't help myself."

CHAPTER NINETEEN

By the end of May, Nannie had been in the sanitarium for almost two months and life had returned to normal. Despite whatever awkwardness might have transpired between Arthur and Marsh, the men now appeared to be as close as ever.

After Marsh returned from Rochester, the two men picked up right where they'd left off. Twice a week or so, they met up for a game of chess. Marsh had even invited Arthur to go fishing. Delia, Arthur and Marsh had resumed their routine, but now with a different undertone. The three of them were often seen dining together or sharing the Fields' theater box. At night they would return to their neighborhood and often Marsh would accompany Delia and Arthur to their home. What happened after that was never spoken of. Delia and Arthur had an understanding; when it came to such matters they could each do as they pleased, no questions asked.

The other night the three of them had returned from dinner and were in the drawing room having a brandy.

"Well," said Arthur, setting his empty glass down, "I'm going to call it a night." He stood up and placed his hand on Marsh's shoulder. "See you both in the morning."

Delia and Marsh sat up talking, finishing their drinks. It was half past eleven, which was an early night for them. They'd been up the night before, talking in bed, until four in the morning and the night before that, it was nearly five a.m. She feared that Marsh would drop from exhaustion, putting in full days at work on as little as two or three hours of sleep a night.

"We could both use a good night's rest," said Delia as they retreated upstairs to her bedroom. "And that means we go straight to sleep tonight, right?"

"Absolutely. I promise I won't touch you," he said with a laugh, sliding under the covers. "I won't even think about it. Well," he said a moment later, "I might think about it. But that's it."

Delia reached over and turned down the light.

He offered her a quick kiss good night, and as his foot drifted over to her side of the bed, she slipped her leg onto his hip. She kissed him back, and before they knew it, they were locked in a breathless embrace. It was impossible for them to resist each other. They made love that night, and as usual it left them both feeling relaxed and invigorated at the same time. So afterward they lay arm in arm, and Marsh told her about the time his father caught him sleeping on the job.

"We were out in the field and I was supposed to be cradling the crop—that's when you uproot the whole thing after it's done growing. Anyway, I hated cradling and I was beat, so I went under a tree and took a nap. My father caught me and he was furious. He made me sleep outside under that tree for a week. It even rained one night. He wouldn't let me back inside. That was the last time I ever took a nap on the job. He had a tough work ethic, but I'm glad he did. I learned a lot from him. More than he ever knew . . ."

They lay in each other's arms, fading into a comfortable silence. When Delia glanced over at the clock she was surprised by the hour. "It's almost three," she said. "We should really try and get some sleep."

But still they found things to talk about for another twenty minutes or so before she heard him starting to snore. She had just closed her eyes and had begun to drift off when she heard him starting to stir. The sun wasn't even up yet as he reached for his trousers.

"Go back to sleep," he whispered. "I'm going home before the servants wake up. They know I didn't come home the other night and I don't want to stir gossip." He leaned over and kissed her as he shrugged on his jacket. "I'll see you later tonight."

Delia watched him slip out the door and out into the world. She drifted back to sleep thinking how it was becoming more and more difficult for them to be discreet. Their relationship seemed to intensify daily. He was forever on her mind, and she swore she could feel him thinking about her as well. When they were together, they shared secrets and inside jokes, and while they were apart, she carried him with her in her heart. She'd watch the clock in the afternoons, waiting for him to return from work, anticipating being held in his arms. When the separation grew too maddening, Arthur was always there to distract her with a hand of cards, a horse ride or even just a bit of chitchat.

She was lucky. She had the best of both her men.

Arthur turned twenty-five that spring and in honor of his birthday Delia threw a coaching party. At noon, a dozen of the city's finest horse-drawn carriages lined up on Calumet Avenue, outside the Caton mansion. The plan was to caravan up to Highland Park for a picnic before coaching back to the city, where

Delia's staff was preparing an elaborate dinner for their forty-seven guests.

Arthur's four-in-hand took the lead with his prized black stallions harnessed and gleaming, and his coachman dressed in his finest red uniform with brass buttons and a matching cap. Abby and Augustus rode behind them with the Palmers in their white carriage. The Pullmans, Swifts, Armours, McCormicks, Leiters, Glessners, Perkinses and several others all followed suit. A carriage of servants tailed behind the caravan.

Arthur sat up on the box, alongside his coachman, while Delia and Marsh remained inside the carriage with its plush velvet seats and matching fringed curtains. It had been at Arthur's insistence that Marsh ride along with them.

When they all arrived in Highland Park they picnicked on the lawn beneath the shade from the nearby trees. The horses grazed off to the side. Delia's staff set out wheels of cheese and crusts of bread, summer sausages and fruit, while several of their guests played croquet and badminton. After the games were done and the last of the wine had been finished, they all climbed into their carriages and made their way back to Delia and Arthur's home.

Delia had transformed her dining room into a floral garden with two long tables draped in lilies and violets. After dinner they moved into the ballroom, where a ten-piece orchestra accompanied the dancing. The whole event was magnificent, and Delia was thrilled to see Arthur so happy. When the orchestra took a brief break, the footmen rolled out an enormous cake and Delia looked on as the candles illuminated Arthur's boyish smile. He so adored the attention.

After the cake was served, a group of men circled around Arthur. They sat off to the side, all a bit tipsy, especially Arthur, who raised his glass as Lionel Perkins launched into a toast in his honor. As soon as he finished, Gustavus Swift stood and made the next toast. The men carried on, laughing and drinking, oblivious that the orchestra had started playing again and the dancing had resumed.

The hour grew late and some of their guests had already left, but the same group of men still sat off to the side where they'd been the majority of the evening. They were quieter now, slouched down in their chairs, blurry eyed with fresh drinks in their hands. Arthur looked groggy, but still had a smile on his face.

When the orchestra finished its last number, Delia heard a sudden burst of laughter coming from the men. She turned and saw all the men cackling, rocking back and forth, holding their sides. All of them, that was, except for Arthur. He was alert now and after another burst of laughter Delia watched his face turn dark red.

"Arthur, darling," she called to rescue him. "Can you help me here for a moment?" She reached for his arm and pulled him to the side. "Is everything all right?"

He glanced at her hands circled about his forearm. "I'd say you've already put on enough of a show for everyone. And this"—he indicated her hold on him—"is only making matters worse." He pulled himself free.

"Arthur—"

"Do you know what they just asked me? Do you have any idea? They wanted to know if I just watch or if I climb into bed with you and Marsh." He turned and started for the stairs.

"Arthur, wait—they're drunk. They don't know—"

He gave her a sharp look and she realized there was nothing she could say. There was no way to make it better. This was the world they had made for themselves.

CHAPTER TWENTY

Mrs. Caton paid Delia a visit the following week. Before she arrived Delia rearranged her Émile Gallé vase of flowers, straightened the sofa doilies and inspected for dust in anticipation of what her mother-in-law would find fault with that day.

But ten minutes into their visit not a critical comment had been made. In fact, they were sitting in the parlor having tea when Mrs. Caton said, "I have something for you."

"For me?" Delia was taken aback. Could it be that Mrs. Caton was finally coming around? Delia watched her mother-in-law check her hair in the beveled mirror on the wall before she reached inside her satchel and pulled out a bottle. "Here." She handed it to Delia. "This is for you."

Delia held the blue bottle of Ayer's Sarsaparilla. She didn't know what to say.

"It comes from Massachusetts," Mrs. Caton said, pointing to

the cherubs on the label. "They say it's very good for woman problems."

"But I'm not unwell. I'm perfectly fine."

Mrs. Caton raised an eyebrow. "They say it's very effective for women in your condition."

"My condition?"

"Delia, my dear, let's not pretend, shall we? After all this time, at the very least I would have expected to have a grandchild on the way by now."

Delia swallowed hard. Naturally they assumed *she* was the problem. *She* was the reason they were barren. She graciously accepted the bottle of Ayer's Sarsaparilla knowing that Arthur's family would never suspect the true nature of her marriage. Or of their son.

After Mrs. Caton left, Delia paced about the parlor. Obviously this issue wasn't going to go away. And she did want a child every bit as much as her in-laws wanted an heir. All this time she and Marsh had been so careful. They practiced coitus interruptus as taught in the pages of Robert Dale Owen's *Moral Physiology.* But now it occurred to her that if she were to become pregnant—with Marsh's child—it could alleviate so many problems, and remove the speculation and blame. It would do the same for Arthur. And even Marsh said he longed for more children. In many ways if she became pregnant, it would be the best thing that could happen for all three of them.

That night when Arthur came home, Delia followed him into his bedroom. She caught her reflection in the mirrored doors of his armoire and drew a deep breath to help with her resolve. "Your mother and father are very eager for an heir. Your mother stopped by today. She gave me something to help things along." Delia handed Arthur the bottle of Ayer's Sarsaparilla.

Arthur looked at the bottle and set it on the nightstand. "I believe it's going to take more than this."

"Maybe. But it *could* still happen." She tilted her head to catch his eye. "It could, you know. Given our"—she struggled for the right word before settling on—"situation."

He looked toward the ceiling, deliberately avoiding her gaze. "Is this your way of telling me you're with child?"

"No." She laughed sadly, got up and went to his side. "But, Arthur, think about it." She placed her hands on either side of his face, her fingers buried in his muttonchops. "If I were to become pregnant, it would certainly pacify your family. You could give them an heir and it would put all this pressure to rest. And you love children. You'd be a wonderful father."

"This is about Marsh, isn't it? You're talking about having a child with him, not me?"

"But the child would be ours. All of ours."

"So I'm assuming you and Marsh have talked this over."

"No. I just—I haven't talked to him about it. I just know he's always wanted more children. You know that too. But this is between us right now. This is something that you and I need to discuss first."

He grew quiet for a moment and she thought he was about to dismiss the whole idea when he turned and asked, "How would this work if you were to become pregnant?"

"You would raise the child as your own. It would be a Caton heir, not a Field. And I would make sure Marsh knew that up front."

"Oh, Dell." He picked up the bottle of sarsaparilla and examined the label. "You know I want an heir. I don't want to let my family down, and you make it sound so easy. Surely you know it would be so much more complicated than that. How would Marsh feel about this? How would Nannie handle it? What if people found out the truth? What if the child looked like him? You have to take all that into consideration."

"Well, it hasn't happened yet. And it may not. But"—she took the bottle from his hand—"I'm asking if I can have your blessings to at least try. For all our sakes."

Arthur sat on the side of the bed and hung his head low for a long time. Finally he raised his eyes and looked at her. "And if I say no?"

"Then I'll never mention it again."

"But even so, it could still happen. At least I assume that's a possibility."

She nodded. "I suppose it could."

He nodded back. "Then, if it should happen and that's what you want—and if that's what Marsh wants—I won't stand in your way."

"I want us to try," she said to Marsh the following night. He was in her bed. Arthur wasn't home, having made an abrupt departure for Ottawa that morning.

Marsh was sitting up, knees bent with his arms looped around them. He hadn't said anything yet. It was warm inside Delia's bedroom and a welcome breeze blew in through the windows, making the drapes balloon out.

Delia propped herself up on one elbow. "I mean it, Marsh. I want us to try."

"You're asking me to father your child. A child that would be raised as a Caton?" Marsh stroked his mustache, staring ahead, his eyes half-closed. She thought he was going to tell her no, but then he leaned over and kissed her, slipping his arm about her waist and sliding his body up against hers. In the midst of that kiss he said in a breathy voice, "Let's try. Let's try right now."

He parted the fabric of her wrapper and brought his mouth to her bare breast, his fingers dancing over her skin and sending shivers down the slope of her hip and to her core. He took his time with her that night, making love to her with a purpose, his kisses deeper, his touch more intense, his desire consuming her. His body fit around hers soft and warm, holding her close. His breath whispered along her neck, his lips against her ear, while her rib cage heaved in and out as she clung to him. The heat built up inside her as she cried out his name, her mouth pressed to his collarbone. There was a ripple of pleasure and then another, ringing out within her, until at last he broke and she took all of him in. He dropped down in her arms, his heart thumping against hers. They fell asleep that night bathed in sweat and blissfully spent.

All that spring and into the summer, while Arthur split his time between Ottawa and Chicago, Delia faithfully took her two tablespoons of Ayer's Sarsaparilla each morning and tried to make a baby with Marsh.

One morning she awoke before Marsh and stole the quiet to observe him undetected while he slept. She considered it a privilege to be so close to his genius, to the mind that thought like none other. She ran her fingertips along the wisps of white hair on his forehead and watched him, lost in his dreams, wondering what he was conjuring up, as she knew his was a mind that never truly stopped. It was one of the things she loved most about him.

That astute mind must have sensed her staring because he began to stir. She eased up off her elbow and rested her head on his chest, content when she felt his arm absentmindedly circle about her waist, turning her skin to gooseflesh even in the summer's heat. Marsh mumbled something and rolled over.

She smiled and lightly ran her fingers through his hair again before she got up and went to the bathroom. It was then, without any warning, without the hint of her usual monthly symptoms, that she saw the blood. All the warmth left her body. She felt herself an empty husk, a meaningless woman. Her purpose had passed her by. She was no closer to being with child now than she had been before she started her mother-in-law's tonic. Her eyes filled with tears as she reached for a vial of Ayer's Sarsaparilla and threw it against the marble floor, shattering it into shards that skidded halfway across the room.

She was staring at the mess when Marsh rushed into the bathroom, his hair rumpled. "What happened? Dell? Are you all right?" He stepped around the broken glass and reached for her, pulling her to him. "What's wrong?"

She sobbed into her hands. "I'm never going to have a baby. I'm barren." She collapsed into his arms, dropping her head to his shoulder as he guided her back to the bedroom.

He sat her down on the side of the bed. She stared at a portrait on the wall, never before noticing the mother-of-pearl buttons on the woman's bodice or the gilt acanthus leaves on the frame. She was absorbed in the most infinitesimal of details, hoping to make her mind go blank.

"Come back to bed," he said, coaxing her. He kissed her and pulled her body close to his. "I'll make you a baby. I'll make you pregnant or I'll die trying."

Arthur broke ground for the solarium in July of that year. After the comments at their coaching party and knowing that Delia was trying to conceive Marsh's child, Arthur wanted to send up a smoke signal to the neighbors indicating that everything was fine inside his home. So fine, in fact, that they were building a fancy solarium onto the back of their house.

Nannie was sending up smoke signals of her own as well. After six months of being away, she'd been released from the sanitarium in August. She returned to Chicago wanting to prove to all that she was fine, never better. In fact, Frances Glessner was hosting an elaborate luncheon in Nannie's honor to welcome her back. All the members of the Chicago Women's Club had been invited. Delia didn't relish the thought of seeing Nannie. She was sick inside over betraying her and had wanted to back out of the party. But she reluctantly attended, knowing that it would look suspicious if she wasn't there.

When she arrived, Nannie and Frances stood in the front parlor receiving their guests. Nannie looked well rested with a vibrant, healthy glow, but Delia could hardly make eye contact with her. All she could think was, *My Lord, I'm in love with this woman's husband. I'm trying to have his child.*

Marsh still hadn't told Nannie about the affair. He wanted to wait until she was stronger before he broke the news to her. Delia had no choice but to go along with the charade, but she was certain that Nannie and everyone else could see the deceit on her face, hear it in her voice, smell it seeping through her pores. Oh, how she wished that Nannie knew the truth. She just wanted it out in the open whatever the retribution might be. Then maybe she could breathe again, look at herself in the mirror and not see a despicable liar and sneak.

"Are you unwell?" Abby asked.

"No, no. I'm fine."

During the luncheon while Nannie spun stories about her fabricated shopping sprees in London and Paris, going on and on about her supposed travels through Europe, Delia felt the deepest pangs of sadness and guilt. Did anyone even suspect that she'd been locked away in a sanitarium this whole time? The more Delia listened, the more upset she became. She tried to appear amused and engaged with each new tale Nannie delivered, but it was wearing her down.

Before dessert was served, Delia feigned a sore throat, left the luncheon and went to see Marsh down at the store.

"I don't know how many more of these social encounters I can handle," she said to Marsh after he closed his office door. "Look at me—" She held out her fingers. "I'm still shaking."

Marsh reached for her hands, covering them with his own. "I told you, I can't tell her yet. I need to wait until she's more stable. The doctors warned that the slightest upset could cause a setback. Believe me, I'm not afraid of the consequences for myself. Only for her and for the children. I need you to be patient a little while longer and then I'll tell her. I'll tell her *everything*."

"And then what? She won't divorce you. I can't leave Arthur—what are we doing? What can we even hope for?"

Someone was at the door. Delia jumped away from Marsh just as Levi Leiter stormed inside.

"There you are," he said, jamming a cigar in his mouth and heading over to Marsh. Levi was worked up, and if he did notice Delia standing there, he didn't bother with her. "Your cashboys are standing around downstairs complaining about wanting a raise."

"Then fire them," said Marsh, planting his hands on his hips. "Fire the whole lot of them. I don't need that kind of chatter on the floor."

"Maybe if the Merchant Prince could climb down off his throne long enough to deal with this, they wouldn't be complaining." Levi butted his barrel chest up against Marsh.

"For your information, you hired half those boys yourself."

They were both talking over each other and Delia knew that she'd lost Marsh. He was every bit as oblivious to her standing there as was Levi. She reached for her things and without a word she let herself out of his office.

CHAPTER TWENTY-ONE

Delia and Marsh stole their time together, trying to be discreet for Nannie's sake. There were early morning rendezvous when he should have been at the store and midafternoon breaks when he would have been at the Chicago Club, but it was always rushed, always cloaked in risk of being caught. Gone were their leisurely nights together, lying in each other's arms, talking until three, sometimes four in the morning. The whole thing didn't sit well with her, but she loved Marsh and there was no other way.

Meanwhile she watched Marsh and Nannie carry on as if everything were fine and in turn she paraded about town as Arthur Caton's dutiful wife, attending charity balls, joining him for family affairs and entertaining guests in their new solarium. It went on like that throughout the rest of the summer and into the fall.

Delia did her best to avoid socializing with Nannie and

Marsh, but every now and again, the four of them turned up at the same party. One night, at the Glessners' charity ball they were even seated at the same table along with Abby and Augustus. Delia felt woozy as she unfolded her napkin, smoothing it across her lap. Nannie chattered on innocently, obliviously, even complimenting Delia on her gown and her necklace—a Carlo Giuliano—that had been a gift from Marsh for her twenty-third birthday. She remembered that Nannie had been stowed away in a sanitarium the day he walked into her bedroom, the box hidden behind his back. She'd been seated at her dressing table and saw him through the mirror. He bent down and kissed her on the neck, setting the box on the vanity before her.

"We'd love for you to join us at the theater next week to see *The Black Pearl*," said Nannie.

"How lovely," said Delia. A stab of guilt grabbed hold of her as it did each time Nannie extended a kindness her way. She looked quickly at Marsh, her eyes begging for a way out.

"It's short notice," said Marsh. "They may have other plans."

"Oh, nonsense. Cancel them whatever they are." Nannie laughed. "We insist you come and be our guests, don't we, Marshall? We won't take no for an answer." Nannie raised her wineglass and took a delicate sip.

Delia could scarcely look at her. Poor Nannie. She was the one left in the dark, the only one unaware of what was really going on. They were all betraying her, even Arthur.

As the first course of melon and consommé royale was served, Augustus asked Marsh about his business. "I hear talk that Lord & Taylor and a few other outfits from New York are thinking of coming to Chicago."

"If the competition comes to town," said Marsh, "we'll be ready for them."

Delia offered a half smile, as she tried not to appear overly interested in Marsh, and yet not too indifferent, either. It was a delicate balance. She found the evening exhausting and painful. All she could hope for was that Nannie would get well enough soon so Marsh could tell her the truth.

It stormed the night of the play. Rain pelted against the windows in Delia's room while Therese finished helping her dress. She had selected a magnolia satin Morin-Blossier gown with a beaded train and a series of bouffant folds cascading from her waist.

"Are you almost ready, Dell?" Arthur asked, standing in the doorway of her bedroom. He was handsomely dressed in a silk waistcoat and red ascot, his walking stick in hand. "You look beautiful," he told her.

"I'm dreading this evening," she said, turning while Therese snapped the clasp on her diamond necklace.

"It's one night," he said, extending his arm to her. "We'll get through it."

The heavy downpour continued as they left, riding to McVicker's Theatre with Marsh and Nannie in their coach. The streets were a sloppy mess with carriages stuck everywhere, the horses unable to pull free from the mud.

Despite the weather, there was a full house at that evening's performance. Delia always adored McVicker's. She felt as if she were in Greece each time she passed by the marble pillars in the mezzanine and the enormous murals of Greek gods and goddesses running floor to ceiling.

They entered the theater and took their seats in the Fields' gilt-trimmed box. As soon as the play began, Nannie and Delia peered at the stage through their gem-encrusted lorgnettes. When Delia wasn't watching the actors, she stole glimpses at Marsh, sitting one seat over. She studied his strong profile, his firm jaw and aquiline nose, his full white mustache. It was a face she loved like none other. She was still staring at him when Nannie caught her, holding Delia's gaze long enough to make her flush. She didn't dare look at Marsh for the rest of the performance.

After the play, they were about to go for a late supper at Rector's on Clark and Monroe when Marsh's office boy came running into the theater. He was soaking wet, panting hard as droplets of rain fell from the tips of his hair.

"I'm sorry," said the boy, wheezing as he spoke, "but there's trouble down at the store. A fire's broken out on the top floor."

Delia watched Marsh's face go chalk white. They were all thinking the same thing. *Not again.* Nannie fisted up her hands, hunched her shoulders close to her ears and began pacing in the mezzanine.

"Is anyone hurt?" Marsh asked.

"No. The store was closed. The alarm bells were sounded and the fire trucks just got there. Mr. Leiter's been told and he's on his way down there, too. We've got a few clerks trying to save the merchandise, but we're going to need more help."

Everything happened so quickly then. They hurried toward State and Washington in the Fields' carriage. It was still pouring and the main roads were turning into mud-packed creeks. When their carriage approached the store, the four of them looked up at the flames shooting twenty feet into the sky, defying the downpour of rain. A fire engine, drawn by three white horses, pulled up in front of the building with its bells clanking as steam belched from the boiler beneath the water tank in the truck. One of the horses shook its head, rattling its bridle, sending off a spray of rain in all directions.

The alarm bells rang out again while the fire raged on. The air filled with a choking smoke and the stench that Chicagoans knew all too well. Dragging their hoses along, the firemen entered the building while onlookers stood beneath awnings and umbrellas.

Levi Leiter came outside with his sleeves rolled up and hair matted down with sweat. Two clerks followed him, carrying crates stuffed with carpets and lamps, bolts of fabric, lace and other merchandise.

Leiter saw Marsh and shouted, "I've got men on the third floor. The fourth and fifth floors are already gone. So are the elevator shafts. We're trying to haul everything down to the first floor."

Marsh called over to his office boy and a handful of clerks who were there to help salvage the merchandise. "We need horses, wagons, drivers—get anyone willing to help us. Find some old barns or empty buildings where we can house everything once we get it out of here. Otherwise the rain will ruin it just as surely as the flames."

As Marsh started for the doorway, Delia reached for his arm. "Oh, Marsh—"

Nannie let out a shrill cry and Delia's pulse jumped. She had forgotten her place, forgotten that she was just the neighbor, the friend. But Nannie hadn't noticed the inappropriate gesture. "Marshall," she cried out again, "I can't breathe!" She was clawing at her neck. "I'm burning! It's my hair—my hair's on fire!"

Marsh went over and grabbed Nannie by the shoulders, shaking her firmly. "You're fine, you hear me. You're not on fire. Go wait in the carriage." Marsh turned back to Delia. "It's because of what happened to her sister."

"I'll watch her for you."

He nodded. "I'm going down to the basement to see if the boilers and pumps are working."

This time Delia blatantly reached for his arm. "Be careful."

"Noooo!" Nannie cried as Marsh rushed into the store with Arthur following behind him.

Delia couldn't watch. She needed to distract herself and helped Nannie back inside the carriage. When she returned to the front of the building, she gripped onto her umbrella, feeling the cold mud seeping through the soles of her shoes as she looked for signs of Marsh and Arthur. Her heart lurched each time someone came outside. More firemen appeared with extinguishers and axes in hand. As they all headed for the upper floors, Delia tried not to think about Marsh and Arthur putting themselves in danger. There were no flames on the first floor yet, but she could see them torching the sky from the upper floors.

Meanwhile a group of young men hefted up crates of merchandise and hauled them outside where two drivers jumped in to relieve them and loaded the crates into the backs of drays. It went on like this, the filling up of crates, dragging them out to the wagons and going back inside for more. Delia had no idea what time it was when she saw Marsh appear in the doorway. He looked haggard, his white hair covered in soot, ashes perched on his shoulders and sleeves, streaks of black across his chin and forehead.

"Are you all right?" She rushed over to his side. "Where's Arthur? Is he safe?"

Marsh nodded and coughed. "He's okay—he's with Levi. But it's bad in there." He dragged his arm across his forehead. "We've lost the top floors, the third is almost gone. There's nothing left." He hung his head and started to cough.

It was still raining. Big quarter-size drops pelted everything. Marsh leaned over, hands planted on his knees, hacking while Delia rubbed circles over his back, urging him to breathe.

"Just rest for a minute." She had her arm around him when he straightened up and that's when Delia noticed a newspaperman standing in front of them, pencil poised above his notepad.

"Would you care to make a comment, Mr. Field?" asked the reporter.

"Why don't you put your pencil down, for God's sake, and help!" Delia snapped. She kept her arm about Marsh's waist and the two of them walked away while the reporter shouted out more questions.

While Marsh went back inside to get what could be salvaged, Delia went to check on Nannie and found her passed out inside the carriage. An empty bottle of laudanum lay on the seat next to her. Delia was shocked. She thought that Nannie was done with all that and doubted that Marsh even knew she still carried laudanum with her.

Meanwhile the race to save the merchandise continued and Delia went back to the front of the building. Men came outside to cough and catch their breath. One of them told Delia that half of the second floor was already engulfed in flames. A thick, choking smoke was everywhere. Clerks soaked their handkerchiefs in rainwater and covered their noses and mouths so they could keep pulling out merchandise. The flames on the second floor forced Arthur, Marsh and the others down to the first floor. The smoke turned from gray to black. Arthur finally came out to get some air. Delia could see Marsh from the doorway, still filling a crate with shirt collars, neckties, perfumes, atomizers.

"Enough, Marsh," Delia called to him from the doorway. "It's too dangerous in there. Come outside."

He didn't respond.

The smoke was getting to her even though she was outside. Each breath felt like a blast of fire on her lungs. She saw the red and orange flames licking at the corners of the ceiling, working their way down the back wall.

"You have to get him out of there," she said to Arthur, a sob escaping from her. "Please, get him out of there."

"Come on now, Marsh," Arthur shouted, his hands cupped about his mouth. "Leave it be."

But Marsh kept going.

"I mean it, Marsh," said Arthur. "Get out of there now!"

When he still didn't respond, Arthur darted inside. Delia watched Marsh twisting out of Arthur's hold when someone screamed, "Look out!"

Delia froze. She couldn't move. She was certain they were both going to die.

Arthur yanked Marsh to the side just as a flaming wooden beam came crashing down through the ceiling, missing Marsh's leg by inches. Both Marsh and Arthur stared at it in shock. Arthur pulled at Marsh's arm again and finally they both stumbled out of the store.

Marsh leaned up against Arthur's shoulder, panting, trying to catch his breath. Branches of lightning lit up the sky and through a curtain of rain Delia saw something in Marsh's face that she'd never seen before: fear. He was genuinely afraid as if he'd just realized what a close call it had been. Arthur continued to hold on to him, saying, "It's okay, Marsh. You're okay now."

Marsh nodded and looked at the building burning and turned back around. "Thank you. Thank you for pulling me out of there."

It was going on two in the morning when the firemen finally put out the last of the flames. Ambulances took those who had breathed in too much smoke off to the hospital. Delia had wanted Arthur and Marsh to go to the hospital, too, but they'd both refused. It was cold and damp, and people stood outside in clusters shivering. Someone brought over pots of hot coffee to pass around. Nannie was still in the carriage, passed out, oblivious.

Marsh looked exhausted and Delia was concerned for him. "Marsh," she said, handing him a cup of coffee, "why don't you let us take you home. There's nothing more you can do here now."

He brushed the coffee aside with the back of his hand. "I need to stay. I need to see the damage in the daylight. I want to be here when the insurance adjusters arrive."

But Delia knew it was more than that. She knew how his mind worked and he couldn't bring himself to leave.

"I'll stay with you, then," she said, as Arthur came up behind her.

"Dell"—Arthur gently tugged at her arm—"it's time to go. We need to get Nannie home and you need your rest."

Delia looked at Arthur and then back at Marsh, who simply nodded, indicating that Arthur was right. It was time for her to go. She reached out and squeezed Marsh's hand while Arthur tugged at her arm again, a bit more emphatically.

Nannie was still woozy on the ride home, her head lolling from side to side as she murmured, "What's burning now? Don't let me catch fire. Don't, don't . . ." More incoherent chattering followed.

When they pulled up to the Field mansion, it had stopped raining. Nannie was slumped down in the seat, her head pressed to the window, her breath fogging up the glass each time she exhaled. Arthur hoisted her in his arms and carried her into the house.

Delia followed behind, explaining the night's events to the butler. "Please have Mrs. Field's maid put her to bed. She's had a very emotional evening. I wouldn't expect Mr. Field back any time soon. He's still down at the store."

"Don't worry about Marsh," Arthur said when they finally made it home. "He's been through far worse than this." He climbed the stairs, heading up to bed. He could barely keep his eyes open.

Delia had Therese draw a hot bath for her, and afterward she dressed for the day and went back downstairs. She couldn't sleep, unable to turn off her mind. Her lungs still ached each time she took a deep breath. To think Marsh could have died had Arthur not saved him. How ironic. She'd never thought of Arthur as the brave, fearless type, but that night he had been a hero and she would never forget the way Marsh looked at him, his eyes filled with new respect and gratitude.

Over several cups of tea she worried how Marsh would bounce back from the devastation of a fire for a second time. Even a man as strong as Marshall Field had his limits.

She was still awake when Williams brought in the morning papers. When she turned to the society page of the *Daily News*, she nearly spilled her tea. There was the headline: "Mrs. Arthur Caton Consoles Marshall Field as Fire Destroys State Street Store." Delia's eyes skimmed the article as the knot in her stomach twisted with each sentence. How was she going to explain this?

> Mrs. Arthur Caton appeared to be the only personal friend of Mr. Field's at the store when the fire broke out. . . . When asked where Mrs. Field was, there was no comment. . . . Mrs. Caton and Mr. Field rushed away, refusing to answer any additional questions. . . .

Delia reread the article. Her gut felt like she'd swallowed a fist. She could only guess what Nannie would think when she saw it. Nannie and everyone else. And poor Marsh, a scandal was the last thing he needed right now. And what about Arthur? How would he feel about seeing something like this?

When Arthur stumbled downstairs Delia went to him with the paper in hand. "You might as well see this now," she said, pushing the newspaper toward him.

"I haven't even had my coffee—" He stopped once he saw the headline. Delia watched his eyes grow wide and his mouth drop open as he read. "They printed this about you!" He slapped the newspaper against the table. "As if there wasn't enough talk about the two of you already."

"Oh, Arthur, I don't know what to say. I'm sick over it, too."

"They're already laughing at me. Now this."

Delia couldn't think of anything to say. She was overwhelmed with guilt.

Rubbing the sleep from his eyes, he stood up and shook his head. "I'm exhausted. I'm going back upstairs to lie down."

Delia waited anxiously for the afternoon editions to arrive. The *Daily News* led with another story of the fire. An estimated $1,200,000 in merchandise was lost. She knew Marsh had a $1,000,000 insurance policy, something he had taken out after the fire of 1871. She hoped it would be enough for him to rebuild the store.

Delia skimmed the entire article, grateful that her name did not appear.

Then she moved on to the *Chicago Tribune*:

> The Destruction of St. Peter's at Rome could hardly have aroused an apparently deeper interest than the destruction of this palatial dry goods establishment. It is questionable whether the death of the Pope or the burning up of the Vatican could have excited such a keen local interest. . . . This was the place of worship of thousands of our female fellow-citizens. It was the only shrine at which they paid their devotions.

Delia folded the newspaper and clutched it to her chest. She felt a surge of pride for Marsh. This was the only article that should have appeared. This one said it all.

CHAPTER TWENTY-TWO

The day after the fire Marsh stopped by to see Arthur and Delia. He looked exhausted and probably hadn't slept at all. Had Williams not been standing there waiting to take Marsh's overcoat and hat, Delia would have run and thrown her arms around him.

"Is Arthur here?" he asked. "I want to apologize to him about all this business in the newspaper."

Delia motioned to Williams, and after he'd gone to get him, she led Marsh into the parlor and closed the doors. "What did Nannie say about the newspaper article?"

He lowered his eyes. "She came right out and asked if I was having an affair with you."

Delia drew a sharp breath. "What did you say?"

"I told her the truth." He gazed back up at her. "I said I was in love with you."

"Oh, Marsh." She clutched her heart. "She's too fragile. I thought you couldn't tell her yet."

"She's already back on the laudanum anyway. And besides, I had no choice. I had to tell her. She backed me into a corner. And frankly I'm relieved. It was time. I can't stand this sneaking around. I don't like to think of myself as a liar. And I want to be with you. I can't stay married to her. I told her I want a divorce."

Delia took another deep breath. "And?"

"She won't hear of it."

Delia's shoulders slumped forward. She wasn't surprised that Nannie wouldn't divorce him. "She must despise me. I have to speak with her."

"I doubt she'll hear you out. She's not even speaking to me at the moment. She says we've humiliated her."

Delia closed her eyes, fighting the throbbing pain behind her temples. Bertha's words from long ago came rushing back to her: *You don't want to cross Nannie.*

Arthur joined them in the parlor, and when Marsh thanked him for his help the night before and extended his hand, Arthur ignored the gesture.

"So what is it that I can do for you *now*?" Arthur asked him, folding his arms across his chest.

"I want to apologize for the article that appeared. And I want you to know that I fully intend to have the *Daily News* retract the story and—"

"Afraid the damage has already been done," said Arthur. His voice was tight. He hadn't looked at Delia once.

"That's precisely why I want them to retract the article."

"Ah yes, but you *are* in fact having an affair with my wife. And now everyone's suspicions have been confirmed." Arthur gave a woeful laugh.

"Fair enough," Marsh conceded, his hands raised in surrender.

Arthur stepped forward, closer to Marsh. "You know, this is something I should have done a long, long time ago." And without warning, Arthur drew back his fist and punched Marsh in the face.

Delia shrieked as Marsh reeled backward, losing his balance and landing on his backside. He looked more shocked than injured, even as he reached for his handkerchief and dabbed his mouth. Marsh made no attempt to get up and defend himself and Arthur didn't make another attack. He just held his hand, his knuckles raw and already swelling.

"There's your hero," Arthur said to Delia. Then he turned and walked out of the room.

After the incident with Marsh, Arthur went upstairs and stayed there all day. It was only later that evening that Delia went to check on him.

"Arthur?" She knocked gently on his bedroom door. "Arthur, are you all right? You haven't eaten anything all day." She looked at the dumbwaiter. "Do you want to have supper sent up to you?"

There was no answer. Delia slowly turned the doorknob. The room was dark, the curtains drawn. Delia found Arthur in his union suit curled into a ball, the bedsheets twisted about his torso. He had his back toward her. "Go away."

"Oh, please don't be like that."

He lifted his head off the pillow, his eyes red and swollen. "What kind of man stands back and does nothing while his wife carries on with his friend? I'm a fool."

He started to break down and Delia went to his bed, wrapping her arms about his waist and comforting him like she would a child who'd had a bad dream. "Shhh," she said soothingly. "Everything will be all right."

"How?" Arthur rolled over. "How can I show my face at the club, or anywhere else in this town?"

She held him tighter, unable to speak past the lump in her throat.

"Oh God," he sighed from deep within himself. "I can't bear to have everyone laughing at me."

"No one's laughing at you. It's me they despise."

"What will my father say? What will I tell my parents?"

"This is our business. No one else's. You don't have to say a word about it to anyone."

"Oh, Dell." He howled in agony as he placed his hand on her stomach. His touch was hot, so hot that she could feel every finger through the fabric of her dress. "I can change," he said. "I know I can. I want to. I do. I can give you a baby."

"Arthur, no."

"But I can. I know I can." Slowly he worked his hand down to her thigh.

"Arthur, no." She tried to stop him.

"I've missed you, Dell." Now both his hands were groping her.

She hated the feel of him on her. He didn't want her. He was only doing this to prove something to himself, something to everyone. Arthur sighed again as he caressed her neck and then her breasts.

"Arthur . . ." She began to squirm. "Come on, now . . ."

"I can change. I can give you a baby. I'll change."

When he leaned in to kiss her, his teeth gnashed against hers. She turned away and his dry lips brushed against the side of her cheek. He reached for her face and held it in place while he covered her mouth with his. She kept her lips pursed, thrashing her head from side to side.

"Don't shut me out like this." He grabbed hold of her and in one swift move he had hurled his body on top of hers. "You're my wife."

"Arthur, please. You don't want this." She tried prying herself out from under him, but she was pinned beneath his weight. His breath was hot on her face and neck. "Arthur, no! Stop it!" She heard the fabric of her dress rip as he tugged on her corset. He kissed her with a full, wet mouth and reached for her exposed breasts. He smothered her with another gagging kiss. He was sweating and she could smell the sour scent of the liquor he'd been drinking. When he yanked down her drawers, she cried out, thinking: *This is not happening. This can't be happening.* "Arthur, stop it! You're hurting me! Please—*stop*!"

"You're still my wife, dammit! You're still mine."

She twisted and tossed beneath him. He was grinding his body into hers as the stays in her corset dug into her rib cage. She could barely breathe as he bore down on her. He had managed to free his penis from his union suit and was prying her legs open with his thigh, trying to work his way inside her.

She locked eyes with him. He looked like a crazed man as he froze in place, his face just inches from hers. She felt helpless and weak, all the struggle draining out of her. She couldn't fight him off anymore. "If you insist on doing this, just hurry up and get it over with," she said, biting back tears.

In that instant his pupils constricted and the wild, menacing glare left his eyes, replaced by a look of disbelief and then disgrace. His face contorted into a terrible grimace as he rolled off her.

She climbed off the bed, clutching her torn dress, covering her breasts. "What's the matter with you?"

"Delia, I'm—"

"How could you do that?" She was trembling.

Arthur sat up, dropped his head to his hands and sobbed. "I'm sorry. I'm so sorry. Forgive me, Dell. It won't happen again. I promise."

By then she was crying, too. He turned to face her, his eyes red, a strand of spittle hanging off his lip. His hair was flat on his forehead like in the photographs she'd seen of him as a young boy. She could picture him as a child then, crouched down in a corner of his room, bawling because of something his father had said or done until his mother came and coddled him.

Delia saw the scene play out in her mind and she understood what had gone wrong with Arthur, why he was the way he was. He was still just a child—in some twisted way, he was *her* child—and that was what finally broke her and made her go to his side. Taking him in her arms, she stroked his hair and pressed her lips to his damp temple while she rocked him back and forth, promising that everything would be okay.

CHAPTER TWENTY-THREE

Delia stared out her back window, past the stables, looking through the sinewy branches of the elms and sycamores that lined her yard, framing her view of the Field mansion. Her body was stiff and sore from what had happened in Arthur's bedroom the other night. She still felt dirty and soiled. It was hard to imagine that she'd ever once craved Arthur in that way. Filled with remorse, he'd apologized again and again, wincing each time he looked at the bruises on her arms. She'd told him she didn't want to speak of it again. She didn't want to even think of it. Besides, she was more concerned about Marsh. She hadn't seen or spoken to him in two days, not since the fire and not since Arthur had struck him.

She grabbed onto the velvet pleats of her draperies, fearing that Marsh had fallen into a deep depression. After all, how could he not be discouraged? He'd already rebuilt his store once after the Great Fire and now this. And then of course there was Nannie, back on laudanum and finding out about his affair, not to mention the newspaper article and his falling-out with Arthur. It was just too much.

Everything was unraveling. She wanted to make things right, only she didn't know where to begin or if it was even possible to repair the damage. Delia wanted to talk to Nannie about the newspaper article. She didn't know what she'd say to her, but she knew that the incident could not go ignored. She'd left her calling card for Nannie the day after the fire but hadn't yet received a response.

Therese came up from behind her and draped a shawl over her shoulders. Delia reached up and patted her maid's hand.

"You have a visitor, Mrs. Caton. Mr. Field is in the parlor."

Delia was both relieved and concerned. She braced herself to find a broken man waiting for her as she followed Therese to the front of the house. She found him standing in the doorway of the parlor and she gasped when she first saw his lip, bruised and swollen.

"Oh, Marsh—" Even before Therese had left the parlor, Delia ran into his arms. "I've been so worried about you." She willed herself not to cry, wanting to be strong for him.

"Now why are you looking so blue?" he asked.

"Don't be glib at a time like this. Where have you been? I was worried sick."

"You should know better than to worry about me." He cracked a sly smile, making his eyes crinkle. "I've been busy getting my new store ready to open."

"What?" Delia reached for his cheek, feeling the bristle of whiskers from his unshaven face. He wasn't broken. Far from it.

He looked at her and placed his hand on top of hers. "You didn't think I'd let something like a little fire close me down? And especially not during the Christmas season."

How could she have doubted him? Just like after the first fire, he'd wasted no time in rebuilding. It was his resilience, his strength, that made her love him all the more.

"I found an abandoned building down on Michigan and Adams. It's the old Lakefront Exposition Hall. It's not perfect but it's the best I could find. It'll be a temporary space until I can figure out our next move. And in the meantime I'm rounding up as many men as I can find to help me get the place in shape."

"What all needs to be done?" came a voice from behind them.

They both turned around and there was Arthur, leaning against the doorjamb with a drink in his hand.

"I can help," he said. "That is, if you want me to."

Delia saw the edges of Marsh's lip curl up and then she saw Arthur's eyes turn misty.

"You ever sand a floor before?" Marsh asked.

"Never."

"Perfect." His smile broadened. "I don't suppose you've buffed one, either," he said with a laugh.

"Well, what are we waiting for?" said Arthur. "We've got work to do."

Later that day, Arthur went down to Michigan Boulevard and spent ten hours whitewashing the walls. For the next two weeks, he faithfully reported to Marsh, eager to help. He learned to work a lathe, and a circular saw. He built cabinets and hung mirrors. He came home at night with calluses and blisters covering hands that had never before known a day of manual labor.

And by the end of November, to everyone's delight and astonishment, Field, Leiter & Company reopened its doors.

Even though things between Arthur and Marsh had returned to normal, Delia's life was anything but. It was the start of the holiday season and her schedule was noticeably thin. Typically she and Arthur would have had two and three engagements a night, not to mention the regular meetings she usually attended each week for the Chicago Women's Club and Fortnightly Club. But since the article about her and Marsh appeared in the *Daily News,* she hadn't had the stomach to show her face at any meetings. And she hadn't been getting their usual invitations, aside from charitable organizations looking for money.

Delia was on the committee for the Chicago Women's Club's annual book drive that year along with Nannie, Abby, Bertha and several other members. She thought about backing out, but it was the one committee she truly enjoyed. Books had always been her companions, her escape. The pages she turned had taken her places and taught her to dream. The books they collected went to orphanages and needy families that couldn't afford to buy them. Out of all the luncheons and teas, the speaking engagements and social events, this was the one that was most important to her and she wasn't about to shirk her responsibilities because of that newspaper article.

The story had appeared a little over three weeks ago, and since then, Delia hadn't spoken to any of her women friends other than Abby and Bertha. She could understand her sister's loyalty, but when she questioned Bertha's, she told Delia about her own tales of being ostracized by the ladies of their social set.

"When I became engaged to Potter they wanted nothing to do with me," Bertha had explained one day while having tea in Delia's parlor. "They were appalled that such a young girl would marry a man old enough to be her father." Bertha had laughed as she toyed with her necklace. "Of course once they saw that hotel, those women changed their tune. But I know how it feels to be shunned by them. It can be very lonely. Those women, especially Nannie, have a cruel streak. And believe me, if she weren't married to the most powerful man in Chicago, those women wouldn't tolerate her, either."

Bertha never directly asked about her affair with Marsh. Not that she was above gossip. Heavens, no. She and Delia had passed many an afternoon sipping sherry and sharing all they'd seen, heard, read and suspected. When it came to particularly salacious tidbits, Bertha would get that look in her eye and say with a giggle, "Oh my, but we're going to the devil now!" Delia assumed that Bertha was too good a friend to get involved in her relationship and had remained quiet out of respect for both her and Marsh.

So aside from Bertha and of course Abby, Delia kept to herself. On those occasions when she came across Sybil or Frances or any of the others, they passed by her without a word, pretending they hadn't seen her. She knew that she'd been removed from the guest list for Malvina Armour's annual Christmas luncheon and the Swifts' holiday pageant. The Glessners hadn't sent an invitation for their New Year's Eve party, either.

They were all punishing Delia and she wanted desperately to defend herself. It enraged her that she was being judged without them knowing the whole story. If only those women understood the truth about Nannie and Arthur, they'd understand that she wasn't some wicked, scheming adulteress. But it was pointless. She'd never tell anyone that her marriage was a sham. She wouldn't do that to Arthur and she knew Marsh would never reveal the truth about Nannie, either.

One afternoon as she sat at her secretary going through her empty calendar, something new occurred to her. She looked back through December and into November and October, counting and recounting the days. She set down her dip pen and closed her engagement book. Could it be possible? She'd given up on the Ayer's Sarsaparilla and had stopped marking down her cycle, but if she wasn't mistaken, she had missed her monthlies twice in a row.

She sat still, all too aware of her shallow breathing, of the sound of the clock in the corner ticking off the seconds. She was stunned as she rose and made her way upstairs, holding on to the banister for support. She counted the steps as she went, too afraid to let herself be hopeful, too overwhelmed by what this could mean to her, to Marsh and to Arthur.

She walked into her dressing room and stood before the cheval mirror. With hands splayed against her flat abdomen, she turned to the left and then the right. She unbuttoned her dress and unlaced her corset. When she slid the straps of her chemise off her shoulders, she raised a hand to her breasts and noticed they were swollen and tender. Her nipples were darker, larger than she remembered. This would explain why she'd felt nauseated and tired the past few days. How had she not noticed the symptoms? Maybe she'd been too afraid to even let herself speculate. Tears sprang to her eyes. Now that she was paying attention, she knew there could be no doubt. She was pregnant. Pregnant with Marsh's baby.

Delia gazed out the carriage window as her driver rambled down Wabash Avenue. Her news was only then just hours old and she couldn't wait to share it with Marsh.

Men and women scurried along the sidewalks, wincing at the frigid winter weather. It was sleeting and the fierce winds coming off the lake battered the coach, gently rocking her from side to side. Despite the conditions outside, Delia had her driver drop her at the corner of Wabash and Adams.

She was always careful about visiting Marsh at work, and now, thanks to that newspaper article, she needed to be more discreet than ever. Recently, Arthur had been seen around town with Marsh at the Chicago Club and in restaurants, but Delia had kept her distance. The only times she'd seen Marsh over the past two weeks was when Arthur brought him by the house. She knew even that was enough to rouse the neighborhood gossips, who no doubt kept their binoculars on the ledges of their windows. She didn't need any of them seeing her carriage dropping her off outside the Exposition Hall store. Instead she walked around the corner, heading into the wind and sleet, gritting her teeth as ice pellets stung her cheeks and patches of slush challenged her every step.

Once inside the store Delia shook the sleet from her coat and muff, and stomped the slush off her boots while pretending she didn't notice Malvina Armour and Annie Swift standing just a few feet behind her.

"She has some nerve coming down here," she heard Annie saying.

"Can you believe she's still going to participate in the book drive?"

Delia spotted Marsh right away, standing by a makeshift counter piled high with bloomers. She knew Annie and Malvina were watching her, but she'd come there with news and what she had to tell Marsh was bigger than their petty gossip.

She went over to his side, tentatively tapping him on the shoulder. "Excuse me, Mr. Field? May I have a word with you?"

As soon as they were alone in his office, he closed his door and pulled her to him, embracing her. He traced the curve of her back with his fingertips as he kissed her slowly, tenderly at first, before letting it build into a fierce passion that she knew would be hard to interrupt. She couldn't stop herself either. They hadn't been alone for so long. He didn't even ask what she'd needed to talk to him about. She took a moment to savor the feel of his arms around her and lost herself in the familiar scent of his aftershave. How she had missed him! As those feelings of love welled inside her, she thought about the wonderful news she'd come to share with him. Taking a deep breath, she took a step back and stared into his eyes.

"Marsh, there's something I have to tell you."

His expression turned to one of alarm.

"No, no." She reached up for his face. "It's nothing bad. It's . . . it's wonderful." But the words—the actual words—just wouldn't come. Instead she brought her hand to her stomach and smiled.

He did a double take, looking down to her belly and then back up into her eyes. He seemed to almost stagger then, and he stepped back to sit in his chair.

"Are you sure?" he asked, finally.

"I haven't been to the doctor yet, but I know. I'm certain of it."

He pulled her onto his lap and kissed her full on the mouth. "I can't believe it—a child. With you."

They sat with that for a moment. Delia was letting it all sink in: one astonishing realization that gave way to another. She was going to be a mother. She was right now, at that very moment, carrying Marsh's child. There was only one downside and she looked at him and asked the inevitable: "Do you think Nannie will suspect it's yours?"

"I'm sure she'll figure it out. I suppose I have to tell her."

"And then what?"

He sighed and shook his head. "There's no way to predict what she'll do. But handling delicate situations with grace and dignity is not her forte." He ran his hand along his jaw, his fingertips brushing up against his whiskers. "Have you told Arthur yet?"

"Not yet. I wanted to tell you first."

He placed his hands on her belly and they stayed like that, Delia sitting in his lap with her head resting on his shoulder. Marsh leaned in and kissed her hair. "Do you want me with you when you tell Arthur?"

Delia looked up at him and smiled. She wanted Arthur to feel included, to know that this child was his, too, and she couldn't think of a better way to convey that. "Yes, let's tell him together tonight."

The three of them were in the drawing room, waiting for dinner to be served.

Arthur was in a jovial mood, already on his second cocktail, talking about a polo match that had taken place in Palm Beach. "It was all over the newspapers earlier today. Of all the matches to miss . . ."

Delia stole a quick glance at Marsh. It was time. She went and joined Arthur on the settee, placing her hand on top of his. "Arthur, darling, Marsh and I have some news."

"Oh?" Arthur looked first at Delia and then at Marsh.

Delia cleared her throat and curled her fingers about his. "Arthur, honey, I'm pregnant. We're going to have a baby. All of us."

"A baby?" Arthur's expression went blank. It was impossible to read. He shot up off the settee, stuffed his hands in his pockets and walked into the center of the room before he abruptly turned and faced the windows. "A baby," he said, with his back toward Delia and Marsh. "You're having a baby."

Delia nodded though she knew he couldn't see her. She stole a glance at Marsh who kept his eyes trained on Arthur's back. They were waiting, in a standoff, and all Delia could think was that they'd made a terrible mistake. She was holding her breath when Arthur turned back around. He looked at Delia and then at Marsh. Then he raised his fists above his head and laughed. Tears clung to his lashes as he rushed over and hugged them both.

"We're having a baby," he said, his cheeks damp from crying. "Champagne—" He called to Williams. "We need champagne!"

When the glasses were poured, Arthur raised his first in a toast. "To you," he said, looking at Delia and then Marsh. "Both of you. And to the baby. Our baby."

They finished that bottle of champagne and opened another. The hour was growing later. They were giddy to begin with and now they were getting tipsy.

"If it's a boy," said Arthur, "I say we call him Rufus."

"Rufus?" Marsh shook his head and laughed. "That'll never do. I had an uncle Rufus once. And if you'd known him, you'd understand my objection."

"And besides," said Delia, "what if it's a girl? I like the name Constance or Ophelia."

"Ophelia and Delia. You want your names to rhyme?" Marsh questioned her teasingly.

"And what do you suggest?" asked Arthur.

Marsh thought for a moment. "I've always liked the name Newton."

"New*ton* Ca*ton*?" Delia wrinkled up her nose.

"She's right," said Arthur, laughing, "too many *tons* for one name."

Marsh started laughing, too, slapping Arthur on the back.

Delia held out her glass for more champagne. As she watched Marsh and Arthur sitting side by side, laughing, she got a warm feeling, right where their baby was. There wasn't a doubt in her mind that this was the right thing for them—all three of them.

The next morning Delia had a slight headache from all the champagne. Therese brought her a tray with her morning coffee and the newspaper. As Delia lay back in bed, she turned to the society page, and read about all the Christmas parties and balls from the night before that she hadn't been invited to. And honestly, she didn't care. Her body felt alive and magical. *It was making a baby! Marsh's baby!*

After breakfast, she bathed and dressed and went down to State Street to finish up her Christmas shopping. All the stores had put up their Christmas decorations and she walked by garlands in the windows, wreaths on the front doors. Normally the Field & Leiter windows were the most spectacular of all with golden trumpets and a Nativity scene resting upon blankets of snow. Shoppers would stand on the sidewalk, four and five rows deep, just to get a look at their Christmas windows. But this year, the Exposition Hall was only modestly decorated; it didn't have the type of windows that allowed for Christmas displays.

She moved on, going in and out of stores, looking for last-minute gifts. She had just purchased a velocipede cycle for her nephew, Spencer, and Shiebler silver hair combs for Abby. Thankfully she had already gotten presents for her parents and all of Arthur's family, too. Now she was shopping for her other family, for Marsh and his children. She even looked at the baby sections of several stores in anticipation of buying bassinets, rattles and buggies. With a smile on her face all she could think was that the three of them, Arthur, Marsh and her, were getting what they wanted for Christmas.

CHAPTER TWENTY-FOUR

1878

Delia awoke one morning feeling tired and queasy. She was entering her fourth month and soon she'd be showing and would need to wear a maternity corset. An icy chill swept across the floorboards as she forced herself to ring for Therese. It was time to get dressed. After all, it was cataloging day for the book drive and Delia wasn't about to shirk her responsibilities.

She planned to meet Bertha and Abby and some of the other women—the few members who were still speaking to her—at the community center to sort through the book donations. Typically, cataloging day was a big event for the Chicago Women's Club, but because of the recent surge of gossip about her, she knew better than to expect much of a turnout that year. If it weren't for Bertha and Abby, she feared she might end up there by herself.

It was snowing hard that day, the middle of January. Looking out the carriage window, Delia took in the scenery. Calumet Avenue was a stretch of endless white with fresh carriage tracks running down the center of the street. The community center on Dearborn was even prettier: a majestic limestone building with a splendid cupola and six massive pillars all perched upon a steep flight of snow-covered steps.

As she alighted from her carriage Delia noticed a woman standing near the doorway, pacing back and forth. She wondered if perhaps the front doors were locked and continued on, carefully navigating the slick steps covered with snow and patches of ice. She was almost to the top when the woman turned around. Delia took one look and almost slipped. It was Nannie. *Nannie!* Delia never thought she'd show up that day. Despite the cold weather she felt a rush of heat filling up her body. Delia hadn't seen her in over two months, not since the night of the fire. Since then Nannie had ignored all of Delia's calling cards.

"Nannie," she said, teetering on the top step. "I didn't expect you here today."

"I'm on this committee, too. In case you've forgotten." Nannie was standing right in front of her, blocking her way from stepping up to the landing.

"No. No, I haven't forgotten." Delia cleared her throat, gripping onto the railing. "Actually, it's a good thing that you're here. I think maybe it's time the two of us talked about a few things."

"As if I'd believe anything you have to say. I asked a long time ago if you were having an affair with my husband and you flat-out denied it. You're a liar. You've been sneaking around behind my back for God knows how long. And you call yourself a friend."

Delia's cheeks burned hot as she squeezed the banister harder. She wanted to set Nannie straight. She wanted to remind her that she was not the cause of Nannie's troubled marriage. The problems were there long before Delia had come along.

Before Delia could respond, Nannie narrowed her eyes and said, "And now I hear you're with child."

Delia went light-headed as she searched Nannie's eyes. How did she know? Had she overheard them talking? She was certain that Marsh hadn't said anything to her yet.

"Just understand one thing—" Nannie leaned forward with daggers in her eyes. "I can and will ruin you in this town."

Delia didn't doubt it. Her nerves unraveled. She was still on the step and Nannie was staring down at her. Delia was shaking and hoped that Nannie would think it was from the cold.

"Well, then," said Delia, "shall we go organize the books?" She started to sidestep around Nannie when she felt a jolt from behind that took her off-balance. Her heel slipped out from under her and she felt her body reeling backward as if in slow motion. She heard herself scream as her arms flailed and she began to tumble. A flash of white stars blinded her each time she struck a step. Her body spiraled down the stairs, going faster and faster until she stopped with a deafening thud.

She realized she must have passed out for a minute. When she opened her eyes, the whiteness of the snow was blinding. The metallic taste of blood filled her mouth and she couldn't feel her lips or teeth. Her head throbbed; her eyes stung with tears as splintering pain shot through her back and limbs. Her carriage driver raced over, asking if she was okay. Delia could hardly speak. She tried to move and that's when she felt the flood of hot wetness between her legs, soaking through her drawers and petticoat. She looked down and saw that the snow beneath her was turning crimson.

The last thing she remembered before she lost consciousness

was Nannie, standing at the top of the steps, glaring down at her with a stone-cold look on her face.

When she came to, Delia was in the hospital. Her eyes landed on a pitcher and basin on a table next to her bed. Each time she tried to move the metal bed frame squeaked and just a turn of her head sent the room whirling. Even blinking made her skull throb. Every breath made her feel as if her body would crack in two. She still had the taste of blood in her mouth and her lips were swollen. She ran her tongue along her teeth, checking to see if they were all there.

She hadn't noticed the doctor in the room, but now he spoke and with his words, he came into focus. He was tall and stocky and stood at the foot of her bed looking over her chart.

"You're very lucky," he said. "It's a miracle you didn't break any bones." He set her chart back down. "There was some internal damage, however."

Delia then became aware of the warm liquid oozing from between her legs. "My baby?" she asked, or maybe she only thought she did. Either way, she already knew the answer. She already knew it was too late.

"I'm sorry." He shook his head. "It's unlikely that you would be able to conceive again."

Delia burst into tears. It felt like a pane of glass shattered inside her chest. The sobs rumbled up from deep within her and there was nothing she could do to stop them.

"Your husband was here all day," said the doctor. "I finally sent him home to get some rest."

He was still speaking, warning her about something, saying she had a rough time ahead of her, but Delia was too distraught to comprehend anything other than the fact that she'd lost her baby and probably wouldn't be able to have another one.

The nurse came in and gave her something for the pain, but later that night, the medicine wore off and the cramps began. In the following hours the pain was piercing and the blood seemed endless. The nurse changed the rag bag towels every ten minutes because they were soaked through. But worse than that were the contractions. Spasms and convulsions racked her body. She cried out in panic realizing that she was actually going into labor. She was going to have to deliver a baby that was already dead. Tears streamed down her face as more contractions came with searing bands of pain that made her scream in agony.

While the nurse was giving her a sponge bath, Delia turned her head and gasped at what she saw. Nannie was standing in the doorway. And that's when the horror came rushing back to her and she remembered the feel of Nannie's hand on her back and the sudden jolt just before her foot slipped out from under her. She wanted to scream, to cry for help—but she was too drained.

"What's with all the fussing, dear? You're fine. I'm right here." The nurse turned around, and when Delia looked again, Nannie was gone. "You're just having fever dreams," she said, patting a cool cloth down Delia's arm.

Another contraction was coming on. Stronger this time. Delia closed her eyes and moaned through gritted teeth and to her horror, she felt it she felt her baby slip out of her womb.

After the doctor examined her, Delia turned her head toward the pillow and sobbed. She'd barely gotten used to the idea of having the child and now it was over. She wanted Marsh there with her. She wanted Arthur, too. She needed them both. The doctor said Arthur was in the waiting room but that she needed her rest before he'd let her see him. But Delia couldn't rest. She was so upset that the doctor eventually had to give her something to quiet her down. She fought the sedative for nearly an hour before it finally conquered her, sending her into a deep, dreamless sleep.

When she awoke, it was dark inside the hospital room. She was still groggy, and as her eyes began to focus, she became aware of Arthur sitting alongside her bed.

"The doctor said you're going to be all right." He reached for her hand and gently squeezed it. "He said you're very lucky you didn't break your neck."

She swallowed hard. Her mouth was dry.

"The doctor told me about the baby." His voice cracked. She could smell the whiskey on his breath. "I'm so sorry, Dell."

Delia felt the tears building up behind her eyes. "Oh, Arthur, I've let you down and . . ."

"Shhh." He shook his head to silence her and squeezed her hand. "It's no one's fault."

"But, Arthur, it is. It was—"

"Shhh. These things happen. It was an accident. There's no one to blame for—"

"Nannie," she said.

"What?"

"It was Nannie. She pushed me. She knew about the baby and she pushed me down those stairs."

"Oh, Dell—you don't know what you're saying. You poor thing. You're exhausted. Delirious."

"But—"

"Even Nannie would never do something like that. Your imagination is running wild. I know you want someone to blame, but you have no proof. You need to rest now. You can't afford to get yourself worked up."

Was he right? Was she delirious? Just looking for someone to blame? She knew it was a terrible accusation, but why would she imagine that Nannie pushed her? Why could she feel the ghost of Nannie's hand on her back? She rolled over and faced the wall, fighting to keep her eyes open. She was so drained that she honestly didn't know what was real anymore.

Arthur stayed at her bedside for a long time, gently holding her hand, not saying a word. Finally, he turned to her, his eyes rimmed red. "Marsh should be here by now. I'll go get him for you."

Arthur waited outside in the hall when Marsh came inside, pulled up a chair close to the bedside and reached for her hand. Delia could hear the sound of Arthur's shoes pacing back and forth outside in the hallway.

"It was a boy," she said. "The nurse told me."

He pressed her fingers to his lips and closed his eyes, bringing her hand from his mouth to his cheek. "I wanted this with you. I wanted this so much."

"I know." Her voice was breaking as she stroked his hair. She thought again about Nannie, thought about saying something to Marsh, but Arthur was right. She had no proof. And even Nannie—as dark as her soul was—could not have done anything that horrid. It was too cruel to fathom.

"We'll try again," he said.

Delia felt her eyes tearing up. She didn't have the heart to tell him that she might never be able to conceive another child.

The nurse came in her room, and when Delia glanced through the open door out into the hallway, she saw Arthur. He was standing with his face to the wall, his shoulders shaking as he sobbed into his hands.

Delia tried not to think about the baby. It was too painful. For two weeks, she could barely get out of bed. She passed her days staring at the William Morris wallpaper until she started seeing a clown's face in the pattern. And the clown's eerie grin became superimposed in her mind on a picture of Nannie's face as she'd stared at her falling down the stairs.

She tried not to think about Nannie because doing so brought on hot waves of hate that nearly overwhelmed her. Instead, she turned her mind to God. God had done this to her, punishing her for loving another woman's husband. *Are you happy now?* she said, fists drawn up toward the heavens. *Have you settled the score?* And then her bursts of anger always, always gave way to bouts of tears before leading her back to despondency.

As the days turned to weeks, Arthur and Marsh managed to resume their routines. Marsh worked more than usual and Arthur drank more. But Delia could not shake her melancholy. Abby assured her that time would ease the pain and Delia glared at her, wanting to scream, "What do you know about it? You've never lost a child." Delia's parents, especially her father, had tried to lift her spirits with tickets to the ballet and the opera. Mrs. Caton had even come by with flowers and more tonics, but nothing helped.

It was about a month after she'd lost the baby that Arthur walked into the parlor with a surprise. "For you," he said, handing her a white wicker basket with a pink ribbon tied to the handle.

Delia peered inside and clutched her heart as a tiny, furry gray-and-beige face popped up and barked. "Oh, Arthur!"

"She's a Yorkshire terrier," he said, joining her on the settee.

"Well, look at you," said Delia, scooping the tiny puppy into her arms. "How old is she?"

"Just five months. But she won't get much bigger. I thought she would cheer you up."

Delia held the puppy closer, laughing as it licked her face. The dog didn't weigh more than four or five pounds. "Oh, Arthur!

Look at that precious face. She's perfect! I love her. I just love her." She looked up at Arthur with tears in her eyes. "How did you know I . . ." She choked up, unable to finish her thought.

"Because I know my wife." He leaned in and kissed her forehead. "I know what you need right now."

And that was the beginning of Delia's relationship with Flossie, her faithful companion. From that day on, wherever Delia went, Flossie went with her.

CHAPTER TWENTY-FIVE

1879

On a cold January evening Delia and Marsh sat before a crackling fireplace in the drawing room at the Field mansion. The flickering firelight danced off the coffered ceiling squares and the room smelled of hickory and pine. Nannie had taken the children back to Europe with her for the winter. Arthur was in New York for a horse show. But Flossie was there, resting on the floor at Delia's feet.

It had been a year, and the rawest of Delia's pain had finally faded. But she still thought about the baby she'd lost all the time. She supposed she'd never really stop grieving. She knew Marsh would always feel the pain of their loss, too, but his way of dealing with it was to throw himself into his work. The last year had been incredible for him. He'd turned an astounding profit, and had invested in more real estate around town. Among his many conquests was the newly rebuilt Singer Building—the very building that they'd occupied before it burned down two years before.

Marsh had persuaded Levi to go along with the purchase and now Field, Leiter & Company was preparing to move from the exposition building on Michigan Boulevard back to State Street.

"That's where all the shopping is. That's where we've got to be." Marsh leaned in toward the fire, rubbing his hands, palm against palm.

She studied his face and saw that spark of magic flickering behind his eyes. Her pulse quickened when he got like that because she knew that something grand was in the works. She could almost see the future formulating inside his head, gathering strength like a twister. She fed off his creativity as much as he fed off her enthusiasm.

"We have to stay one step ahead of the competition," he said. "I have it on good authority that Carson Pirie Scott just sublet a building a few doors down from us. Plus, Lord & Taylor and Arnold Constable are looking for space on State Street, too."

"All the more reason to do something extraordinary with the new store," she said.

"Exactly. I want us to offer an experience that ladies in this town can't find anywhere else. I want Field, Leiter & Company to be a sophisticated, elegant place to shop with the finest merchandise—items that can't be found anywhere else. Levi doesn't know this yet, but I'm going to gut the whole interior and rebuild it."

"You're asking for a fight, you know."

"And I'll win. I always do." He smiled.

"But wouldn't it be better if you didn't have to fight with him at all? Honestly, I've never understood this partnership of yours."

"I feel a sense of loyalty toward Levi."

"Aw, and to think everyone says you're just a cold, hard-nosed businessman."

"They do?" He looked at her slightly amused, with genuine surprise, his eyebrows raised.

"Oh come now, Marsh," she said with a laugh. "Don't tell me you don't know you have a reputation as being a wee bit tough when it comes to business."

He smiled as if he liked the sound of that. "So I have a reputation, do I? But I do have a heart."

"Oh, yes. For select people—of which I'm pleased to be included—you have a very big heart." She rested her head on his shoulder and patted his chest. "And Levi is lucky that you've put him in that circle."

"It's just that Levi and I have built this company together."

"And we both know he couldn't have gotten it off the ground without you. If I were you, I would have bought him out years ago."

Marsh reached over and cupped her face. "You talk about me being hard and callous when it comes to these things. My Lord, you would have made one hell of a shrewd businessman, Dell."

"Businesswoman," she corrected him. "And I tell you something else—"

"Oh boy." Marsh squinted jokingly as if bracing himself for a lecture.

"I'm serious. If you want to keep us women shopping all day, you need lavatories. And feed us, for God's sake."

He sat up, forcing her to raise her head and look at him. Marsh shook his head. "I'll never get Levi to go along with a tearoom. But lavatories—"

"Oh, and a lounge where the women can relax, maybe read a newspaper or magazine—"

"Now that would be something. I'd like to see Carson Pirie Scott try to match that. I dare any of them to even try. There's going to be one grand store—grander than all the others on State Street and . . ." He looked at the smile on her face. "What?"

"Nothing," she said, leaning in to kiss him. "I just love it when you get so competitive. It's very seductive. Very alluring. New York merchants be damned!"

Marsh grinned, obviously liking the sound of that.

All that winter and into the spring, Delia and Marsh were preoccupied with the new store. Marsh included Delia in all the planning, showing her the blueprints, the inventory for new merchandise, even the fixtures and displays.

One afternoon in April Delia went down to State Street with Flossie scampering alongside her, her diamond leash swinging back and forth like a jump rope. The city had grown so much in recent years she hardly recognized it. New stone buildings had appeared on every corner, and they spread farther west along streets that Delia had never ventured down. She still couldn't believe the fire had been less than a decade before.

It had stormed earlier that day and the sidewalks were still damp, peppered with puddles here and there. The sun was coming out now and so were the shoppers who had ducked inside during the rain. Delia paused before a display window and caught a reflection of the new Field, Leiter & Company across the way. It was preparing to open in less than a week.

Delia knew that other merchants were moving to town soon, but up until then there wasn't a store on State Street that even came close to Field & Leiter. By comparison, they were downright shoddy. The Ed Ahlswede Company had dragged half their merchandise onto the sidewalk. Some of it had gotten soaked in the rain, but that didn't seem to matter. Their clerks sat on the front stoop while women sorted through the bins of damp fabrics, knitting needles, thimbles, pincushions and other notions, searching for what they needed. A few doors down was Hinckley & Brothers. It was another mishmash of merchandise. The lace was mixed in with the silks, the wools in with the linens. The aisles were cluttered with boxes and litter and a film of dust covered the counters, clinging to items that you'd have to shake out and clean once you got them home. Even her father's store, over on Lake Street, was cramped with overcrowded shelves. It was a treasure hunt even for the clerks to find items. Though her father had been a dry goods pioneer, Hibbard & Spencer was from another place in time. They couldn't begin to match the kind of luxury service and quality that shoppers had come to expect from Field & Leiter.

"Hello, Delia." A shrill voice from behind called to her.

Delia turned around and her jaw dropped. "Nannie—" She was so startled, so caught off guard, she didn't know what to say.

"You look pale."

"Just surprised is all. I didn't know you were back in town."

"I had to come back for the store opening."

Delia nodded. Of course Nannie wouldn't miss an opportunity to wear her crown as Mrs. Marshall Field.

Flossie jumped up on Nannie, leaving damp paw prints on the bottom of her dress. "Flossie," Delia said, tugging on her leash. "Down. Flossie, get down."

A series of carriages rambled down the street, the horses' bridles and harnesses jangling as they passed. The noise made the silence between the two women almost eerie.

Nannie smiled as if struck by some great revelation. "I don't love him anymore," she said. "I don't love Marshall."

Delia was taken aback by her words, blurted out and in the middle of the busy downtown street where anyone passing by could overhear them.

"So you see," said Nannie, "you're not *taking* anything away from me that I haven't already willingly given up."

Suddenly Delia found the smug look on Nannie's face more than she could bear. The hate she'd worked so hard to control and bury came raging back. It was all she could do to remain calm enough to say, "If that's the case, then why not divorce him?"

"Because I have children," she snapped. "That's something you will never understand. You couldn't even hold on to the child you had."

That cut deeply. Delia lost her power to control herself. "No thanks to you."

"I beg your pardon." Nannie shot her an indignant look.

"You think I don't remember? You think I don't know you pushed me down those stairs?"

"That's absurd. You're not in your right mind. You must have fallen on your head—you don't know what you're talking about." Before she turned to walk away, Nannie stepped closer to Delia and said, "Just so you know, I will never give Marshall a divorce. I will be the one and only Mrs. Marshall Field until the day I die."

Nannie brushed past her, leaving Delia standing alone on the sidewalk, shaking.

Ever since her run-in with Nannie, Delia had talked herself in and out of going to the grand opening party at least a dozen times. Now it was the night of the party and at Marsh's insistence and Arthur's encouragement, she was going.

Therese helped dress Delia in a royal blue velvet gown with rhinestone detailing and a silk ribbon at the waist. A diamond choker graced her long neck and her hair was done up, held in place with sapphire combs. The pale blue gloves she wore came up past her elbows.

With a drink in hand—his second, she suspected—Arthur stepped into the doorway of her bedroom in a new well-tailored suit. His diamond stickpin sparkled in the flickering glow of the lamp on her dressing table. She noticed also that Arthur had gotten a shave earlier that day and that his muttonchops had been trimmed, cut quite close to his jowls.

"No Flossie tonight?" he asked, looking at the puppy, who was up on her hind legs and dancing about his feet.

"Not tonight." Delia told the dog to stay put. It was one of the few times she'd left her behind and neither one was happy about it. Flossie lay flat on the floor, whimpering and covering her nose with her paws. A pang of guilt shot through Delia and she scooped up the dog, cuddling her, planting kisses on her head.

"When I die," said Arthur, "I want to come back as Flossie."

With regret Delia set Flossie down and they were on their way.

The carriages were lined up on State Street as men and women dressed in all their finery entered the Field, Leiter & Company store. The new building, now six stories high, had an impressive mansard roof accented by a series of small domes. Delia was nervous for Marsh, wanting everything to go perfectly. The whole idea of having a society party to open a dry goods store had never been done before, just as a store as elegant and beautiful as Field & Leiter had never existed before, either. Marsh was creating something completely new. Her pulse raced and she wrung her sweating hands together.

Inside, the store was magnificent. Delia couldn't get over the transformation. It was hard to believe this was the same space that had been devoured by flames just two years before. The well light overhead let the moonlight shine down. Beautiful plush carpets ran the length of the aisles. Rich mahogany counters and glassed-in shelves lined the exterior of the room. Large mirrors were stationed around the elaborate displays. Delia's eyes landed on everything from Alexandre kid gloves to front-fastening Machree corsets to bustle pads. The gentlemen's department, she noted, was filled with collars, suspenders and smoking caps.

She remembered how Marsh fretted over the expense of the

renovation. But in the end, he had decided that the store needed to be equipped with all the latest amenities, including electric lights. That feature alone amazed the guests as they made their way through the aisles.

A twenty-piece orchestra played while people filtered throughout the store, taking in the latest merchandise from Europe and the Orient. Champagne was served along with platters of oysters, caviar and other seafood delicacies. Uniformed security guards stood watch from various points around the room, on the lookout for pickpockets and shoplifters who had managed to obtain a coveted invitation to the event.

Every newspaper reporter in town clustered around Marsh and Levi, taking turns asking questions. That's when Marsh spotted Delia. With just a glance they both acknowledged that this was a shared victory. The rest of the party blurred into the backdrop for Delia as she savored the moment, the fruit of all their hard work. She was reveling in this when she spotted Nannie's hand reaching over, resting on Marsh's forearm. The moment had been ruined. Just thinking about the things Nannie said to her on the street, that Nannie's push caused her to lose her baby, filled Delia with rage. She couldn't look at her anymore. She had to turn away.

"Let's go see the rest of the store," suggested Arthur, tugging at Delia's arm. She knew he could tell how upset she was. It wasn't until he had fetched her a second glass of champagne that she began to calm down.

"Go easy with that, my pet," he said, watching her take two large sips.

For most of the evening, Delia stayed off to the side, insulated by Arthur, Abby and Augustus, Bertha and Potter. Some people, like Frances and Annie, were cordial, but they still let Delia know they disapproved of her being there. Delia had expected a cool reception and tried not to let it spoil her evening. After all, this was a celebration. But still, it stung that she was slighted, especially when she had contributed so much to the design of the store. She deserved to be there more than they could have imagined.

At one point Delia excused herself and went upstairs to see the new lavatory on the second floor. After months of looking at sketches, she found it a thrill to view the finished product, including the marble she'd help select along with the gilt-trimmed mirror. She especially liked the Blaise and Millet vanity table accessorized with dusting powder, a silver paddle brush and a tray of French perfumes. A uniformed attendant rose from a gold velvet stool in the corner. Delia was taking it all in when the lavatory door swung open and in walked Nannie.

She brushed past the attendant and went straight up to Delia, forcing her back against the wall. "What do you think you're doing here?"

Delia was so caught off guard she couldn't speak. Her composure was beginning to unravel.

"You have no business being here." Nannie grabbed hold of her and Delia shrieked as she shook her hard, banging her shoulders against the marble wall.

Nannie's fingers felt like claws clamping down on her shoulders, just like her cockatiel's talons. Delia looked to the attendant for help, but she only stood back with a panicked expression on her face. Delia squirmed and twisted until at last she managed to push Nannie off.

"I'm not finished with you yet." Nannie grabbed onto Delia's shoulder and spun her around. "You're nothing to him, you hear me? You're nothing! Nothing but a used-up little tart! He didn't even want that baby."

Delia's hatred suddenly exploded inside her. She didn't even remember slapping Nannie across the face. Her fingers and palm stung before she even realized what she'd done. She looked at her gloved hand and then up at Nannie. A red welt had already come up on her cheek.

Nannie looked stunned and ran out the door calling, "Guard! Guard!"

With the help of the attendant, Delia salvaged what was left of her appearance. As soon as she stepped out of the lavatory, Nannie thrust her finger at her. "That's her!" Two uniformed security guards were standing at her side. "She's the one. That's the woman who assaulted me."

"That's ridiculous," said Delia.

Turning to the security guards, Nannie said, "I'm Mrs. Marshall Field and I demand that you arrest this woman."

Delia was speechless as the guards grabbed hold of her by either arm, cuffing her in their bare hands. She froze in a state of disbelief as they tugged her along, escorting her down the long staircase. She'd never been handled like that before, treated with such disrespect. Her hair had come undone and she realized how disheveled she must appear. The guards were walking so fast she tripped on the stairs as the entire party watched her being led down to the first floor. Her sister and Augustus, Bertha and Potter, Sybil and Annie were looking at her aghast.

Arthur rushed up, meeting them at the foot of the stairs. "What happened? Are you all right? What's going on here?"

Marsh cut in front of him. "What's the meaning of this?"

"I'm afraid this woman caused an incident with your wife upstairs in the lavatory, Mr. Field."

"Incident? What sort of incident?" Marsh shifted his gaze from Delia to Nannie and back to Delia.

"This woman assaulted Mrs. Field."

There was a gasp from the onlookers. Delia was too overwhelmed to speak up and defend herself.

"That's absurd." Marsh reached over and pulled the guard's hand off Delia's wrist. "Do you know who this woman is?"

As soon as her arms were freed, Delia hugged herself about the middle. She felt as though she heard the whole room inhale while she inched her way down the rest of the stairs, keeping her eyes low. She was battling against breaking down in tears, but on top of everything else, she didn't want to give the crowd the satisfaction of seeing her cry.

When she reached the bottom step, Marsh caught up with her. "I'm so sorry this—"

Delia looked up and shook her head to stop him. She grabbed hold of Arthur's arm and said, "Get me out of here. Please, just get me out of here."

CHAPTER TWENTY-SIX

Three months later, Delia found herself amid a group of men standing outside Field & Leiter dressed in bib overalls, scuffed-up boots and unkempt beards. They were chanting, calling for the workingman to rise up. She'd heard about this group of socialists, but this was the first time she'd ever encountered them. They were all part of the growing labor union movement, a schism that was widening between the workers and the capitalists.

Marsh was keeping a close eye on the situation, as were Potter Palmer and George Pullman. She recalled them discussing it quite passionately at a dinner party she hosted a few weeks back.

"I tell you," Marsh had said at they sat around the Catons' dining room table, "we'd better quash them before they get out of hand. If we're not careful, the labor organizers will be our undoing."

"It's the capitalists who have built this city—this country," Potter said. "Where would the workingman be without us?"

"Exactly!" George Pullman had practically leaped out of his

chair. "How dare these socialists try to tell us how to run the very businesses we created. And now they're asking for an eight-hour workday. Eight hours for the same pay they're getting now for working ten hours."

"That Albert Parsons is nothing but trouble." Marsh had pounded the table with his fist. "He's the one organizing all this. He and those Germans need to be stopped."

"We don't need labor unions," said Pullman. "Labor unions will destroy everything we've established."

"We're in the midst of a depression, so they're bound to blame us," Potter had added.

"Did you see that they've taken to calling themselves 'wage slaves'?" said Marsh, shaking his head as if it were absurd. "They're making themselves out to be victims and turning us into monsters."

Delia remembered how she had glanced over at Arthur, who sat mildly detached, brushing crumbs off the tablecloth. She wasn't surprised that he wouldn't join in. After all, he was neither a worker nor a capitalist. But what about Abby's husband? Augustus hadn't said a word and she found his silence puzzling.

The protestors interrupted her thoughts as she stood at the street corner, listening to them chanting, "Down with capitalists! Let the workingman rise!" She hurried past them. All their talk made her nervous.

She tried to clear her mind as she set Flossie on the sidewalk and closed her parasol, letting the sunlight radiate on her face and the crown of her head. It was July, not a cloud to be seen. Clearly, she needed a new sunbonnet. All the more reason why she needed to be down there. She drew a deep breath, scooped up Flossie and smiled at the doorman as she entered Field & Leiter. It was the first time she'd stepped foot inside the store since the incident at the party.

The main floor bustled with women standing at the counters, sampling toilet waters, trying on earrings, inspecting lace and embroidered fabrics. Delia realized how much she'd missed being among pretty new things. Seeing something in *Vogue* or *Harper's Bazaar* wasn't the same as being here to feel the different textures, smell the latest fragrances and take into her possession anything she desired.

Delia felt self-conscious as she walked down the center aisle, wondering whom she'd run into that day. Thankfully she hadn't seen Nannie since the night of the party, though she knew she was still in town. That in and of itself was unsettling. Nannie had succeeded in humiliating Delia in front of Chicago high society and there wasn't a thing she could do to redeem herself. Time was her only defense and she hoped that in the past three months people had forgotten and moved on to some more salacious piece of gossip, like Mr. Samuels running off with a chambermaid or even all this talk of social revolution.

Delia kept her eyes straight ahead as she approached the millinery counter. With Flossie resting in the crook of her arm she looked at the new summer hats by Caroline Reboux from Paris in beautiful teal blues, buttercup yellows and mint greens. Just as she was about to try on one of the latest three-story flowerpot styles, Delia heard the familiar voices of Frances Glessner, Harriet Pullman and Malvina Armour standing just a few feet away. Aside from Abby and Bertha, the three of them were the only ones from her old group that would still socialize with her. Delia hadn't seen any of them since the incident with Nannie and was about to go over and say hello when Malvina looked up. The queer expression on her face caught Delia by surprise.

"Just looking at the new hats," Delia offered clumsily, aware that the others were staring at her as well.

"You have some nerve showing your face back here," said Harriet. "We thought you had the decency to know better."

A rush of angry heat filled Delia's chest. "And I thought you'd know better than to believe Nannie's lies about me."

Frances gasped. "Nannie should have banned you from this store."

"Come now." Malvina turned to the others. "Let's move on."

"You don't have to leave on my account," said Delia, willing her voice not to crack. "I was just on my way out." She didn't wait to see their reaction. She dropped the hat she'd been looking at and headed for the doorway with Flossie in tow.

It was a blistering hot day outside, but Delia's face was hotter still from humiliation. She rushed away from the store, and at the corner of State and Washington, she came upon the same group of protestors. She noticed that more men had joined their gathering. A man at the center of them all stood atop a wooden crate shouting with his hands cupped about his mouth, calling: "Death to the plutocrats. War on the capitalists. Workingmen, put down your tools and join the labor movement. We will fight these capitalists to the bitter end. . . ."

Normally the socialists' tirades upset Delia, knowing they aimed their hatred at men like Marshall Field, but on that day she was so distraught, she hardly gave them a second thought. Instead, all she could think was that she had been snubbed by the last of her friends. Not that snubbing was anything new to Delia. So many of the society women had looked down on her for a long time now. But thanks to Nannie, their scorn seemed to have intensified. Going by the reaction of Harriet, Frances and Malvina, she'd clearly lost the support of the last few people willing to claim her as a friend. Thankfully she still had Bertha and Abby. And of course, Arthur.

She and Arthur continued to socialize with Marsh. Sometimes Abby and Augustus or the Palmers would join them and they'd all go to plays or the opera. Delia managed to keep busy, but she dearly missed her meetings with the Fortnightly Club and the Chicago Women's Club. But those were organizations that Nannie had brought her into and Delia knew better than to attend one of those gatherings now.

Delia's driver wasn't supposed to pick her up for at least another hour, so she decided to walk, thinking it might clear her head. She opened her parasol to block the sun, but oh, what she wouldn't have given for a little shade. But all the lush trees that had once lined State Street had been lost to the Great Fire and to the ways of progress. Every time Delia turned around, there was another building going up. There seemed no end to the masonry fortress or the influx of immigrants who'd flocked to Chicago to build it. Marsh told her there were entire neighborhoods where no one spoke English, and all the stores filled their windows with signs written in only German or Polish, Yiddish or Hebrew. Once again, she marveled at how much the city had changed since the fire.

When she arrived back home, Williams took her parasol and Flossie's leash. Delia heard voices coming from the library and when she entered the room, Arthur smiled and said, "Look who's back."

"Delia, my darling. It's been far too long." Paxton Lowry, handsome as ever, rose from the sofa and gave her a tight embrace as the sweet scent of his shaving soap circled around her. No sooner had Paxton released her than Arthur came and planted a kiss on her cheek.

"It's wonderful to see you again," she said to Paxton. And it was. She'd always been fond of him, amused by his cynical view of the world. She was feeling down and Paxton was the perfect person to lift her spirits. "What a lovely surprise. What brings you back to Chicago?"

"I grew bored with New York."

"So it didn't work out with the girl, I gather."

He shrugged. "I guess you could say I grew homesick. Anyway, I'm back here now for good." He looked at Arthur and smiled.

"You two can catch up later." Arthur tossed Paxton his hat. "We have to run."

"Oh, don't leave yet," Delia pleaded. "I just got home."

"Sorry," said Arthur, "but we're going to meet an old friend for a drink."

"I'm an old friend. Don't I count?" Delia tried to pass it off as a lighthearted comment, but inside, she was sickened by her own neediness. Her desperation to be included was pathetic.

"We'll be back soon. Come on now," Arthur said to Paxton. "We don't have all day."

"We'll catch up later," Paxton called back to her just before the front door shut.

The sound of the door closing reverberated in her chest as if she were hollowed out inside. Between the ladies snubbing her earlier and now this, Delia had never felt so utterly alone. With Nannie still in Chicago she couldn't go to the Field mansion to see Marsh whenever she pleased anymore. And Marsh coming to the Catons' was nearly impossible. Each time he tried to leave the house, Nannie went on one of her tirades or feigned some near-death sickness. One night she started pulling out her hair in clumps until her fingers were covered in blood. Other times she would drop to the ground in hysterics, barricading herself in front of the doorway. It frightened Ethel and Junior to see her that way, and Delia and Marsh agreed that it was better for the sake of the children not to agitate Nannie. And that meant that she and Marsh were rarely able to be alone together. Now their meetings had to be scheduled and planned. And even though Nannie was well aware of their affair, this new development made

Delia feel cheap and deceitful. Each time Marsh had to leave her side to return to Nannie, Delia lost a piece of herself.

That night Delia wandered through the house trying to distract herself. She wondered where Arthur and Paxton had gone. She wondered why Arthur hadn't told her Paxton was coming back to Chicago—unless of course he hadn't known, which she found doubtful. She thought about Arthur's last visit to New York. He'd said he was going for a horse show, but she now suspected that he'd gone solely to see Paxton. She'd never allowed herself to ponder the nature of Arthur's friendship with Paxton, but now she couldn't help herself. Paxton always had a girl, but then again, Arthur had always had Delia.

She thought back to their early courtship. There was hardly a time when Paxton wasn't with them. How many times had she sat with one of Paxton's dates making small talk while the two men entertained themselves? How could she have been so naive? Of course they hadn't wanted her to come with them tonight—or perhaps they'd never wanted her to come along. Ever. She was the outsider. For the first time, she understood how Arthur must have felt whenever Marsh was around. That made her feel guilty. It was just one more offense to heap onto the pile of mistakes she'd made.

She went into the parlor and sat in her favorite chair with Flossie. She tried reading but couldn't concentrate. The same was true for drawing. All she could think about was how lonely and isolated she felt and how it was different for Marsh. For a man. The other men didn't ostracize him, nor did the women. It was all on Delia. She was the culprit, the one responsible for all the wrongdoing.

She was still feeling glum and abandoned several hours later when Arthur and Paxton returned home. They were drunk and laughing, their arms clasped about each other's shoulders.

"You'll never guess where we ended up tonight," said Paxton.

"She won't like it," said Arthur.

"We went to a séance!"

"You did what?" Delia sat back and pressed a hand to her chest.

"I told you," said Arthur. "Dell hates that sort of thing."

And it was true. She told herself it was all a bunch of bunk and yet she grew tense at the very notion of ghosts and conjuring up the dead.

"But wait until we tell you—"

"No." Delia covered her ears. "I don't want to hear it."

"I told you."

"Okay, all right," said Paxton, "we'll drop it. Forget we ever said a word about it. Tell us about your night."

"Quiet," she said. "I've been alone all evening."

"Well, then," said Paxton, reaching for her hands and pulling her to her feet, "up, up, up!"

"I'm up. I'm up," she said with a laugh. "What are we doing?"

"We're going to raid the pantry," said Paxton. "I'm famished."

"We forgot to eat dinner tonight," said Arthur.

"Well, don't raid the pantry," said Delia. "I'll have the kitchen maid—"

"No, no, no," said Paxton. "It's much more fun this way."

With each of them taking hold of her hands, they whisked her off to the kitchen. She so rarely stepped foot inside her own kitchen that she had to take a moment to observe the room. Copper pots and kettles lined the shelf above the basins with stacked bowls of every size stashed below. Ladles and spatulas, giant spoons and strainers hung from the tiled wall behind the stove. There was a long wooden worktable in the center, its surface scarred with knife wounds. A meat grinder was fastened to the far end. As the three of them pulled out jars of olives, wedges of cheese, sausages and loaves of bread, Delia had newfound respect for her kitchen staff, who produced three lavish meals a day in that room, day after day.

The three of them ate standing up with their fingers, laughing between bites. Arthur began pitching olives toward Paxton, who caught them in his mouth. Delia turned giddy and had all but forgotten how lonely she'd been earlier.

"Now's your turn," said Arthur, aiming an olive in Delia's direction. "Come on now."

After a mild protest, Delia leaned her head back and opened her mouth to catch the olive. It bounced off her chin and landed near her feet. She picked it up off the floor and was still laughing when she looked up and screamed.

Just outside the kitchen window, she saw Nannie standing in the dark, staring in at her.

"What's wrong?" Paxton was still laughing.

"What is it?" Arthur dabbed the sweat from his brow.

Delia turned around and pointed to the window but Nannie was gone.

"Please tell me I'm not losing my mind," Delia said to Marsh later that night. She had been so distraught over what she'd seen or—according to Arthur and Paxton—what she thought she'd seen that they couldn't calm her down. That's when Paxton suggested that Arthur find Marsh and bring him back to the house.

"I know you think I'm being foolish," she said, clutching his handkerchief, "but I feel like she's out there right now. I feel like she's standing in the dark watching me."

"I highly doubt that," said Marsh, rubbing his hands over Delia's shoulders and down her arms. "She was sound asleep when I left the house."

"See?" said Arthur. "What did I tell you? Nothing to worry about."

"Except that I *am* crazy. I *am* seeing things."

"I didn't say that," said Arthur.

It went on like that for another half an hour or so until, finally, at half past midnight, Delia and Marsh said good night to Arthur and Paxton and then to Williams before making their way up the grand staircase. The servants, at both the Catons' and the Fields' mansions, were accustomed to Delia's and Marsh's comings and goings. If they found it peculiar or the subject of scandal, Delia would have never known it. She trusted her staff. She was generous to them and kind and received their loyalty and discretion in return.

After they were in Delia's bedroom, Marsh held out his arms. "Now would you please come over here and kiss me."

Delia crossed the room and slipped into his embrace. It was the first time she had seen him in almost a week. Nannie had already interfered enough with their precious time together and Delia didn't want her to take anything more away from them.

That night Delia and Marsh made love quickly, efficiently. The hunger they'd once felt for each other had changed over the past two years, gradually being replaced with a comforting, familiar need for each other.

Marsh rolled onto his back and Delia scooted over, resting her head on his chest, her ear picking up on every heartbeat. They were talking about Ethel, who had just lost another tooth.

"You'd think she was losing an arm," said Marsh. "That tooth's been loose, just dangling by a thread. I wanted to pull it two days ago and Ethel wouldn't let me. Just clamped her lips together and refused to open her mouth."

"Don't forget to put a silver dollar beneath her pillow before she wakes up."

Marsh gave her a puzzled look. "What for?"

"The tooth fairy," she explained with a laugh. "Didn't you ever do that for Junior?"

"I haven't a clue as to what you're talking about."

"When we were little, my father always put a silver dollar under our pillows each time we lost a tooth. We thought it was from the tooth fairy."

"That's a very expensive practice," he said.

"I thought all parents did that."

"Not this parent. And not my parents, either. My father used to go after our loose teeth with a pair of pliers. And heaven help you if you cried. The first sound of a snivel and he'd threaten to take out another tooth whether it was loose or not."

Delia laughed.

They talked some more as they lay in each other's arms, holding each other until the last possible moment when they both knew he had to leave her bed and return home to Nannie.

When she finally dozed off that night, she had a nightmare about Nannie standing in her closet, watching her every move. Delia woke up in a cold sweat and turned the lamp on until it was daylight. For the next week or so she found herself always looking for Nannie, half expecting her to appear on every street corner, inside her favorite tearooms and restaurants. Delia supposed it was foolish, but still that eerie feeling of being followed never fully left her. There were nights when she asked Arthur to check the grounds, making sure that Nannie wasn't there, somewhere, watching her.

CHAPTER TWENTY-SEVEN

1881

Delia cuddled the baby, kissing her tiny curled fingers, pressing her lips to her button of a nose. As far as she was concerned, this was the most beautiful, perfect baby girl in the world. "She looks just like you," she said to Abby.

"Oh, no. I think little Catherine here looks more like Augustus. Look at those cheeks." Abby reached down and lifted her daughter from Delia's arms. Delia wasn't ready to let go and tried to mask her disappointment as Abby set the baby back in her buggy.

"I wish we could stay longer," said Abby, "but I have to take Spencer to a friend's birthday party."

Delia looked at her sister, lost in her motherly bliss. As happy as she was for Abby, she couldn't help but feel a little sorry for herself. It was as if everyone in her world was moving forward, progressing, maybe even passing her by: Abby now had two children, Arthur spent all his free time with Paxton, and Marsh's business affairs consumed most of his time. As for Delia, she was paying the price for love as her social circle continued to narrow and the rumors continued to spread.

It was ironic, but despite the nearly half a million people who now lived in the city, Delia found Chicago to be a very small place—especially among their elite group. Avoiding Nannie indefinitely was impossible. Every now and again their paths would cross, in the neighborhood, at the theater or at a tearoom. They both kept to themselves, steering clear of each other.

And yet, despite it all, Delia felt more connected to Marsh than ever. When he was restless she felt it, even without him having to say a word. In separate bedrooms, in separate houses, she felt him tossing and turning through the night as if he lay beside her. From around the corner she sensed him pacing, brooding, contemplating.

And so, when Delia saw Marsh that evening, she already knew something was on his mind. It was after ten when he arrived. She offered him a drink, but he declined, and after they'd gone upstairs, he sat on the side of the bed, hung his head and rubbed his eyes.

Delia closed her bedroom door and stood before him, stepping into the opening between his legs and pressing his head against her breasts as he wrapped his arms around her waist. "What's wrong? Something's bothering you."

He stood up and pulled her close for a kiss. "We have such little time together these days, I don't want to spoil it by talking."

They made love that night and afterward as they lay in each other's arms she asked again what was bothering him.

"Oh, I had a falling out with Levi today. Why can't he see that it's not good enough to be *good enough*." He dragged a hand over his face. "The man is an imbecile and he's rude. Rude to me, rude to our customers. I told him so and he stormed out of my office and slammed the door so hard he broke the frosted glass panel. I went by his office later in the day and he wouldn't speak to me."

"I don't understand why you put up with him." She was lying close to him, stroking his hair. "His values are completely incompatible with yours. How long can you go on running a company with a man you're not on speaking terms with?" Delia asked, as she rolled onto her side, pulling the bedsheet up over her breasts.

Marsh didn't answer.

"You've succeeded all these years in spite of Levi. Imagine what you could do if you didn't have to work around him."

"What are you suggesting?"

"You know very well what I'm going to say. It's what I've been telling you all along. I think you should buy him out. You don't need Levi. He's only holding you back."

"He's been my partner for sixteen years. We've built something very solid together, very good."

"But you said yourself: 'It's not good enough to be good enough.' You want to achieve more and you're capable of it."

"It's just that I see what this store can be. I know the kind of experience we can create for shoppers. You know I always say 'Give the lady what she wants.' I believe that's the key to our success and Levi fights me on it all the way. Just refuses to cooperate."

Delia reached up and traced Marsh's cheek with her fingertips. "Then buy him out. Open your own store. You can do it right this time. Exactly the way you want."

He stretched his arms and then crossed them behind his head. Then something shifted in his eyes and he looked at her, his expression open and filled with curiosity. "What would I call this new store?"

Delia propped herself up on her elbow and laughed, "Why, Marshall Field & Company—what else?"

One month later, in February of 1881, Field, Leiter & Company closed its doors for good and the renovation of the new Marshall Field & Company got under way.

Marsh unrolled the blueprints while Delia and Arthur looked on over his shoulder. Paxton stood off to the side, checking his pocket watch. The four of them were going to a play that evening, but Marsh wanted to show them the new floor plans first.

"This is going to cost a fortune," said Arthur.

"A million, to be exact," Marsh said with a satisfied smile. "But I don't care. It has to be perfect. Everything from the fixtures to the flooring has to be perfect."

Delia stood back, taking in this new extravagant side of Marsh as he rolled up the plans.

They were about to leave for the theater when the butler came in the drawing room. "Mrs. Field is here," said Williams.

Mrs. Field? They all turned around. Delia couldn't imagine what Nannie was doing at her home. No doubt she knew Marsh had plans that night and that she was not included. She wouldn't have expected to be, either, for Nannie hadn't joined her husband socially in years. According to Marsh she'd been fairly civil as of late, but usually that just meant that something else was brewing beneath the surface.

"She has her children with her," said Williams. "Shall I show them in?"

Delia looked at Marsh and then at Williams. "Of course."

Arthur and Paxton stood protectively on either side of Delia as her heart beat wildly. Marsh finished rolling up the blueprints and fastening them with an elastic band while Nannie marched into the drawing room.

"Wait here," she told the children as she stormed up to Marsh. Her jaw was set, her eyes were glaring, and through gritted teeth she said, "Look after your children. I'm going to France."

Delia was dumbstruck as Nannie went back over to Junior and Ethel, kissed them both on the cheeks and said she'd be back soon.

No one knew what Nannie meant by "soon."

She just disappeared after that and with each passing week the children became more traumatized by their mother's departure. All that spring and into the summer Delia tried to help Junior and Ethel cope by spending as much time with them as possible.

Of course, she quickly realized that at thirteen, Junior preferred the company of his friends or going fishing or hunting with his uncle Arthur, whereas Ethel was just eight and in desperate need of her mother. Over the past six months, Nannie had sent letters and the occasional telegram, but Delia knew that wasn't enough for Ethel. Delia also knew she couldn't take the place of Ethel's mother, but she tried to be a source of comfort for the girl. She took her to matinees and out shopping. She attended her ballet and piano recitals and sat up with her all night when she had a fever and cried out for her mother.

Delia even took Ethel with her to visit Abby and the new baby. Abby and Augustus still lived with Delia's parents at the house on Sixteenth and Michigan, the house they'd built after the Great Fire. It was hard for Delia to imagine still living at home, but Augustus had made some poor investments and been nearly ruined in the depression of '77. On top of that, he had been fired from the railroad company, and though he secured another position with a competitor several months later, Augustus had never quite gotten back on his feet.

They'd turned one of the guest rooms into a nursery. A walnut crib rested in the corner next to a matching hutch with a stack of baby blankets, booties, bibs and a silver rattle on top. The room smelled sweetly of baby talc. As Ethel sat in the rocking chair, holding baby Catherine, Delia's mother came into room. As soon as she saw Ethel, Mrs. Spencer frowned and summoned Delia out to the hallway.

"Really, Delia, you brought *his* child here. To my house!" Her mother folded her arms across her chest and paced back and forth. "You've got the whole town talking about you as it is and now you're parading around with *his* daughter. I won't be a part of this. I can't be."

Delia received a similar response from Annie Swift the following day when she took Ethel down to State Street to buy her a new Easter bonnet. Annie spotted them from down the block and quickened her step to catch up to them, her white blond ringlets bobbing up and down.

"Isn't that Marshall's daughter?" Annie asked, nearly out of breath as she gave Delia a hard glance.

As Delia introduced Ethel she noticed that a group of socialists had begun to congregate along State Street. Their signs and banners crowded around the construction team's wheelbarrows, ladders and sawhorses parked on the sidewalk. One of the new electric cable cars rumbled by, adding to the confusion and chaos around them.

"I don't think Nannie would approve of you spending time with her daughter. Do you?" Annie pursed her lips.

"I think under the circumstances, it's fine."

"You can be sure I'm going to write Nannie right away and let her know."

"I assure you that won't be—"

But before Delia could finish her sentence, Annie cut her off and said, "I can't imagine what it's like being you—just going through life, doing whatever you please, without a care in the world for anyone else. Really, Delia, you are the epitome of selfishness."

"Annie, that's not—"

"Good day." She brushed past her, leaving Delia at a loss.

"Who was that lady?" Ethel asked, looking back over her shoulder. "Why was she talking about Mama?"

"Oh, she's no one. Don't you give her a second thought." Delia put her arm around Ethel and quickly walked her in the opposite direction, away from the protestors, who any minute would surely be calling for her father's death.

CHAPTER TWENTY-EIGHT

It was the start of another holiday season, and with Nannie still in Europe, Delia anticipated sharing it with Arthur, Paxton, Marsh and the children. She envisioned them all sitting around the table at Thanksgiving and then weeks later trimming the tree on Christmas Eve. She had stockings made with their names embroidered along the tops and was going to hang them along the fireplace hearth. They would open presents and sing Christmas carols.

This was what she was thinking as she walked with Junior, Ethel and Spencer. She'd just taken them skating at the frozen harbor not far from the Prairie Avenue District. Now they marched through the snow alongside her, their skates tied together by their laces and slung over their shoulders like scarves.

The city was a blanket of white with smoke puffing from chimneys and foot-long icicles hanging down from rooftops. Flossie shivered in Delia's arms despite the cashmere sweater covering her little body.

When they entered the Field mansion, Delia heard the cockatiels squawking and beating their wings wildly.

"There you are," came a voice from across the room.

Delia looked up and did a double take.

Ethel dropped her skates and shouted, "Mama!"

She ran across the room into Nannie's open arms. Junior followed suit, charging toward his mother and fiercely wrapping his arms about her.

Delia swallowed past the lump in her throat. She was so unprepared for this. She'd never felt so jealous of Nannie or of any other woman. One look at Nannie and all the ice cream sodas, the baseball games, the new toys, were forgotten. No matter how rotten Nannie was, no matter how neglectful, she was still their mother and that was a bond that Delia could never compete with.

While gripping Spencer's hand and holding tight to Flossie's leash, Delia tried to be gracious and welcomed Nannie home.

"You can run along now, Delia," said Nannie with a dismissive wave of her hand before turning back to the children. "Mama's home and we're going to have a marvelous family holiday."

Delia was still in a stupor after dropping Spencer off at his home. She decided to head down to State Street to warn Marsh that Nannie was back. The store still wasn't open to the public yet but that didn't stop the labor organizers. They were out front, stirring up trouble.

One of the leaders, standing in the middle of the crowd, was shouting, "Marshall Field has got to go! He refuses to hire immigrant workers! Marshall Field is anti-America!"

This was met with a chorus of cheers.

Luckily one of Marsh's office boys recognized her out front and let her in through a side door. There was a haze of dust floating through the air and scaffolds and ladders scattered about the floor, but still, she could see what was taking place inside those walls. Giant white marble pilasters were stationed every ten feet within the aisles and an enormous grand staircase swept upward from the first floor. Wires stuck out of the ceiling in all directions like crazy tentacles awaiting the crystal chandeliers from France. The walls and the main aisles were set in Italian marble and fourteen-karat-gold wall sconces were on a table, waiting to be mounted.

The office boy led Delia into Marsh's makeshift office on the lower level. She found him leaning over a desk, his shirtsleeves rolled up, a ledger before him. He'd been so busy working, getting ready to open the store in less than two months, that she'd hardly seen him lately, and now here she was, turning up uninvited and with news about his estranged wife.

When she told him that Nannie was back in town, Marsh cursed and slammed the ledger shut, sending it and various papers to the floor. She knew that he was angry with Nannie, not her, and that she'd been right to tell him. He stood back, blew out a deep breath and ran his hands back through his hair, trying to regain his composure.

"Damn that woman." He kicked a heap of papers out of his path and planted his hands on his hips. "She knows exactly how to infuriate me. It's just like her to swoop back into town and disrupt everything."

"If it helps at all, I can tell you that the children were happy to see her."

"Of course they were. They don't know what kind of witch their mother is." Marsh reached for his suit jacket and muttered, "I suppose I should go home and find out what she wants this time."

As they headed for their neighborhood, Delia felt the holiday magic drifting away even before the season had begun.

And later that night, Arthur felt it, too.

They were having cocktails at home with Paxton and one of his new girls. Her name was Penelope Briggs and she was a young socialite, the daughter of a banker. She had just celebrated her twenty-first birthday. She sat very close to Paxton on the settee, and when Arthur made a toast, the two of them, Paxton and Penelope, gazed at each other over the rims of their glasses. She had a perfect heart-shaped face and even longer lashes than Paxton did.

"Say," said Arthur, turning to Paxton, "I've got a new rifle. Come have a look."

"In a bit," he said. "Relax. We just got here. Let us enjoy our drinks first."

Delia saw the disappointment on Arthur's face and she knew what he was thinking. They were used to Paxton bringing his girls around, but something about this one was different. It was making Arthur nervous and with good reason. Clearly, Paxton was smitten with Penelope and she was obviously quite taken with him, too.

In many ways Penelope reminded Delia of herself and she desperately wanted to warn her, encourage her to move on. Keep Paxton as her friend but move on. She wanted to tell this young girl that even if Paxton was to fall for her, even if he was to marry her, she might never be fulfilled. She might never have children. She might never be loved and desired the way that every woman wanted and needed to be.

The following week, Paxton joined Penelope and her family for Thanksgiving, leaving Arthur in such a state of jealousy that he drank away half the holiday afternoon.

"I don't even feel like having Thanksgiving this year," he said, refilling his glass. "Let's just cancel and not go to my parents' tonight."

"I would love to, but it's Thanksgiving and my family will be there, too. I promised Abby I would protect her from your mother."

As they were leaving their house to walk next door to the Catons', they heard a blast of loud music along with an army of voices chanting, "Fair Pay for a Fair Day" and "Death to Capitalism."

She grabbed hold of Arthur's hand and they raced to the corner; what Delia saw there stopped her heart. There were hundreds of men and women whose tattered coats and hats were so out of place on Prairie Avenue. Some were beating drums or blowing horns, while others hoisted black and red flags—the flags of the anarchists—into the air. The anarchists were here! In her neighborhood! Her whole being flooded with panic.

"We will fight with dynamite! You will die!" They shouted these hideous threats over and over again.

Delia watched in horror as they stormed the Pullman mansion, surrounding all the entrances, pounding on their drums and the front door, calling for Pullman's assassination. They did the same thing to the Perkins mansion and when they arrived outside the Field mansion, they pushed open the gate and took to the stairs, fists pounding on the door. Delia could hear the *brring brrring brrrring* of the doorbell ringing while they chanted, "Death to the Merchant Prince."

"Come on," said Arthur, tugging at her arm. "It's not safe out here. Let's go."

They scurried back to their house and locked all the doors just moments before the demonstration bled over onto Calumet Avenue. Delia heard the music and chanting as she clutched Flossie to her chest. The protestors pounded on the doors and windows. She was afraid they would break them down. The buzzer on the doorbell rang so shrilly it nearly made her come out of her skin.

"Stay away from the windows and doors," she heard Arthur telling Williams. She could see the staff was as terrified as she was.

Delia huddled in the safety of the parlor, praying that Marsh wouldn't be foolish enough to go outside and engage them. If he did, she was certain that they would kill him.

Eventually the police arrived. The pounding eased up and the shouting grew fainter and fainter as the demonstrators moved on, leaving the lawns and gardens trampled. Delia was still shaking even after the last of them had left the Prairie Avenue District.

The terror of it stayed with her for weeks afterward and she feared the anarchists weren't finished with them yet. And though Delia had long since been excluded from the city's biggest holiday parties, that year she was relieved to stay home on Christmas Eve with Arthur.

But Arthur wasn't quite as content to spend the night home alone with her. Paxton had stopped by earlier in the evening, but said he couldn't stay long. He was expected to join Penelope at her family's home.

"Just one more drink," Arthur had begged when Paxton got up to leave forty-five minutes after arriving.

Paxton looked at his pocket watch and twisted his handsome lips as he slumped back down on the sofa. "Just a quick one," he said. "And then I really do have to go."

Paxton left two hours and two drinks later and afterward Arthur turned to Delia and said, "Look at us. We're all alone on the holidays."

"No, we're not," she said. "We have each other."

So they decorated their tree and exchanged gifts: a collection of leather-bound novels for her, a new saddle for him. Before ten o'clock that night Arthur was passed out on the sofa. After his valet helped him to bed, Delia stayed in the parlor, seated before the fireplace with all the stockings hanging down, filled and waiting for the children who never came. The tree stood off to the side, only adding to the absurdity of it all. Arthur had been right: she was alone for Christmas. She sipped her sherry and watched the snow falling outside the window, stacking up on the ledge. Eventually she got up and looked out the window, wondering what was happening across the way at the Field mansion.

She'd never felt like a mistress before, the second tier, the next in line after the wife. But she knew that children trumped all else on a holiday. It was Christmas and Marsh's place was with them.

CHAPTER TWENTY-NINE

1882

The festivities were over and Delia tucked away her melancholy along with the tinsel, the ornaments and the other holiday decorations. Even though Nannie was still holed up in the Field mansion, Delia paid her little mind. She was focused on one thing and that was the grand opening of Marshall Field & Company.

At first she'd questioned why Marsh didn't get the store ready in time for the Christmas shopping season. But he was a perfectionist and refused to open his doors until every last detail was in place. Plus, he had enough faith in his customers to believe that women would come to shop no matter what the season.

And now it was the beginning of January and the opening was just three weeks away. Delia and her father had just come from lunch and were now standing across the street from the new store. A massive green awning and four enormous granite pillars had recently been installed at the main entrance. The brass placard sign was mounted to the limestone and the flagpoles had been set up. It looked spectacular and everyone was enthralled with anticipation for Marshall Field & Company. Even though the ten-story Montauk Building, which the newspapers were calling a skyscraper, was under construction just a few blocks away on Monroe, everyone on State Street was talking about Marshall Field & Company, including the socialists. They stood across the street, at the southeast corner of Washington and State, chanting, "Long live the workingman! Death to the Merchant Prince!"

"They make me nervous," Delia said to her father, holding Flossie close.

"Oh, they're harmless."

"I don't know. You heard what happened on Thanksgiving and now they've joined forces with anarchists from Germany."

"That's just talk. That's what they want you to think. Those workers and labor organizers have been out there protesting for ages. Nothing's come of it. Nobody pays them any mind," said her father, glancing over at the crowd and shaking his head. "But the thing that's making the neighbors here nervous—and it's got nothing to do with the labor movement—is the Merchant Prince. Just look at that." Her father pointed to the left of the protestors, to the future Marshall Field & Company. "He's building a palace compared to all the other dry goods stores on this street. He's changing the face of State Street and putting the rest of the merchants to shame."

Her father paused and blew into his hands to warm them. "My, what an accomplishment that is. I remember when all us merchants were down on Lake Street. We thought it was something to have a second floor. We never could have imagined something like what Marshall's building." Her father whistled through his teeth. "Just goes to show, there's no limit to what modern man can create. It all starts up here—" He pointed to his temple. "Yes indeed, that Marshall Field is something else. Now, there's a man who doesn't believe in the status quo. I can only imagine what he's going to do with the inside."

The protestors began chanting again, "This is war! The plutocrats must die!"

"I'll tell you another thing about Marshall Field. He hates those labor organizers with a passion. He'll do whatever it takes to break them. He refuses to even do business with them."

"Wouldn't any merchant worth his salt?" she said, defensively.

"Yes, but ole Marsh won't even sell a labor member a toothpick." He laughed.

"And why should he? After everything he's done for this city and after all the people he's provided jobs to, is he supposed to just roll over and let the unions tell him how to run his business?"

"My, oh my," said her father, giving her a close look. "You're becoming very politically minded these days, aren't you?"

"I just think it's wrong. That's all." She agreed with Marsh and the other industrialists; these men—mostly the anarchist immigrants—were dangerous. They needed to be stopped.

Mr. Spencer stopped and turned toward her with a serious expression on his face. "Dell, you're a grown woman and I've never wanted to meddle in your private affairs but . . ." His voice trailed off.

Delia busied herself with Flossie, holding her breath because she knew what was coming.

"Do be careful," he said. "All this talk, it's not good for you or Arthur. It's not good for any of us."

Delia gazed down at the sidewalk. She hated the thought of disappointing her father. They drifted to the corner of State and Randolph and she still hadn't said a word to him.

"Be careful. That's all I ask." Mr. Spencer leaned over and

kissed her on the cheek before they parted ways and he headed down Randolph.

A few moments later, despite her father's warning, Delia turned around and headed back down State Street. She found one of Marsh's office boys to let her inside to see him. Even from upstairs in his office she could hear the chatter from the protestors rising up from the street level, leaking in through the window.

He looked out the panes of glass, his hands braced on the ledge. "Do you know what Junior told me last night?"

She sighed and nodded. "That he'd rather take art classes than work at your store?"

Marsh looked at her from over his shoulder. "So you already knew, huh?"

"Oh, Marsh, he was scared to death to tell you. Arthur was the one who encouraged him to talk to you about it."

"The boy needs discipline, not art classes."

Delia got up and placed her hands on his shoulders. "He's only a teenager."

"He's fourteen, and when I was his age, I was working."

"Times are different now. You can't force him to become a merchant."

But no matter how many times Delia reminded him of that, Marsh continued to scoff at the drawings Junior brought home from art class and tacked up on the wall in his room. On more than one occasion Delia had seen Marsh reduce his son to a puddle of tears, calling him lazy and spoiled. It reminded her of the way the judge talked to Arthur. She tried to intervene, but that only threatened to drive a wedge between Marsh and her.

Finally, thankfully, instead of berating his son, Marsh decided to concentrate on training his five hundred new Marshall Field employees, including doormen, cashboys, supervisors, clerks and elevator boys. He was strict with them, insisting that they address one another properly as Mr., Mrs. or Miss. They were expected to know all regular customers by name as well as learn each and every piece of merchandise in their department, memorizing colors, sizes and styles. He insisted that they become experts on every item they sold. He promised that in exchange for their hard work, he could make a merchant out of any of them.

Delia had always known that Marsh was a stickler for perfection, but the longer she listened to him, the more she wondered if his staff would be able to live up to such steep expectations.

The night before the store opening, Delia and Marsh went for dinner at an out-of-the-way restaurant down on Toothpick Alley at Madison and Clark. It was at one of those new cafeteria-style places that none of their friends or colleagues would have ever stepped foot in.

"I've decided to invest in Charles Yerkes's new cable car system," Marsh said, arranging the salt and pepper shakers as if they were chess pieces.

"Oh, Marsh, why?" Delia made a face and pushed her tray aside. She had read all about Yerkes in the newspapers. He'd come to Chicago from Philadelphia and used unscrupulous measures to obtain the capital needed to build his cable car lines. "The man is a thief."

"Yes, but by investing in his cable cars I can insist that they stop in front of my store." He raised one eyebrow. "They'll stop in front of the store and then loop back around and make a big circle and bring the next carload of passengers right to my front door."

"So all day long you'll have his cable cars making one big circle—one giant loop—around your store?"

"Exactly."

He spoke with such enthusiasm she could see it bubbling up inside him. Usually her excitement rose to match his, but this time he was too far out in front. With all her eagerness she'd never be able to catch up to him.

After dinner they walked down Clark Street with January's frigid chill in the air. The clouds were moving swiftly to the south and it looked as though it was going to snow.

"I meant it when I said I can turn any clerk into a merchant."

"I know you did."

"And now I've got a new clerk who seems determined to prove me right. His name's Harry Selfridge. He's young, maybe twenty or twenty-one years old. Certainly ambitious. He comes up to me today and presents me with a list of merchandising ideas. 'I had some thoughts about the display windows out front, Mr. Field,' he says to me. I couldn't believe this young man's gall."

"But don't you want ambitious clerks like that? I thought that was the whole point."

"It is, but I tell you there's something about this Harry Selfridge that rubs me the wrong way."

"Then why not get rid of him?"

"Because the fact of the matter is, I looked at the list he gave me, and his ideas aren't half-bad. I wish I'd thought of them myself."

She wanted to put her arms around him but knew she couldn't. It was bad enough that they were together in the evening, strolling along where anyone could have seen them. But something about that night emboldened them. They cut over to State Street and stood on the sidewalk outside the store. The drapes were drawn over the giant display windows, only adding to the mystique of what was about to be revealed to all of Chicago in just a matter of hours.

She discreetly slipped her hand in his and leaned in, whispering, "Look at what you've done, Mr. Field."

They were still standing admiring the front of the store when two men darted around the corner. Delia noticed them from the corner of her eye and the hair on the back of her neck prickled her skin.

"Field," they began shouting, "you're a dead man. We'll destroy you and your store!"

"Go on," Marsh called after them as they scampered around the corner. "Run away, you cowards! I dare you to come back here." He raised his fists in fury while Delia held him back from going after them. She was trembling, but Marsh didn't appear to be frightened at all. Just angry. "I will fight those damn socialists with everything I've got."

The next morning, January 26, 1882, was one of the coldest days of the year, but that didn't derail Marsh's plans. At eight o'clock precisely, the display window draperies parted and Marshall Field & Company officially opened its doors for business.

Delia was enthralled by what Marsh had been able to do to the old Singer Building. The doorman standing out front in his green and gold uniform held the door and bowed as Delia, Flossie and Abby stepped inside. A potpourri of perfumes, toilet waters and scented sachets enveloped them and Delia felt as though she had just entered a royal palace, or been wrapped in cashmere.

"Oh my goodness," said Abby, her eyes wide, taking it all in. "I've never seen anything like this."

"Didn't I tell you?" Delia said, hugging Flossie.

Despite a grand opening gala that was planned for the following week, all the society ladies were there that first day, not wanting to miss a thing. They were coolly polite to Delia, merely acknowledging her before moving on to Abby. When Sybil Perkins and Annie Swift arrived, they brushed past her as if she were invisible. Another woman, Thelma Moyer, glared at her and that's when Delia motioned to her sister, indicating that she and Flossie were going up to the second floor. Anything to get away from those women.

Delia browsed through the stationery and fountain pens. She was admiring the ambergris-scented sealing wax when she glanced up and gasped, nearly dropping the stamper she was holding. There was Nannie. Standing just three feet away.

"Nannie—" That was all she could manage to say.

Nannie said nothing in response. She simply stared at Delia with a cold, eerie glare. It was as if her face were a mask, frozen with a smirk in place. The silence lingered too long, adding to the tension.

"Well, say something, for God's sake!"

But Nannie only tilted her head and continued with that eerie stare of hers, her menacing smile more disturbing than any words could have been. Finally, Delia couldn't bear it any longer. She clutched Flossie closer to her chest and scurried away toward the first floor, past the doorman and out onto the street.

Once outside she held Flossie tight and reminded herself to breathe. She was so disturbed by Nannie's behavior that it took a moment before she became aware of the chaos swarming around her. A group of protestors had formed an angry demonstration that stretched half a block long. Red and black anarchist flags waved in the air as they chanted, "Death to the capitalists," and, "Down with the rich, let the working class rise."

Delia felt so vulnerable. They hated the wealthy and all they'd have to do was look at her in her fine tailored dress and her dog with the diamond collar, and they would know that she was the enemy. She feared they would see her and turn their rage toward her. Her palms began to sweat. She wanted to get away from them as quickly as possible and hurried away from the store entrance.

As she turned the corner at State and Washington, she spotted Augustus standing there among the crowd, listening intently to the speaker. He'd recently grown a scraggly beard and replaced his stylish monocle with a pair of spectacles. He looked more like one of them than a high-priced railroad executive. He hadn't seen her and she couldn't imagine what he was doing there. She knew he'd been unhappy with his position and supposed her brother-in-law identified more with the men who worked under him than with his fellow executives. But still, these socialists and anarchists were violent men. Could Augustus have been in favor of their movement? Was he getting involved with them? It wasn't possible. Or was it?

". . . And we shall win this war at any price," cried the man in the center of the group. There was a burst of applause and cheering and Delia was relieved that Augustus didn't join in. He stood neutral, but she knew that even neutrality was an adversary as far as Marsh was concerned.

CHAPTER THIRTY

1886

It was because of Paxton that she would always remember the date, Saturday, May 1, 1886. The night before, much to Arthur's distress, Paxton married Penelope Briggs. The ceremony took place at her family's country estate in Highland Park and immediately following the reception, Arthur escaped and headed downstate to Ottawa for a few days to avoid the hoopla surrounding the affair. Delia offered to go with him, but he said he needed to be alone.

Delia had just come from seeing her sister, her mother and her five-year-old niece, Catherine. It was a beautiful spring day with trees in bloom and the smell of fresh grass in the air. Delia and Flossie decided to stroll along Michigan Boulevard and slowly make their way back to Calumet Avenue.

As she reached Eighteenth and Michigan, she was stopped by a police officer. "I'm sorry, ma'am," he said, running his gloved hands over the brass buttons on his uniform. "This street is closed."

"Whatever for?"

"The demonstrators," he said, pointing north. "They're marching down Michigan Boulevard. We're expecting some eighty thousand protestors to come through here."

"Eighty *thousand*?" Delia looked down the boulevard and noticed another policeman stationed on the roof of a building, a rifle at his side. She looked across the way and spotted two more riot officers, both armed with guns.

"If I were you," he said, "I'd go home and stay there until it's safe."

But she didn't go home. Arthur was in Ottawa and she couldn't bear the thought of being alone, not when the city was on the brink of revolution. Nannie was back in Europe with the children, so Delia went to the Field mansion.

She knew it was a bad sign that Marsh was already home from the store and in a meeting with the police inspector, Captain Bonfield, and General Sheridan. After the butler announced her, Marsh came out of the library and asked Delia to wait. She took a seat on the settee just outside the closed door where she could overhear the three men. Their conversation sent a chill running through her body.

". . . We know it's going to take force to stop them," said one of the men.

"They've gotten ahold of dynamite now," said the other.

"And I don't doubt for a second that they're prepared to use it," said the first.

"You tell me what you need," she heard Marsh saying. "I don't care what it costs. I'll give you whatever additional financial backing necessary to stop these bastards."

Delia raised her hand to her mouth. Marsh was going to fund

the riot police? There was more talk, some of which she could hear, some muffled and hushed. Her anxiety mounted. Whatever was happening in the city today was more serious and dangerous than she'd realized.

She recalled an argument that Marsh and Augustus had a few weeks back. They were all riding to the country in Arthur's coach when Marsh opened a copy of *The Alarm*, a weekly newspaper published by the anarchists.

"Did you see the story in there, instructing new recruits on how to use dynamite?" Augustus asked.

"Damn those fools," said Marsh. "They're telling people to kill us with explosives. They're even teaching them how to do it. We have to stop them."

"But really," said Augustus, "is an eight-hour workday so unreasonable?"

Marsh had clenched his jaw and Delia could see that he was offended. "It is if you're the one paying them."

The voices coming from inside the library broke into Delia's thoughts. She glanced at the clock in the hallway, listening to it tick off the minutes. The cockatiels in the next room squawked. She heard the hushed footsteps of the servants in other corners of the house. Everything was still, but not at all tranquil. Even Flossie picked up on the tension.

Twenty excruciating minutes later, the door opened and out walked the general and the inspector. They were so preoccupied that they seemed not to notice her sitting there.

After they'd gone, Delia rushed to Marsh's side. "Dear God, Marsh, what's happening?" She followed him back into the library. It smelled of cigar smoke and she saw the embers smoldering on a stub left in a crystal ashtray.

Marsh sat in his wingback chair and rubbed his eyes. "The damn workers have called a general strike. The whole blasted city's come to a standstill. The streetcars aren't running. Trains aren't letting people into town. The restaurants have all closed their doors. All my clerks, my shopgirls, my cashboys, even some of my supervisors, never showed up for work today. We had to close the store. All this over wanting an eight-hour workday. They'll get eight hours," he said through gritted teeth, "over my dead body."

She had never seen him so agitated, not even when it came to Nannie. His fury was ferocious. This was a side of him she didn't even know existed.

By nightfall, the marchers dispersed and there was an eerie calm left in their wake. But the streetcars still weren't operating and no one was going to leave their house. The whole city was terrorized.

On the night of May 4, Delia braced herself while Marsh went to a public meeting that the anarchists were holding at the open market on Haymarket Square. This rally was in reaction to the police retaliation that had occurred the day before at the McCormick Reaper Works. The riot police—whom Marsh had financially backed—killed six striking workers during a demonstration outside the plant.

Before he had left for the meeting, Delia tried to persuade Marsh not to go down to Haymarket Square. "Please," she'd said, grabbing hold of his lapels, "don't go to the rally tonight."

"Delia"—he pried her fingers free—"these people are calling for my death."

"Exactly."

"Running away and hiding isn't going to make them back down. The only way is to stand up to them. I'm doing this for all our benefits. This entire city is in jeopardy and those rebels have to be stopped."

After he left, she headed around the corner to her house on

Calumet Avenue. She so wished Arthur were home. She hadn't heard from him in nearly a week and she knew he was sick inside over Paxton's marriage. She imagined him in the drawing room down in Ottawa, lost in a drunken stupor.

It started to rain, the kind of steady drizzle where the dampness seeped into her bones. The next several hours dragged on as she sat with Flossie in the library, thumbing through the latest issue of *Vogue*, trying to keep her mind busy. The second hand on the wall clock seemed to take forever to move. She sat down and played piano for the first time in ages, then played solitaire before she reached for her sketch pad and tried to draw. But nothing would distract her.

Two hours later, not wanting to be alone, she packed up Flossie and went over to her family's home.

"This is nerve-racking," Delia said to Abby and her parents as she removed her gloves, one finger at a time.

Abby set her needlepoint aside and sighed. "Augustus is attending the rally. I couldn't stop him from going."

"I just pray no one gets hurt," said Delia.

"Don't forget, the mayor is down there tonight, too," said Abby. "Augustus told me the city is taking every precaution to make certain it's a peaceful demonstration."

But that did little to calm Delia. She kept repeating over and over again in her mind, *Please, please let it be peaceful. Keep Marsh safe.*

"I suppose all we can do is wait," said Mrs. Spencer.

"I'd be down there myself right now except your mother has forbidden me to leave the house," said Mr. Spencer. "Personally, I hope they crush the rebels."

Delia looked at her father in disbelief. He sounded just like Marsh. When it came to their business, men like Marsh and her father were as fierce as a mother bear protecting her cubs.

The rain picked up in the evening hours, pelting the windows like a steady hand of pebbles being thrown at the glass. Spencer, now twelve years old, lay on the floor in the drawing room reading, and Catherine, just five, was already asleep upstairs. Abby and Mrs. Spencer picked up their needlepoint, and Delia and her father read. It reminded Delia of her childhood and how they used to pass the time, and she found some comfort in that. She gradualy began to relax and had even grown sleepy when suddenly Augustus stormed through the front door.

He panted as the rainwater dripped off his hat and shirtsleeves, puddling at his feet. The right lens of his spectacles was cracked, the frames bent. Abby shot up off the settee and rushed to his side, with Delia and her parents close behind. Augustus was pale. His eyes seemed unfocused; his clothes were splattered with mud.

"They set off a bomb!" cried Augustus. "The anarchists threw a bomb into the crowd. I've never seen anything like it. People are dying down there. They're killing people."

Delia went light-headed. She knew Marsh was a target. The anarchists wanted him dead. She grabbed hold of his sleeve. "Did you see him? Did you see Marsh? Is he all right?"

Augustus shook his head. "I saw him earlier, but once they threw that bomb, I lost track of everyone. . . ."

He kept talking, but Delia could no longer listen. The room was spinning around her as she let go of his sleeve and started for the door.

Her hand was reaching for the knob when Mr. Spencer grabbed her from behind. "Where do you think you're going?"

"I have to go to him. I have to see him," she said, turning to free herself.

"Now, you listen to me." Her father moved to block her from leaving. "It's dangerous out there," he said, shaking her by the shoulders. "You're not going anywhere. And don't forget, you are a married woman."

Delia gave her struggle one last attempt before the fight drained out of her and she dropped into her father's arms, willing herself not to cry.

"You'll stay here tonight," he said, patting her back. "There's nothing you can do right now anyway."

The room she'd once called her own had long since been occupied by Spencer, so she stayed in a guest room down the hall. She was staring out the window when Abby knocked on the door and came inside.

"Are you all right?" she asked, sitting on the side of the bed.

Delia nodded, too afraid to speak, for fear she'd start crying.

"I want to discuss something with you," Abby said. Her sister met her gaze and took a deep breath, as if to steady her nerves. "I've never said anything about this to you before, but you must realize that I know about you and Marshall. Everyone does."

"Oh, Abby, must we—"

"I have and will continue to defend you against the gossip, but I have to ask, what are you doing? How can you do this to your poor husband?"

Delia pressed her fingertips to her temples. Her husband was heartsick over another man getting married. How could she begin to explain it all to her sister? "Things with Arthur and me are not as they appear."

"I know he drinks but—"

"It's not just the drinking. Please, Abby"—she was begging with her eyes—"I've already said too much."

"But I'm your sister, Dell. If you can't tell me, who can you tell?"

"No one."

Abby gave a slight nod. She knew the discussion was over. "I'm sorry. I won't pry anymore." She got up and kissed Delia's cheek good night.

With the sound of rain still hitting the windows, Delia crawled beneath the covers and turned down the lamp. As her eyes adjusted to the dark, the tears began to flow. She was terrified that Marsh had been among the wounded or, God forbid, killed. It wasn't fair. Marsh was being punished for having built his business. He'd given people jobs, he'd put a city to work, he'd made Chicago a better place for everyone and now, in exchange for all his efforts, they wanted him dead. These thoughts spun inside her head until just before dawn when she finally fell asleep.

The next morning, once they were certain the streets were safe, Delia raced over to the Field mansion. She found Marsh in the library sitting before a stack of newspapers strewn across the center table. A tray of coffee and an untouched plate of eggs with a rasher of bacon had been pushed aside.

Even before the butler announced her, Delia rushed to Marsh with tears collecting in her eyes. Her legs went weak with relief as she knelt at his side, clutching his hand, pressing it to her cheek. "Thank God you're all right."

Marsh stood up and lifted her to her feet and wrapped his arms around her. "Come on now, I need you to be strong," he said, his mouth pressed to her ear. "Things are going to get ugly from this point on."

Delia clung to him thinking, *How could things possibly get any uglier?*

"We're in the fight of our lives," he said in a tight voice. "And I don't intend to lose." He looked worn through. She saw there was a gray cast to his skin and circles beneath his eyes.

"Why don't you try and get some rest?" she said, stroking his hair.

"There's no time for rest." He released her from his embrace and walked over to his desk. "Those bastards are trying to blame it on the police now. I saw what happened. I was standing right there. Their last speaker was on the platform, spouting off about killing every last capitalist. Then they threw the goddamn bomb and now they're going to pay for it." He clenched his jaw as he reached for the telephone.

He was as angry as she'd ever seen him. He was a force and she knew the anarchists were about to get a dose of just how powerful Marshall Field really was.

Delia stood off to the side, overhearing his half of a conversation with Captain Bonfield: ". . . Well, of course the public is outraged. Their security has been challenged. No one feels safe anymore. The Knights of Labor and the IWPA are a direct threat to everything this city and this country stand for. . . . We have to stop the hysteria and the only way to do that is to destroy this movement. I want those labor newspapers shut down. I want the people responsible for this arrested and thrown in jail. . . . I don't care—whatever it takes. I want that labor union crushed."

He slammed down the telephone base and Delia jumped.

Marsh drew a deep breath and calmed himself before he telephoned Mayor Harrison. ". . . Search their houses, arrest them on sight. . . . Declare martial law. Do whatever you have to do to put an end to the anarchists and the labor organizers once and for all."

Delia sat by Marsh's side watching as all his demands unfolded. Later that day, the city of Chicago declared martial law, and the police set out like hunters, searching for anyone and everyone suspected of participating in the uprising. She would always wonder how much of what happened in the coming weeks and months was a result of Mr. Marshall Field making those telephone calls on the morning of May 5, 1886.

All that spring and into the summer, the city police hauled more people off to jail. Delia picked up the newspaper each morning and cheered on more arrests. The more anarchists and socialists that were in jail, the safer she and the rest of Chicago felt. Like everyone else, she experienced an enormous sigh of relief when the men responsible were condemned for the bombings and stood trial. At last there was a face to the violence.

Delia followed the trial closely. When they announced the jury selection, she noted that it was comprised of businessmen, all capitalists themselves. There wasn't one laborer included. It was obvious that every juror had the prosecution's best interest at heart. Indeed, it would be advantageous for each juror to convict the anarchists. But as the summer stretched on, she couldn't help noticing that there didn't seem to be any actual evidence that the men on trial were involved with the bombing. Two of the men hadn't even been at Haymarket Square when the bomb went off. How could that possibly be? It seemed as though they were holding those few men responsible for the entire socialist and anarchist movement, and that they had been chosen almost arbitrarily to be the sacrificial lambs.

That August when the verdict came back, Marsh rushed into the Catons' drawing room and announced the news to Delia and Arthur. "Guilty! Death by hanging!"

"Guilty? The jury found them guilty? Death by hanging!" Delia repeated his words back to him in disbelief.

"Thank God," said Marsh, slapping Arthur on the shoulder, as if congratulations were in order, as if they were in this together.

"But they don't even know who threw the bomb," said Delia. "How can they say those men are guilty when they have no proof?"

"Somebody's got to pay for what happened," Marsh said as he reached for the evening edition of the *Tribune* lying on the table and snapped it open.

As news of the verdict spread, Delia realized she wasn't alone in her thinking. At first it was just a handful of journalists and scholars calling for leniency. But then more and more people began to see the trial as a sham.

One morning after reading another article calling for clemency, Delia watched as Marsh took the paper from her and ripped it in two. "They're the organizers," Marsh said. "They're going to be held responsible."

"I'm not so sure," challenged Delia, and she was right.

In the days and weeks ahead more and more people declared the trial a travesty. Governor Oglesby was beginning to buckle under the pressure.

"Come back to bed," Delia called to Marsh, propping herself up against the pillows. They had been spending the late morning in bed when the telephone call came, disrupting their mood, summoning Marsh down to city hall.

"The governor is looking for a consensus from the business leaders," said Marsh, turning up his collar and looping his silk tie around his neck. "Mark my words, he's going to ask us to back down from our position. His argument is going to be that setting those men free will resolve the labor dispute. I suspect that if we agree, he'll grant clemency to those bastards." Marsh scowled in the mirror while knotting his tie.

"But the trial wasn't just."

"Not just!" His eyes flashed wide. "Those men had their followers threaten my life, for God's sake. The lives of others. They deserve to die." He released a heavy sigh as he reached for his hat. "Don't look at me like I'm some heartless beast."

Delia spent the rest of the afternoon with her stomach upset, twisted in a bundle of nerves. She understood why Marsh felt so strongly. But there was no evidence tying the accused men to the bomb, and now the fate of the reformers was in the hands of the very capitalists they had been fighting all along.

After the meeting with Governor Oglesby, Marsh was in a foul mood, practically throwing his hat and overcoat at Williams, then brushing past Flossie, ignoring her when she jumped up to greet him.

"Dare I ask how the meeting went?" Delia followed him into the library and was standing in the doorway, her arms folded across her chest.

"It was a farce. The whole thing was a sham. A complete waste of time. I sat there listening to a bunch of rationalizations just so Oglesby can get reelected." He went over to the bar and poured himself a whiskey. "By the end of the meeting Palmer and Pullman were starting to side with Oglesby." He took a long pull from his glass, wincing as he swallowed. "You wait and see, Swift and Armour are going to fold. They're going to agree to release those men and I won't have it. It's a matter of principle. We have to hold our ground. If we back down now, after the trial, after the jury already reached a verdict, then we're undermining our entire justice system. Someone has to be held up as an example. It's up to us to send a message loud and clear to those revolutionaries. If we turn a blind eye, the anarchists win and we lose. And if that happens, progress in this city and across the country will come to a halt. It's the capitalists that took us from a trading post to a metropolis. If we let those men walk, we're leaving ourselves open for more violence, more attacks farther down the road. They're going to be the ones in charge. Is that what you want?"

Delia held her tongue. She understood what Marsh was saying but disagreed that executing innocent men was the way to punish the anarchists and quell the labor movement.

As the days passed it became evident that Marsh was the only man standing in the way of letting the men go free. What's more, Nannie had recently returned to Chicago with the children, and Delia desperately wanted to protect Junior and Ethel from the dreadful things being written about their father in the newspapers.

Ethel was fourteen and much less interested in the news than in going shopping and attending matinees with her aunt Dell—something that must have infuriated Nannie. Nineteen-year-old Junior, however, was very much aware of the fact that his father was the only industrialist not willing to grant the men clemency. And no one, not even the governor, was willing to go up against Marsh. Instead, people came to Delia, urging her to speak with him.

"Talk some sense into him," was what Augustus said to her.

"Even my mother thinks you're the only one who can reach him," said Junior.

Delia tried again and again to reason with Marsh. One Sunday afternoon at the end of October she and Marsh found themselves in a standoff. They were in the sitting room at the Caton mansion, locked into a silent battle they couldn't seem to escape. Delia knew she would be the first to break, just as he was the first to break their embraces.

She had called him impossible and foolish just a few minutes before. But now, his face was set in obstinate lines as he turned his attention to a carriage passing by outside the window.

She felt herself weakening. "I wish you'd reconsider," she said at last.

Nothing.

"Marsh," she pleaded, "these are human beings we're talking about."

"And they organized a violent revolution against me and everything I stand for. Everything this city stands for. Why can't you understand that?"

She looked into those blue gray eyes and realized that the very things she'd initially fallen in love with—his drive, his ambition, his power and determination—were the very things affecting his stance—a stance that she found so distasteful. Through all the years and all the obstacles they'd faced, if something was going to make her turn and walk away from him, she never thought it would come down to his politics. And yet, she found she couldn't understand or respect what he was doing.

"Well," he said, "whose side *are* you on?"

"Honestly, I don't know."

BOOK TWO

1890–1899

CHAPTER THIRTY-ONE

1890

Delia and Abby had just come out of a year's mourning following the death of their father and then the passing of their mother a few weeks later. It was now November 11, the three-year anniversary of the execution of the four men found guilty for the Haymarket bombing.

Delia was dressing in her room, preparing to go check on Marsh, though she knew this would be a more painful day for her than it would be for him. For the past three years this date had spawned a flurry of newspaper articles rehashing the trial of the accused men and their ultimate execution—and vilifying Marshall Field.

Despite how she'd felt at the time, Delia stood by Marsh, who seemed impervious to his critics. Though she was relieved that the outcome of the Haymarket Affair didn't incite more rioting among the labor organizers, she knew they weren't done pointing fingers. After the hangings, as their movement unraveled and they temporarily gave up their fight for the eight-hour workday, people continued to condemn Marsh. It pained her to know that everyone blamed him for the hanging of those men. She was accustomed to being the subject of nasty gossip herself, but she found it harder to watch people attack the man she loved. She couldn't dispute the truth, though: it was because of him that those men were hanged.

Delia was beside herself when she went downstairs and Arthur handed her the newspaper. "Why must they dredge this up every year?" he said. "They've already crucified Marsh enough. Can't they leave well enough alone?"

She couldn't read the article and opted instead to focus on the piece about bringing the World's Columbian Exposition to Chicago. They were still in the very early planning stages—the fair was three years off and Chicago was competing with New York, St. Louis and a slew of other cities to host the event. It was all anyone was talking about. Marsh, Potter, Cyrus McCormick and the other men who helped rebuild the city after the Great Fire were determined to be awarded the host city and shine a spotlight on what they had built in Chicago. This was especially important to Marsh given the outcome of what everyone was now referring to as the Haymarket Affair.

She handed the paper back to Arthur, reached for her hat and headed for State Street. Walking along, she passed by a string of dry goods stores: Chas Grossage and Mandel's, Schlesinger & Mayer's, Siegel & Cooper's. But none of them could measure up to Marshall Field's. His store dominated them all, but collectively these merchants had taken over State Street and nicknamed it the Ladies' Half Mile.

When Delia approached Marshall Field's, Eddie Anderson, the head doorman, greeted her at the curb and led her to the door. "Good day, Mrs. Caton. Welcome to Marshall Field & Company."

"Good day, Eddie."

Shoppers filled the store. Women ogled the latest arrivals of bumbershoots and Chantilly lace parasols, folding fans with ivory and gold handles, and satchels made of silk and beading. The clerks were impeccably dressed, the women in black dresses, the men in suits. They were all hard at work, assisting customers, tidying up the displays and setting out new merchandise. Sunlight streamed in from the well light above, and as Delia made her way down the center aisle, she was spotted by Harry Selfridge. Over the years Harry had worked his way up from a clerk to the general retail manager. He adored mingling with the customers, especially the women customers.

"Why, Mrs. Caton," he said, bowing and kissing her hand. "So very good to see you."

Delia couldn't help but smile. Harry Selfridge was a charmer with a merchant's spark. And a good-looking man, too, with dark hair parted down the center and a captivating smile. He was quite flirtatious with Delia and the other women at the store, married or single, young or old. He was very presumptuous, thinking that everyone welcomed his attention.

And yet, despite his overbearing manner, Delia had to admit that he'd made many fine contributions to the store. Because of Harry Selfridge, if Delia had so desired, she could check her coat and packages when she entered the store. She could have her jewelry cleaned or her gloves and other garments repaired while she shopped. She could drop off her shoes to be shined, her letters to be mailed, too. People purchased their theater tickets through Marshall Field & Company. They made their travel arrangements there, reserving train tickets and steamer fares. There was a nursery where young mothers deposited their children while they shopped. There was even talk about creating a library on the top floor where women could read magazines and novels in a room with plush seats and good lighting. With Harry's influence, Marshall Field & Company had become the center of the city and a destination, where a lady need never leave the store.

And thanks to Delia and a clever salesclerk, they didn't need to leave for lunch anymore, either. It had started with one of the clerks, an astute woman named Mrs. Hering, who worked in the millinery department. One morning she brought a potpie into work with her. When her customers got hungry and were about to leave the store, Mrs. Hering brought them to the back room and served them a helping of her potpie. She promised the women lunch again the next day if they agreed to come back and shop. Word caught on and soon more and more women were stopping by the millinery counter at noon looking for lunch. The demand became too much for one person, so Mrs. Hering recruited other salesclerks to bring in potpies as well. One day, Marsh happened to stumble upon the back room and found nearly two dozen women, seated on crates and boxes, eating potpies. He became enraged and threatened to fire Mrs. Hering and the other clerks, too.

"But why?" Delia had said. "This is what I've been saying to you for years now. I'll bet every one of those women stayed the afternoon and did more shopping after eating those potpies."

Marsh and Harry checked the sales tallies and Delia's theory was proved correct. Mrs. Hering was promoted and became the supervisor of the first ever dry goods store tearoom.

Harry stayed on the main floor and chatted with Delia about the latest Persian rugs and china arrivals until one of the clerks called him away. Finally, Delia made her way to the bank of elevators in the rear, eager to see Marsh. The elevator boys, dressed in green and gold uniforms similar to the doorman's, pulled the brass gates open and waited, stiff as soldiers, while the passengers stepped into the cars. Securing the outer gate, the elevator boy in Delia's car pulled the lever, letting the car rise before delivering her to the executive offices on the fifth floor.

Though Delia was a regular customer at Marshall Field's, she rarely visited Marsh upstairs in his office. Usually she ran into him on the lower levels while he conducted his routine floor checks. If he so much as found a fingerprint on the glass display case, or spotted one of the clerks leaning on a counter, there was hell to pay.

Coming to his office now, Delia found him seated behind his desk, eyes fixed on a stack of documents. She was always struck by how humble Marsh's office was. Just a small room with one window and a modest desk upon which his plug hat sat upside down, collecting mail, messages and other business of the day. Opposite his desk sat two simple straight-back chairs. Certainly a man of his wealth who commanded a business as large as his could have had a more opulent office, but Marsh didn't want or need one.

His brow furrowed. "What's wrong?"

"Nothing." Delia shook her head. "I guess I just wanted to see how you were doing."

Marsh darted his fountain pen into the stack of papers on his desk. "I haven't looked at the newspapers yet today, if that's what you mean. I suppose there's a story or two about me."

Before Delia could respond, the office door burst open and in barged Harry Selfridge. "We have news—"

"Harry, how many times do I have to tell you to knock first?" Marsh gestured toward Delia.

"Apologies, Mrs. Caton, but this can't wait."

"Nothing can wait according to you," said Marsh, squaring his elbows on his desk.

"Have you seen this yet?" he asked, waving a copy of the

Tribune. "They've narrowed it down to two cities. It's now between New York and Chicago to host the world's fair."

"Of course I knew about it. I got the call before the newspapermen did." Marsh grabbed the *Tribune* from Harry and scanned the article, paying no attention to the other headline: "Breach of Justice, Remembering the Haymarket Hangings."

"Do you know what this will mean for us if we get it?" Harry said. "Millions of people from all over the world will come to Chicago, and ultimately, they'll come to Marshall Field & Company." Harry was so excited he couldn't stand still.

"Trust me when I say we'll be awarded the fair," Marsh said. "Chicago can put on a world's fair better than New York. Besides," he added with a sly smile, "we're putting up more money for it than New York. We've already raised over five million dollars."

After Marsh sent Harry on his way, he closed his office door. "That man exhausts me," he said, squeezing Delia's hand. "He makes me a lot of money, but he exhausts me."

CHAPTER THIRTY-TWO

Six weeks later, seventeen-year-old Ethel Field married Arthur Tree. He was a fine young man from a respectable family. Just like Delia's Arthur, Ethel's Arthur was the son of a judge. The Trees were patrons of the arts and Ethel had met Arthur at a gallery opening his parents hosted just three months before.

They had a small wedding, held at noon at the Field mansion. The guest list was quite exclusive; not more than fifty people were in attendance along with a few select members of the press. Ethel wanted something small and private, whereas Nannie had wanted something that would appear on the society pages. Small but lavish was what they settled on.

Delia was certain that if it had been left to Nannie, she and Arthur would have been excluded. But Ethel said her day would not be complete without having Aunt Dell and Uncle Arthur there. Truly it was only because of Ethel and Junior that Delia and Nannie managed to be civil to each other whenever their paths crossed. And there would soon be another such occasion, as Junior had been courting a lovely young lady, Albertine Huck, for nearly a year. She was twenty-one and startlingly beautiful with a flawless complexion and the features of a china doll. Junior had recently turned twenty-two and told his aunt Dell that he was ready to settle down.

Nannie had decided on an Oriental theme for Ethel's wedding, and when Delia stepped inside the Field mansion, she felt as though she were walking into an Asian garden. Everywhere she turned she saw garlands and flowers, and their blossoms heavily perfumed the air. Delia and Arthur passed by a series of enormous palms flanking the entranceway to the drawing room where the ceremony would take place.

Junior, looking tall and handsome, walked his mother down the aisle. Nannie's dress was stunning—a white velvet gown trimmed in white fur along her train. Her face was nearly as pale as her dress. Over the past several years Nannie had been plagued with more migraines, which always led to more laudanum. It had been months since Delia had seen Nannie and she was shocked by how much she'd aged. But then again, she reminded herself that Nannie was fifty now, fourteen years older than Delia. Marsh was fifty-six, but despite his white hair, to Delia he hadn't aged a bit.

Nannie kept her eyes straight ahead, her chin lifted, as she glided on her son's arm, pausing just long enough for the photographers to take their picture before Junior showed her to a chair in the front row.

Ethel was a beautiful bride in her white tulle gown. It was understated but exquisite. With her brilliant blue gray eyes, she was every bit her father's daughter. Following the ceremony, Nannie hosted an elaborate luncheon in the ballroom. Guests were ushered inside to take their places. Marsh sat at the head table with the bridal party and immediate family members. He was seated next to his daughter and the empty chair to his right was reserved for Nannie. Everyone else sat at heart-shaped tables, waiting for the luncheon to begin.

Delia and Arthur were with the Eddys, the Palmers and Mr. and Mrs. Paxton Lowry. Arthur was antsy, ready for a drink. Even though he and Paxton were still as close as ever, having recently gone to New York and down to Ottawa together, there was tension between them whenever Penelope was present.

They were all making small talk, but as time passed, the empty chair next to Marsh became too obvious to overlook. A breeze coming through the windows made the curtain sheers swell out into the room while the candles stationed about burned at an accelerated rate. Water glasses were refilled, but people grew bored and started wandering around, speaking to guests at other tables. It had been nearly forty minutes and everyone was whispering, wondering what had happened to the mother of the bride.

Marsh got up from the head table and went to Delia. "I say we start the luncheon without her. Will you tell the staff to start serving? I'm going to go find Nannie."

But before she could get to the kitchen, Ethel stopped her. "I can't have a wedding luncheon without my mother." She narrowed her eyes, pulling her brows close together.

"Go on," said Delia. "Go and be with your guests. I'll take care of this."

Delia went into the kitchen, where she was met by a burst of steam and dozens of servants scurrying about. The smell of garlic, caramelized onions and other seasonings was overwhelming. The chef was frazzled, worried that her Selle d'Agneau Forestière and Pommes à la Crème would be ruined.

It was while she was back in the kitchen that Delia glimpsed the train of Nannie's white velvet gown trailing down the back stairwell. A dreadful feeling rose up in her chest as she rushed over and found Nannie slumped on the bottom step, her arm propped up on the banister, her chin resting on her chest.

"Oh, Nannie." Delia bent down and shook her by the shoulders. "Nannie, please, get up."

Nannie lifted her head, letting it roll from side to side. "I'll be there right away. Just give me a minute here."

"Nannie, don't do this. Not now. Not today."

Delia was still shaking her awake when Marsh appeared behind her.

"Goddammit, Nannie!" Marsh stepped in and yanked her up by her underarms.

Nannie's eyes flashed open with a start as she stumbled on the bottom step. "You're hurting me."

"I'd like to kill you right now, is what I'd like to do," Marsh hissed.

"Then go on," she said with a sudden burst of defiant energy, jutting her face up close to his. "Kill me! Get it over with already, you bastard." She slapped his chest and then his arm.

Marsh grabbed her by her forearm. "Keep your voice down—you want everyone to hear you?"

"I don't care!" she shouted. "You've already ruined my life, so just go on and kill me. That way you and your precious Delia can finally be together. I'm leaving you, you hear me? I've had it. I'm moving to Europe and this time I'm not coming back. And, no, Delia"—she turned and glared at her—"I won't give him a divorce since I know that's all you care about." Nannie looked back at Marsh. "I'm done with you."

Delia sensed someone crowding in behind her and as she turned around, her heart dropped. Ethel was standing there.

"So it's true," Ethel said, as tears collected in her eyes. "All the rumors. All these years, I didn't believe what people said, but it's true."

"Of course it's true," shouted Nannie. "That's why I'm leaving him. I'm leaving your father. And it'll be for good this time."

Marsh was standing next to Nannie, still holding on to her arm. His cheeks darkened as Delia watched the rage rising up inside of him.

"Ethel," Delia said, going to her side. "You don't understand. It's so much more complicated than—"

"Oh, Mother!" Ethel turned and sobbed, her shoulders shaking. "This was supposed to be my day. My day!" She tapped her open hand to her chest. "Mother, you promised. You promised me you wouldn't take anything and now look at you. You've ruined my wedding day." Then she pointed to Delia. "And it's all your fault! Look at her!" Ethel pushed past her mother and ran up the back stairs sobbing, the train of her wedding dress trailing behind her. Marsh let go of Nannie's arm and she stumbled, grasping on to the banister for balance.

"Are you satisfied now?" he said to Nannie.

Delia was speechless. She wanted to go after Ethel, but she knew it wasn't her place to do so. For a moment, all three of them stood frozen. But then Marsh headed back toward the reception and Delia followed him.

"Don't you dare walk away from me!" Nannie shouted.

Delia and Marsh kept walking with Nannie now close behind, still screaming at them. She was out of control. "I'm warning you—Marshall! Come back here, Delia!" Neither one responded, which infuriated her all the more. She shouted after them once more, "You can both go to hell! You hear me! Go. To. Hell."

When Delia and Marsh reached the ballroom, all the wedding guests were hovering in the doorway wanting to know what was going on. Arthur was standing right in front, next to Spencer and one of the newspapermen.

Nannie grabbed hold of Marsh's jacket, and when he shrugged her away, she lost her balance and fell, taking down one of the potted palms with her. And that's when the flash lamp went off.

While Delia tried to help Nannie up, Marsh grabbed hold of the photographer. "You were invited into my home as a guest," he said through gritted teeth. "And if that photograph turns up in your newspaper or anywhere else, you tell your editor he won't see another advertising penny from Marshall Field & Company. Is that understood?"

The photographer went ashen-faced and nodded.

Nannie was on her feet now, sobbing, potting soil crushed into her white velvet dress. Pointing her finger she shouted, "He pushed me. You saw it. You all saw it!"

Delia cringed, instantly recalling the night of the Field & Leiter opening party when Nannie had accused her of assault. Nannie continued hollering at Marsh while their guests quickly made their excuses. Everyone left without one course of the luncheon being served.

CHAPTER THIRTY-THREE

1891

"I need your advice," said Abby.

It was a cold January afternoon and the sisters were in the sitting room, warming themselves by the fire while sipping tea from the Wedgwood gilt-rimmed cups that had belonged to their mother.

Abby crossed her ankles and leaned forward. "I've been thinking about my inheritance, and I'm contemplating giving it to Augustus to invest."

"Invest?" Delia gave her a questioning look. "But it's already been invested for us. And quite wisely. It's nearly a million dollars that Father left you. And me. And forgive me, but Augustus hasn't proven himself very astute when it comes to investing. He's already lost a great deal of his own money. Why would you even think of giving him access to yours?"

Abby looked away and began fiddling with the buttons running along her dress.

Delia became suspicious. "What's this really all about?"

Abby twisted a button so hard, it fell off and rolled onto the floor. Flossie, who had been lounging on the sofa next to Delia, got up to investigate.

"Abby?" Delia leaned forward and reached for her sister's twitching fingers. "What on earth is going on?"

"Augustus has a wonderful opportunity and—"

Delia let go of Abby's hand, sat back and folded her arms. "And he's asking for the money."

"Not all of it."

"Why does he need you to provide the funds? He has a new position now." Delia couldn't understand. Yes, it was true that Augustus had made some poor financial decisions in the past and yes, they were still living in her parents' home. But they lived well, even by Delia's standards.

"It's just going to take more capital than what he can pull together on his own right now," Abby explained.

Delia reminded Abby about one of Augustus's previous business ventures involving food service on railcars. "Don't you remember I arranged for Augustus to speak with Marsh about it? Marsh came right out and said, 'The problem isn't the business plan. It's the proprietor. Augustus, you're not a businessman.' Marsh was very clear when he said he didn't think Augustus was cut out to be a proprietor."

"But that's only one man's opinion," said Abby.

"One man who happens to be the most successful businessman in this city."

"You know Augustus respects Marshall's opinion," said Abby. "And he appreciated you arranging to have them speak. But Augustus isn't like him. He couldn't run a business the way Marsh does. He doesn't have that killer instinct." Abby lowered her eyes and chewed on her lower lip. "I'm sorry. I didn't mean that the way it sounded."

Delia knew she was referring to the Haymarket executions. Never mind all that he had done for State Street and the rest of Chicago, she worried that in the end, the Haymarket Affair was all people would remember about Marshall Field.

"He's my husband, Dell. How can I say no?"

"You just have to, Abby. Don't do it. Promise me you won't give him access to your inheritance."

Abby squeezed Delia's hand and nodded. "I know you're right. I know it."

"Promise me."

Abby nodded. "All right. I promise—I won't do it."

"Where's Penelope tonight?" Delia asked as she entered the drawing room where Arthur and Paxton sat across from each other, both with a fresh drink in their hands. Flossie ran to Paxton's side, rising up on her hind legs, her tail thrashing back and forth.

"I'm afraid she's under the weather," said Paxton, reaching down to pet Flossie's head. "She's been in bed all afternoon."

"Poor thing," said Delia. "I hope it's nothing serious."

"She'll be fine," said Paxton. "She just needs some rest."

"You're looking rather natty tonight," said Arthur, raising his glass to her. "Give Marsh my best."

Delia bid them both adieu and went over to the Field mansion. Now that Nannie had moved to London, Delia spent more and more time there with Marsh.

That evening when she arrived, he met her in the drawing room with a glass of champagne.

"What's the occasion?" she asked, setting Flossie down and accepting the glass from him.

"We're celebrating. I received some excellent news today. I just found out that we won the bid for the Columbian Exposition.

Chicago is going to host the world's fair." He raised his glass and kissed it to the rim of hers.

"Oh, Marsh, that's wonderful." She leaned over and hugged him. She was pleased but not surprised. Once again her Merchant Prince had accomplished something so grand, so beyond what any ordinary man could do. She truly had come to see him as someone with mythical powers. He was the most influential force in the city, and now that he was bringing the world's fair to Chicago, maybe people would stop thinking of him as a monster for letting them hang those men for the Haymarket Affair.

"I'm leaving for D.C. late tonight with Potter. We need to finalize everything with Washington and then we'll go straight on to Europe to meet with the heads of state from France, England and Italy."

"You're leaving? Tonight?" She felt a stab of disappointment.

"On the eleven-thirty train."

"How long will you be gone for?" She cringed, hating how pathetic she sounded.

"Hard to say right now. At least six weeks, I suspect."

"Oh." Delia turned away, afraid she wouldn't be able to hide her disappointment. Instead she busied herself with Flossie's ruby barrette, straightening it between her ears.

"Of course," Marsh continued in a blasé fashion, "Selfridge is ecstatic that I'll be gone for so long. I told John Shedd he's in charge and he'd better keep a close eye on Harry." He walked over to her and smiled. "Now why are you looking so sad?"

Delia shook her head, afraid she'd start to blubber if she dared speak.

"Hmmm." He started to laugh. "I suppose you're thinking six weeks is too long to be away."

"Now you're just making fun of me."

"Not at all." He went over and sat on the settee, and gave Flossie's chin a scratch. "I'm just wondering what it would take to get you to come meet me in Europe."

Delia looked at him, her eyes growing as wide as her smile. She rushed onto his lap and wrapped her arms around him. "Why, Mr. Field, I thought you'd never ask."

When Delia returned home that night she was excited, already starting to plan what outfits she would pack for Europe. After Williams removed Flossie's leash, the dog went scampering through the hallway and into the drawing room. Delia followed and found Arthur and Paxton right where she'd left them earlier that night. Arthur was still sitting on the sofa and Paxton was in the chair across from him. Neither one of them spoke. They both had drinks in their hands. Paxton's was nearly full. Arthur's was just about empty. Flossie took turns going back and forth between the two men, who hadn't blinked, hadn't taken their eyes off each other.

"Hello?" Delia bent slightly trying to catch Arthur's eye and then did the same to Paxton. "Should I leave and come back?" she asked, halfheartedly.

"No need," said Paxton as he finally broke his pose and reached for his hat. "I was just leaving anyway. I'm late as it is." He came over and squeezed Delia's shoulders, kissing her on the cheek.

"Is everything all right?" she asked. "I didn't mean to intrude."

"No. We're done here." Paxton adjusted his hat, and without so much as a glance back at Arthur, he walked out of the room.

She went and sat next to Arthur. "What happened with you

two?" She tried to brush his hair out of his eyes, but Arthur shrugged her away. "Please tell me what's wrong."

"Nothing." Arthur drained his drink and shook the melted ice in his glass before he got up and fixed himself another one.

"Obviously something just happened."

"If you must know, Penelope's pregnant. All right?"

"Oh, I see." Delia sat back and took this in. "And Paxton's the father?"

"Of course he's the father," Arthur snapped as he slumped back down in his chair, nearly spilling his drink. "Not everyone's wife takes a lover, you know."

"Okay, all right. Calm down." She drew a deep breath and smoothed down the front of her dress. "Surely you knew this was a possibility when he married her."

"That's not the point. The point is that it's happened. She's pregnant."

"But that doesn't have to change things—"

"Oh, come now, Delia. It changes *everything*." He stood up and nearly tumbled over as he headed for the doorway.

"Where are you going?"

"What do you care?" He stormed out of the drawing room and a moment later she heard the front door slam behind him.

"Mrs. Caton—"

Delia woke with a start. Therese was standing over her bed, shaking her awake. "What is it? What time is it?" It was still dark in her bedroom as her sleepy eyes registered the grave expression on Therese's face. She sat up abruptly. "What's wrong? Tell me. What is it?"

"I'm afraid there's been an accident. Mr. Caton took a bad fall on his horse. He's in the hospital. They just telephoned. They said it's best if you get down there right away."

It was half past two when Delia arrived at the hospital. Arthur had just come out of surgery. The doctor met her outside his room and told her what little he knew about the accident.

"He was still conscious when they brought him in. Someone found him on the side of the road. Apparently his horse got spooked and threw him. He was dragged for a quarter mile before he was able to free himself from his stirrups. I should also tell you, Mrs. Caton, that your husband was very intoxicated."

"How bad are his injuries?"

The doctor consulted his chart. "He has a concussion, a collapsed lung, a ruptured spleen." He flipped the page over. "He broke his collarbone and both legs."

"Oh, my God!" She splayed an open hand against her chest. "He must be in terrible pain. Can I see him now?"

"He's still heavily sedated," the doctor warned as he gestured toward the sickroom.

Delia nodded, steeling herself for what she'd find. But when she entered the room and saw the oxygen canopy tented over the upper half of his body, she gasped. "Is he going to be okay?"

The doctor adjusted something on the side of Arthur's bed. "The next forty-eight hours are critical. Let's just hope he pulls through."

Delia went light-headed and weak-kneed. She didn't even hear the doctor as he continued speaking, nor was she aware of him leaving the room. All she could think was, *He can't die. He can't.*

It was still the middle of the night, but she couldn't face this alone. Marsh was already on a train bound for D.C., so she telephoned Paxton. He rushed to the hospital, and she met him in the waiting room. The two of them sat there, drinking bad coffee, while the doctor examined Arthur again.

"It's my fault," said Paxton, his head in his hands. "If Arthur hadn't been so upset with me, he wouldn't have gotten so drunk. He wouldn't have gotten on a horse in that state."

"You can't blame yourself. It was an accident."

"It's just so damn complicated, Dell." Paxton leaned forward with his elbows on his knees, his knuckles pressed to his eyes as the tears leaked out.

Delia scooted closer to him and put her arm around his shoulder. "He's going to be okay. He has to be okay."

She sat with Paxton in the waiting room thinking of all the things she should have told Arthur, or should have told him more often. Did he know he was her best friend? Did he know how much she loved him? Did he trust that she would always keep his secret? Had she ever told him that she would have married him anyway, even knowing the truth about him? Their life together worked. For them both. She realized that she couldn't be with Marsh and he couldn't have been with Paxton if it weren't for their marriage. Given the circumstances, they were a blessing to each other. Did he understand that?

At half past six Paxton left the hospital and Delia stayed alone in Arthur's sickroom. She was still at his bedside when her in-laws arrived. She had waited until the sun was up before she telephoned them with the news.

When Mrs. Caton saw her son, she let out a cry and buried her face in the judge's chest. Delia got up from her chair and offered it to her mother-in-law. The judge, stoic as ever, went down the hall to find the doctor.

"How could this have happened?" Mrs. Caton cried. "Arthur's such an excellent rider."

"I have no idea." Delia didn't say that he'd been drinking all day and had no business getting on a horse in the first place.

The rest of the day passed without any change in Arthur's

condition. Even after the judge and Mrs. Caton left for the night, Delia stayed in the sickroom with Arthur. Occasionally she dozed off in the chair. Her neck and back were stiff, but she didn't dare complain. She wanted to be there when Arthur woke up. And finally he did. At two in the morning, his eyes fluttered open, groggy and unfocused.

"Oh, my God. Arthur?" Delia was on her feet. She called out for a doctor, not wanting to leave his side. She could tell that he was in enormous pain, wincing each time he breathed. Delia raced into the hallway and called to one of the nurses. "He's awake. Quick! Get the doctor!"

"Oh Arthur," she said, running back inside, leaning in as close as she could to the oxygen tent. "Hang on. The doctor's coming. He's on his way."

Arthur blinked and she thought he was trying to say something.

"Don't try to speak, darling. You're going to be fine." Her eyes glazed over. "Don't you worry about a thing. Paxton was here earlier. So were your parents."

He closed his eyes and tried to move his lips. He tried to say something. It was a soft murmur. She thought she heard him asking for Marsh.

"Be still, darling. Don't move." Tears were streaming down her face. "I love you, Arthur. You're not alone. You're our family, you hear me? You, me and Marsh. You have us and you always will."

Arthur closed his eyes again as a tear leaked out.

The doctor rushed in and Delia stepped aside, crying freely now as she watched him reach inside the oxygen tent, checking Arthur's pulse, holding his eyelids open with his thumb. He filled a syringe, and before he had even finished administering it, Arthur drifted away.

"What happened?" she asked in a panic. "What's wrong?"

"I just gave him more morphine for the pain. Sleep is the best thing for him. We'll see if we can get him breathing on his own later."

For the next two days Delia stayed by Arthur's side. Gradually he began to improve and as his pain eased up they lowered the morphine dose. By the end of the week, Arthur's sisters had come and gone along with the judge and Paxton. Now it was just Delia and her mother-in-law in the sickroom. Delia waited until Arthur fell asleep before she announced that she was going home for the evening. After nearly a week of being at his bedside, she was in desperate need of a good night's sleep.

"But I'll be back in the morning."

"You needn't come back," Mrs. Caton said as she rearranged a bouquet of flowers that Abby had dropped off for Arthur earlier.

"Of course I'm coming back," said Delia.

"I'd appreciate it if you didn't."

"I beg your pardon?"

Mrs. Caton looked at Arthur, sleeping. "I think you've done enough damage already. You've dragged my son and my family's good name into your disgrace. This entire city knows about you and Marshall Field."

Delia didn't even consider denying it. "For your information, I've never kept any secrets from Arthur. I've never been anything but honest with him from the very beginning. We have an understanding."

"That's absurd." Mrs. Caton scowled, her faint eyebrows knitted together.

"I don't expect you to understand, but your son and I have a very special love for each other. It may not be the kind of love either of us expected, but it's genuine and I will be here for him, just as I know he would be here for me."

"He never should have married you."

"Maybe he shouldn't have, but I wouldn't trade the life we have together for anything." Delia grabbed her hat and bag. "I'm leaving now, but whether you like it or not, I will be back."

CHAPTER THIRTY-FOUR

Delia never met Marsh in Europe that winter. Instead she stayed in Chicago and looked after Arthur, who by the end of February was recuperating back at home. Since he was unable to manage the stairs, she had the servants convert one of the sitting rooms into a temporary bedroom for him.

Not long after Arthur returned home, she came into his room. "You have a visitor," she said with a smile, sidestepping around the rickety cane wheelchair just inside the doorway. "Can I show him in?"

"Who is it?"

"Who do you think?"

"Tell him to go away."

"Oh, Arthur . . . really?"

But Arthur just turned away and stared at the wall.

Delia glanced back to Paxton, who was waiting out in the hallway. She shook her head sadly. "I'm sorry," she whispered as she walked him back toward the parlor.

Paxton frowned. "I guess I'll try again tomorrow."

"Don't take it personally," she said, grabbing hold of his arm. "He's terribly depressed. He's in a great deal of pain. He still can't walk and he loathes that wheelchair."

"What does he do all day?"

"He drinks," she said matter-of-factly. "And I can't blame him for that."

"And how are you holding up?" he asked.

"Me?" She almost laughed. "I'm fine."

Fine. That was the answer she gave everyone, but in truth she was far from it. Delia was tired of having to be strong. And it wasn't just for Arthur's sake. Lately she felt as though her entire family leaned on her for support.

Her sister was in a state over whether to fund Augustus's latest business venture, a post office car sorting system for the rail lines. It was a subject that had come up time and time again and Delia was tired of arguing with Abby about it. All she could think was, *Thank God Father isn't here to see this.* It would have broken his heart to see his daughter squander away everything that he'd worked so hard for.

And then there was Marsh and his children. Ethel and her husband never returned to Chicago. Instead, immediately after their honeymoon they took up residence in London so Ethel could be closer to her mother. Delia had started to write to Ethel after the wedding fiasco, trying to apologize, hoping to explain. But in the end, she never sent a single letter or telegram, realizing that Ethel was in an impossible position. Any act of kindness or even diplomacy toward Delia would be a slap in the face to Nannie. Though it broke her heart, Delia knew the best thing she could do for Ethel was leave her alone.

Shortly after the wedding Ethel found out she was pregnant. "She's not even eighteen yet. A child having a child," Marsh said upon hearing the news. They were in the solarium working in Delia's indoor garden, planting primrose seeds. Gardening had become a favorite pastime of theirs and reminded Marsh of his childhood days back on his father's farm. Usually he found it relaxing, but that day Delia could see it was having no soothing effect at all.

"Maybe this is just the thing she needs to make her grow up."

"Doubtful," grunted Marsh, lifting the watering can. "And on top of that, Junior told me he's ready to propose to Albertine and—"

"Marsh, that's wonderful." She dropped her shovel and went to hug him, but he went on watering the seeds.

"And—are you ready for this?" He raised one eyebrow. "They're going to move to London, too. Nannie's request." He set the can down hard, sending the water sloshing about. "If he goes to London, he'll never come back and take over the business."

"Oh, Marsh, even if he stayed here, do you really think he'd come work for you?"

Marsh removed his gardening gloves and slapped them onto the ledge. "Why can't he see what's he's throwing away? Doesn't he understand that I'm trying to build something here? The boy is twenty-two and has never worked a day in his life. My father worked me—out in the fields—and you know what that taught me? It taught me how to grow something, from scratch. I always wanted to grow something that would last. Forever."

"Sounds like you're seeking immortality, Mr. Field."

He tilted his head and smiled in a sad way. "I always thought of the store as something that Junior would take over. I was building a business that would stand for generations to come. Junior's supposed to carry on and then his son will pick up where he leaves off. That's always been the dream. And now Nannie's got him turning his back on me and running off to London. Why can't he see what I'm trying to do here?"

After the engagement party several weeks later, Junior came by to visit with his uncle Arthur. And unlike the times Paxton came by, Delia knew Arthur would welcome a visit from Junior. The two played chess in the parlor while Delia read in the next room. She couldn't help but overhear them talking about Marsh.

"He doesn't listen," said Junior. "He's never once asked me what *I* want. . . ."

She knew that no one understood his predicament better than his uncle Arthur. Perhaps that's what made the two of them so close. Arthur saw himself in Junior, and he had always seen a bit of the judge in Marsh. In fact, she'd long suspected that Arthur had initially sought out Marsh's friendship because of his longing for a relationship with the judge.

Arthur still tired easily in those days and he needed to lie down after their first game of chess. After helping Arthur back to bed, Junior joined Delia out in the solarium.

"He's getting better each time I see him," said Junior.

"We're hoping that he'll be able to graduate to crutches soon. Getting out of that wheelchair would certainly cheer him up."

"He doesn't like that chair, that's for sure."

"Can you blame him? It's been two and a half months."

"I'm sorry you and Uncle Arthur won't be able to come aboard for the wedding. I told Albertine we should just get married here, but her family wants the wedding in Europe."

"We're disappointed, too. But he can't make the crossing and I won't leave him here alone." She smiled and gave Flossie a few strokes on her head. "I'm going to miss you, though," said Delia. "I selfishly wish you and Albertine were staying in Chicago."

"Mother asked us to come there. I couldn't bring myself to say no. It's no secret that she's not well," he said. "And Albertine is quite fond of Mother, as you know." Junior opened his silver cigarette case and propped a Duke's Best between his lips.

Delia remembered the days when it would have been a lollipop. Smoking was one of his latest eccentricities. He said he preferred Duke's Best to other popular cigarette brands or cigars. My goodness, she thought, how had he grown up so quickly?

"You'll come visit, though, won't you, Aunt Dell? And of course, we'll be back for the fair." He lit his cigarette and waved the smoke away from Delia's face. "I think it's for the best that I go. I need to get out from under my father's shadow."

"Is that the real reason you're leaving?"

Junior fiddled with his cigarette case. "I won't lie, it's a big part of it." He gazed up at Delia and she saw the sadness in his eyes. "Do you have any idea what it's like being his son? His *only* son? Let's face it, no matter what I do, I'm never going to accomplish even half of what my father has. Everyone's watching, waiting to see what I'm going to do. And no matter what, it's never going to be enough. Father's set the bar too high. It's too much pressure for me."

Delia didn't know what to say. She'd known that Junior was intimidated by his father since he was a young boy, but she'd never heard him articulate it before. It touched her deeply that he was willing to confide in her. He was telling her the very things he needed to but could never say to his father.

Junior raised his cigarette to his lips and paused before taking a puff. "I'd rather get as far away from his business as I can than try to live up to his standards and end up failing. And I would fail. I'm not like him. I know Father doesn't want to hear it, but even if I wanted to become a merchant, don't you see, he's ruined it for me. I know I've been a huge disappointment to him but—"

"I wouldn't say that."

"Oh, Aunt Dell"—he flicked his ash and laughed—"you're a terrible liar. I *know* he's disappointed. He's told me so from the time I was twelve and didn't want to be a cashboy. And then when I turned sixteen and didn't want to be a clerk. Or a buyer. Or a manager and so on and so on . . ."

Delia recalled an argument she'd witnessed between Marsh and Junior just a few weeks before on that very subject. Marsh had an assistant's position open at the store and offered it to his son. Junior had politely turned him down, which sent Marsh into a rage.

"And why? Because you're lazy, that's why. Just once I'd like to see you get off your duff and do something worthwhile."

Delia wanted to disappear as soon as Marsh raised his voice, but his temper had exploded without warning and there was no place to hide. She watched Junior slouch deeper and deeper into his chair.

"You're spoiled. That's what the problem is. You and your sister—both of you are spoiled rotten."

Junior's expression suddenly changed. "And whose fault is that?"

It was the first time Delia had ever heard Junior talk back to his father and it would be the last, too. Marsh stormed over to his chair and clutched Junior by the collar, thrusting his knuckles into his throat. Junior's eyes were bulging from his sockets in panic. It was Delia who had finally pulled Marsh off him. Junior was in tears and Marsh had nearly put his fist through the wall.

The smoke from Junior's cigarette drifted Delia's way and

brought her back to the moment. "So what will you do now?" she asked.

"I want to travel and take my time thinking about my future. Besides, I'm going to inherit a fortune. I'm rich. I figure I don't need the money, so why should I work?"

Delia shook her head. "Oh, Junior, look at your uncle Arthur. Do you want to end up like him? His father's reputation and the easy fortune he made as a young man have crippled him more than that accident. Don't make the same mistake. You don't have to go work for your father, but find something you can make your own. Don't waste your future. I beg of you."

A tight expression registered on his face. "Well," he said, checking his pocket watch, changing the subject, "I should get going. I have dinner tonight with Albertine's family." He reached over and gave Flossie's head a pat and then leaned in and kissed Delia on the cheek. "Oh, and Aunt Dell?" He straightened up, buttoning his jacket. "Take care of Father after we're gone. I know you will, but I had to say it just the same."

"You have my word." She gave him a smile. It was clear to her that Junior had confessed to her knowing that she would find a way to explain to Marsh why Junior was turning his back and walking away from the family business.

CHAPTER THIRTY-FIVE

Delia looked at the calendar in her engagement book. It was April 18, 1891. Junior's wedding day. Marsh had already departed for France on the *Majestic* over a week ago. From France he was going on to England and Italy to meet with more heads of state on behalf of the world's fair. Had it not been for Arthur's accident, Delia would have joined Marsh in Europe. But she was determined to stay by Arthur's side for as long as he needed her.

She closed her engagement book, smoothing her hand over the leather-bound cover, remembering the days when there was scarcely a blank space left to jot down even the briefest of comments. She'd been ostracized by society for so long now she had to admit she hardly missed the endless chatter at the luncheons and teas, the petty scrutinizing over everyone's gowns at the galas and balls. No, she didn't miss that at all. And besides, caring for Arthur kept her so busy now, she wouldn't have had time for her old schedule anyway. She sat back in her chair watching as

Arthur made his way into the library. Four months after the accident he had finally graduated from the wheelchair to crutches.

"You're doing much better on those," she said.

"I'm getting the hang of it."

She helped him get situated in his chair.

"I still wish you would have gone to France for the wedding," he said.

"And leave you behind? You know I wouldn't do that. Besides, can you imagine what Nannie would do if I showed up? Not to mention Ethel."

"Ethel will come around. She loves you." He yawned and rubbed his eyes. "But seriously, Dell, you've got to get on with things. You can't just sit around the house and look after me."

"Maybe I like looking after you. Did you ever consider that?"

Arthur gave her a skeptical look. "I know better than to believe that."

Delia smiled. "Right now you need me and that's all there is to it."

Williams came into the library and announced that Mr. Caton had a visitor.

Delia turned to Arthur. "You know it's him. Won't you please just speak to him? He comes by nearly every day. It's breaking his heart."

Arthur went silent. He pursed his lips and looked out the window.

"Please? Just say hello to him."

"I can't. I can't have him see me like this. Like a cripple."

"Oh, Arthur, this is temporary. He knows that. It won't matter. I promise you that. Please say hello to him. Please? Do it for me."

He sighed, keeping his gaze focused on the window.

"Arthur, please?" She tried again.

He turned back around and she could tell he was beginning to give in.

"Please? For me?"

At last he offered a barely perceptible nod.

Before he had a chance to change his mind, Delia followed Williams out to get Paxton. When she told him Arthur would see him, Paxton's face came to life.

"Now I'm nervous," he said to Delia. "I don't even know what to say to him."

"It'll be fine. I promise." Delia took his hand in hers. It was clammy.

In a moment of vanity, Arthur must have been trying to hide his crutches because when they came back into the room, the one crutch was stuck under the chair. He was leaning on the chair, frantically tugging on it, hoping to free it. The frustration and humiliation on his face was heartbreaking. It was Paxton who walked over, helped Arthur back into his chair before he bent down and pulled the crutch free, setting it out of the way, behind the door.

"Thank you," Arthur said, unable to look at Paxton.

Delia could see his eyes turning glassy. She excused herself and went to send a telegram to Marsh. As she was closing the French doors behind her she heard whispering: "God, do you have any idea how much I've missed you." She couldn't tell if it was Paxton or Arthur who'd said it, and it didn't matter. They both needed to say that and they both needed to hear it, too.

A few weeks later, on a lovely spring morning Delia and Bertha were wheeling through Lincoln Park. Bertha with all her baubles was on a Swift safety bicycle and Delia in her new bloomers was on a Rover safety model with Flossie riding up front in the basket. The sunlight glinted off the diamonds on Flossie's collar, sending prisms of light across the handlebars.

There were dozens of other riders out that day, some still pedaling the old-fashioned three-wheelers. Delia adored cycling, but because Arthur was still recuperating, she went either alone or with Bertha, who also needed a companion since Potter insisted he was too old. Delia thought that was nonsense. Marsh was a fan of wheeling and at fifty-seven he wasn't much younger than Potter.

That day Bertha wanted to ride by the location of her future home up north. It was still just a stretch of barren swampland that butted up against the lakeshore. Delia couldn't imagine how they were going to make this section of town inhabitable.

"What are you going to do with all the frogs?" Delia asked, noting the green, slimy frog ponds collecting in the swampy land.

"Potter assured me that they will be relocated to a lovely new swamp," she said with a confident nod.

The whole move to this no-man's-land reminded Delia of how her father had been a Chicago pioneer in the 1850s. And my, what a different city it was today. Delia looked off in the distance and saw the skyline that seemed to change month by month. The new Rookery Building on LaSalle Street soared eleven stories high and construction was visible on the Monadnock Building on Dearborn. Every day in the papers she read about the ongoing battle with New York to claim the tallest skyscraper in the country.

Delia and Bertha continued cycling and made their way back toward the city. On the way, Bertha shared a bit of gossip that nearly made Delia ride off the sidewalk.

"Surely you're joking," Delia said as she slowed her bike and looked at Bertha. "They really think I have a tunnel? A tunnel in my backyard that connects my house to Marsh's! And they think I meet Marsh inside this so-called tunnel? That's ridiculous!"

"Of course it's ridiculous." Bertha veered to the left and pedaled up a slight incline. "I wasn't even sure if I should say anything to you about it."

"No, no, I'm glad you did," Delia reassured her as she waved to another cyclist coming up the path. "I just can't believe people actually think I built a tunnel in my backyard."

"They say you supposedly built it at the same time you built the solarium. They say that was just a distraction for the construction of the tunnel."

"I know who started this rumor," said Delia as they came to a fork in the pathway. "It was Sybil Perkins, wasn't it?"

Bertha didn't comment one way or the other and instead tried to change the subject. "Mary Leiter says you're not to be trusted. She called you 'a wolf in cheap clothing.'" Bertha burst into peals of laughter.

"So they think we have a love nest, do they?" Delia started to pedal faster with Bertha following. "And what else?"

"Well, they say you've decorated this tunnel in the finest Italian marble. They say it's nicer than your house. There's also been talk about a gold bed frame that Marsh bought for ten thousand dollars."

"Oh, yes, because isn't that just like him. He's just the type to throw ten thousand dollars away on a bed." Delia tried to laugh as she steered over a bump in the path.

"Supposedly you two meet in the tunnel every evening. They say Nannie discovered the tunnel and that's why she left Marshall. Supposedly, supposedly, supposedly . . ." Bertha looked over her shoulder and saw that Delia had brought her cycle to a stop, her one foot on the ground, keeping her balance. "Are you all right?"

"What? Yes. I'm—I'm fine." She looked across the way and did a double take.

"Dell, are you all right?" Bertha asked again.

Delia looked at Bertha and pointed to a man sitting on a park bench beneath a giant elm tree. "Isn't that Augustus over there?"

Bertha shaded her eyes. "Why, yes. It is. Let's go say hello."

As they drew closer, Delia saw that Augustus was carving an apple with a pocketknife, meticulously skinning the peel into long ruby strips that dropped onto a crumpled brown paper sack on the bench beside him. Some of the juice had dribbled onto the newspaper in his lap, making the ink run. He was so engrossed in his apple that he didn't notice when Delia and Bertha pedaled up beside him. It wasn't until Flossie yelped that he looked up, nearly dropping his pocketknife.

"I'm sorry. We didn't mean to startle you," said Delia with a laugh, reaching over to pet Flossie, who was stirring about in her basket.

"Oh, Delia. Mrs. Palmer. My goodness. What a surprise." He set the apple down on the paper sack and grappled with his coat pocket, searching for his handkerchief. His fingers were shiny with apple juice.

"I'll say. What are you doing all the way up here? Don't you have work today?"

"Yes, yes, I do have work today. Lots of work, in fact. Just taking advantage of this beautiful morning." He wiped his hands dry and straightened his spectacles. "It is beautiful, isn't it?" he said, reaching for his pocket watch. "Oh my, look at the time. I had no idea. I am late, aren't I? I have to run. I have a big meeting down at the office."

"We'll have to all get together soon," said Bertha.

"Of course. Of course. Wonderful to see you ladies," he said as he packed up his newspaper, haphazardly stuffing it inside his valise, leaving edges of newsprint jutting out of the top. "I'd best run along now. I have that meeting. Down at the office."

Delia glanced down at the apple resting on the juice-stained paper sack. "Oh wait, you forgot—" But it was too late. Augustus was already hurrying down the pathway.

CHAPTER THIRTY-SIX

Delia had all but forgotten about seeing Augustus in the park that day. A whole season had come and gone since then. And in September of 1891, Delia and Abby were planning a trip to Paris to meet with the famed fashion designer Charles Frederick Worth. Bertha was already in Paris, securing her wardrobe for the upcoming season, along with several other women Delia knew. While she was there, Delia hoped to make it to London to see Junior and Albertine. It had been nearly six months since their wedding and she missed them both. Of course she wanted to see Ethel, too, but she knew better than to hope for that. According to Marsh, Ethel was pregnant and miserable, barely speaking to her husband, let alone anyone else.

Abby came by the house while Delia was in her dressing closet, deciding what gowns to have Therese pack in her steamer trunks. "Which do you prefer?" she asked, holding out two blue satin dresses. "The one with the velvet trim or the one with the lace?"

Abby sat in the tufted chair in the corner, looking at the dresses as if she were seeing through them.

"Well?" Delia gave both hangers a slight shake. "Abby? What's wrong?"

"Oh, nothing." Abby folded her arms across her chest. "I'm just thinking that perhaps I won't go abroad with you after all."

Delia laughed as she hung up the velvet-trimmed dress. "Very funny."

"I'm serious. I think it may be best if I don't go."

"But you need to get outfitted properly for the season." Delia held out the other dress at arm's length and gave it a closer inspection.

"Perhaps not this time."

"Nonsense. Why wouldn't you go?"

"I'm so busy with the children and with . . ." Her voice trailed off and she turned her face away.

"With what?" Delia challenged. "We can't have you gallivanting around town in last year's fashions, now, can we?" Delia looked in the mirror and saw Abby's chin began to crumple. "What is it? Tell me what's wrong?"

"It's just that it's an awfully expensive trip."

"But so worth it. You know your dressmaker here can't match the quality of Worth."

Abby worried her fingers, refusing to look at Delia.

"What on earth is going on?"

Abby looked up, her eyes filling with tears. "Please don't be cross with me, but . . ."

"Oh, Abby." Delia finally understood. "Did Augustus ask you again for the money?"

Abby began to sob.

Delia set her dress down and went to Abby's side.

"He needs the money. He's put everything he has into starting up his mail-sorting business, and if he can't get that off the ground, he'll have nothing. I have to give it to him." Abby lowered her face to her hands and whispered, "He's my husband. I have to help him."

"But I don't understand. His position with the railroad is a very good—"

"He's lost his job, Dell," she blurted out. "He's been out of work for months."

"Oh my, Abby . . ." She remembered questioning her sister that day after she saw Augustus on the park bench. Abby had dismissed it, saying he'd been feeling under the weather and had gone into the office late that day. "Why didn't you tell me about his job?"

"He made me promise not to say anything. But now we have nothing. I have to give him the money. He's got no one else to turn to."

Delia knew by then that Abby had probably already given Augustus the money and that she had to step in and rescue her sister. She took a moment and cleared her throat. "Well, if that's the case, then I'll pay your way to Paris. And I'll pay for your clothes for next season. We have our family name to protect. We're the Spencer girls after all, aren't we?"

Two weeks later Abby and Delia, along with Therese and Abby's maid, Gretchen, completed their ocean crossing and arrived in Paris on a crisp September morning. The next day they visited the House of Worth on rue de la Paix. Abby and Delia sat back in his fine upholstered chairs and sipped tea while the live mannequins modeled the latest gowns from his collection for the upcoming season.

"Now, don't you worry," Delia whispered to Abby. "You get whatever you need. Whatever you see that you like."

Delia selected a black and pink taffeta gown with a lace fichu, a salmon-colored chiffon gown with a vertical motif and a burgundy day dress with a plush polonaise. Those were her favorites, but she ordered dozens more, as did Abby.

After selecting their gowns, they discussed fabrics and trim, buttons and clasps with Worth himself. One of his assistants took their measurements so that each item could be tailored to fit perfectly. Delia adored the dressmaking process, especially with Charles Worth. When he was creating a gown, he was creating art.

"No outfit for this one?" He laughed as he patted Flossie's head where wisps of her fur were collected in a ruby barrette. Her diamond collar was sparkling beneath his chandelier. "Aha, soon she will have as much jewelry as your friend Mrs. Palmer," he said, giving Delia a playful jab with his finger.

Delia laughed, lifting the dog up just high enough to let Flossie lick her chin.

The day after their visit to the House of Worth Delia and Abby visited several boutiques along rue Saint-Honoré. There they purchased dozens of handkerchiefs from one shop and their fans and hair combs from another. The following day she and Abby shopped for their bloomers and corsets before ending up at Louis Vuitton on rue Neuve des Capucines.

By the end of the week, after their fittings and alterations at Worth, Delia realized they were never going to get everything home in their luggage. So they went to Goyard's at the corner of rue Saint-Honoré and rue de Castiglione, where they purchased half a dozen new steamer trunks. While they were there, Delia made arrangements for Edmond Goyard himself to pack their new wardrobes after Worth finished with their gowns.

• • •

Four and a half weeks later when they returned to Chicago, Delia found her new dresses hanging in her closet looking every bit as perfect as they had when Worth presented them. But now, the excitement of Paris was in the past. Delia had returned to the sad news that Ethel had given birth while she was making the crossing back to America and that the child, a boy, had died just three days later. Though she knew she wouldn't get a response, she wrote Ethel a ten-page letter, front and back.

Delia took the news hard. Almost too hard. She felt the space, the gaping hole in the universe, where Ethel's child should have been; playing, laughing, growing up. For days she wandered about listlessly, unable to pull herself out of it. Even she didn't understand why the infant's death was having such an effect on her until Bertha pointed out what the problem was.

"Now don't get me wrong," said Bertha one day, as she plucked a sugar cube from the bowl with a pair of gold tongs, "it's a tragedy to lose a child. I can't imagine the heartache that poor girl is going through." She gave her tea a stir and passed the sugar bowl to Delia. "But it's been several weeks and look at you, dear."

"I can't help it. It's heartbreaking," said Delia, glancing around the tearoom at all the other women oblivious to this unspeakable pain.

"Of course it is, and forgive me for saying this, but you're dwelling on this loss and it makes me wonder if there isn't something else that you're really grieving over."

"Such as?" Delia paused, about to take a sip of tea.

Bertha gave her a knowing look. "Perhaps you have some losses of your own?"

She set her teacup down and contemplated what Bertha said. How could she have not recognized what was really going on? Bertha was right. She was grieving over other losses. Truth was, she was lonely. Marsh was preoccupied, having recently purchased the building next door in order to expand Marshall Field's in time for the fair. And Arthur was now relying on Paxton more than Delia to help with his recovery. While she was pleased to see him walking with a cane now, she couldn't help but feel she'd been replaced. After devoting all her free time to caring for him, she was left with a tremendous void in her life. She was restless and blue, and Bertha had picked up on that.

As they were leaving the tearoom that day, Bertha draped her arm about Delia's waist and walked her down the street to where her landau carriage was waiting.

"I do have something that might help," said Bertha.

"Please, tell me," said Delia. "I need to do something. I can't go on like this."

"Well." Bertha placed her hands on her lap, lacing her fingers together. "I just attended a meeting yesterday for the Columbian Exposition. I've been named the chairman of the Board of Lady Managers."

"Oh, Bertha, what a wonderful honor."

"Thank you. It is an honor. And it's also a great deal of work. I can't possibly handle all the responsibilities myself. So, I wonder, Mrs. Caton, if you would be my assistant?"

CHAPTER THIRTY-SEVEN

One week later Delia found herself in the boardroom at the mayor's office. Portraits of Carter Harrison and the mayors that came before him lined the walls in heavy gilt frames. She counted twelve sweating silver water pitchers stationed about the long boardroom table along with twenty crystal goblets. At each place there was also a pad of paper with the World's Columbian Exposition Fair logo embossed on the top.

This would be Delia and Bertha's first meeting with the executive committee for the world's fair, composed of the top city officials and the men who were helping to finance the event. Delia liked the idea of being in a meeting with Marsh. It gave her a sense of equality to be sitting right across from him at an oversize table along with men like Potter Palmer, Gustavus Swift, Cyrus McCormick and Philip Armour.

Once the meeting started, the mayor asked for a report on

the main attraction. "It's got to be something spectacular," he said. "Something that will rival France's Eiffel Tower."

"We did get a proposal from a railroad engineer," said Marsh.

"Oh, you mean the gentleman working on the giant Pleasure Wheel," said Potter.

"Yes. That's the one."

"You're talking about George Ferris," said Gustavus Swift.

"Is it worth us having a meeting with him?" asked the mayor.

Potter and Marsh exchanged glances and both nodded.

The mayor scratched down his name and then moved on to Cyrus McCormick. "And what about the faulty sewer system near the park? We're going to have to deal with a host of sanitation issues down there and I won't have a cholera outbreak in the midst of this fair. . . ."

When it was finally their turn, Bertha announced that the Board of Lady Managers had selected the architect who would design the Women's Building. "We've decided to award it to a very bright, very talented twenty-one-year-old graduate of MIT named Sophia Hayden."

"Did you say *Sophia*?" Daniel Burnham, the head architect for the fair, leaned back in his chair and cupped his ear.

Delia had known Burnham for years, as she and Arthur had commissioned him to build their home on Calumet Avenue. He hadn't changed much at all, still full and round-faced with a scraggly handlebar mustache.

"Indeed I did," said Bertha.

Burnham folded his arms across his chest. "Do you think she's up for the task?"

"Why do you ask?" Delia said, turning to him. "Because she's so young? Or because she's a *she*?"

There was a ripple of commotion before Gustavus Swift

spoke up. "Mrs. Caton, Mrs. Palmer, please let's be reasonable here."

"Exactly." Burnham wrinkled his brow and leaned forward. "Need I remind you that we have less than two years to build this exposition? This is a monumental task. Do you have any idea what it's going to take to transform Jackson Park into the White City?"

The mayor straightened his tie and spoke up. "And just what is this White City that you keep referring to? I've heard you use that term countless times and I haven't the foggiest idea what you're talking about."

Burnham jotted something down on his notepad before he looked up and began to speak. "The White City is my theme for the fair. It's no secret that our greatest challenge is convincing the Europeans to come to Chicago. All they've ever heard is that our city is dirty. It smells. It's dangerous. They realize that Chicago is a modern city—a glimpse into the future—but let's face it, Chicago frightens them. We need to dispel the belief that Chicago is a dark and dangerous place. We're going to construct more than two hundred buildings—all in white—along the perimeter of the basin. We're literally going to construct a pristine, white, gleaming paradise—the White City. Right now Jackson Park is nothing but swampland. We have to dig a basin and drain the water and transform the whole place. Nothing like this has ever been attempted before and in such a short time period. That's why I'm questioning the women's choice of architect. We need the very best people on these assignments."

Marsh planted one elbow on the table, resting his chin on his knuckles. "Then we'll continue to look for a new architect for the Women's Building. I say we move on with the business at hand and—"

"The business at hand," said Delia, giving Marsh a glaring

look, "is to award the design to the most qualified architect—be it a man or woman."

"And I believe, Mrs. Caton," said Marsh, "that we've already determined that your candidate is not the best architect for this project."

"But you haven't even looked at her proposal." Delia felt Bertha's hand on her arm, trying to calm her down. Delia reached into her file and pulled out Sophia Hayden's sketches and blueprints. For the next thirty minutes the group pored over them.

Finally Potter spoke up. "If the Board of Lady Managers think this Sophia woman is the best person for the project, then I say we proceed."

"But with caution—" Philip Armour raised a finger. "Daniel, if you need to step in and assist—"

"I assure you that won't be necessary," said Delia. "You worry about the men. We'll worry about the women."

Within a month of that initial meeting with the executive committee, Delia and Bertha had set up an office next door to the Chicago Academy of Fine Arts on Michigan and Van Buren. Together they wasted no time decorating their work space. Some may have considered this a silly extravagance, but Delia and Bertha couldn't help themselves. They were both so accustomed to being surrounded by luxury and beautiful things. Besides, they believed that an aesthetically pleasing environment was conducive to their success. They purchased a Persian Mahal carpet and two hand-carved De Morgan walnut partners desks that faced each other with matching marbleized stained-glass desk lamps. Off to the side they had a little seating area with a pair of exquisite mahogany scrolling armchairs, a matching settee and a table with an enormous Mont Joye glass vase of lilies on top.

One morning Delia and Bertha were having their coffee while going through the invites for the Women's Pavilion planning meeting.

"Well," said Delia, looking over the updated list, "we just heard back from Arizona and Nebraska, so we now have our two representatives needed from each state."

"And would you look at all these entries we've already received?" said Bertha. She was surrounded by piles of envelopes and boxes.

As word spread that they would showcase women's achievements throughout the world, applications flooded their office. Each day they received paintings, poetry and short stories, needlepoint and embroidered pieces, fashion designs and inventions all created by women.

"Did you see this?" said Bertha, holding up a sketch they'd just received. It was a sofa built into a bathtub.

They had a good laugh over that as they continued sorting through the letters and cables touting the accomplishments of suffragettes, women in law school, women doctors and women who worked in the man's world.

"Isn't it amazing?" said Bertha. "Just think of all the capabilities these women display."

"Yes, and just think of how many bright, talented women are overlooked in this world, simply because they're females." Delia was just getting a taste of what it meant to work side by side with men. Stubborn, arrogant, pushy men. If there was one thing she hoped the Women's Pavilion would prove, it was that women deserved a chance to excel every bit as much as a man.

CHAPTER THIRTY-EIGHT

1893

Delia looked at the invitation, a hand-drawn note from Frances Glessner requesting her presence at a meeting for the women of the Prairie Avenue District. She crumpled it up and tossed it into the trash. It had been years since she'd attended a meeting with these women and she didn't relish the thought of sitting in a room with all of them now. Bertha and Abby had stopped by her house on their way to the meeting, determined to convince her otherwise.

"It's for the world's fair," Bertha explained. "You have to attend."

"As if we don't have enough meetings right now," said Delia, sorting through a stack of mail. "It's March. The fair opens in three months. What could they possibly want to meet about?"

"Dancing lessons," said Abby with a shrug.

Delia stopped shuffling the mail and looked up. "Dancing lessons?"

Bertha nodded. "The women all agree that if we are to present a regal image of Chicago at the world's fair, our men had best master their dance steps."

Delia laughed, trying to picture some of the men like Gustavus Swift and Lionel Perkins taking waltzing lessons.

"As a member of the Board of Lady Managers, you have to be there," said Bertha.

"And don't worry," added Abby, handing Delia her hat and gloves. "I won't leave your side for a minute."

Half an hour later Delia felt all eyes on her as the three of them stepped inside Frances Glessner's library. There were fifteen women already there, perched on their chairs, teacups balanced on their laps, necks craned her way. Delia couldn't read their expressions and had a mind to turn around and leave when Frances rose from her seat and walked over. Delia froze in place thinking, *Here it comes.*

But a smile spread across Frances's face as she took hold of both Delia's hands, kissing her on either cheek. "I'm so glad you could make it today."

While Frances greeted Bertha and Abby, Malvina Armour went up to Delia. "It's so wonderful to see you," she said. "It's been too long."

Another woman stepped up and introduced herself. "I don't know if you'd remember me," she said, clasping Delia's hand. Delia had indeed remembered her. She was Thelma Moyer and she had snubbed Delia on several occasions. "I think the work you've done on behalf of the women in this town is outstanding." She smiled, still holding Delia's hands. "Just outstanding."

And no sooner had she finished speaking with Thelma than the other women lined up, waiting to pay homage to Delia, thanking her for all her efforts on behalf of the fair. She was especially taken aback when Sybil Perkins invited her to a luncheon the following week and Annie Swift asked if she would have time to sit on a committee for the Fortnightly Club.

"I don't know," said Delia. "Am I still a member?"

Annie and Sybil laughed as if Delia's exclusion had never been a possibility. "Of course you're still a member," said Sybil. "We've all missed you terribly. Haven't we, ladies?"

"Oh, of course," said Malvina as several others all chimed in, circling around Delia and agreeing emphatically.

"And you know the Chicago Women's Club still meets every Tuesday," said Harriet Pullman.

"So there you have it," said Mary Leiter. "Time to let fly-gones be bygones."

Delia graciously accepted all their attention and invitations though she knew it was only because she was part of the Board of Lady Managers. Now all the women who had previously spurned her were welcoming her back into their circle.

"Come now, everyone," said Frances Glessner, calling the meeting to order. "We have a great many items to discuss. . . ."

Delia sat in between Abby and Bertha, listening to the elaborate plans for the opening ball.

At one point Harriet Pullman looked at Delia and frowned. "Oh dear, I'm sorry. I just realized something. We forgot about Arthur's injury. He won't be able to join in on the dancing, will he?"

"Afraid not," said Delia. "He still relies quite heavily on his cane."

"Well, we simply must find you a partner," said Frances.

"Yes. Yes." The others all agreed.

"There's Mr. Howton," said Annie Swift.

"He's arthritic," said Abby, shaking her head.

"What about Mr. Beauregard?" suggested Harriet.

"Mr. Beauregard?" Malvina made a face. "We can't do that to Delia. He'll barely come up to her shoulders."

"Mr. Fitzsimons?" said Frances.

"Oh no," said Sybil. "He'll be drunk and passed out in a corner before the orchestra finishes the first waltz."

Delia sat back, not saying a word, fascinated by everyone's preposterous attempts to pair her off.

Finally Bertha spoke up, cutting through the chatter. "What about Mr. Field? We all know Nannie won't be in town for this."

The room went quiet and Delia held her breath waiting for the outrage to strike. But it never came. The women grew very still, but no one gasped; no one raised even the slightest protest. After all, they all knew that Arthur couldn't dance and Marsh was separated from Nannie and had no partner of his own.

"It's settled, then," said Frances. "Delia's partner for the opening ball will be Mr. Field."

The round of applause that followed took her completely by surprise.

After that meeting at Frances Glessner's, Delia's engagement book was flooded as never before with invitations to dinner parties, luncheons, teas and meetings. How ironic, she thought: the very women who had torn her down now—because of all her work on the fair and the Board of Lady Managers—regarded her as an advocate for women worldwide. Like their queen, Bertha Palmer, Delia Caton was seen as a feminist and as one of the most progressive and influential women in the city.

This was a wondrous time for Delia. She'd never felt stronger or more self-assured. She couldn't tell whether the women had changed toward her because she herself had changed, or whether it was the women who had changed her. All she knew was that with her fortieth birthday fast approaching, she was finally feeling grown-up. She saw the world differently and the world in turn treated her differently.

After that meeting, once a week for the next six weeks Delia and her neighbors congregated at the Bournique Dance Academy near Prairie Avenue. Before a wall of mirrors, the couples stood in two straight lines facing each other. Delia was directly across from Marsh.

A pianist played various waltzes while Miss Bournique walked around the room, calling out instructions and inspecting their form. "Shoulders back," she said, tapping George Pullman's arm. "Look at your partner, Mr. Eddy," she said to Augustus as he turned Abby in a circle.

Delia watched her sister and brother-in-law across the way. They smiled, looking as though they hadn't a care in the world. No one would have guessed that Delia had paid for their clothes, their shoes and even their dancing lessons.

Miss Bournique continued to weave in and out of the couples going, "And one, two, three. One, two, three . . . and twirl to the left. Your other left, Mr. Swift . . ."

Delia gazed over at Arthur, his cane lying flat across his lap. He'd had quite a lot to drink before they'd left the house and she could see that even though his eyes were heavy-lidded and bloodshot, he never once lost sight of Paxton and Penelope Lowry dancing.

Finally, on Tuesday, May 2, 1893, Delia watched the World's Columbian Exposition open with fireworks, marching bands and parades. A grand pageant of two dozen carriages delivered President Cleveland and the other officials and dignitaries to the fair. Delia and Bertha, representing the Board of Lady Managers, rode together in the procession that was accompanied by Chicago's mounted guard.

Delia glanced out the carriage window at the patriotic bunting and banners hanging from the storefront windows, including $10,000 worth outside the new Marshall Field & Company building. Crowds of people lined the sidewalks, cheering them on as the cavalry moved alongside the carriages. The air still carried the mossy scent of rain from two consecutive days of downpour. But the clouds were parting and the sun was on their side now.

When they arrived at the Administration Building, where the opening ceremony and dedication took place, Delia was overwhelmed. She and Bertha emerged from their carriage as she took in all the sights. The faux facades of the buildings looked like white marble. No one would guess that they were made mostly of plaster and that they'd been designed as only temporary structures. To see those white gleaming buildings positioned about the grand basin gave Delia a rush of pride. This was her city, on display for the world to see, and there was no place like it on earth.

And the proof was in the grandstands that overflowed with people who had paid twenty-five cents apiece to hear President Cleveland's speech and join in the singing of "My Country 'Tis of Thee." As the fairgrounds officially opened, more fireworks ignited and fountains throughout the midway sprang to life as electrical lights illuminated every building, thrilling the crowd of people, many of whom had never seen so much as a single lightbulb before. The whole experience was magical.

That evening Delia, Arthur and five thousand other prominent guests attended a ball held at the Auditorium Theatre. The Auditorium was the tallest building in the country. It had opened in 1889 and Delia had always enjoyed seeing the Chicago Symphony and the ballet there, as well as other productions. The theater was attached to a hotel and housed a glamorous ballroom with a golden ceiling and crystal chandeliers.

The opening ball was the event of the decade and one where all their dance lessons were put to good use. Dressed in one of the Worth gowns she'd purchased while in Paris, Delia danced with Marsh and then her brother-in-law. She danced with Potter and George Pullman and even Paxton while Arthur sat at a nearby table, tapping his cane to the beat of the music.

Delia was finishing up her dance with Paxton when she saw Ethel Field go over to Arthur. Her heart began to race. This was the first time she'd seen Ethel since her wedding. During the past week Delia had telephoned and sent cards inviting Ethel to tea and lunch, but all had gone unanswered. Ethel's husband didn't make the crossing with her and Delia knew there were rumors circulating around London that Ethel was having an affair with a Royal Navy officer named David Beatty. Whether or not there was any truth to it, Delia hoped the rumors would have at least made Ethel more compassionate about her father's circumstances.

Junior and Albertine also returned to Chicago for the fair, and while Delia was delighted to visit with them, she still longed to see Ethel and patch things up.

Delia finally excused herself from Paxton and went over to see Ethel, who was still speaking with Arthur.

"Thank goodness you're all right," Ethel said, hugging her uncle Arthur for the second time. "Will you need that dreadful thing much longer?" she asked, gesturing toward his cane.

"Hopefully not," he said, reaching for Delia's hand.

"Well," said Ethel, "I think it's just dreadful that you have to use it at all. . . ."

Delia stood back, holding on to Arthur's hand, while Ethel chattered on, not once acknowledging her presence. When Delia did manage to capture Ethel's attention she went over and gave her cheek a kiss. "It's so good to see you, dear."

She felt Ethel tensing up, her body going stiff, her eyes narrowing just before she abruptly pulled away. "If you'll excuse me."

That was it? Not so much as a hello? Delia was stunned. A sinking feeling settled into her gut as she watched Ethel walk away, the train from her dress disappearing into the crowd.

"Aw, Dell," said Arthur, "try not to take it personally. You know how stubborn she is."

"Not take it personally? She wasn't even cordial. What if she never forgives me? What then?"

Delia sat at the table next to Arthur, willing herself not to cry.

It wasn't until Marsh came to get her for the final dance that Delia's spirits began to lift. As they glided about to Valisi's "Waltz-Polka," twirling this way and that, Delia smiled at Marsh. Gazing into his blue gray eyes, she was savoring this moment. It was a victory for them both on so many levels. He had succeeded in bringing the world's fair to Chicago and by so doing had put the Haymarket hangings behind him. The Women's Pavilion was a success, and Delia had restored her reputation. What's more, here she was dancing in front of the whole world with the man she loved.

CHAPTER THIRTY-NINE

1896

There was a draft coming in from the library windows even with the drapes drawn. Delia's fingers were cold as she signed her name and set her fountain pen down on her desk blotter. For a moment she thought she heard the jangling of little Flossie's collar, but it was only Abby's bracelets. Poor Flossie. Her old age had finally caught up with her, and though she'd been gone for nearly two years now, Delia still expected her to come circle about her legs before settling down at her feet.

"Are you sure that will be enough?" she asked as she handed Abby the check.

Abby looked at the amount and nodded sheepishly. "Thank you."

"If you find yourself running short again this month, you have to tell me. I won't have you going without."

"This should be more than enough. I just hadn't counted on

Spencer needing extra money. I'm trying to get him to live within his means but . . ." She shook her head and let the unfinished thought linger in the air like dust motes.

They both knew she couldn't blame it on Spencer. Yes, it was true that the boy had no sense of money. He was twenty-two and expected his parents would supplement his extravagant whims. He'd been raised on the false assumption that his family was wealthier than they were and Abby never had the heart to tell him otherwise. And it wasn't just Spencer. All the Eddys were living beyond their means.

"Well," said Delia, closing her ledger book, "if you need more, you just let me know."

"Thank you, Dell," said Abby as she carefully folded the check, slipping it inside the pocket of her satchel. "I don't know what we'd do without—"

Delia stopped her with a raised hand. "I'm glad I can help."

After Abby left, Delia went into the drawing room and visited with Arthur, who had started in on his second cocktail for the day.

"Sure you won't join me?" he asked, gesturing with his empty glass.

"Not tonight. I'm afraid I don't have time."

"Well, then, do give Marsh my best."

She kissed him on the cheek and retreated to the hallway, where Williams helped her on with her coat.

She felt the shock of the freezing cold on her cheeks the instant she stepped outside. A fine but heavy snow fell in thick flakes, making it hard to see even just a few feet ahead. The only images she could make out were the streetlamps glowing in the distance. By the time she'd made her way down Calumet and over to Prairie Avenue, she could barely feel her fingers or toes.

The Fields' butler seemed especially somber as he helped Delia off with her things.

"Is everything all right?" she asked as he led her into the library.

"Pity," was what he said with a shake of his head as he stood in the doorway and announced her.

Marsh was sitting on the sofa, a telegram in his hand. The sight of it gave her a chill. It was just a sheet of paper, yet she knew how a single telegram could change the course of people's lives.

She ran to his side. "What's going on? Marsh? What's happened?"

He handed the telegram to her.

She read it over, each word sinking in, filling her with a sense of sadness and, at the same time, relief. Nannie was dead. At the age of fifty-six she overdosed on laudanum while vacationing in the south of France. She passed earlier that day, February 23, 1896. Delia closed her eyes trying to picture Nannie's face, trying to comprehend that that face no longer existed.

"I shouldn't be surprised. We knew something like this would happen sooner or later."

She looked up at him. "Oh, Marsh. How are the children?"

"Ethel's devastated. Junior's holding her together." Marsh looked at Delia and said, "I couldn't stand the sight of her in the end. Couldn't tolerate the sound of her voice. I keep asking myself how I ever could have loved her. The anger I've felt toward her filled up so much of my life for so long—and now she's gone, but the anger's still here. Shouldn't she have taken it with her?"

"You know Nannie would never let you off the hook that easily. She always did love to make you suffer."

While Marsh got up and fixed them drinks she glanced

about the library. She'd been in the Field mansion thousands of times before, but now that Nannie was gone, it seemed haunted. She swore she felt the ghostly touch of a hand on her shoulder as she sat on Nannie's sofa, drinking from Nannie's glasses. She even thought she detected a sudden burst of Nannie's perfume.

At one point Marsh leaned over to kiss her and the desk lamp flickered. Delia nearly dropped her glass. The lamp had never done that before. She immediately took it as a sign that Nannie was watching. It sent a chill through her.

She took a sip of the scotch to calm herself. It was strong and burned her throat as the heat spread throughout her chest.

She didn't say a word to Marsh. He didn't believe in anything or anyone other than things he could see and touch; he'd scoff at her. She knew he would call her fears foolish, but Delia couldn't shake them.

She sat beside Marsh, hardly speaking, lost in her own thoughts. Nannie's passing was making her think about death in a whole new way. She suddenly found herself questioning what would become of Nannie's soul. Would she be reunited with God or turned away for her addictions and weaknesses and for all the wrongdoings she'd caused? Nannie lived with demons—did that mean those demons would follow her in death?

Delia had never shared Arthur and Paxton's curiosity with séances, but now she had to wonder if the dead might actually be all-powerful in some way. What if Nannie now had the final say over Delia and Marsh's fate? What if she could bestow blessings and punishments on them? Delia no longer felt in control of her destiny. She felt doomed and subject to the ruling hand of Nannie Field.

Later that night, after they'd picked through dinner, they retired to the parlor, where a roaring fire threw shadows about the room and warmed them in its glow. Delia sank into Marsh's arms and nuzzled her head against his shoulder. With the moonlight peeking through the parting of the drapes, Delia began to relax and even felt a bit foolish. There was no such thing as ghosts. She was sure of it. And as crass as it sounded, she was glad Nannie was gone.

CHAPTER FORTY

1899

Delia stood beneath the giant patina clock suspended overhead outside Marshall Field's. She turned up her collar to block the winter chill as she waited for Abby, who was meeting her for a day of shopping. Marsh had installed the giant clock just two years before and it had since become the meeting point for shoppers up and down State Street.

She heard the rivet guns down the street where the new Carson Pirie Scott building was under construction. Marsh told her that Sullivan, the architect who had criticized the latest renovations to the Marshall Field & Company building, was designing a dry goods store with nothing but glass along the first floor. She couldn't imagine it. But then again, she couldn't have imagined skyscrapers like the Reliance Building or the Masonic Temple, either. She never could have predicted half the changes that had taken place in the past few years. There were over a million people in Chicago now and the city had stretched to accommodate them all with more el cars and cable cars that ran from the outskirts into the heart of the Loop. There were more homes and neighborhoods springing up in places people used to consider the countryside. Motorcars were increasingly replacing carriages on the roads. It was all progress, visible everywhere but Delia still longed for the familiar Chicago in which she had been raised.

She shaded her eyes from the sun and waved to her sister as her new driver helped her down from the coach and onto the sidewalk. After learning that Augustus had to let their old driver go, Delia had insisted on hiring a new coachman and paying his salary.

Delia and Abby hurried up to the doorman, who greeted them by name before letting them inside. Marsh had recently installed a newfangled circular doorway at the main entrance that revolved around and around. The doorman gave it a push, and with a magical whoosh, the glass doors rotated and there they were, standing in the main entrance, humming with busy shoppers and tempting displays. Delia and Abby rode the moving staircase—another new addition to Field's—up to the eighth floor and worked their way down. After several hours of shopping, Delia had several parcels and half a dozen others that would be delivered to her house. She had also purchased some items for Abby, including a black velvet reticule she'd been admiring, a tortoiseshell hair comb and an abalone spangled silk fan.

At the end of the day, Delia reached into her satchel, took out two twenty-dollar bills and handed them to her sister. "Please, treat yourself to something nice. Do it for me. Otherwise, I'll just have to go buy you something that you probably won't like."

Abby made a halfhearted attempt to resist before she clutched the bills and said, "Thank you. Thank you. I'll pay you back every penny." But of course they both knew she never would. What's more, they both knew it wouldn't matter.

When Delia arrived home after dropping off Abby, Williams lowered his voice and said, "I believe Mr. Caton could use your help."

"Is he all right? Where is he?" she asked quickly, handing him her parcels, hat and gloves.

"I'm afraid he's upstairs." Williams gestured with his eyes toward the grand staircase. "In the tub."

Delia rushed the staircase and found Arthur shivering in a bath that had long since turned cold. He rocked back and forth as he hugged his arms around his shins, his knees pulled up close to his chest. Tears dripped down his cheeks.

"Arthur? What is it? What's wrong?" She reached for a towel and draped it over his shoulders.

"It's the judge." He grabbed her hand, gripping it tight. "He's gone. He's dead. Mother said he was sitting in his chair, reading the newspaper, and that was it. She thought he was napping. But he never woke up." His words came out like a burst of hiccups.

"Oh, Arthur. I'm so sorry." She leaned in and helped him to his feet, wrapping the towel closer about his body.

"What am I supposed to do now?" he asked, weeping, stepping out of the tub, his fingertips pruned, his arms and legs covered in gooseflesh. "He died thinking I was nothing but a loser."

"Shssh."

"He thought I was lazy and weak."

"Come on now, don't think like that."

But he couldn't stop himself. "I never once stood up to that son of a bitch and now I never can. What am I supposed to do? I was supposed to prove something to him. I just needed a little more time. I was going to make him proud. I just needed time." His legs began to buckle as he sobbed harder and sank to the floor.

Delia sat with him on the wet marble floor and held him while he cried.

Throughout the wake and the funeral, she never left his side.

Arthur was haunted by all the unfinished, unresolved matters with the judge. Delia knew that, and as the weeks and months passed, he continued to grieve and struggle with a loss that was still as raw as the day he'd received the news. She feared for him, knowing that he could never win the approval he so desperately needed. He felt frustrated, angry and cheated out of the chance to set the record straight with his father.

One evening, about six months after the judge's passing, Delia heard a commotion coming from the drawing room. Arthur was in there with Paxton, and as she drew closer to the door, she overheard the two of them arguing.

"You're fooling yourself, Paxton. It'll never work. I know it won't. No one knows that better than I."

"But I have to try."

"Why? Why, when you know it won't do any good? Why are you torturing yourself like this? Why are you torturing me?"

"Maybe I'm not like you. Did you ever think of that? I have a child now. He's getting older. I can't go on living two separate lives."

Delia always feared that something like this would happen, that Paxton would leave Arthur for a more conventional, acceptable way to conduct himself. She drew a sharp breath and prayed that she was wrong. Given everything he was going through with the judge, she didn't think he could bear losing Paxton now, too.

". . . It'll never work and you know it," said Arthur.

Delia couldn't bring herself to interrupt them and instead she went to the sitting room down the hall and distracted herself with a book. One chapter in, she started to doze off. It was half past ten when Williams appeared in the doorway and announced that Mr. Field had arrived.

Delia met him in the foyer. It had snowed quite a bit in the few hours since she'd been outside and Marsh stood in the foyer shaking the flakes off his coat and hat before Williams hung them up. The house smelled faintly of cigar smoke and they heard mumblings coming from the drawing room down the hall.

"Is Mr. Lowry still here?" she asked Williams with surprise.

"Yes, ma'am."

"They were having an argument earlier," she explained to Marsh. "They've been in there for hours."

Delia and Marsh were starting down the hall to the sitting room when they heard a loud crash coming from the drawing room and raced down the hall.

Delia heard Paxton shouting at Arthur. "Just calm down! You're acting like a madman."

"Maybe I am a madman!" Arthur shouted back. She could tell by the sound of their voices that they were drunk. "Did you ever think I just might be mad after all?"

A moment later the drawing room door flew open, and from the hallway, Delia saw the buffalo head once mounted above the fireplace lying on the floor.

"Arthur?" Delia called to him. "Arthur, what happened?"

He brushed past her, leaning on his cane.

Marsh reached for his arm. "Are you all right?"

Arthur shrugged him away and kept walking down the hall.

Delia and Marsh stepped inside the drawing room, where Paxton sat on the sofa, cradling his head in his hands. Next to the buffalo head, a table had been overturned and her Émile Gallé vase lay shattered on the carpet, flowers scattered everywhere.

"Talk some sense into him, would you, please?" When Paxton looked up at them, Delia saw a bright red welt on his cheek.

Delia excused Williams, and after he'd closed the door behind him, she turned to Paxton. "What on earth is going on?"

"He's got to understand. I have a child. He can't be jealous of a child. Penelope, yes, but of a child?"

"I'll talk to him. I'll—"

"Mr. Caton, sir—" They heard Williams cry out from the hallway. "Oh, my God, no!" Williams's voice turned sharp with panic. "Mr. Caton—"

Arthur burst back into the drawing room with a crazed look in his eye, swinging his cane in one hand and a revolver in the other. Paxton jumped up from the divan. Delia and Marsh froze in place. Arthur waved the gun in their direction and Delia shrieked, grabbing hold of Marsh.

"Arthur, please . . ." Marsh started toward him.

"Don't!" Arthur swerved on his cane, raising the revolver, aiming it at Marsh. "Don't. You. Move."

Marsh raised his hands in surrender.

Delia's legs turned weak. Stars swam before her eyes as if she was about to faint. She could smell the scotch coming off Arthur and it made her almost vomit. He was swaying, turning on his heels, moving the gun from Marsh to Delia and then to Paxton, who was plastered up against the wall, his arms stretched out to his sides. He seemed unable to move.

"Arthur, be reasonable," said Marsh. "This won't solve anything."

Arthur staggered closer to Marsh, the gun steady in his hand. "Shut up! Shut up, goddammit!" He inched the barrel closer.

Delia's heart nearly stopped. "Arthur, please, I beg of you, put the gun down."

Arthur shifted the revolver back on Delia. She was barely

able to breathe. Her whole body trembled. She could hear her heart beating up inside her head. She didn't recognize this man before her and she was terrified.

Arthur turned to Paxton. "You're a coward. Nothing but a coward." He slurred his words as sweat trickled down his face. Arthur began to shake as he took turns pointing the barrel at Paxton and then Marsh and Delia. His grip floundered as if the gun were suddenly too heavy for him. His eyes began filling with tears.

"It's okay," said Marsh, again trying to reason with him. But that only seemed to agitate him more.

Arthur thrust the gun even closer to Marsh and put his finger on the trigger. Just when Delia thought he'd shoot, Arthur let out an agonizing cry and turned the gun on himself, aiming it at his temple.

"Arthur, no!" Delia shrieked as Marsh lunged toward him and wrestled him to the ground, knocking over a chair. Delia jumped out of the way just as she heard the gun go off.

No one was killed. Or even injured. The bookshelf took the brunt of the punishment that day in the drawing room, and then of course, so did Arthur. Poor Arthur.

Immediately after the gun went off, Marsh kept Arthur pinned to the floor while Paxton secured the gun. Delia stood in the corner, stunned by what she was seeing, what she was hearing. Arthur howled like a wild beast, kicking and clawing at Marsh's back, trying to get free. His face went red as the veins in his neck stood out, pulsing.

It seemed to go on endlessly. Arthur was tireless in his struggle, forcing Paxton to take over for Marsh and hold him down until, finally, Arthur began to tremble and cried out in one long agonizing growl that shattered into tears. Delia had never seen him like that before. He was losing his mind right before their eyes. She was terrified of being near him. She couldn't bear to look at him that way. Paxton still had Arthur pinned down in the drawing room while Marsh led her out into the hall.

"We need to get him help. He can't stay here. It's not safe for you. Or him."

Later on she would hardly remember making the telephone call, but within an hour, the ambulance arrived. By then the three of them had managed to calm Arthur down. He sat in a chair in the library, all the rage drained out of him and the glazed look gone from his eyes. Seeing him restored to the Arthur she knew made her think they'd all just overreacted. Yes, he'd brought a gun into the drawing room, but anyone who knew Arthur—sweet, gentle Arthur—knew he never would have used it. She told herself all this and more, fearing that she'd made a terrible mistake, especially when she saw the alarm take hold of his face when the men arrived in their hospital whites, carrying a stretcher.

"Who are these people? Who are you!" Arthur jumped out of his chair and began to back away from them, crying, "Don't let them take me away, Dell. Don't let them."

When the one man reached for his arm, Arthur took a swing at him while the other attendant wrestled him to the ground. The first man pulled out a syringe and injected him straight through his trousers. Moments later all the muscles in Arthur's body seemed to soften and he became as docile as a baby. They moved him onto a stretcher and restrained his arms and legs in case the sedative wore off.

BOOK THREE

1900–1906

CHAPTER FORTY-ONE

1900

Arthur had been in the asylum in Batavia for three months, and during that time, Delia grappled with every possible emotion. After struggling through the sadness, the anger and the guilt, she emerged with a sense of fearlessness. She accepted that there was little she could do for Arthur, but the time had come to take charge of her own life. She had begun doing this at the world's fair when Marsh was her dance partner, but now she was about to take an even bolder step.

Abby and Augustus were hosting a party that Saturday evening at the Palmer House Hotel. It was in honor of nineteen-year-old Catherine's debut party and Delia decided she would arrive on the arm of Marshall Field. After all, she was paying for the party. She could damn well do as she pleased.

When they arrived, Delia saw Catherine posing for a photograph with her parents. She was a beautiful girl with her mother's blond coloring and large blue eyes. Abby and Augustus smiled as they stood on either side of their daughter, looking proud and regal. For this Delia was grateful. While her father would have been sick over Abby's losing her inheritance, he would have been pleased to see that Delia had stood by her sister.

"Aunt Dell," Spencer said, coming up to give her a hug and shake Marsh's hand. He had a girl on his arm. "I'd like you to meet Miss Lurline Spreckels."

"Charmed," said Delia. "I've heard so much about you." And she had. This was the young lady that Spencer had been courting for the past few months. Abby didn't care for her, though Delia couldn't see why. She was extremely pretty with soft brown hair and wistful eyes. She came from a well-to-do family in San Francisco, the daughter of a sugarcane mogul, and she appeared just as sweet as the product her family produced. Delia suspected Abby wouldn't deem anyone good enough for her children. She'd already rejected several of Spencer's previous girlfriends and more than one of Catherine's suitors, too.

Delia was still talking with Spencer and Lurline when she noticed Paxton and Penelope entering the ballroom. Delia couldn't look at the two of them without thinking about Arthur. Poor Arthur.

Marsh must have known this, for he came up to her and whispered, "Don't think about it. You know he's best off where he is right now."

Delia looked up and nodded.

"Come," he said, holding out his hand. "Dance with me."

Without another word, he led her onto the dance floor. As the music took hold, they waltzed together in the way that lovers did, knowing each other's bodies, anticipating each other's moves. Delia was very much aware of Malvina Armour and Frances Glessner standing off to the side watching her. They weren't snickering, though. They weren't pointing and whispering, either. She feared that everyone would think, *How dare she abandon her sick husband and shamelessly step out in public with another man whose wife just died!* But instead Delia sensed that they were on her side. Ever since her work on the Board of Lady Managers, she had managed to rise above the gossip and the scandal. And so, Delia danced with her man for all to see. *To hell with everyone,* she said to herself. *I'm Marshall Field's mistress and at last I'm going to own it.*

Three days later Delia tried to distract herself, still thinking about Catherine's party as she stood in the hallway of the asylum. The glaring electric lights and an antiseptic smell permeated the corridor. The atmosphere of the place was something she'd never get used to. She drew a deep breath and braced herself for her weekly visit with Arthur.

She found him sitting in the main room staring out a window covered in chicken wire. He'd lost weight, and the hollows of his cheeks were sunk in. Placing her hand on his shoulder, she bent down to kiss his cheek.

He looked at her and smiled weakly. "Say, it's good to see you. Thanks for coming by."

Delia reached for a nearby chair and pulled it up close to him. "How are you feeling?"

"I'm fine." He forced a smile. "Is Paxton here with you?"

This was the question she dreaded the most. The question he always asked. A stab of pity pinched her heart as she shook her head.

"Will you tell him I asked about him? He hasn't returned any of my letters."

She couldn't bring herself to tell Arthur that Paxton destroyed them all. "I can't have his letters lying around," Paxton had said. "What if Penelope saw them? I can't be part of his life anymore. Not after what happened that night."

Delia understood. She couldn't exactly blame Paxton. But still, she knew how much Arthur needed him now. "Marsh is going to come by and see you this weekend," she said, hoping to change the subject.

"When you see him—Paxton, that is—tell him to come see me."

Delia tried again to change the subject and asked about his mother and sisters. "Did they come by this week?"

Arthur nodded and turned quiet for a moment and lowered his head. "Have they said anything to you about Paxton?"

Delia shook her head. No matter how hard she tried, Arthur kept driving the conversation back to Paxton, as he always did when she visited him. She knew Arthur was fixated on him and that it was a sign of his illness. She sat with Arthur for another hour, but it felt more like three. For two people who'd never run out of conversation, it seemed now there was nothing for them to talk about other than Paxton. Before she left him, Delia leaned over to kiss his forehead and hugged him close.

She left him in the sitting room and hurried toward the train depot, reminding herself that Arthur could have killed Paxton that day in the drawing room. He could have killed her and Marsh, too. And possibly himself. He needed to be in that asylum, as god-awful as it was.

Later that evening Abby stopped by to see Delia. She was instantly alarmed when her sister stepped into the parlor. Abby looked tired, her skin pale and her eyes shadowed by the dark circles underneath them.

"Abby, darling, what's wrong? Come." She rang for Williams, asking for tea.

"I'm sorry to be calling on you so late," she said. "I'm sure you must be exhausted from seeing Arthur."

"You know my door is always open to you. Day or night."

"Well, as a matter of fact, that's exactly what I wanted to talk to you about. You know the neighborhood where we are has taken a turn lately. There's just so much crime these days. Even Augustus is concerned." Abby chewed on her lower lip. "I just don't think it's safe for us there anymore. Especially not for Catherine . . ."

Abby was going on and on and Delia hated to see her sister like this. Yes, the neighborhood at Sixteenth and Michigan had waned in recent years, but they both knew it wasn't the crime that was the problem. It was that Augustus was in danger of losing the house.

"Abby," she said with a compassionate smile, "would you like to all stay here?"

"Oh, Dell," she gasped as if she'd been holding her breath. "Could we? It would just be until we find a suitable—"

Delia raised her hand to stop her. "It's me, remember? I know. You're all welcome to stay. You can tell people whatever you like, but you don't have to pretend with me."

Abby began to cry. "But I can't let Catherine know. Or Spencer. Even though he doesn't live at home anymore, he still can't know."

"I understand." Catherine and Spencer had both been so protected, so sheltered from their parents' realities. Especially Catherine. Though she was an Eddy, Abby and Delia had raised her like a Spencer girl. She had no knowledge of her father's financial problems. She moved through society with the entitled edge of a socialite and Delia wasn't about to shatter that illusion. Catherine was their only hope, according to Abby. She had told Delia how she feared Spencer would marry Lurline, and despite her father's money, Abby didn't feel Lurline had the proper breeding. "She may be rich, but she's lacking the grace and elegance that Spencer deserves," Abby had said on many occasions. That placed all the Eddys' expectations on Catherine marrying well and preserving the family name.

Though preserving the family name had now fallen on Delia's shoulders and the next day she instructed her staff to make room for the Eddys, Delia truly didn't mind. Aside from the fact that her home was plenty large enough for them all, she was, for all intents and purposes, living at the Field mansion with Marsh.

That evening, when the Eddys arrived, Delia had dinner with them and stayed until Marsh picked her up on his way home from work. After she said her good-nights to her sister, brother-in-law and niece, she and Marsh went around the corner to Prairie Avenue.

As Delia stepped inside the Field mansion, she was greeted as if she'd entered her own home. The servants regarded her as the lady of the house. Therese would now be traveling between both houses, since she would be tending to Abby as well as Delia.

Delia went upstairs to the master bedroom, which she now shared with Marsh. After changing into her wrapper, she sat at the dressing table and unpinned her hair, letting it spill onto her shoulders and fall down to the center of her back. In the mirror she looked at her reflection, and except for a few soft lines around her eyes and a strand or two of gray hair, her appearance hadn't changed much through the years. But oh, on the inside, she felt very different from the young girl who met Marsh the night of the Great Fire. All the hardships, the struggles and loss had forged her, making her tougher, stronger, able to withstand more. She brought a hand to her cheek and dragged her fingertips over her jaw and down her neck, grateful that the hardness didn't show on her face.

She sat back and gazed around the bedroom. It was a deeply masculine room with a four-poster mahogany bed, a marble-topped commode, heavy red velvet drapes and a thick Persian carpet. Delia had added her own touches, insisting on a vase of fresh flowers, decorative pillows and a picture of the two of them taken years ago at the Columbian Exposition ball. For her, the room was theirs now.

She got up and gazed out the window. Instead of facing her own house on Calumet, she saw the lot next door, already under construction. Marsh had purchased it for Junior and Albertine and the boys. They had two sons, Marshall III and Henry, and now that Nannie was gone, they had decided to return to Chicago.

Delia knew, despite trying to tell him otherwise, that Marsh expected Junior to come work with him at the store. She could almost hear the arguments now. She also worried about what this move would do to Marsh's relationship with Ethel. Ethel had divorced Arthur Tree and then just three months later married her lover, David Beatty, the Royal Navy officer whom Marsh had taken to calling Jack the Sailor. Marsh hadn't spoken to her since. Why Marsh disapproved of David was a mystery to Delia. Perhaps he feared that Ethel was leaving one bad marriage and entering impulsively into another. Delia did know, however, that Ethel would be infuriated when she found out her father had built a home for Junior. She felt he played favorites as it was.

Delia removed her wrapper and climbed into bed, waiting for Marsh to finish working downstairs in the library. He had such hopes for his children and yet he couldn't see his own hand in their failures. He'd spoiled them, made their lives too easy, robbing them of a sense of appreciation or accomplishment. Marsh had tried to give them everything, and in doing so he had taken something from them that was far more valuable. He was so bright and yet Marsh couldn't see that he had become the very reason that his children were destined to fall short of his expectations.

CHAPTER FORTY-TWO

Delia stared out the chicken-wired windows while she waited for the attendants to get Arthur. It was foggy and all she could see was a blur of green in the courtyard. Four months before, when they'd admitted Arthur to the asylum in Batavia, the trees had been bare, their branches etched in snow. Now it was spring and the weather called for rain.

It was on that dreary afternoon that Arthur walked out to greet her without his cane. "Look at me," he said, doing a jaunty dip, arms out to his side. "Good as new."

"Oh, Arthur." She hugged him close and pressed her cheek to his. "I'm so proud of you."

"Did I tell you about this new exercise routine they put me on? I'm up to a hundred push-ups a day now and two hundred sit-ups. Haven't been in this kind of shape since I was in law school," he said, patting his taut stomach. "Not bad for forty-eight, huh?"

"Not bad at all," she said.

They'd just settled into the stiff chairs in the corner when Arthur asked about Paxton. "Have you seen him lately?"

"Not since Catherine's party."

"Oh. I see." His shoulders dropped and for a moment he just stared at the chicken wire.

"Junior and Albertine will be back in town in just a few weeks. Marsh is almost finished with the construction on the new house for them. I know they'll want to come see you."

"Not here," he said, shaking his head. "I don't want them to see me in here." He turned quiet and somber after that. "Funny, isn't it, that I'd let Paxton see me like this but not them? Remember how I was afraid to let Paxton see me after I had my accident. So afraid that he wouldn't love me as a cripple, and here I am"—he looked around—"in this place and all I want is to see him. Paxton, that is. Not the children."

"I understand. So, then you'll go see them when you're well and they're in the new house."

He nodded and held out his hands, studying the veins running under the skin like rivers on a map.

She reached over and tugged his sleeve. "I bet you'll be back home before the summer. Won't that be nice?"

He nodded and dragged a hand over his face. "Did I tell you we started up a nightly poker game here? We don't play for money, of course. There's a fellow here named Stroker. Used to be a banker. Tried to commit suicide after his son died. And my buddy Henry down the hall, he's an accountant. His father was just like the judge," he said with a gentle laugh.

"Arthur," she said, now holding on to his hands. "Why are you changing the subject? Don't you want to come home?"

He looked at her and pursed his lips. "If I come home, what do I have to look forward to? Tell me, what do I have to come home to?"

"You have me. You have Marsh."

"And you have each other. I have no one. No one just for me. At least I fit in here. We're all in the same boat."

That thought stayed with Delia long after she'd said goodbye to Arthur. And later that night, as she lay awake next to Marsh watching him sleep, all she could think was that Arthur didn't want to come home. He was going to let life pass him by. What a sad and sorry shame and there was nothing she could do about it. And to think she thought he'd been wasting his potential before.

In the morning she went back to the house on Calumet to have breakfast with Abby and Catherine. Augustus had already left for the day to try and find work. The three of them were just sitting down to coffee when Williams announced a visitor.

Delia excused herself and went into the parlor, where she found Paxton waiting for her. The sunlight coming in from the windows showed the first hints of gray around his temples. He saw Delia and stood up, rushing over to embrace her.

"I don't believe I've ever seen you up this early," Delia said, keeping her arms to her side. Even though she understood Paxton's predicament, she couldn't help but be annoyed by the way he'd turned his back on Arthur.

"I had to come see you, Dell. I keep having this terrible recurring dream about Arthur."

"Perhaps that's just your guilty conscience."

"I have nothing to feel guilty about."

"Oh no? He asks about you every time I'm there. He writes to you every week, sometimes twice a week. It's been four months and you haven't gone to see him once."

"You don't understand. I'm married. I have a child. It isn't natural."

"It isn't natural to go visit your friend who's been unwell?"

Paxton dropped his head to his hands. "I'm torn, Dell. I don't know what to do. I miss him. I do. But he's not himself anymore. Even you've told me that."

"But he's getting better. Much better and he needs you right now. Can't you at least still be his friend? He needs something to live for."

Paxton shook his head and ran his fingers back through his hair. She could see the battle going on inside him. He truly was torn. "All right." He swallowed hard and looked at Delia with tears in his eyes. "Take me to him."

Later that week, Paxton and Delia went to the asylum. Delia spotted Arthur in the sitting room and Paxton stood back while she went to speak with him. He brightened as soon as he saw her.

She hugged him and kissed him on the cheek, and after exchanging a few pleasantries, she said, "I have a surprise for you. Someone's here to see you."

Arthur craned his neck, and when Paxton came around the corner, his eyes grew wide and instantly glassy. "You came," he said. His voice was breathy and light, almost like a whisper.

Paxton hung his head, unable to look at Arthur. Delia inhaled sharply, worried that this had been a terrible mistake. Should he raise his head, Delia feared that Arthur would see only pity reflected in Paxton's eyes. He felt sorry for Arthur. She was sure that's what it was. But then Paxton took a step forward and then another before he broke out in a jog and rushed to Arthur's side, barely able to speak as the two embraced. It didn't take long before all three of them had tears running down their faces.

Delia left the two men alone and went to see Arthur's doctor at the opposite end of the corridor.

"We're very encouraged," said Dr. Brooks. "Your husband is making significant improvement, Mrs. Caton."

"Yes, I can see."

"Outside of any setbacks—which we don't anticipate," Dr. Brooks continued, "we see no reason why we would not be able to release Mr. Caton sometime within the next few weeks."

"That's wonderful." She clasped her hands together. "Have you told him yet?"

"We thought perhaps you'd like to tell him the good news yourself."

Delia left the doctor's office and went back down to the sitting room. Arthur and Paxton were seated across from each other, talking and laughing. It was the happiest she'd seen him in months. She could hardly wait to tell him that he would be coming home soon.

"Arthur," she said, taking the empty seat next to him, "they're going to release you. Within a few weeks."

"That's fantastic," said Paxton, clasping his hands. "Let's get you out of this godforsaken place and back home where you belong."

Arthur studied the backs of his hands.

"Well, say something." Delia reached over and jiggled his knee. "What's wrong? I thought you would be happy. You can come home soon."

Arthur twisted up his mouth and shook his head. "I don't know. . . ."

"What don't you know?" asked Paxton.

"Maybe I'm not ready to go home. I have a routine in here. I have people in here who know what I've been through."

"But you have people back home who love you," said Delia.

"But I don't know how to be out there." He gestured with his chin toward the chicken-wired windows. "I'm scared. What if it happens again? I lost my mind inside that house. What if something else happens and I can't control myself?"

"No, no," Delia said, squeezing his hand and swallowing

hard. She knew what he was saying. He'd been trying to tell her for weeks. The truth was that he felt safe inside the asylum, but she had hoped seeing Paxton would get him past his fears. It was too awful for her to imagine that he preferred his life behind chicken wire to the life they'd had together, with or without Paxton. She wanted to take away his doubt, to protect him and make him feel safe. "You mustn't think like that," she said. "The doctors wouldn't be releasing you if they thought you weren't ready."

"And you'll see," added Paxton, "things will be different this time."

"That's what I'm afraid of," said Arthur. "It won't be the same. Nothing will be the same ever again."

Paxton looked at him and said, "Maybe the way things were before was part of the problem."

Six weeks later, at the start of July, Arthur returned home to Calumet Avenue. Many things had changed in the six months that he'd been away and Delia had tried to prepare him as best she could.

"You're sure you don't mind having Abby, Augustus and Catherine here?" Delia asked the first morning he was home. She was sitting on a stool in his bathroom watching while he shaved. As a child she used to sit that way, with her feet on the rungs of a step stool watching her father shave.

"I told you I don't mind. It's nice to have the company," he said, soaping up his shaving brush and spreading the lather across his cheeks and neck.

"You're sure, now, because if you want I can make other—"

"Dell"—he exchanged his soap brush for the straight blade—"it's fine. I'm okay. Honestly, I am."

"Well, then," she said, setting her elbows on her knees, "what would you like to do today? We could go visit Junior and Albertine. Their new house is lovely. Or we could go to Washington Park. Or if you'd like we could go to—"

"Dell, please. You don't have to babysit me. I'm fine. I'm going to go to the stable, maybe go for a ride. I've missed my horses. I'll be fine. Don't worry."

But how could she not worry? She'd tried so hard to prepare Arthur for coming home, but no one had prepared her. She was relieved about never having to step foot inside that asylum again, but now that he was home, she felt an enormous responsibility to keep him well. The asylum was safe for him. All the sharp objects were hidden, but here, back home Delia feared a million things that could harm him, an insensitive comment, a bottle of brandy, a poor night's sleep. Not wanting to leave him alone, she explained to Marsh that for now it was better if she slept in her old room on Calumet. She talked with the servants and with Abby and Augustus, asking them to keep an eye on him. She hated to admit that it had been easier when he was away. Now the responsibility was all on her.

In the days and weeks ahead she was forever asking Junior and Marsh to invite Arthur out with them and she was relieved whenever Paxton turned up for a hand of cards or a game of chess. Every morning she observed as Arthur adhered to a strict daily routine, rising at six and doing calisthenics before breakfast, then he'd visit his stable and groom his horses.

Things gradually returned to normal or as close to normal as they could be. After about a month, Delia returned to Marsh's bed and by October the three of them, Arthur, Delia and Marsh, began going to plays and out to dinners again. On quiet evenings Arthur and Augustus played cards or read aloud to each other. At the start of December, Delia, Marsh and Arthur attended the Swift holiday pageant and as Delia watched Arthur guardedly mingling with old friends, clumsily fielding questions about his state of mind, she realized that it was a big, cold world out there and that she could only protect him so much.

Toward the end of year, in between Christmas and New Year's, Arthur went down to Ottawa and even took Paxton with him. Delia took that as a sign that it was all right for her to get on with her life.

CHAPTER FORTY-THREE

1902

On May 6, 1902, Delia found herself surrounded by hushed voices, solemn faces and muffled tears. She had already buried her parents and her father-in-law and now she was burying her friend's husband. She looked at Bertha, stoic as ever, surrounded by her grown sons, Honoré and Potter Jr., while Potter lay in state.

The funeral services, held two days after he'd passed, were at the Palmers' home, which they referred to as their castle. Bertha and Potter had transformed that plot of swampland into the most enviable address in the city. Even more enviable than Prairie Avenue. Between Potter's money and Bertha's flair for spending it, they had established a neighborhood that people now called the Gold Coast. The home Potter built for Bertha overlooked Lake Michigan. It was the largest residence in Chicago and certainly the most elaborate.

Everywhere Delia looked she saw more flowers, enormous wreaths and oversize arrangements. She and Marsh stood off to the side with Arthur, Paxton and Penelope while mourners waited in a line that reached down the grand staircase, to the first floor and out the front door.

That night Delia followed Marsh upstairs to their bedroom. It had been a long, emotional day and they were both exhausted. The staircase had never seemed so steep and her legs ached when she reached the top.

"At a time like this," Marsh said as he unfastened his cuff links, "I can't help but be reminded of my own mortality."

Marsh's mortality. That was all Delia had been able to think about since Potter passed. It was the curse of loving an older man. She watched as he undressed, aware of how his body had changed through the years. His once lean, hard build had grown slack, with a slight paunch around his middle. His thick head of white hair was thinning in the back. The third toe on his left foot had grown crooked and now overlapped the one next to it. Recently he'd begun to suffer from indigestion if they ate rich foods too late at night. Yet, his was the body she wanted, the one she had loved through all its changes just as he had loved hers. He was sixty-seven, she was forty-seven, and oddly, it wasn't until Potter died that she thought of Marsh as someone twenty years her senior.

Marsh pulled back the covers and climbed into bed. "Once I'm dead and gone," he said, "what will be left of me?"

"Oh, Marsh, don't talk like that." Delia slid beneath the sheets and turned off the lamp on her night table.

"It's a fair question," he said. "Comes a time in every man's life when he has to evaluate what he's done. What he hasn't done. Yes, I built a business, but now I have no one to leave it to. I'll be damned if I'm going to keep begging Junior to come work for me. I guess it just goes to show that I haven't been much of a father. I've worked my whole life to build this business and my son—my only son—wants nothing to do with it."

"But that doesn't mean he doesn't want you. Junior's living right next door now," she said, rolling onto her side. His face was half-lit by his bedside lamp. She noticed how his jaw slacked and the wrinkles that now ringed his neck. "You never go over there. And Albertine's pregnant again. I would think you'd want to spend time with them. Junior is right there, just waiting for you."

"But he doesn't want what I have to offer."

"You have more to offer your son than just your store."

"And what about Ethel?" he said, as if he hadn't heard her. "She married that damn sailor."

"He was a Royal Naval officer," Delia corrected him.

"Makes no damn difference to me. He's still a sailor as far as I'm concerned."

"And your daughter loves him very much. It's no different than how you felt about me—only she was in a position to marry him. If anyone should understand, I would think it would be you."

"And how can I possibly tell her I understand? She isn't speaking to me now."

"Write to her. You have to be the bigger person here. You're the father."

He reached up and turned off the light by his side of the bed. Delia knew he didn't want to talk about it anymore. He was just as stubborn as Ethel. He went silent and Delia looked for him in the dark, waiting for him to come into focus while her eyes adjusted. She felt afraid just then. She didn't want to lose him. Not ever. Delia lay awake that night long after Marsh had fallen asleep. She stared over at her aging love, watching the top sheet rise and fall, so aware of his every breath.

After Potter died, Marsh began making changes in his life, especially where his children and grandchildren were concerned.

Much to Delia's surprise, he sat down and wrote Ethel a letter. And then another one, and another one after that. It had been over a month now and he was still waiting, checking the post every day, for her reply.

And then there was Junior and his family. Albertine had just given birth to his first and only granddaughter, Gwendolin. She was three months old and Marsh doted on her, always hoisting her up in his arms, bouncing her on his knee. "Every time I see this little one," he'd said one day, "she changes." Setting her back in her bassinet, he turned to Delia and Albertine and said, "I don't even remember Junior and Ethel being this age." Delia detected the sadness in his voice. His grandsons were growing up fast, too. Marshall III was eleven already and Henry was nine.

"Come here," Marsh said to Henry, grabbing hold of the boy's chin. "Let me have a look at that tooth."

Henry opened wide, giving him an "awwww" while Marsh wiggled the tooth.

"She's ready to come out," Marsh said.

"Noooo, Grandpa. Not yet," Henry protested, and Marsh laughed.

The following Sunday Delia invited the whole family, including Arthur, over for supper. She and Albertine sat together on the sofa waiting for dinner to be served. They were watching Marsh, lying on the floor, on his stomach, propped up on his elbows, playing marbles with Marshall III.

"Would you look at them?" said Albertine. "Do you know that last night he stopped by after he left the store just to read Gwendolin a bedtime story? And then he went into Henry's room and put a fifty-cent piece under his pillow. He said to tell Henry that the tooth fairy had been there."

"Can you imagine that?" said Junior, coming over to join them. "My father the tooth fairy." He shook his head in amazement and laughed. "I don't think he ever played a game of marbles with me or read me a story."

"I'd say he's just making up for lost years," said Delia.

And it was true. Marsh did the things with his grandchildren that he'd done with his father and older brothers back on the farm in Massachusetts. He hiked and fished and went horseback riding with Junior and Marshall III. For the first time in his life, Marshall Field was becoming a family man.

"We've never seen him like this," Albertine said, hoisting the baby up in her arms.

"I just hope he's happy," said Delia.

"He's a Field," said Albertine with a knowing glance. "Are any of them ever really happy? But," she said with a smile, "if anyone can make him happy, it's you."

Delia blinked back her tears as she reached over, patting the baby's back. Unlike Ethel, Junior and Albertine had accepted Delia as the woman in Marsh's life. They never questioned the nature of Delia's marriage, though she was certain they found it perplexing.

What they did question, however, was why Abby, Augustus and Catherine were still living at Delia's home.

"Surely they could have found a home or built a new one by now," said Junior, turning to his uncle Arthur. "Don't you find it odd that they've stayed on? Even Spencer thinks it's strange. He can't for the life of him understand why."

"They're not in my way," said Arthur.

"But that's not the point," Junior persisted. "Why are they *still* living at the house on Calumet?"

"They've been talking about buying a town house in Washington, D.C.," said Delia. It came out a bit more defensively than she intended, but at least that seemed to settle it. Delia of course would be the one purchasing the town house out of her own inheritance, and she was doing it so that Abby could be closer to her children. She wanted to keep an eye on Spencer, who worked in D.C., and on Catherine, who, on the pretense of seeing her brother, made frequent trips to the capital in order to see Senator Albert Beveridge. He'd been courting Catherine for several months and Abby disapproved.

After the children and Arthur left for the night, Marsh came up behind Delia and put his arms around her. "We're going to do more of this," he said. "Birthdays, holidays, anniversaries—I want us all to celebrate them together. And I want to spend more time with you, too. We'll travel. Go see the world."

She leaned into his chest and reached up to stroke his face. "And what about the store?"

"Shedd and Selfridge are more than capable of running the day-to-day duties."

"Really?" She did a quarter turn, looking into his blue gray eyes. "My goodness, you're serious."

"I am. It's time for me to pass the baton. I would have liked to hand it over to Junior, but for now it will go to John Shedd."

"You're going to make John the new president of Marshall Field's?"

"I didn't say that. I'm still president, but John will be running things from now on. So like it or not, I'll be spending more time with you these days."

About a month after they had that conversation, Delia could sense that Marsh was growing restless. He'd already shown the boys how to clean their hunting rifles, how to bait their fishing lines. Now he was looking for the next project, the next challenge. After nearly fifty years of running his store, overseeing hundreds of departments and supervisors and thousands of employees, cutting back on his work schedule quickly went from liberating to outright befuddling.

Delia observed him struggling to fill his days. He read newspapers front to back including the obituaries of people he'd never known. At half past ten he started talking about lunch. At four in the afternoon he was thinking about dinner. He became overly involved in the affairs of the house, even holding meetings with the butler and head housekeeper, looking for ways they could be more efficient. He was forever in search of the next thing to cross off his list. Accomplishment was what fueled him. Ordinary life didn't suit him. Leisure was an enigma.

It was during Henry's tenth birthday party that Delia knew Marsh couldn't sustain this unstructured, unproductive way of life. She noticed he stifled yawns while the children played party games and stole glances at his pocket watch when they brought out the cake. While opening the presents, he leaned over and whispered, "I'm just going to step outside for a little air."

"Are you unwell?" Delia asked.

"I'm fine. Just going to take a little walk is all."

By three o'clock the party was over. The servants were stacking up plates and presents, pulling down streamers and balloons. Marsh still hadn't returned, so Delia went to find him. She knew exactly where to look, too.

Ever since he'd handed the controls over to John Shedd, he was afraid that something would go terribly wrong. She suspected that he'd snuck out of the party to go down to the store. And she was right. When she entered Marshall Field & Company, she found him on the main floor berating Harry Selfridge and another clerk for moving a display of evening gloves.

"I want these put back where they were immediately. And just because I'm not here every minute of the day, don't you dare forget whose name is on the door."

"My name should be on that door, too," Harry snapped back.

"I've been with Marshall Field & Company for twenty-four years now and I deserve to have my name on the door."

Marsh looked at him, his jaw twitching. "You know what, Selfridge, I think you're absolutely right. It's high time you had your name on the door. Someone *else's* door. Now get your things and get out."

Delia watched Harry storm off in one direction while Marsh took off out the front door. She caught up to him at Washington and State. "Was that really necessary?" she asked. "Harry's been with you a long time."

"I don't need Harry. It's still my store."

"Of course it's still your store." She stopped and reached for his arm, making him turn toward her. "What's really bothering you?" she asked.

He looked up and down State Street and his brilliant eyes came close to clouding over with tears.

"Marsh? My goodness—what is it?"

He shook his head and then raised his chin. "I'm scared, Dell. I don't want this to be the end. I'm not finished yet."

She slipped her arms in the opening of his coat and pulled him close. He was gripped with fear. She could see it on his face. Her own eyes filled with tears as she tried to reassure him. "It's not the end, you hear me. This is not the end."

He dropped his head to her shoulder and drew a deep breath. "I still have ideas and plans. I still have dreams. I still have things to do. I have to make my mark."

"You have made your mark. Look around here, Marsh. You turned State Street into the Ladies' Half Mile. You created a palace of a store—nothing like it existed before, and now others have copied you in New York, in Boston. You even created the Loop. You made Chicago what it is. None of that would have happened without you. And you're not done yet. I know you aren't."

"Then what now?" Marsh pulled back from her, raised his hands and let them drop to his sides. "I'm not a young man anymore. My friends are dying, and goddammit, I want my last hurrah. I don't want to be written off just yet."

She studied his face, his eyes, the pulsing of his temples. The answer was so simple. She reached up and stroked his face. "Go. Go back to work. Full-time."

He looked at her, puzzled. "But we were going to travel and spend more time together. Isn't that what you want?"

"I mean it. You're no good to me this way. Go back to work. It's what you love. It's what you do. It's who you are."

He nodded, kissed her cheek and turned around and went back into Marshall Field & Company. He worked until ten o'clock that night and was back in the store by seven the next morning.

Soon he was back to working twelve- and fourteen-hour days. He worked through his grandsons' baseball games and track meets and Delia wasn't surprised. As much as he tried to be a family man, it was a lie. He would always be who he truly was: the Merchant Prince.

CHAPTER FORTY-FOUR

1905

Delia was back at the house on Calumet Avenue to get a necklace from her jewelry box when she heard the horn blast. Rushing to the bedroom window, she gazed out and saw that Paxton had just pulled up in his new motorcar. It had a gleaming white body with red leather interior and a wooden steering device.

"But I don't need to go for a ride in that contraption," she heard Arthur saying as she came down the stairs. "I'll take my coach over that iron horse any day."

"You're jealous," said Paxton. "Just admit it."

"Please," said Arthur. "I'm not even going to dignify that with a response."

"What's all the commotion about?" asked Delia as she joined the men in the foyer.

"Arthur here is being an old stick-in-the-mud is all," said Paxton.

"Why? Because I don't want to go for a ride in that ridiculous machine of yours?"

"You're just jealous. Now come for a ride. Delia, you too."

"I don't want to ride in that thing," said Arthur.

"That *thing* is a brand-new 1905 Studebaker, I'll have you know."

Delia laughed. "You two are something else. Come," she said, looping her arms through both of theirs, "let's go have some tea."

They moved into the parlor and Delia and Arthur sipped tea while Paxton had a whiskey. The two men continued to battle over coaches versus motorcars.

"I'm telling you there's no way that heap of metal is ever going to replace the horse," said Arthur.

"I agree," said Abby as she and Catherine came in to join them.

"I don't," said Catherine, sitting on the sofa next to Delia. "Sorry, Uncle Arthur, but I do think motoring is the way of the future."

"You mean to say that you'd rather ride in that box than in my coach," said Arthur, a hand splayed over his heart.

They laughed but a few minutes later the argument between Arthur and Paxton heated up again. Delia was always struck by how competitive they were. A good horse race or a round of golf always managed to rile them up. Perhaps that was just the male ego or maybe they longed to be each other's heroes.

The following week they were at it again. The two of them were playing lawn tennis while Delia and Penelope sat in a gazebo, sipping lemonade and watching, listening to the steady *ping, ping, ping* of the ball playing off their rackets.

"It's amazing how Arthur can get around now. I mean after his accident and all."

"It still hurts him plenty, though," said Delia. "Especially when it's damp out."

Paxton let out a yelp after missing a shot.

"They're so very close, aren't they?" said Penelope. "Truly the very best of friends."

Delia nodded as she shaded her eyes and watched the two of them.

"Hardly any room for anyone else, is there?"

Delia turned around and looked at her. Penelope's eyes grew wide, pleading for reassurance or perhaps just answers.

Delia pressed her hand to her chest. They had never discussed this. She never thought they would. "They share a bond," she said finally. "They always have."

Penelope reached for her lemonade and then thought better of it and set the glass back down. "I've tried my best to be a good wife."

Delia looked at Penelope, at all the confusion and frustration on her face. It was as if she were looking into a mirror from years gone by. "I'm certain that you are a good wife."

"Obviously not good enough." Penelope twisted up her mouth and wrinkled the bridge of her nose. "All these years I've been trying to compete."

Delia shooed a fly away, stalling. She was unprepared to have this conversation. "Oh, honey," she said finally, "but you can't compete. You just can't."

"It hurts me so to know that his son and I aren't enough."

"You mustn't think like that. It's so much more complex. It's something you and I can't understand."

"Aren't you angry?"

Delia thought for a moment. "No. Not anymore."

Paxton missed another shot and leaned over, hands on his knees, trying to catch his breath.

"Oh, come on now," Arthur teased. "Don't tell me you're getting tired already. . . ."

Delia saw Penelope's eyes tearing up. That could have been her, the long-suffering wife, had it not been for Marsh. "I think in this case, in a situation like ours," said Delia, "it's perfectly fine for you to seek out your own happiness."

Penelope looked at her, stunned.

"All right," said Arthur, "your serve. Hurry it up now."

"But Paxton *is* my happiness," said Penelope. "I'll never love anyone the way I love him."

"Come on now," said Arthur. "I don't have all day. Paxton? Hey, Paxton—very funny. Cut it out."

Delia gazed over at the court. Paxton had dropped his racket, his arms flailing in the air.

"It's true, you won't," she said, turning back to Penelope. "But there are other kinds of loves in this world. Don't deny your own chance at happiness."

"Hey, Paxton," shouted Arthur. "Come on now. Paxton? Paxton! Oh my God—PAXTON!"

Penelope let out a scream and Delia turned around just as Paxton's legs buckled and he collapsed onto the lawn.

A week after Paxton's funeral, Delia was sitting with Arthur in the solarium. A shadow veiled his face and she could almost see the darkness coming from inside of him. He was still in his bathrobe in the middle of the afternoon, starting in on his second drink of the day. She didn't say a word. How could she stop him from drinking at a time like this? His world had just been shattered and there was nothing she could do to comfort him. Or herself. Delia couldn't begin to address her own feelings of grief, for she, too, had lost a dear friend.

So they sat together and stared out at the garden, watching the bees fluttering in and out of the rose blossoms, listening to the breeze rustle the sycamore leaves. Life was going on without even a pause. People died every second of every day, but this was Arthur's loss and thus Delia's, and she resented the nonchalance of the universe, just accepting Paxton Lowry's death as a matter of course.

She also resented the sounds of Abby and Catherine's bickering filtering in from the other room. It all seemed so trivial to her. Mother and daughter were once again arguing about Albert Beveridge.

"But he is a good man," she heard Catherine telling her mother.

"If he makes it to the White House, that's one thing," said Abby. "And if he doesn't, then what? What kind of a life will you have?"

"Spencer warned me that you wouldn't like him," said Catherine. "It's just like with Lurline. You don't think anyone's good enough for your children and it's just not true. You refuse to give anyone a chance. . . ."

Delia got up and closed the door. "Can I get you anything?" she asked Arthur.

He stared into the amber liquor in his glass and said, "I've been thinking . . . I've given this a lot of thought and well, I've decided to grant you a divorce."

At first she thought she hadn't heard right. It was so out of the blue, so unexpected. She looked into his eyes as if seeking confirmation.

"I want you to be happy," he said. "And life is much too short. Much too unpredictable."

"But, but . . ." She had a million questions. "What about your mother?"

"As I say, life is much too short."

She always thought that if this moment ever came, she would

have been elated. Instead, it felt bittersweet. There were so many tentacles to their situation; they were all tied to one another in such complexity.

"Thank you," she said solemnly, her voice barely above a whisper.

"But I won't kid you, I'm terrified. I'm afraid to go it alone without you. I'm not sure how to manage without you in my life."

"I'll always be in your life, Arthur. You know that. You and Marsh and I are a family. That will never change."

He smiled but his eyes were weeping and it nearly split her down the center. She sat with him while he finished his drink, the two of them holding hands. *This is friendship*, thought Delia. *This is love.* They would always be there for each other.

Marsh was leaving in the morning for a business trip to Europe and Delia waited until he was out of the store to tell him the news. They were walking arm in arm along the lakefront, south of Grant Park to the site of the Columbian Museum of Chicago that was soon to be renamed the Field Museum. Delia could already see it coming into view. It was one of only two buildings that remained from the world's fair.

On that beautiful summer evening just as the sun was setting, Delia turned to Marsh and said, "Mr. Field, will you do me the honor of marrying me?"

He stood back and gave her a quizzical look.

"Arthur has agreed to grant me a divorce. I'm going to be a free woman." She was smiling. He was not. This gave her a scare. Her heart began to hammer. It had never occurred to her that he wouldn't be pleased. His blue gray eyes narrowed and she nearly stopped breathing. "You *do* want to marry me, don't you?" He hesitated for an agonizing minute and she braced herself for a fall.

"Now what do you think?" He began to laugh as he picked her up and whirled her in a circle.

They were giddy as they made their way back to the Field mansion. He rang for his butler, asking for champagne, and as he cupped Delia's face in his hands, he kissed either cheek and then finally her lips. Through the years there had been millions of kisses between them, some quick like a punctuation mark, others long and exploring and still others filled with urgency and passion. Yet, this kiss was different from all the others. This one kiss said that in the world filled of people, you are my very favorite one. You are my one and only.

She didn't think she could possibly love him any more or any deeper and yet here she was, in his arms, falling for him all over again. He was going to be her husband and suddenly it was more than just a label.

Just as their kisses had taken on every expression imaginable, so had their lovemaking. In the early years they relied on the intensity and fiery passion to convey their feelings and desire for each other. But as their love matured they no longer needed to ravish each other to prove their affection. Like a vivid painting whose definition blurs and softens the closer you stand to it, so was their love. Intimacy had taken on a different kind of pleasure now. A richer, deeper, more satisfying pleasure. That night they made love slowly, tenderly, like two old souls dancing.

The next morning after they said good-bye Delia made her way around the corner to the house on Calumet. With each step the elation over wedding plans seemed to fade. Delia couldn't stop thinking about Arthur. Even though he had given her his blessings, she felt she was betraying him, abandoning him, leaving him behind.

Arthur was in the sitting room when she returned, still in

the same bathrobe he'd been wearing the day before. He hadn't shaved or bathed in days. An untouched newspaper, neatly folded, sat at his side along with a glass of bourbon.

"I'm sure Marsh was pleased," he said.

She went over and put her arms around him, leaning in to kiss the top of his head. "You're a good man, Arthur."

He gave off a soft sound, half laugh, half sob.

"How about a hand of cards?" she asked, desperate to lift his spirits.

"Can I ask one final favor of you?" he said as if he hadn't heard her.

"A *final* favor. You know I'll always do anything for you."

"I want you to accompany me to New York next week. There's a dinner, in honor of my father. A memorial. They're presenting him with an award and I told Mother I would go and accept on behalf of the family. I'd like you to accompany me, as my wife, just this one last time."

"Are you sure you're up for this?" She was surprised that Arthur had agreed to it and that his mother would have encouraged it. But then again, as far as Mrs. Caton was concerned, her son had *only* lost a close friend, nothing more.

"I think it'll be good for me. I owe it to Mother and to the judge."

"Then of course I'll go to New York with you. Of course I will."

CHAPTER FORTY-FIVE

Just one month after Paxton passed away, at the end of July, on a balmy, steamy afternoon, Delia and Arthur headed for New York City. The train station smelled of creosol and Delia brought a handkerchief to her nose as passengers rushed in and about them, boarding the train.

She had reserved a first-class Pullman coach for the two of them with plush velvet seats, crystal chandeliers and a private sleeper car. Two porters were on hand for anything they needed.

Arthur spent much of the trip talking about Paxton. "Remember how he loved the theater? Loved going to plays? Couldn't stand to be a moment late . . . The last time I was in New York, it was with him. . . ."

The train rolled on as the hours passed, and the next day, the flashing red lights blinked and the bells began clanging as they approached their stop. The porters opened the doors at Grand

Central Station, letting a rush of hot air in along with the heady smell of coal and smoke.

When they arrived at the Waldorf Astoria, Arthur stood in the lobby and sighed woefully. "Paxton always loved to stay at this hotel."

"Oh, Arthur." Delia felt a sting. She knew this was where they stayed when they were in Manhattan. "I'm sorry. I should have made a reservation somewhere else."

"No, no. I love the Waldorf. This is perfect. Just perfect."

The bellhop showed them to their rooms, a penthouse suite with adjoining bedrooms. It was beautifully appointed with bouquets of fresh flowers and baskets of fruit, cheese and a bottle of wine, which Arthur asked the bellboy to open.

They had a glass of wine and talked about the award for his father and about getting tickets to see *Little Johnny Jones* on Broadway. Arthur then rose to go change for dinner, but before he left he went over to Delia and gave her a tight embrace and a long kiss on the cheek.

"I do you love you, my pet. Always know that much is true."

She looked into his face, sensing that something was off, something in his tone, in his eyes. "Is everything all right?"

"Everything's perfect."

He had said the word *perfect* a few too many times since they'd arrived in New York. Delia watched him go into his room. "Arthur?" she called to him, and when he turned back around she simply said, "I love you, too." She stood there for a moment, waiting until he disappeared before she went into her adjoining room to get ready for the dinner.

She took her time getting dressed, and after considering two gowns that she'd brought for that night, she chose a beautiful blue satin by Worth embellished with crystal beading along the bodice. Having not brought Therese along, Delia was struggling with her buttons and needed Arthur's help.

"Arthur? Arthur, can you help me with these but—"

She heard a blast. A blast so loud and sharp and piercing, her whole body went stiff. She froze in place, afraid to move. *Please dear God, don't let that be a gunshot.* A moment later, all was quiet. Too quiet.

"Arthur?" Delia's heart was racing as she got hold of herself and ran through the suite, calling for him. "Arthur!"

He didn't answer.

She tore into the second bedroom, frantically looking and calling for him. The bed looked untouched, the pillows fluffed. She saw that the bathroom door was closed and rushed toward it. As she reached for the glass doorknob, her hand began to shake. It was as if she knew what she'd find on the other side. The longer she took, the longer she waited to turn that knob, the longer it wouldn't be true.

She drew a deep breath and threw the door open. Everything seemed fine. The white fluffy towels were hanging on their gold racks. Arthur's shaving kit was laid out on the vanity with his brush resting in the soap dish. His slippers were tucked in the corner. All was in its place. But then she shifted her eyes and saw the spray of blood on the wall. When she looked in the mirror she screamed. She saw Arthur's reflection, faceup on the marbled bathroom floor. A pool of blood was collecting beneath his head, soaking his blond hair dark and spreading out in all directions. The gun was lying next to his hand.

She was still screaming and keening when she heard the pounding on the penthouse door. She crawled across the suite, unable to stand. Her head was in a fog of shock and horror. When she managed to open the door, she saw two men from hotel security. They said they'd heard the gunshot and rushed upstairs. Delia pointed toward the bathroom and watched from the doorway as they stepped over Arthur's body. The one man leaned over to take Arthur's pulse. Delia turned away, unable to watch. She already knew.

It wasn't until after they'd removed his body and the hotel manager had been up to see her, to see if he could do anything for her, that she noticed the letter sitting on Arthur's bedside, addressed to her:

> My Dearest Delia, my Dell, my pet,
>
> Don't hate me for this. And don't be sad. For me this is relief. I just can't go on this way any longer. You know I've never found a true, honest place for myself in this world and the pain of continuing on has been too great. I'm just not strong enough. Forgive me for that. You and Marsh can be together now as you should have been all along, and this gives me peace as I say good-bye. Don't blame yourself. This one is on me, my dear sweet Dell.
>
> Yours for all eternity,
> Arthur

Delia sank down on the edge of the bed. The room turned hazy before her eyes. She was suddenly aware of the motorcars twelve stories below, blasting their horns. She heard a guest keying into the suite across the way and the ding of the elevator car down the hall. She heard water running through the pipes and the creaking, settling of the building. There was so much noise inside her head she couldn't shut it out.

She clutched Arthur's letter to her chest and squeezed her eyes shut. She should have known. He had probably been planning this ever since Paxton died, ever since he said he'd give her a divorce. She thought they'd gotten rid of all his guns after he went into the asylum. She was sure that they had. She tried to read his note again but couldn't make out the words through the blurring of her tears.

She started to telephone Marsh but remembered that he was in Europe. She slammed the base of the phone down hard and started to sob. After a while she composed herself enough to telephone Junior.

"I'll call Spencer," he said. "We'll be on the next train. We'll make all the arrangements. You just sit tight."

Delia was still numb on Monday morning when the boys arrived in New York. They found her in the suite, unable to bring herself to change hotels or even switch rooms. She was paralyzed and felt that leaving that room was in some way leaving Arthur behind and she wasn't ready to do that.

The first thing Spencer and Junior did was get Delia away from the Waldorf.

"We'll go over to the Carlton," suggested Junior. "The change of scenery will do you good."

Delia docilely did as they instructed. Having Junior and Spencer there afforded her the chance to give in to her sorrow and she sobbed in their arms, barely able to stand. After that, she let them take charge of matters. While she sat in the lounge with Junior, Spencer was at the front desk, on the telephone, making the arrangements to have Arthur's body sent back to Chicago.

"You can't blame yourself for this, Aunt Dell," Junior said.

Delia just shook her head. How could she not blame herself? "I didn't know he was in such a state. I wish he would have talked to me about it. Maybe I only saw what I wanted to. I was just so sure that he was ready to start a new life. But then he lost Paxton and . . ." She couldn't finish her thought and dropped her head to her hands.

Even after his death she wouldn't betray Arthur's confidence.

CHAPTER FORTY-SIX

After the funeral, the Caton mansion felt unbearably empty to Delia, even though Abby, Augustus and Catherine still lived there. Delia wandered through the hallways and in and out of rooms as if in a trance. Just like when Nannie passed away, Delia felt the house was haunted with Arthur's spirit. While sitting in the library, she was certain she heard his voice, or saw his shadow move across the room, smelled his shaving soap. It got to be too upsetting for her in the house and she retreated back to the Field mansion.

Delia's grief was deep and unrelenting. As she expected, Marsh's only way of dealing with his pain was to throw himself into his work. But Delia had no such distractions. Bertha and Abby tried to take her mind off things, insisting she join them for lunch and shopping or a walk through the Art Institute. But it was no good. Delia couldn't shake her sorrow, couldn't let any joy inside her life.

Every day she asked herself the same question: What was she to do now? Go about her life as if her husband hadn't killed himself? How could one's pain be so great as to think it would be better to not exist? Why, oh why, hadn't he talked to her about it? She felt guilty for every breath she could still take, for every bit of this earth that she still inhabited. Something as simple as a cup of coffee felt like an undue pleasure. Nothing was untouched by the loss. How was she supposed to be all right with this world, let alone be happy about anything now? The minute she'd catch herself laughing, or not dwelling on poor Arthur, she would rein herself back in, reminding herself that she didn't deserve to feel any semblance of joy.

She confessed all this to Marsh one night when he found her crying out in the garden, looking across the way at her house.

"That's ridiculous," said Marsh. "Arthur wouldn't want you to punish yourself like this."

It was ten o'clock at night, just three weeks after Arthur's suicide. The August night air was still, motionless. Fireflies flickered around the rosebushes while crickets chirped in the dark. The moon was just a sliver, a toenail of light suspended overhead. Marsh pulled a lawn chair up close to where Delia was sitting.

"Life goes on. It simply has to," he said matter-of-factly, as if he were discussing a failed sales event.

She tried to let the comment pass, but for Arthur's sake she couldn't. "How dare you be so callous. We're not talking about Nannie here. This is about Arthur! He's dead! Don't you understand that?"

"Oh, Delia." He leaned back and let out an exasperated sigh as he looked up at the stars. "Of course I understand that Arthur is dead. He was my friend. But you can't torture yourself like this. It isn't fair to you. Or to me."

"To you!" She bolted up straight. "Who gives a damn about

what's fair to you? You're still alive. You have everything you want now."

She started to get up, but he reached for her arm and stopped her. "For God's sake, woman! I don't have you. I've waited a long, long time to make you my wife. I'm tired of waiting. I say we get married and we do it now."

She struggled to pull away from him. "How can you even think about that now?"

"He gave you his blessing." Marsh was on his feet then, too, standing in front of her, holding her still. "He wants us to be together."

"But it's too soon." She could feel the grief mounting beneath her rage as she twisted herself free from his hold, dropped to her knees and let her tears flow.

He knelt down beside her. "Don't do this to us, Delia. Don't sabotage us. For the first time there's no one standing in our way."

"What is the big rush? Why so soon?"

He brought his hands to the top of his head as if to keep it from exploding. "So soon? Good God, woman. I've been waiting thirty years for you."

She looked at him and in spite of herself she was struck by the absurdity of it all. She began to laugh. At first he stared at her in shock, but then gradually he began to laugh as well. They stayed there in the garden laughing until the tears poured from their eyes.

They agreed to marry right away, in Europe, where they could escape the scrutiny of the press. Delia and Marsh set sail for London on August 25. Delia still grieved, but she had come to see her marrying Marsh as a tribute to Arthur, as if she was carrying out his final wish for her.

The crossing was peaceful and Marsh and Delia stayed in

the Fields' stateroom on board the *Baltic.* Everything from the furnishings to the silver and china was of the finest quality. The seas were calm and the gentle breeze upon the deck was refreshing. They made love in the middle of the afternoon and lingered in bed until dinnertime. There was no pressing business, no meetings, just time for each other, and for once the quiet, the stillness of it all, was enough for Marsh.

They arrived in London on Saturday, September 2, three days before they were to be married. They stayed at Claridge's with Junior and Albertine, who arrived the next day, along with Abby, Augustus, Spencer and Catherine.

Ethel did not take the news of her father's marriage very well. The day before the wedding they went to Ethel's home on Eaton Square. After being introduced to her new husband, David Beatty, Marsh slipped his arm about Delia's waist and announced their wedding plans.

Ethel stared at her father. "What do you expect me to say?"

"A simple congratulations would do," he said, tightening his hold about Delia's waist.

"How can you do this to Mother and to poor Uncle Arthur?" Ethel theatrically covered her face in her hands and began weeping. Her husband tried to calm her down, but she just sobbed into his chest.

Delia had hoped that Ethel would understand—especially since she herself had had an affair and was now married to that man. Surely she wouldn't stand back in judgment any longer. But Ethel's stubborn streak wasn't about to give.

When Ethel pulled away from David she addressed Delia for the first time. "Uncle Arthur hasn't even been gone a month! You drove him and Mother to their graves."

Delia felt the sting of her words, but she didn't say anything.

She wouldn't dare betray Arthur's secret. If Ethel wanted to blame it on her, then so be it.

Later that night they all dined at Forman's and the evening was a disaster. Delia burned her tongue on the bisque and then Marsh spilled a glass of red wine down the front of his suit. Ethel pouted the whole time. On their way back to the hotel, their motorcar got into an accident—no one was hurt—but an accident just the same. Ethel's words haunted Delia, and images of Nannie rose up unbidden. Delia couldn't help but think Nannie was sabotaging them from the grave.

The next day, Tuesday morning, September 5, 1905, was their wedding day and by ten o'clock Delia had experienced even more mishaps. While Therese helped her into her dress, the clasp on her bracelet caught on her cuff and tore a section of the lace trim. She stuck herself with her brooch, sending a droplet of blood onto her cream-colored shoe. The snag in her stocking seemed minor in comparison. Delia couldn't help but think their union was cursed.

Of course she didn't dare share her fears with Marsh. He always pooh-poohed her superstitions. But still she worried that the ghost of Nannie would see to it that they didn't have a moment's peace. Delia was waiting for something—something bad—to catch up with them. If only she'd known that stain on her shoe and a snag in her stocking would be the least of it.

Three hours later, Delia, at fifty-one, married her seventy-one-year-old groom. They said their vows at London's St. Margaret's Church in a private ceremony for just their family. Ethel reluctantly attended and cried during the ceremony. Delia and everyone else knew they were not tears of joy.

Word of the nuptials had somehow leaked to the press, and immediately following the ceremony, newspapermen swarmed

Delia and Marsh with a host of questions while camera flashed, releasing a smokeless powder in the air. Spencer and Junior held the reporters and photographers at bay while the newlyweds made their escape and began their honeymoon.

They took the train from London to Chur and then on to St. Moritz. En route they traveled through Paris, Dijon and Zurich and other cities that charmed them with their breathtaking scenery. At stops along the way they shopped for clothes, for furniture and antiquities.

St. Moritz was everything they'd hoped it would be. Though they had missed the height of the season, they were thrilled by the privacy. No reporters, no obligations to attend luncheons and balls. They had just each other and the Alps.

One afternoon they went to see the Leaning Tower of St. Moritz. Standing on the stone walkway they were surrounded by evergreens and the Alps. It was breathtaking. As the funiculars in the distance strained their way up the mountainside, Marsh pointed to the peak of Corviglia and said to his new wife, "Mrs. Field, when I look at that mountaintop, I think of you and me."

"Oh, and why is that?"

"Because we've climbed and crawled our way up just as steep a mountain to get to where we are now."

"Why, that's almost poetic, Mr. Field." She laughed as she settled into his arms, loving the feel of his lips and mustache on her cool cheek as he kissed her. This was contentment. This was pure happiness. All she'd ever wanted. It was as if after thirty years, she could at last breathe freely. She'd finally left the ghosts of Nannie and Arthur behind.

She realized that she and Marsh were the opposite of most newly married couples. Most newlyweds were excited about sharing their lives together, whereas Delia and Marsh were excited about finally sharing the life they'd been living with the rest of the world. She was so proud that they had stuck it out together, that they were now free to be man and wife and that their love for each other was even stronger now than it had been thirty years ago.

"I want to climb that mountain," he said, his arms still wrapped around her.

"I can't picture you as a mountaineer," she said.

"Do I detect a challenge?" He laughed. "I'll tell you what, next year—on our anniversary—I shall climb that very mountain. And if you're so inclined, Mrs. Field, you may join me."

Marsh stood behind her, their bodies pressed together, his arms about her waist. She looked down at his wedding band and smiled. "I'm glad you're wearing that," she said, running her thumb over the gold band. "You never wore your wedding ring when you were married to Nannie."

"Oh, I did in the beginning, but something happened early on and I took it off and never wore it again."

"What happened?"

Marsh held up his right hand, extending his crooked index finger. "That's what happened."

"Nannie did that to your finger?"

"We'd been married about six months and we were in the midst of our first truly grand argument. I'd never heard her raise her voice before. It was shocking, I tell you."

"What were you arguing about?"

He laughed. "Can't for the life of me remember. But I do remember that it was hot as the devil that night. All the windows were open, but it didn't help much. We were living in a dump of a place with poor ventilation. Anyway, Nannie was having a fit. And I do mean a genuine fit. I'd never seen her like that before. The soft-spoken Southern girl I married had turned into a ranting lunatic. At one point, I told her to go to hell or something equally as endearing. I got up and went over to the window to get some air. I had my hands on the ledge and Nannie came charging up behind me and slammed the window shut. I got all my fingers out of the way in time but this one. Later she swore up and down that it was an accident, but she did it with malice. That's when I knew I'd married an evil woman. I took off my wedding band and never put it back on."

Something about what he said struck Delia and struck her hard. Nannie did have an evil streak. No doubt about that. Delia remembered how she'd set the birds loose, terrifying her, and of course Delia would never forget that look of smug satisfaction on her face the day she fell down the stairs and lost her baby. All these years Delia questioned whether Nannie could have really pushed her. Could she have possibly done something that wicked, that malicious? Because she had no proof, she never said anything to Marsh, but now she knew that Nannie was to blame. Now she had her answer.

Six weeks later when they returned to Chicago, Delia wanted all traces of Nannie removed from their life. She walked through the Field mansion with the head housekeeper, who took copious notes as Delia made her comments.

"Please see to it that all the King Louis XVI pieces in the parlor are removed," she said. "And I want those birds out of this house, too."

"Right away, Mrs. Field."

Mrs. Field. It still sounded foreign to her, but she was the new Mrs. Field and she had every right to make this house into a real home for Marsh and her.

After finishing up with the head housekeeper, Delia returned to the house on Calumet, where she planned to divvy up the staff with Abby, deciding which servants would follow Delia to Prairie Avenue and which ones would remain on Calumet.

As soon as she stepped inside, Abby and Catherine rushed to her side.

"We tried to stop them," said Abby.

"They're just helping themselves to all your things, Aunt Dell." Catherine pointed toward the library.

Both Abby and Catherine followed Delia inside, where she came face-to-face with Mrs. Caton and Arthur's sisters along with several members of the Caton Colony staff.

"All the books," said Mrs. Caton. "And that sculpture on the desk. In fact, take the desk, too."

"Excuse me," said Delia. "What do you think you're doing?"

"Oh, and the Tiffany lamp."

"Mrs. Caton"—Delia stepped in front of her—"this is still my house."

"And thanks to you, my son is dead. He would have rather killed himself than stay in this house with you. This is all we have left of him and we're taking it."

Delia faltered as if she'd been struck. All the wind had been knocked out of her. "Fine," she said, trying to recover. She wasn't about to argue this point with Arthur's mother. She knew the truth and that had to be enough. "Fine. Take it. Take it all."

"What!" Abby was alarmed. "But we won't have any furniture left. We'll be here in an empty—"

Delia raised her hand to stop her sister and then turned back to Mrs. Caton. "Take everything. And once you're done, do me a kindness and never step foot inside this home again."

She went to the drawing room on the other side of the house with Abby and Catherine trailing after her.

"But, Aunt Dell, they *will* take it all. They will."

"You should see what they've already done to the upstairs," said Abby.

Delia was cool and collected. "Let them take it all. I'll redecorate the house. It's worth it for me just to have them out of my life once and for all."

CHAPTER FORTY-SEVEN

A month after Delia and Marsh returned from their honeymoon, they went to New York for a gallery opening. It was Delia's first time back in New York since Arthur's suicide.

They stayed at the opulent Holland House on Fifth Avenue near Thirtieth Street. From the moment they stepped through the front doors until they reached their suite, they were surrounded by Siena marble, bronze and stained-glass accents. Only the Palmer House could rival the Holland House's amenities.

Their first night in the city, they went with the Astors to see *Oliver Twist* at the New York Theater on Forty-fifth Street and afterward the four of them dined at Delmonico's. The next day, despite the brisk November air, Delia and Marsh strolled through Central Park, where the bare trees were already bracing for the coming winter.

"It's getting cold out here. What do you say we get in a cab and go down to Thirty-second Street. There's a couple of new merchants over there. A fellow named Herman Bergdorf and his partner, Edwin Goodman. I'd like to get a look at their store."

Delia found the store to be rather cramped and poorly lit. It was nothing like the bright spacious Marshall Field & Company, but even Marsh had to admit their merchandise was first-rate.

"If they can figure out a way to better display their goods," said Marsh, "I think they might be able to make a go of it."

After Bergdorf Goodman's Marsh wanted to see Macy's new location at Herald Square. As they approached Broadway and Thirty-fourth Street, Delia saw the red awning first, and as they drew closer, she paused to admire the neoclassical facade. Inside it was pure luxury. Marsh kept pulling a notebook from his breast pocket to jot down thoughts to discuss with John Shedd when he got back to Chicago.

Delia and Marsh returned to their suite at the Holland House around three that afternoon, wanting to rest and have time to freshen up before dinner with the Vanderbilts that evening. While Delia waited for the maid to draw her bath, the telephone rang. It was Spencer calling.

"Aunt Dell—" His voice was quaking.

"What is it? What's wrong?" Delia pinched her wrapper closed and gripped onto the armchair. All she could think was that something had happened to Abby or Augustus. Or Catherine.

"It's Junior," Spencer said, throwing a punch to her stomach. "There's been an accident."

"What kind of accident?" She looked over at Marsh, who rushed to her side.

"He's been shot."

"What!" Delia shrieked. "Who shot him? Is he alive?"

"He's in the hospital."

By then Marsh had grabbed the telephone from Delia while she watched the color drain from his face.

Delia and Marsh were on the train at ten o'clock that night. The New York Central would arrive at Chicago's Thirty-first Street Station early the next afternoon. Though it was an express train, the journey seemed to take forever. There were other passengers on board, business travelers and families bound for Chicago, too, but Delia and Marsh kept to themselves in their private compartment.

Marsh tried to distract himself with newspapers, but Delia saw that he hadn't moved off the front page in over half an hour. Delia herself stared out the window as their train barreled through the Pennsylvania mountains. It was a cold, harsh-looking landscape and it gave her the chills.

"I still can't understand how he could have shot himself," Marsh said, folding his newspaper in half. "Junior's been handling guns all his life."

Delia didn't have an explanation. They were both frustrated, not having any details. They didn't even know how serious his injury was. All they knew was that Junior had accidentally shot himself. The bullet was lodged in his abdomen and they were going to operate. Albertine had already been told. She'd been away with the children visiting relatives in New Jersey and was on her way back to Chicago, too.

Their porter managed to find one newspaper with a brief paragraph stating: "Marshall Field, Jr., son of Chicago's mercantile magnate Marshall Field, has been shot and rushed to Mercy Hospital. No family members were available for comment."

When their train pulled into Chicago, the station was filled with reporters awaiting their arrival. Spencer was waiting for them, too, with his Oldsmobile idling at the curb. The November air was raw and punishing with the winds kicking up off the lake. The photographers pushed and shoved, trying to get closer to the couple, asking for a statement. It was a frenzy and Delia was frightened. When one of the photographers reached for her arm, Marsh grabbed hold of his camera and smashed it on the platform before rushing Delia toward Spencer's motorcar.

Marsh and Delia went directly to Mercy Hospital, where another swarm of reporters and photographers were gathered outside, their collars turned up, hats held down in place while they bombarded Delia and Marsh with questions as their flash bags popped off.

"Do you know who shot your son, Mr. Field?"

"What have the doctors told you about Marshall Field Jr.'s condition?"

"How severe is his injury, Mr. Field?"

"No comment," was all Marsh said as he and Delia climbed the stairs trying to get away from the cameras.

Once inside the corridor they were met by the head of the hospital, who ushered them down the hall to a waiting area just outside the sickroom. Albertine sat with Gwendolin on her lap, Marshall III and Henry at her side. Albertine was pale and Delia felt her tremble in her arms when she embraced her.

All Albertine knew was that three doctors were operating on Junior at that very moment. While Delia sat and waited with Albertine, Marsh paced up and down the corridor and then sat, hunched forward with his elbows on his knees, his fingers laced together.

It was an hour later when the head doctor came out and pulled down his surgical mask, letting it hang beneath his chin. "Mr. Field's a very lucky young man," he said. "I'm pleased to report that the wound was not fatal."

There was a gasp of relief as Albertine hugged Delia and then Marsh, tears collecting in their eyes.

Marsh leaned forward, fingers pressed together. "Does that mean he'll be okay?" he asked.

The doctor nodded. "As I said, he's a very lucky man. I think we can expect him to make a full recovery."

Delia looked around the waiting room, feeling the tension leaving her neck and shoulders. Even the air seemed thinner now that they knew Junior would be all right. Still, Albertine insisted on staying at the hospital in the room next door. She wanted to be there when he woke up.

In the meantime, Marsh and Delia took the grandchildren home and got them into bed before they returned to the Field mansion next door. A cluster of reporters was huddled together out front, standing beneath a streetlamp. It had started to snow and a white dusting was collecting on their hats and overcoats. Still they didn't budge. They were waiting for a statement, but Marsh waved them off, asking for privacy.

About an hour after they'd returned home from the hospital, the doorbell rang, and a few moments later, the butler escorted Spencer into the drawing room. He looked like he'd been drinking. His dark hair was ruffled, his necktie loosened about his collar. It was cold and snowing outside, but he was perspiring.

"This is a bit indelicate," he began, pacing back and forth in the drawing room. "I didn't want to say anything over the telephone when I called you in New York, or at the hospital in front of Albertine."

"For God's sake what is it?" Marsh got up and blocked Spencer's pacing.

"Well—" He stopped, his eyes shifting from Marsh to Delia and then back to Marsh. "Junior didn't exactly shoot himself. It was an accident, but he didn't do it."

Delia and Marsh both stared at Spencer. "What in God's name happened?"

"It all started when Junior and I met up with a friend of ours from New York. Miss Scott. Vera Scott. We started out at a dinner and then we decided to go to a party—some friends of hers. Junior and I didn't know any of them. It was getting late and we were all ready to call it a night, but then Vera—Miss Scott—suggested we go to the Everleigh Club."

"The Everleigh Club! What in the devil was my son doing in a place like that?"

The Everleigh Club was Chicago's most exclusive bordello and Delia had heard that it cost fifty dollars just to get in the front door. People said that night after night the two sisters, Minna and Ada Everleigh, entertained celebrities and dignitaries, princes and kings from around the world.

"Well, we ended up there," said Spencer, slicking back his hair with both hands. "Everyone was clowning around and having a good time, when all of a sudden Vera and Junior got into an argument. It was a friendly argument, though—mostly they were just teasing each other. But then, out of nowhere, Vera pulled a pistol out of her handbag. She was still joking around. I swear, it was just in fun. But then Vera kept taunting Junior with the gun, waving it in his face. We both kept telling her enough was enough and to put the gun away. And when she wouldn't listen, Junior tried to take it from her and that's when it accidentally went off and shot Junior right in the stomach."

"This happened inside the Everleigh Club?" Marsh pressed his hands to his forehead. "My son was shot inside a brothel!"

"That's why we moved him."

"What?" Delia and Marsh were both astonished. "What do you mean, you *moved* him?"

"We knew we couldn't leave him there in the club. Minna and Ada didn't want him there, either. I don't need to tell you that the press would have had a heyday with that. So we moved him. It was his idea. Junior was talking the whole time, telling us to take him home. So Vera and I got him into a cab and brought him back to his place. We didn't think he was hurt all that bad. We knew Albertine was out of town with the children and we thought we'd get him fixed up before she got back. Anyway, we took him up to his dressing room and we realized how bad off he was. He lost consciousness shortly after we got him upstairs and that's when we telephoned for the ambulance."

"Now what? You've tampered with everything. How are we going to explain all this!"

Delia had never seen Marsh so rattled. Seeing him—her rock—lose his composure shook her at first. But then it made her tap a reserve of strength that she'd almost forgotten she had. It was the core of strength she'd found the night of the Great Fire nearly thirty-five years before. Marsh needed her now in a way he never had before. Suddenly her mind was cycling, looking for angles, looking for solutions.

"Now wait a minute," she said, placing a reassuring hand on Marsh's arm. "I think they did the right thing."

Marsh and Spencer looked at her, both of them surprised.

"We can figure this out," she told them. "We just need to think it through. Now, did anyone else see her shoot him?"

"It was just the three of us in there. In one of the rooms in the back of the house."

"And did anyone else hear the gun go off?"

"I don't know. It was really noisy in there that night. They had a couple big parties going on and the place was packed. Loud music was playing in all the rooms. I'm the one who went and got the sisters. They hadn't heard a thing."

"This is absurd," said Marsh. "Of course someone had to have heard something, seen something. And what about this Vera Scott woman? What the devil are we supposed to do about her?"

"I took her to a hotel up north," said Spencer. "She's waiting there to hear from me."

"Do you think she'll talk to the reporters? Do you think she'll talk to *anyone*?" Delia asked.

"I told her not to say a word. Not to anyone."

"And you trust her?" Marsh was horrified.

"She's scared to death," said Spencer. "She thinks she's going to jail. Trust me, she's not going to talk."

"This will work," said Delia.

Marsh stood up, stuffed his hands inside his pockets and walked around the room. Finally he stopped and looked at Delia. "Just tell me exactly what you're suggesting."

"I'm suggesting that we stick with Spencer's original story and tell the press that Junior accidentally shot himself."

"Actually," said Spencer, "that was Junior's idea, too. He said he'd just bought a new gun. It's still up in his room. He said to tell you he'd shot himself by accident while he was cleaning it."

"Then that's our story," said Delia, slapping her hands to her lap. "We'll come up with a statement for the press and we'll stick to it. And don't look at me like that, Marshall. We can't have this in the papers. We can't do that to Albertine or to the children."

"And what about the taxi driver and the servants?" asked Marsh. "Surely they must have seen that Junior was shot when you brought him back home."

"We told them he was drunk. Even we didn't notice *that* much blood until we got him upstairs, so I highly doubt they did," said Spencer.

"And what about that Vera Scott woman?" asked Marsh. "I don't trust her."

"Then we get rid of her. We send her away—overseas somewhere." Delia said this as if she were disposing trash in a bin. She was shocked that she was so coolheaded and so was Marsh.

Again, he shot her a mortified look. "Well?" she said. "Can you think of a better way to handle her?"

"We'll never get away with this. I've never lied to the press before," said Marsh. "They have ways of finding things out."

"You've also never been put in this kind of predicament before," Delia reminded him. "This is more about protecting your family than lying to the press."

CHAPTER FORTY-EIGHT

Delia stayed up with Marsh most of the night, going over the statement he would give to the press, looking for loopholes, anything that could trip them up.

Before he gave an official statement and before Marsh talked to his friends at the police station, Spencer made the travel arrangements for Vera Scott and took Marsh and Delia to the hotel where she was waiting. Thankfully the number of reporters looming outside their mansion had thinned and Spencer was able to appease them by simply saying he was taking Mr. and Mrs. Field to the hospital.

Later that morning they arrived at a shoddy-looking hotel up on Diversey Parkway with peeling paint on the walls and threadbare carpets in the lobby. A musty smell hung in the air. Vera Scott's room was up on the second floor at the very end, and while they waited out in the drafty hallway, the door opened just a crack. The chain latch was still in place, letting a sliver of Vera Scott's face show through.

"Who else is with you?" she asked.

"I've brought Mr. and Mrs. Field," said Spencer.

"No police?" she asked.

"No police."

Delia heard the chain slide across the latch and then the door opened. Vera let them into the tiny hotel room with a radiator clacking and condensation climbing up the windows. Vera's dark hair was tousled and her lip rouge was smeared. It was barely ten o'clock in the morning and Vera was dressed in a flashy sequined dress, presumably the very dress she'd worn the night of the shooting. The bed was unmade and the sheets were rumpled; her shoes were lying under a chair, soles up.

After they were all inside, Vera asked about Junior. "Is he going to be all right?"

Spencer nodded. "The operation was a success."

"Oh, thank God." She rested her open hand across her chest. "I don't know what I would have done if he'd died. You're not going to turn me in to the police, are you? It was an accident. I swear it was. I never even held a gun before in my life. You won't turn me in, will you?"

"That depends on you," said Marsh.

"What do you mean? What do I have to do?"

"Leave Chicago. Leave the country," he said, matter-of-factly. "If you agree to leave and keep your mouth shut, you'll stay out of jail."

Vera's eyes grew wide and Delia watched her go from being a shrewd New York City woman to a frightened little girl. "But I don't have any money to leave town, let alone get out of the country."

Marsh reached for an envelope tucked inside his breast pocket. "This should cover your needs and ensure your silence."

"How much?" she asked.

"There's twenty thousand dollars."

Vera Scott took a deep breath as she looked inside the envelope. It was probably more money than she'd ever seen in one place, at one time. It was probably more money than she'd expected to ever see in her lifetime.

"You'll go to San Francisco and then take a steamer bound for the Orient."

"The Orient!" There was that frightened little girl again, looking at them with alarm in her eyes.

"Hong Kong," Spencer clarified. "We've made all the arrangements. And in the meantime, I need you to stick around here. Don't go anywhere."

"You mean I have to stay in this hotel room like a prisoner?"

"Unless you prefer a jail cell," offered Marsh.

"Okay, fine." She folded her arms across her chest.

"I'll come back and get you tomorrow," said Spencer.

"And now, Miss Scott," Marsh said, replacing his hat, "I'll expect to never see or hear of you again."

On Saturday, November 25, Marsh and Delia paid a visit to Marsh's longtime friend, the police chief, Stephen Collins. By noon that same day, the official statement was made to the press, and immediately after that, word of Junior's accidental gunshot wound was on the front page of every newspaper. The story caught on, the details expanding with each edition.

The *Chicago Tribune* was the first to report that:

> Police Chief Collins stated that his detectives had conducted a thorough investigation that included question-

ing members of the Field mansion staff as well as neighbors. After examining all the evidence, Collins was satisfied that the shooting was the result of a self-inflicted accident.

Delia spent the balance of the day keeping tabs on all the newspapers. The *Chicago Daily News* seemed to corroborate the story by reporting that Junior had recently purchased the automatic revolver from Roach, Hirth & Company on Wabash and Monroe. By six o'clock that evening Delia was satisfied that the press was under control, though a slew of reporters still hovered outside the hospital and both of the Field mansions, their pens and cameras ready, hoping for updates. But as it stood, there was little to report. Thankfully Junior's condition had stabilized. Delia and Marsh went back home to get some rest and suggested the same to Albertine, but she refused to leave the sickroom.

Early the next day, on Sunday, November 26, while Marsh went back to the hospital, Delia accompanied Spencer to take Vera Scott to the train. By the time they left the depot, it had started to snow again, light flakes that spiraled down, landing on the windshield of Spencer's motorcar. The leather upholstery was stiff and so cold it seemed as if it were on the verge of cracking. They could see their breath in the air.

"Is he in love with her?" Delia asked.

"Who?"

"Junior. Is Junior in love with that woman?"

"They're just friends."

Delia gave him a knowing look. "A man and a woman are never *just* friends. Even when they are."

Spencer gripped onto the steering wheel and sighed. "He talked about leaving Albertine for her." He stole a worrisome look at Delia. "You won't say anything to his father, will you?"

"What, and crush him? Absolutely not."

After that, Delia hardly said a word on the drive back to the hospital. When they arrived, she and Spencer worked their way through a handful of reporters that were clustered together at the entranceway. Once inside, they headed down the long corridor of shiny tiled walls and found Albertine waiting outside Junior's sickroom. As soon as she saw her, Delia felt a panic creep up her spine. Albertine looked pale and drained, her eyes rimmed red, a handkerchief clutched in her hand.

"What's wrong?" Delia asked, rushing over to her. "What's happened?"

"Junior's fever spiked." Albertine dabbed her eyes with her handkerchief. "He has an infection now."

Delia dropped into the chair next to her. "How serious is it?"

"The doctors are in with him now," said Albertine. "They said it's not good."

"Does Marsh know?"

Albertine nodded.

"Has anyone notified Ethel?"

"We wired her and she's on her way from London." Albertine's voice began to crack. "I don't think she'll make it here in time."

Spencer went over to Albertine and sat with his arm around her shoulder.

"Where's Marsh?" Delia asked.

"He's in with the doctors," Albertine managed to say before she broke down completely, sobbing into Spencer's shoulder.

Delia entered the sickroom, shocked by the change in Junior's condition. When last she'd seen him, just the day before, he'd been weak, but alert. He was sitting up and talking, making plans for when he got out of the hospital. Now he was frail, his breathing labored and shallow, his skin mottled.

Marsh turned when he heard Delia come in. He looked exhausted; deep lines had formed around his eyes and across his brow. His skin was nearly as white as his hair. He held her tight and just shook his head. No words were needed to tell her that his thirty-seven-year-old son was dying.

The family stayed at the hospital Sunday night, taking turns sitting with Junior. It all seemed so final, so unreal. When it was just Delia alone with Junior, she reached over for his hand and pressed it to her cheek. She didn't know if he could hear her, but still she spoke to him.

"I couldn't have loved you more if you'd been my own son. I remember when I first saw you with your governess in the neighborhood. After that, I always tried to keep a piece of chocolate or a lollipop in my pocket just in case I'd run into you. . . ." She continued to reminisce, sitting at his side, holding his limp hand in hers. Before she got up to leave she leaned over and whispered in his ear, "And don't worry about Vera Scott. No one will ever know. That will be our little secret. . . ."

On Monday morning, Father Hugh McGuire entered the sickroom and administered the last rites. Afterward, unable to bear it any longer, Delia and Spencer helped Albertine into the hallway, where she collapsed in a chair sobbing. Marsh stayed with Junior.

Twenty minutes later, the door to Junior's room opened and everyone held their breath. When Marsh stepped out into the hallway, his blue gray eyes were misted over. He seemed lost. Delia had never seen him that way before. He looked at them all and nodded. It was over.

At first no one questioned the family's explanation that Junior had accidentally shot himself. Delia was beginning to believe that they would escape the scandal unscathed. But then, not three days after they'd buried Junior, Marsh walked into the sitting room and handed Delia the latest edition of the *Daily News.*

"Now what?" he asked, dropping down in the chair next to hers.

Delia scanned the headline: "Reenactment of Field Shooting Leads to More Questions Than Answers." Her skin turned clammy as she read the article. Her eyes scanned the words in disbelief.

"They're asking how Junior's gun could have caused that type of injury," said Marsh, wringing his hands. "All the experts agree that even if the gun had been dropped and dislodged, it would be impossible for the bullet to have entered Junior's body at that angle."

Delia set the newspaper down and reached for his hands. She didn't know what to say.

"And lastly," added Marsh, pulling his hand away, "they're questioning how a seasoned gunman like Junior could have accidentally shot himself. What are we going to do? I knew this wouldn't work."

"It's going to be okay. It has to be okay."

Marsh paced before the windows. Neither one of them spoke.

They were locked into their silence when Spencer rushed into the sitting room, his dark hair slick with sweat, a newspaper tucked under his arm. "Did you see the *Chicago Defender*?" he asked.

"Oh God," said Marsh. "What now?"

Delia felt sick.

Spencer pulled the newspaper from under his arm and snapped it open. "They're claiming that an anonymous witness said that Junior was shot during a poker game. Supposedly he'd won a lot of money off some man who turned around and shot him. They're just making that up. It's a blatant lie."

Delia didn't have the heart to remind Spencer that everything they'd conjured up was a lie as well.

Spencer folded the newspaper and slapped it on the coffee table. "And that's better than the *Eagle.* They're calling it a suicide."

Delia felt everything inside her begin to sink. It had taken all her strength to get through the funeral, and now this. They had to start defending their position all over again. She glanced across the room. Spencer was slumped down in the chair, running his hands through his hair. Marsh stared out the window, hardly blinking at all. Spencer was coming unglued and Marsh was too grief-stricken to think clearly. It was up to her. She summoned all her will and felt everything inside her pull together, propping herself up.

"Now listen to me," she said, looking first at Spencer and then at Marsh. "Junior accidentally shot himself. In his home. That's what happened. Nothing else. Do you hear me?"

"And what am I supposed to tell the reporters?" asked Marsh. "They won't go away."

"You tell them exactly what I just said. And then you do whatever it takes to *make* them go away."

"Are you suggesting what I think you're . . ." He couldn't finish the thought.

"It's the only way, Marsh. Thank God you're in a position to do it."

Only Delia, Marsh and Spencer knew the truth and they, along with the rest of the Field family, stood firm. Delia had told the lie to herself and everyone else so many times she was starting to believe it herself. An infection as a result of an accidental self-inflicted gunshot wound was the cause of death. No dispute. It was backed up in full by the police and the coroner's office and everyone else that Marsh paid to preserve his family's honor.

Still Delia searched the newspapers every day, holding her breath, waiting and fearful that someone else would question their story. She was antsy and couldn't relax. The truth was, she felt cursed. It had been one tragedy, one loss, after another. First Nannie and then Arthur and now Junior. She was afraid to ask what could possibly happen next. Here she and Marsh had finally found their happiness and now it was already buried beneath their grief and sorrow.

Marsh was destroyed by the death of his son. She'd never seen him so broken or overcome with emotion. There were days he couldn't get out of bed. One afternoon she found him sitting in the chair with an unopened newspaper on his lap. He was still there an hour later.

Delia went over to his side. "Would you like to go down to the store today? "

Marsh stared out the window and shook his head.

"How about a game of chess?"

"Not now," he said, barely moving his lips. He shook his head again, his eyes as empty as his heart. "What the hell was I thinking? Who the hell cares if Junior worked in the business or not? I'm just now starting to realize that I didn't even know my own son. I didn't know what he wanted, what he hoped for. What did he want for his family? I have no idea." Marsh shook his head, bewildered. "I've lost my boy and now it's too late to tell him that I don't give a damn that he didn't become a merchant. Why was that so goddamned important to me all those years?"

Delia pulled over the ottoman and sat across from him. He seemed to have aged so after losing Junior. "You were only doing what you thought was best for him."

"For him. Or for me?" He shook his head. "I squandered all that time. And for what?"

Delia sat with him the rest of the afternoon. The daylight

streaming in through the windows threw changing shadows about the room as she tried everything she could to console Marsh. No matter what she said, what she did, he'd just shake his head. The man who had rebuilt Chicago after the Great Fire now could not rebuild himself. Part of him had died right along with his son.

CHAPTER FORTY-NINE

1906

Six weeks after Junior's death, the day after New Year's, Marsh was talked into going golfing with his good friend Robert Todd Lincoln and Spencer. Marsh was actually just starting to come out of his darkness and told Delia he thought this was just the thing he needed.

"But it's the middle of winter. No one golfs in the wintertime." Delia stood in the hallway with all of them, protesting. "And besides, you said you were getting a sore throat."

"It's a sore throat, woman, not pneumonia," he said, adjusting his cap.

"I don't want you getting sick, we're leaving for New York tomorrow."

"Delia," he said with a grin, "you're beginning to sound like a wife."

"Well, I am a wife—your wife—so get used to it. And I think

this is foolish. There's snow on the course. You won't even be able to see the ball when you're out there."

Spencer reached in his pocket and pulled out a red golf ball.

She set her hands on her hips. "Well, I see you boys have thought of everything, haven't you?"

"You're just jealous that you're not coming along," joked Marsh.

"Not a chance. Go. Go." She kissed her husband good-bye and shooed him out the door.

When Marsh came home later that afternoon, his nose was red, and his fingers and toes were stiff and numb from the cold. Delia delivered a big *I told you so* and ordered him upstairs to take a hot bath.

When he appeared in his robe and slippers, she said, "That was a silly thing you did today."

"It was," he admitted, still chilled to the bone. "But I have to say, it's the first time I've laughed in weeks."

Delia smiled, though she felt a pinch inside her heart. She'd been trying everything she knew to get him to smile, to laugh, to feel like himself again. Nothing had worked, but a ridiculous round of golf in the snow with red balls had managed to do what she could not.

The next morning Marsh woke up with swollen glands and a raw sore throat.

Delia placed her hand on his forehead. "You are a little warm. Maybe we should put off the trip to New York."

Marsh had a meeting with some merchants that had been scheduled six months before. "Nonsense," he said. "I'll be fine. I'll rest on the train."

Marsh was running a fever, she was sure of it, but he insisted he was up for the trip. She knew this was his attempt to get back on with his life, with their life together, and she couldn't fault him for that. After all, he was a survivor and she knew better than to question his will.

As scheduled, they boarded the Pennsylvania Limited at noon on January 3. Marsh ended up sleeping for the first three hours of the journey while Delia alternated reading and watching the landscape pass by outside her window. When he awoke somewhere in Ohio, he was shivering so much his teeth were chattering. Delia ordered him hot tea and extra blankets. She noticed, too, that he was developing a raspy cough that made his lungs give off a rumbling sound.

By the time their train arrived in Pittsburgh, Marsh was coughing up blood. Delia was alarmed and asked for a physician. Before they left the station, a young doctor by the name of Richards came on board and was kind enough to tend to Marsh the rest of the way.

Once they were in New York, they were met with blustery winds and a steady snowfall that accompanied them on their way to the Holland House Hotel. As soon as they arrived they were shown to their usual penthouse suite, where Marsh was immediately put to bed.

Dr. Richards said that despite his high fever, it was little more than a bad cold. There was a slight danger that it might turn into bronchitis, but he doubted it. He recommended bed rest. "A few days and he'll be good as new."

The next day, Tuesday, Marsh was indeed resting comfortably and Delia began to relax. Marsh's physician, Dr. Billings, had since arrived from Chicago and met with Dr. Richards to discuss Marsh's condition.

Since he appeared to be improving, Delia decided to leave the hotel for a bit of shopping along Fifth Avenue. She knew that

Marsh would love hearing all about the displays in Macy's and Bergdorf's.

New York had come to represent the darkest of times for her and Marsh. On their last visit, they'd heard about Junior's shooting. The time before that, Arthur had taken his life in the Waldorf Astoria. She and Marsh had talked about needing to reclaim Manhattan and replace the bad memories with happy new ones.

And so in that spirit, Delia walked through Macy's, taking note of the merchandise, of how they'd displayed their wares. She found a lovely necktie for Marsh, and when she went to purchase it, she caught a reflection of herself in the mirror. Her hair was streaked with strands of gray and lines had crept into her face around her mouth and eyes. It was as if she'd never noticed herself aging, but now she looked every day of her fifty-one years. It sent a chill through her body.

She couldn't explain it, but she saw herself alone and suddenly she had the premonition that Marsh would never have the chance to wear the tie. She was going to lose him, she could feel it. Fear gripped her body as she leaned into the counter for support. She dropped the necktie and fled back to the hotel. She was praying silently to herself, hoping she made it back to the hotel in time. When she arrived back at the Holland House she was nearly in tears.

Dr. Billings was leaving the suite as she stepped off the elevator. She rushed toward him, frantically asking, "How is he, Doctor? Is everything okay? I was out and I had this horrible feeling that . . ."

The doctor smiled. "Delia, he's fine. Better in fact. His fever is down. He just woke up from a nap and had a good hearty lunch. He was asking for you."

Delia was flooded with relief. Her shoulders settled down

where they belonged and the knot in her stomach began to untie. She went in the hotel room and sat on the edge of the bed and brushed his white hair back off his forehead.

His eyes flickered open at her touch. "Oh, there you are."

"I love you," she said. "I've always loved you." She leaned forward and pressed her cheek to the back of his hand. "Thank God you're going to be all right because I simply forbid you to leave me this early on in our marriage."

Three days later, everything had changed.

Delia telephoned Abby right away. She could hear the doctors in the background, muttering among themselves, while she waited for the long-distance operator to connect her call.

"It's pneumonia," she said when Abby came on the line. Her voice was tight, strained. Each word felt thick and foreign in her mouth. "And they tell me it's spread to both lungs. They're going to try and keep him comfortable." The sound of that last statement turned her bones to ice. "Will you contact Albertine for me? And Ethel, too?"

"Of course. Ethel's still stateside with David. I'll find her and tell her what's happened. And Dell," said Abby, "Augustus and I will be on the next train."

For the next two days Delia sat at Marsh's side. She could hear him wheezing as he breathed. He was weak and hadn't been able to walk on his own since they'd arrived in New York.

"Why isn't Marshall in the hospital?" Augustus asked after they arrived at the Holland House.

"I'm afraid there's nothing more that can be done for him there," said the doctor. "We felt he'd be more comfortable here and didn't want to risk moving him. We have a full staff of nurses and doctors here—we've been with him round the clock, ever since he took this turn."

The next day there was little change in Marsh's condition. Delia excused herself and went into the outer room of their suite. As soon as she was alone, Delia hugged herself about her waist and doubled over as the tears tumbled out. How could they be at the end of their road so quickly and after they'd only just started their journey together? How could she say good-bye to him so soon? She didn't care what the doctors were telling her. He couldn't be leaving her, not yet. He had to beat this illness and recover. He just had to.

Augustus came into her room and placed his hand on her shoulder. "Delia, we're going to have to give a statement to the press soon."

Delia looked straight ahead. "I can't. I'm sorry," she said, shaking her head, "but I just can't face them now."

"I'll take care of it. I'll talk to them."

Delia's back was still turned to the door when the next person entered the room. She heard the faint footsteps first, then the timid voice. "Aunt Dell?"

Delia turned around and there was Ethel.

"Oh, Aunt Dell." She ran into Delia's arms, sobbing on her shoulder. "He can't be dying. He just can't be."

She held the girl tightly in her arms and began to cry herself, too overwhelmed to speak.

Ethel's face shone with tears as she pulled herself back. "I've been so awful to him," she said. "Do you think he'll forgive me? I'm scared, Aunt Dell. I'm going to be an orphan now. I'm going to be all alone."

Delia stroked Ethel's hair and then her cheek as if to reassure her. "You'll never be alone. Not while I'm here."

"But I've been awful to you, too. I'm so ashamed, Aunt Dell."

"Shssh." Delia tried to stop her.

Ethel shook her head. "I'm so sorry for the way I've behaved.

I was just so angry and I needed someone to blame. It wasn't fair of me. I'd never been in love—I didn't understand. And then I met David and I realized . . . But I was too stubborn, too proud to say I was wrong. I know how much he loves you. He's always loved you. He always has. I knew it, but I just—I was just . . . You made him happier than I've ever seen him."

This bit of recognition went right to Delia's heart as she hugged the girl even tighter. "Come," she said, wiping Ethel's tears and trying to compose herself. "Let's go see your father. Together."

When they entered the sickroom, two doctors and three nurses were at his side. Delia had her arm about Ethel's waist and could feel her trembling. Marsh had his eyes closed. White whiskers covered his handsome face and Delia made a note to ask one of the nurses to shave him.

"How is he?" Delia asked Dr. Billings.

Marsh opened one eye and said, "I'm right here. You can ask me. Don't rule me out yet."

She smiled and went to his side, with Ethel trailing behind her. "I'm sorry, darling, I didn't know you were awake."

"Awake and feisty," said Dr. Billings.

"We'll take that as a good sign, then," said Delia, stepping aside so Marsh could see that Ethel was with her.

"Ah," he said, a smile rising on his lips. "My girls, together at last."

Both Delia and Ethel began to weep quietly again. Marsh was tiring quickly and the doctor asked them to wait outside while they finished conducting the examination.

The family was sequestered in the living room area of their suite. The hotel staff had brought them fresh pots of coffee, sandwiches and trays of fruit and cheese that went untouched.

Dr. Billings came out of the sickroom and asked if he could

have a word with Mrs. Field. Delia's stomach dropped. She felt light-headed as she stood up and followed him into the corridor.

"I'm afraid we're in the home stretch," he said.

Delia clasped a hand over her mouth. "But he was alert just now. You saw him. He was sitting up and talking."

"He rallied for you, for his daughter. But despite that burst of energy, his condition is rapidly deteriorating."

"No." Delia shook her head fiercely. "You don't know how strong he is. He's going to beat this. I know he is."

He placed his hands on her shoulders. "I'm afraid even Marshall Field is not going to be able to recover from this. I just want to prepare you."

Delia swallowed past the lump in her throat. "How long do we have?"

Dr. Billings held her hand gently. "My guess is a matter of hours."

"Hours!" Delia nearly dropped to the ground. She looked into the doctor's eyes, hoping for a different answer.

"Your husband is a strong man, a real fighter. But he is gravely ill. He asked me to tell him when the end is near."

"Then you must do what he asked," she said, feeling everything inside her trying to pull together, to keep from unraveling. "But I'm coming with you when you do."

When the doctor told Marsh the news, he closed his eyes and nodded as he reached for Delia's hand. The two sat like that, quietly together, their hands tightly clasped. As with everything else, they were facing this together. She was scared to death, and couldn't fathom this world without him, but she wouldn't give in to those fears now. There was no choice but to be strong. If ever he needed her, it was now.

She stayed and held his hand while one by one family members came in to say good-bye. Delia didn't move. She and Marsh always knew that he would be the first to go, but it had come too soon. She wasn't ready. How could she let go of his hand, his love? She couldn't believe that tomorrow morning, when she awoke, he wouldn't be on this earth. What would the world look like without Marshall Field in it? What would her life look like without her Marsh?

Three hours later, she was still with him when he took his final breath and the Merchant Prince closed his brilliant blue gray eyes for the last time.

EPILOGUE

1906

Three weeks later, after the reading of Marsh's will, Delia left the lawyer's office with Ethel and Albertine. The other three remaining heirs, Marshall III, Henry and Gwendolin, were with their governess back at the Field mansion.

It was a cold and snowy day. The wind gusted against Delia's cheeks as she stuffed her hands deeper inside her muff and headed down the walkway to where her driver waited.

"It's not fair," said Ethel, who had been granted $6 million of her father's $120 million fortune. "Aunt Dell—what about you? Aren't you upset?"

"I'm upset that I lost your father. That's what I'm upset about." She continued down the icy walkway, feeling the packed snow and slush giving way beneath her footsteps.

"Well, of course, we're all upset about that," said Ethel, trailing a few strides behind. "But, Aunt Dell, you were his wife."

Marsh had left Delia $2 million along with the Field mansion. Delia didn't say anything. Frankly, she was surprised he'd left her that much.

"And poor Albertine," said Ethel. "How will you manage?"

"It looks as though I'll have to borrow money from my children." Marsh had left Albertine one million dollars and the rest of his estate to his grandchildren, primarily his grandsons, Marshall III and Henry.

"But they can't even touch that money until they're thirty-five," said Ethel. "Why would Father have done such a thing?"

Delia reached the motorcar, and before stepping inside she turned and said, "Because he wanted his grandsons to work, to know what it means to build something of their own. Forgive me, Albertine, but he didn't want your boys to end up like their father. I'm sorry, but that's the truth." She turned and climbed inside her Mercedes Simplex.

When they reached the Field mansion, Delia's niece Catherine was waiting for them. Catherine had left the house on Calumet and moved in with Delia right after Marsh's funeral. Everyone assumed that she didn't want her aunt to be alone, but in truth, Catherine was desperate to get out from under her mother's scrutiny, especially where Albert Beveridge was concerned.

Lunch was waiting for them in the dining room, a hearty serving of lobster bisque and watercress sandwiches. While they ate, Ethel and Albertine continued to whine about the will.

"But he only left eight million to the Columbian Museum of Chicago," Ethel said.

"Imagine what people will say when they hear that," said Albertine.

"I doubt they're going to want to rename it after him now," said Ethel.

Delia silently ate her soup, tuning them out as best she could. She was exhausted by her grief. She didn't care what Marsh left behind or to whom. He was gone and she was left with a gaping hole in her heart.

"I still think it's unfair," said Albertine.

"I'm convinced there has to have been a mistake," said Ethel.

Catherine nibbled on her sandwich, her eyes and ears open wide.

"Aunt Dell," said Ethel, "can't you break the will?"

"Oh, please, Aunt Dell," said Albertine. "For us. Please, will you do it?"

Delia set down her soupspoon with a loud clank. "Girls, stop this begging. It's not becoming and it's not going to work. My hands are tied. I couldn't break the will even if I wanted to."

"But why?" asked Ethel.

"Because I had an agreement with your father. We agreed to keep our finances separate and out of our marriage. It was all drawn up in a contract and we both signed it. I have no more power over his estate than either of you. Now I suggest you try being a little more grateful and a little less greedy."

Ethel tossed her napkin onto the table. "But . . ."

Delia glared at Ethel, who finally closed her mouth. "You saw the length of your father's will. It was eighty pages long. Do you really think he hadn't thought this through? Now please, let's discuss something else."

Later that afternoon, Delia was in the back parlor with Albertine. They were seated before a stack of cards and envelopes, working on thank-yous to all the people who sent flowers and cards and paid their respects at the wake.

"Aunt Dell," Albertine said as she sealed an envelope and set it in the finished pile, "I'm sorry for the way I behaved earlier. It was truly shameful."

"Yes, it was."

"I'm sorry that we upset you. And not that this is an excuse, but you have to understand that I'm frightened. I don't know how I'm going to manage without Junior."

"You know very well that I'll give you whatever money you need. I can't take it out of the Field estate, but I can certainly give to you from my own resources. As you know, I have money from Arthur as well."

"It's not just the money. It's that house. I hate the thought of raising my children in the same house where their father shot himself."

Delia set her fountain pen down and reached over to squeeze her hand. She'd been so distraught over Marsh that she hadn't stopped to consider the situation Albertine and the children were in. "Tell me how I can help."

"Well, I was wondering if you would mind if the children and I came and stayed here with you. Just for a little while. They love you so and they love being here. I know you have Catherine here already, but if we could . . ."

There was only one answer. Delia smiled. "I think both Junior and Marsh would like that very much."

Albertine leaned over and kissed Delia's hand. "Thank you, Aunt Dell. My goodness, what would any of us do without you?"

Delia and Bertha were on the back porch at the Field mansion one summer day, enjoying a glass of sherry. It had been eight months since Marsh had died.

"We're too young to be widows," said Bertha. She was fifty-six. Delia had just turned fifty-two.

"Do you think you'll ever remarry?" Delia asked.

Bertha laughed, running her fingertips along her pearl choker as if checking to make sure the gems were all there and accounted for. "I can't imagine it. Can you?"

Delia shook her head. Soon they would have been celebrating

their first wedding anniversary and there was something she needed to do. She turned to Bertha and said, "How would you feel about making a journey to St. Moritz with me?"

Soon the two socialites found themselves in the heart of the Swiss Alps. One afternoon she and Bertha were seated in a café, having coffee with two writers, Manuel and Alvaro. The Corviglia Mountain was in the background, towering over everything, and Delia pointed toward the peak and said, "I'd like to conquer that mountain."

Manuel and Alvaro laughed. "You? A woman? Going mountaineering?"

"Why not?" she said, remembering the day she and Marsh had stood before that mountain, admiring its height, comparing their love affair to reaching the summit. She felt she owed it to him to see the top. "And I wouldn't do it on foot. I'd drive."

The writers laughed even harder. "Impossible. The mountain roads are crude at best. Even a man has never been able to reach the top by car."

That was all Delia needed to hear. She had more of Marsh's spirit in her than she'd suspected. And of course, Bertha was never one to back away from a challenge, either.

"Please, please," Manuel and Alvaro begged the next day when they realized Delia and Bertha were serious about this. "It's very dangerous. You could easily drive over the edge and that would be the end of you both."

Several other people tried talking them out of it as well.

But the ladies' minds were set.

If they'd waited they might have changed their minds, but two days later, they had an automobile and new motoring outfits complete with goggles and gloves.

With their guide map before them, Bertha said, "Well, there's only one way to go and that's up."

And so, on the morning of September 16, 1906, Delia Spencer Caton Field sat at the controls while Bertha Palmer used the hand crank to start the motorcar before she climbed in next to Delia.

With Delia behind the wheel, they started on their journey. The local authorities had insisted on following behind them in a separate motorcar, though Delia and Bertha were not happy about it and made disparaging remarks about them each time they looked through the rearview mirror.

The scenery was breathtaking. They were surrounded by stone overhangs and pine forests that seemed to go on endlessly. As they continued on, the road was filled with surprises. Delia gripped the wheel tighter as unexpected sharp turns gave way to long winding stretches of road. All was fine for a quarter mile when suddenly, without warning, the gradual incline they were on turned into a straight upward climb. Delia gave it full throttle and then the grade eased and they found themselves chugging along again. The second motorcar was still behind them, keeping pace.

The higher up they drove, the more astonishing the views. The air looked gauzelike, an endless sheer cloud that enveloped them, and straight ahead were snowdrifts so deep, they collected like mountains all their own. Three-quarters of the way toward the summit, they met with the steepest incline yet. Delia willed the throttle on, but the machine coughed and sputtered and coughed some more before it died.

The two women turned to each other and had to laugh—what else was there to do? But then Delia got out of the motorcar and leaned against the hood. She folded her arms across her chest and pointed her chin up toward the summit. It looked so close at hand, yet she was still miles away.

She gazed toward the open sky and thought of Marsh, her

Merchant Prince. *Just as well I didn't make it to the top*, she thought to herself. *It wouldn't have been the same without you. Nothing is the same without you, Marsh.*

Six weeks later Delia returned from Europe. She stepped onto the platform at Dearborn Station, watching the fall foliage come into view as the smoke and haze from the train began to clear away.

"Aunt Dell! Aunt Dell!" Catherine waved to her before she rushed to her side, wrapping her arms about her. "I'm so glad you're home. I have so much to tell you."

On the drive back to Prairie Avenue Catherine spoke endlessly about Albert Beveridge and how she planned to marry him with or without her mother's approval. "But don't tell my mother I said that."

"Our secret," Delia promised. She was happy for Catherine even though she knew Abby would be heartsick and that it would be up to her to reassure her sister that it wasn't the end of the world. She would do it, too. Delia understood the power of an inconvenient, unconventional love that couldn't be denied. One look in her niece's eyes and she could see that Catherine understood that, too.

As they entered the Field mansion Delia was met with a chorus of voices.

"Surprise! Welcome home!"

Delia was caught off guard as Abby and Augustus, Albertine and the children circled around her, showering her with hugs. Spencer was there with Lurline Spreckels, along with Ethel and her husband, David Beatty. They were all gathered around her and she didn't know who to speak to first. Her heart felt so big, so full, it couldn't have held any more joy.

Still clustered close to her, they walked Delia into the dining room, where an elaborate table was set. As the smells of sautéed garlic and onions emanated from the kitchen, Delia realized how long it had been since she'd last eaten and yet she was too excited, too pleased to be bothered with something as trivial as food.

Everyone took their seats except for Ethel, who raised her glass of champagne. "To Aunt Dell," she said. "Our matriarch has come home." The glasses went up as the beams of light from the crystal chandelier played off the goblets.

Delia looked around the table and found herself moved to tears. She never thought of herself as the matriarch and yet what else could she have possibly been? For years she had provided for her sister's family. More recently she'd looked after Albertine and her children, who were still living with her. Even Ethel, despite it all, now looked to Delia for motherly advice.

Though she'd never had children of her own, Delia realized that in her own way, she had become their matriarch, everyone's mother. The house Marsh left to her was filled with family, and while it may not have been the way she'd planned it, she had children and grandchildren to enjoy. A gift to her from Marsh and, in the end, the most valuable one he'd ever given her.

Just then she realized something else. When Nannie died, and again when Arthur passed away, she felt their ghosts all around, lingering everywhere. Their sense of presence had frightened her, but now she felt Marsh's life force all around and it was like she'd swallowed the sun, its heat and light filling her soul. As she looked around the table, she had the sensation that Marsh was there with her and she realized that she did have all she had ever wanted.

AUTHOR'S NOTE

What the Lady Wants is a work of fiction, but I did base it largely on the facts of Marshall Field's and Delia Caton's lives. I did most of my research for the book at the Chicago History Museum and the Newberry Library in Chicago. I tried to be faithful to the important historical facts of their lives, but many of the events in the novel as well as the characters' motivations are my suppositions. The Fields and Catons were extremely private people and the truth of their full story will never be known. In the interests of crafting an entertaining novel, I took some creative liberties with their stories and I'd like to clarify the fact from fiction here.

Delia and Marshall's relationship was without question a great scandal for the better part of three decades. It was in fact widely rumored that the two had built a secret lovers' tunnel that connected their properties, though I found no evidence that such a tunnel ever existed. While they were generally known to be lovers, and there's a record of Delia's relationship with Marsh's children, I created the details of their intimate lives. There's no evidence that she was ever pregnant by Marshall Field, although it is true that Delia Caton never had children.

It was also well noted that Marshall and Nannie Field had a very tumultuous relationship and as a result Nannie spent long periods of time in Europe with the children. Though it was quite clear that she had health issues and suffered from migraines, her addiction to laudanum and her stay at the sanitarium are the workings of my imagination. Back in the late 1800s there was no diagnosis for what ailed Nannie Field, but according to *The Marshall Fields: The Evolution of an American Business Dynasty* by Axel Madsen, it was chronic fatigue syndrome.

As for the Catons' marriage, very little was ever recorded. The nature of their relationship here is the work of fiction based upon a study of photographs and documents I found at the Newberry Library, which houses the archives of Delia's niece, Catherine Eddy Beveridge. Based upon my findings, I speculated that Delia and Arthur were friends above all else and that Arthur was aware of his wife's affair with Marshall Field. It should be noted that my portrayal of his acceptance of it is a product of my imagination; there's no record of his private thoughts concerning his wife's long affair. According to *The Chronicle of Catherine Eddy Beveridge: An American Girl Travels into the Twentieth Century* by Albert J. Beveridge III and Susan Radomsky, Marshall Field often traveled with Delia and Arthur and was very much a fixture in their lives.

Arthur Caton, for reasons never disclosed, did commit suicide at the Waldorf Astoria in 1905. My portrayal of him as a homosexual is not based on any historical evidence. Paxton Lowry is a fictitious character.

Above all, Marshall Field was instrumental in shaping the

Chicago we know today. In addition to developing State Street and his retail empire, he was also an early investor in Charles Yerkes's cable cars. By insisting that they continuously circle around his store, he created the famous Chicago Loop.

It's also true that he played a key role in the Haymarket Affair, which was the result of friction between the labor movement wanting an eight-hour workday (among other things) and the capitalists. What started as a peaceful socialist movement turned into a violent uprising and ultimately the deadly riot at Haymarket Square when the anarchists joined their cause. Marshall Field was the one holdout who refused to grant clemency to the convicted men despite the lack of evidence. Also, the anarchists' march on Prairie Avenue actually took place on Thanksgiving Day 1884, not 1881 as I have it here. Lastly, it should be noted that the Haymarket Affair could be and has been the subject of many books in and of itself and that what I've presented here is really just a snapshot of that story.

The same is true of my portrayal of the 1893 Columbian Exposition World's Fair. I also found no specific evidence of Delia's involvement with the fair. While Bertha Palmer was the chairwoman for the Board of Lady Managers, for the sake of this novel, I took the liberty of making Delia Caton her assistant. Marshall Field and other Chicago businessmen such as George Pullman, Philip Armour and Gustavus Swift were extremely instrumental in bringing the fair to Chicago.

The secondary characters in this novel were all real figures except for Sybil and Lionel Perkins, Penelope Lowry and, as noted above, Paxton. Harry Selfridge, the subject of the PBS *Masterpiece Classic* series *Mr. Selfridge*, worked for Marshall Field for twenty-five years before the two parted ways. When Harry moved to London, he established his version of Marshall Field & Company, known as Selfridges.

Marshall Field Jr.'s death to this day remains a mystery. It was believed that he was shot in the Everleigh Club, Chicago's most famous brothel, and that his body was later moved to his home. Based on various newspaper articles that appeared in the *New York Times* as well as *Sin in the Second City: Madams, Ministers, Playboys, and the Battle for America's Soul* by Karen Abbott, it was obvious that the family was involved in covering up the incident, claiming that he accidentally shot himself. Again, in both sources cited above, Vera Scott did come forward years later confessing to the crime, but again, her guilt was never proved.

I relied heavily upon a number of sources in the writing of this book. I would like to note that the excerpt from the *Chicago Tribune* article after the Field & Leiter fire in 1877 is as it appeared in *Give the Lady What She Wants: The Story of Marshall Field & Company*, by Lloyd Wendt and Herman Kogan.

For more about Marshall Field's and Chicago's history, I highly recommend the following:

Give the Lady What She Wants: The Story of Marshall Field & Company, by Lloyd Wendt and Herman Kogan. Chicago: Rand McNally, 1952.

The Marshall Fields: The Evolution of an American Business Dynasty, by Axel Madsen. Hoboken: John Wiley & Sons, 2002.

The Chronicle of Catherine Eddy Beveridge: An American Girl Travels into the Twentieth Century, by Albert J. Beveridge III and Susan Radomsky. Lanham, MD: Hamilton Books, 2005.

Challenging Chicago: Coping with Everyday Life, 1837–1920, by Perry R. Duis. Urbana and Chicago: University of Illinois Press, 1998.

City of the Century: The Epic of Chicago and the Making of America, by Donald L. Miller. New York: Simon & Schuster, 1996.

The Jewel of the Gold Coast: Mrs. Potter Palmer's Chicago, by Sally Sexton Kalmbach. Chicago: Ampersand, 2009.

Remembering Marshall Field's, by Leslie Goddard. Charleston, SC: Arcadia, 2011.

Chicago's Historic Prairie Avenue, by William H. Tyre. Charleston, SC: Arcadia, 2008.

The Devil in the White City: Murder, Magic, and Madness at the Fair That Changed America, by Erik Larson. New York: Random House, 2003.

Chicago by Day and Night: The Pleasure Seeker's Guide to the Paris of America, edited by Paul Durica and Bill Savage. Evanston: Northwestern University Press, 2013.

Bertha Honoré Palmer, by Timothy A. Long. Chicago: Chicago Historical Society, 2009.

The Letters of Pauline Palmer: A Great Lady of Chicago's First Family, by Eleanor Dwight. Easthampton, MA: M.T. Train/Scala Books, 2005.

In addition to all these, I highly recommend touring the Glessner House, which still stands at 1800 South Prairie Avenue and is representative of the grand homes from Chicago's Gilded Age.

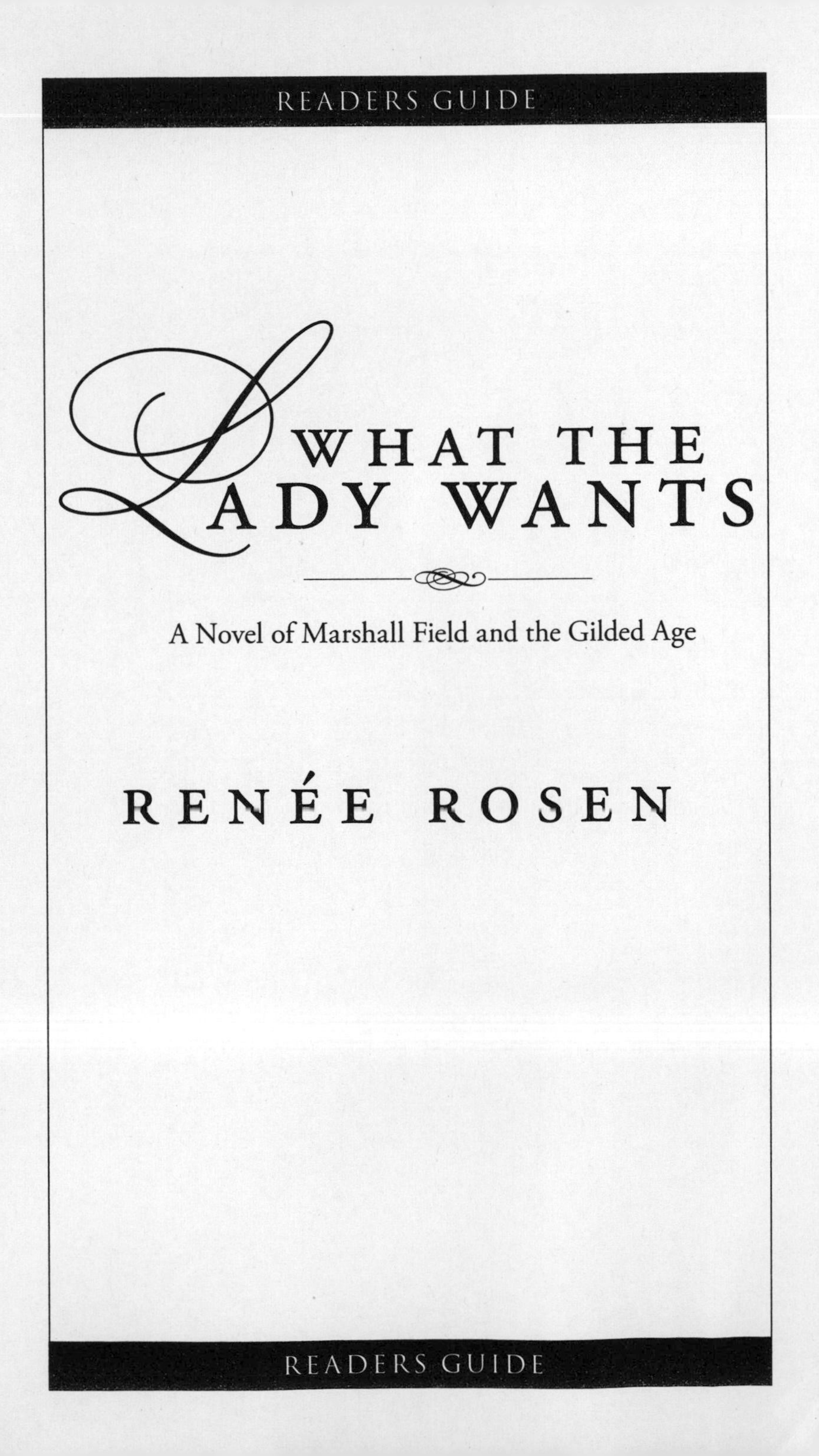

READERS GUIDE

What the Lady Wants

A Novel of Marshall Field and the Gilded Age

RENÉE ROSEN

READERS GUIDE

QUESTIONS FOR DISCUSSION

1. Do you find it acceptable that Marshall and Delia pursued their love affair? Or do you think they were wrong for going outside their marriages? In other words, is adultery ever justified?

2. There's a twenty-year age difference between Delia and Marshall. How do you account for Delia's attraction to him? Was it his money? His power? Or was it something else? Do you think relationships between older men and younger women were more common in the late nineteenth century than they are now?

3. Delia's greatest desire was to be a mother and at one point she sets out to have a child with Marsh that she, Marsh and Arthur will go on to raise. Had she not lost the baby, how do you think this arrangement would have worked out? What do you think Nannie's reaction would have been? What about Arthur's parents? Do you think the children she "had" by the end of the book ultimately fulfilled her desire for motherhood?

4. What do you think about how Delia handled her critics who spread rumors and blackballed her from high society? What

should she have done differently, if anything? What do you think of the different reactions society had to Delia versus Marsh?

5. During the late 1800s a woman could not easily seek a divorce and so Delia chose to stay with Arthur. Do you think she did that solely out of obligation or out of genuine love and friendship? What would you have done if put in the same situation?

6. Loyalty is a big theme in this book. Delia is certainly loyal to Arthur and Marshall, but can you cite other examples in the book? Do you think this is a strength or weakness of hers? Can you think of an instance or instances where you disagree with Delia's sense of devotion?

7. Delia and Marshall Field were part of a very elite social group known as the Prairie Avenue set. Did you find their sense of privilege more enchanting or annoying? What parts did you especially like? What parts did you not like?

8. Had you been alive during the Great Chicago Fire, would you have stayed and helped rebuild the city, or would you have moved on and possibly returned after the city had come back?

9. The Haymarket Riots, which pitted the labor organizers against the capitalists and resulted in a deadly riot, marked a very pivotal time in our nation's history. Delia was clearly opposed to Marshall's decision to execute the accused men. Do you think she should have left him over this? How could she defend him to others when she was so strongly opposed to his position? Was this another case of loyalty and do you think she should have stood by him?

10. Delia has a very definite opinion of what makes a man a man. Do you think this is based upon her father? And how do you think her relationship with her father factors into her relationship with Marshall and how does it impact her feelings toward Arthur?

11. How do you think department stores and retail in general have changed since the early days of Marshall Field & Company? What do you think would have been the best part of shopping in those days? Would you trade the convenience of online shopping for the charm and service offered at a store like Marshall Field & Company?

Photo by Charles Osgood

Renée Rosen is the author of *Dollface* and *Every Crooked Pot.* She lives in Chicago where she is at work on her next novel coming from Penguin/ New American Library in November of 2015.